TRICK ME TWICE

STEPHEN SOLOMITA

Bantam Books

New York Toronto London Sydney Auckland

Trick Me Twice
A Bantam Book

Bantam edition / August 1998

ISBN 0-553-57770-0

Published simultaneously in the United States and Canada

Bantam Books are published by Bantam Books, a division of
Bantam Doubleday Dell Publishing Group, Inc. Its trademark,
consisting of the words "Bantam Books" and the portrayal of a
rooster, is Registered in U.S. Patent and Trademark Office and in
other countries. Marca Registrada. Bantam Books, 1540
Broadway, New York, New York 10036.

PRINTED IN THE UNITED STATES OF AMERICA

OPM 10 9 8 7 6 5 4 3 2 1

TRICK ME TWICE

ONE

Most days it seemed, to Ezekiel McTeague at age seventy-three, that everything he did, he did for the last time. It was a feeling he couldn't shake, and the first thought to enter his mind when the ancient Big Ben on the nightstand woke him from a dreamless sleep at six o'clock on a cold November morning. It stayed with him as he began his day by swallowing a handful of pills, as he turned up the kerosene heater and trudged off to the bathroom, as he coated his upper plate with pink cement and fitted it to his gums.

The feeling was mostly an illusion, of course. Because he'd done the same things yesterday, though not at six o'clock, and the day before and the day before. Maybe that was part of it, of the reason why he saw himself running down like the engines in the rigs he'd been driving since 1947. They went on and on, the big Macks, as if they were determined to run forever. Then, one day, everything fell apart. The valves were clogged with grit, the heads leaked steam, the pistons clanked in their cylinders like chained demons.

Well, if you wanted to stay in business, what you did was go out and find another engine. Too bad he couldn't run down to the junkyard and scavenge another heart. Because without ever actually saying, "Hey, pal, better make a will, get your insurance straight," the docs had made it pretty clear. A big piece of Zeke McTeague's heart was already dead and the rest of him wouldn't be long in following.

Outside, the dog began to bark, a persistent racket that broke through his ruminations, had him shuffling across the room. By the time he opened the door, he was out of breath; his heart—what was left of it—fluttered against his ribs like a frightened bird. Instinctively, he sucked the frigid autumn air down into his lungs.

The cold knifed into his chest, actually backed him into the little house. Zeke tried to reach into his shirt pocket for the vial of nitro pills he was supposed to carry at all times, then remembered that he was still wearing the quilted long johns he used for pajamas in the winter. For a moment, he was close to panic, but then the pain subsided, the band around his chest loosened. As it always had. As, one day in the not too distant future, it would not.

"Goddamn dog." He slammed the door, crossed the room to the chair by his bed, pulled on his shirt and pants, jammed his feet into socks and heavy boots. Then he checked his shirt pocket to make sure he had his pills, walked to the door, and stepped outside.

Without his glasses, which he rarely wore, Zeke McTeague's vision was blurry at best. Standing in the predawn morning, he was virtually blind. He took a hesitant breath, warmed it in his mouth before allowing it down into his lungs. He could hear the wind rattle the few dried leaves clinging to the birches at the edge of the forest. It hissed in the white pine, ticked at his stiff mustache, riffled the coarse gray hair on his head. A perfect beginning to the first day of the Pennsylvania hunt.

The idea seized him then. The first day of his last season, and what he was going to do was get out there into the woods, set himself in place, wait for his trophy to come out of hiding. He was going to do it or die in the attempt.

He looked down the driveway, searched for headlights. Nothing. A visitor now, of course, would ruin his plans, but Zeke didn't get many visitors, never a neighbor, no relatives. The do-gooders came around, fetched him a hot meal, took him shopping, to the doctor, even fixed his roof. They were coming today, around noon, a pack of do-gooders with chain saws to cut the deadfall behind the house into firewood. They'd split and stack it, too. Smiling, their Jesus-loves-me smiles while they busted their do-gooder butts.

He could see the dog now, straining at the end of her chain. She was staring into the woods and not down the driveway, probably spooked by a deer, maybe even a bear. With winter coming on, the bears would be ravenous, desperate to build fat before the long sleep.

"Better watch your ass, Becky," he told the dog. "Old bear'll come down and have you for breakfast."

Zeke took a moment to imagine the bear lumbering out of the forest, rising to smell the dog's hot flesh on the wind, dropping to all fours, charging across the yard.

Be a hell of a fight with that big dog, he thought. Be a *hell* of a fight. Then he backed into the house, closed the door, put on his glasses, began to prepare.

Fifteen minutes later, he was in the barn, installing a set of license plates on an '85 Chevrolet pickup. In defiance of Doctor Kellerman's casual proclamation.

"I'm afraid your driving days are over, Zeke. You could have a heart attack at any time. We have to consider other vehicles." Kellerman had nodded wisely, actually winked. "And, of course, the passengers inside them."

McTeague felt himself grow angry at the memory.

Kellerman had misunderstood everything, had wanted to put Zeke McTeague into a nursing home, leave him there to rot. Well, that just wasn't gonna be his fate. Not in this life or any other.

He forced himself to go slowly, to conserve his strength. The mornings, once he got his heart off and running, were his best times, but he didn't want to push his luck. He wouldn't have survived all these years if he hadn't been able to resist temptation.

When the license plates were firmly attached, he fetched a small air pump from beneath the loose planks at the rear of the barn where the roof had pushed in, clamped its hose into the flat rear tire on the right side of the truck, then plugged the pump into the socket of an extension cord hanging against the wall. While the tire filled, he opened the hood and reattached the coil wire.

His fingers were cold now, almost numb; his feet were cold, too, even jammed into heavy socks. He got into the cab of the pickup, started the engine. The heater blew a wave of icy air across his left foot and for a few very long moments he wasn't sure he could make it. The rocker and the TV in the house beckoned to him. He could turn up the heat, wrap his body in a flannel robe, catch the morning talk shows, die before lunch.

It wouldn't be as bad as it sounded. Zeke McTeague had been close enough to know that death was really quite peaceful, a gentle slide into . . . Well, he hadn't gotten close enough to see where it all went before the docs slammed a couple of shock paddles onto his chest, blew him right back up the slide. Gave him life is what they did. Gave him life, then told him he couldn't do anything with it except die.

Gradually, almost grudgingly, the heater began to push out warm air. McTeague raised his toes, held them in the stream. He was staring out through the barn door at the sun rising between the branches of the old maple hanging over the driveway. As he watched, the wind stirred the bare branches, scattering them like drumsticks across a cloudless sky. It was a perfect day for a hunt, to get set, face up into the breeze, wait for your prey to come out of hiding.

The air pump kicked off with a final hiss, rousing McTeague. He moved a bit more confidently now, put the pump away, fetched an ancient Winchester 30–30 fitted with a 4X scope, dropped it behind the seat. Then he slid the gearshift into first, let out the clutch, and eased the pickup down the driveway and onto a dirt and gravel road. He took his time about it, knowing anything above fifteen miles an hour would raise a cloud of dust, that many of his neighbors would be stirring as they prepared for hunts of their own.

McTeague heard the first gunshot before he traveled a mile over Route 196. A few minutes later he heard another, then a whole fusillade. "Bad loser," he said aloud, imagining the white flash of a deer's retreating tail, some New York City asshole desperately snatching at the trigger. Probably stoned to the gills, him and his buddies come up to get the big trophy.

His father had never hunted for trophies. *Meat on the table, boy.* That was the way his old man had put it in '32 when McTeague was twelve years old and preparing for his first hunt.

The tourists never got this far in those days. Days when Route 196 had a name, Drinker Turnpike, instead of a number, when it was two lanes of dirt, impassable in winter, choked with mud in the spring. The forest was darker then, Zeke remembered, the little towns and farms hacked out of that darkness.

He passed a strip mall and a few houses set well back from the road. A video store-grocery, a pizza parlor, a real estate office, a beauty parlor. The rest of the stores were empty, their dusty windows set aglow by a cold sun that sat just above the treetops.

McTeague opened the glove compartment, took out a Hershey bar, peeled off the wrapper, and took a bite. It tasted so good that he began to laugh out loud. It was a candy bar to remember, the last candy bar until you bit into another one.

The way he figured it, Zeke McTeague decided as he came to the end of his life, everything you did was the last thing you did. Until you did something else. Hoard your memories? Great. But you couldn't take them with you. No, you could empty your bank accounts, stuff the coffin with greenbacks, but your memories were as dead as you were.

He heard more gunshots as he made his way south, through Sterling and Dreher townships toward the game lands in northern Monroe County. State Game Lands No. 127.

"Don't nothin' have a name no more," Zeke McTeague said aloud. "Not in the great State of Pennsylvania. Nope, in the great State of Pennsylvania the guvmint took the names away, gave everythin' numbers." He tried to hawk a wad of phlegm, wanted to spit his contempt through the window. The effort set off a coughing spasm that forced him to pull off the road, that had him bent over the steering wheel, clutching his chest.

He got the vial out of his shirt pocket, managed to control his shaking fingers long enough to pop it open, shove a nitro tablet beneath his tongue. Cars passed without slowing, other hunters, maybe, anxious to get into the field, or commuters heading for jobs in Scranton or Wilkes-Barre. Just as well, because the last thing he wanted was to have some do-gooder drag his sorry ass into the hospital, let the doctors play with their pills and their tubes. The docs would have their role, all right, but not until Zeke McTeague was ready for them. Not until there was nothing else left for him to do.

The pain eased as the nitro took effect and McTeague slowly raised his head to look out over a rocky field covered almost entirely with wood fern. Bright gold and stirred by the wind, the interlaced fronds shivered in the angled light; they lifted his heart, piercing it as firmly as the pain that had, a moment before, stolen his very breath.

"A perfect day," the old man called to the aspens at the edge of the forest, to the birches and oaks and maples behind them, to the beech and the pin cherry, to the white pine, the hemlock, the naked larch. "A perfect day for a hunt."

Thirty minutes later, McTeague pulled off Route 507 and onto a dirt road that ran for miles through the northern end of the game lands. A hundred yards inside, he turned into a gravel-covered parking area, one of dozens scattered along the road. A number of other vehicles, mostly four-by-fours, were already parked there; Zeke scanned each as he pulled the truck in a slow circle through the lot. When he was sure he was alone, he parked his truck a few feet from the road, retrieved the Winchester, and stepped out.

It was much warmer, now, the air crisp enough to stir the senses without slicing into his lungs. McTeague could see two houses through the trees, part of a small development huddled on the northwestern boundary of the game lands. He watched for a moment, wondering if the people who lived in those houses felt vulnerable, if they listened to the rifle and shotgun fire in the distance, thought about just how far a bullet could travel and still retain its killing power, how a slug from a 30–30 could rip through the walls of their double-wides and prefabs, tear their hearts out while they watched the morning news.

He wanted to take the images further, flesh them out with husbands, wives, and children, with pets and aging grandparents, but the sound of a shotgun exploding a few hundred yards to the east got him into gear. Cradling the rifle against his chest, he moved off into the woods. The way was easier than it had been the first time he'd been here a month before. The leaves had been up then, the forest aflame with color, dense enough to taste. Now, he had clear sight lines as he made his way to a pair of boulders set at the edge of a patch of laurel.

As he walked, slowly and deliberately, McTeague raked

the forest with his eyes. Though most of the deer hunters would expect their prey to head for deep cover with the first gunshots, as far from humans as they could get, there was always the chance that one or two fools had settled at the edge of the forest, too lazy or drunk to get any farther.

In his brown plaid jacket and brown corduroy pants, his green woolen cap, McTeague felt nearly invisible. The deer hunters, of course, would be wearing a touch of red-orange somewhere, hats or vests, even camouflage, a safety precaution that had become universal over the years. It was the color he looked for, the flaming orange, as he made his way through the woods, stopping now and again to catch his breath. The wind rattled through dried branches, stirred the brown leaves at his feet, fleshed out his confidence as if blowing into an open parachute. He felt good about what he was doing, what he was about to do. Better, in fact, he finally decided, than he had in years.

By the time he settled down behind the rocks, McTeague was certain that he was entirely alone. Still, he swept the forest one more time, raising his eyes to search for deer hunters in tree stands. Again, he found nothing, no evidence that he shared this patch of ground, that anyone had seen him coming in or would see him going out. He jacked a round into the chamber of the rifle, brought the scope to his right eye, swept the three houses clearly visible fifty yards away.

McTeague found his prey on the first sweep. A woman, standing in front of a stove, talking over her shoulder as she worked. He could see her through a sliding glass door at the back of the house, her movements crisp and confident. This was a chore she'd performed many times, though she appeared to be still young, at least through the scope.

Maybe, McTeague thought, she took care of her brothers and sisters when she was a kid, made breakfast while her parents went off to work. Maybe she was a good girl. Shouldered the burden. Didn't try to get out of it.

He pulled away from the window, swept the yard, looking for clues. A pair of trikes caught his attention, one lying on its side, the second upright. They were identical, down to the red-and-white streamers on the handle grips. Farther on, he noted a partially deflated basketball lying beneath an overgrown juniper by the side of the house, and a rusting swing set in the backyard.

McTeague put the rifle down, settled his back against the rock. He imagined twins, a girl and boy, scuttling across the yard on their new trikes, red-and-white streamers flying behind them. Another boy, older, maybe ten or twelve, stands with his buddy at the edge of the road, casually dribbling a basketball. A woman, honey blond and solidly built, pulls the sliding door open, steps onto the deck. She watches the twins for a moment, then calls to her older son, "Tommy? Are you keeping an eye on the kids?"

Tommy, a wise guy to his bones, doesn't hesitate. "They're still alive, aren't they?" Then he grins at his friend, exchanges a high five. "Yessssssss."

The woman's mouth curls into a frown; she starts to speak, stops, wipes her brow with the back of her hand. Finally . . .

The sound of a slamming car door roused McTeague. He slid onto his knees, peered through the cleft that separated the two boulders. For a moment, he thought she was going to get away, maybe take the kids off to school or herself off to work. But no, it was a man in the car, youngish, wearing a green work uniform. As McTeague watched through the scope, the man rolled down the window and shouted in the direction of the house, then, a moment later, backed down the driveway and onto the main road.

"Time to get up and at 'em," McTeague said. He heard the regret in his voice. There was a time when he would have truly possessed this woman, when he would have received the details of her life from her own lips, made her fully aware, in her last moments, of all she was losing.

He brought the rifle up, propped it on the rock, sighted down through the scope, took just a second to enjoy the mix of anticipation, lust, and regret swirling through his body.

Funny, he thought as he squeezed the trigger, done spent my whole damn life makin' an end for other folks and never thought I'd come to an end myself.

TWO

Sometimes it seemed, to Pat Detrick as she entered her thirty-second year, that everything she did, she did for the first time. And not only in the morning, when life has a right to begin afresh, but all through the day. In her lighter moments, she called herself Rip Van Detrick. In her darker moments—and there had been many over the past eighteen months—she felt entirely alienated, as if nothing she'd done in the past had any application in the present, as if she was now starring in an unscripted, unrehearsed play. The oddest part, at least the way she saw it, was that the other characters, despite the mix of pity, advice, and support they offered, had been untouched by the event that'd shaken her life. Their roles went on as before; they knew exactly who they were.

What do I do, she asked herself as she stared into the mirror on her dressing table (as she'd begun to ask herself a dozen times each day), if I never find my place?

An answer popped up: I could always haunt *myself*. I could be the Ghost of Detricks Past, Present, and Future. A shell of my former self. Better yet, my former self's shell, wandering from sleep to sleep, looking for the nut inside.

"Enough," Pat Detrick told her image. "Enough self-pity." She looked at herself for a long moment, then grinned. "And this time I *really* mean it."

She picked up an eyebrow pencil, raised it to her eyes, then hesitated. I need a face, she thought, to charm an irascible septuagenarian with a disabling heart condition. A face to overwhelm his fears and suspicions, to convince him that I approach with love in my heart. Even though I don't know him and am entirely preoccupied with my own problems.

Rounded brows, she decided, to crown my baby blues, soften my Mount Rushmore forehead. And light on the blush and the lipstick. According to Reverend Gauss, Ezekiel McTeague had spent most of his life in the cab of an eighteen-wheeler, pounding down the highway from one truck stop to another. Exotic would not be on his menu.

"Meat loaf," Pat said. "Meat loaf and mashed potatoes, heavy on the gravy. The official look of the day."

And why not? The only (and obvious) benefit of not having an identity was that you could assume any disguise without giving away a self you didn't possess. If you begin with nothing, you can be anything.

That particular happy message had been given, free of charge, by her oldest friend, Betty Hoffmann.

"I know how you feel about transitions," Betty had said. "When I first came to New York, I was rural Pennsylvania and five steps behind the herd. You don't know how much I wanted to go back home, settle back into a comfortable routine. Now, I realize that what I thought was loneliness, was actually freedom. I just wasn't used to it."

Pat had started to say, "You chose to start a new life, Betty. It's not the same when it's forced down your throat."

But she didn't say it, because she didn't want to evoke the little scene hovering at the edge of her consciousness. She didn't want to see Bradford Detrick naked on the edge of the bed, his erection already fading, didn't want to see his bright red face (from shame? from passion?) or his narrowed eyes or the drops of sweat prominent in the hairs on his chest, didn't want to see Marianne Todt, also naked, kneeling on the carpet, her mouth frozen in a perfect circle, her breasts resting on Bradford's knees, her fingers grasping at what remained of his passion.

Those images had haunted Pat for months afterward, rushing up into her mind without warning, a sharply focused video that began with her slowly opening the door of her bedroom, that ended with her panicked retreat. They'd propelled her back and forth, from the purest rage to the blackest despair, only fading when her divorce became final and she realized that every ending short of actual death implies a new beginning. Like it or not.

"You've been a good girl for too long." Betty had stated her case flatly, brooking no contradiction. "When the rest of us were smoking cigarettes in the bathroom, you were up in the library, studying. I swear, lady, you were the only one sober at the senior prom. The *only* one."

"And you were so drunk, you went home with the wrong date."

"I went home with the *better* date. At least the guy knew how to kiss." Betty had paused briefly, then continued. "Come to Manhattan, Pat. Stay with me for a few weeks. There's so much life here."

"And so much dirt, and so much noise, and so much crime. And everybody talking a hundred miles an hour. You forget, Betty, that I've already been to New York."

They'd left it like that, an invitation with no expiration date. And despite her protestations, Pat hadn't rejected the idea of a complete break with a past she couldn't reclaim. In the meantime, and the irony didn't escape her, she was actively pursuing her good-girl inclinations, volunteering four days a week at the Wayne County Senior Aid Mission. SAM was run by William Gauss, who'd been pastor of the Dreher Community Church since Pat was a child. In many ways (even more than her parents, who'd moved to Florida a year before what Pat had come to call *the incident*), Bill Gauss symbolized the continuity, the smooth passages, from child to adolescent to spouse, that had characterized her former life.

"You have time, Pat, time to heal," Gauss had offered. "You don't have to rush into anything."

He was talking about the money, though he didn't actually say it. Bradford Detrick still owned Detrick Motors, the largest car dealership in the Poconos, but only because he'd signed a ten-year note for half its value. The monthly payments met Pat Detrick's needs, paid her rent, put food in the cupboard, clothes on her back. That was the good news. The bad news was that without the pressure of economic necessity forcing her out the door every morning, she felt frozen in place.

What I need, she thought, as she went to the closet, is a dose of poverty. Then she laughed, remembering what Betty Hoffmann had told her: "What you need, lady, is to get laid. And don't forget to use a condom."

"There was a time," Bill Gauss began his spiel, "when rural Pennsylvania families took care of their own. It wasn't something that had to be said, an obligation you had to name: Folks simply did it. When your parents became too old or sick to care for themselves, you stepped up, took them into your own house. That's if you weren't living in the family homestead to begin with."

He paused there, fingertips steepled, gave the message a

chance to sink into the minds and hearts of the couple on the other side of his desk, Mark and Cathy Bouganian, newly moved from suburban Philadelphia to a house on the third fairway at Hillside Village where the homes started at a cool half-million. Gauss thought of them as legitimate prey. Mark and Cathy would never know what it was like to be eighty years old and shivering in the cold because they couldn't afford fuel oil. They would never have to choose which prescriptions to fill and which to leave on the kitchen table until the Social Security check arrived. They would never be carted off to nursing homes because they lacked the strength to prepare a simple meal. But they might—if he pushed just the right buttons—sign a check with enough zeros to keep SAM healthy, to allow Bill Gauss to remedy a small piece of the suffering he saw every day.

"All that," he continued, "began to change in the sixties. I'll leave the why of it to the college professors, but the obvious fact is that families became fragmented. The kids not only moved out of the nest, they moved far away from the nest. When their parents got old, they said, 'Time for the nursing home. Let the professionals do it.' "

Bill stopped again, looked at the Bouganians as if awaiting a response. They were dressed to fit the situation. He in a Harris tweed jacket (elbow patches and all); she in a white cotton blouse, black wool skirt, leather boots supple enough to be gloves for the feet.

"We believe," Cathy Bouganian said, "that people have to begin taking responsibility. If they don't . . ."

Her voice quivered just a bit as it trailed off, hinting at a vulnerability Bill Gauss was quick to exploit.

"I try to avoid moral judgments, Mrs. Bouganian; I try to stick to reality. The other end . . . well, it's a little too much like chasing windmills when there are real dragons out there." He leaned forward, pressed his palms against the desk. "Look, when it's January and there's four feet of snow on the ground, somebody has to get Mrs. Jones over to the doctor in time for her chemotherapy. The political questions—how much the government should do, how much the family should do—they deal with solutions that apply to the future." He smiled, leaned back. "Of course, if the kids decide to reclaim their obligations, I'll be happy to return to my parishioners, tend my own flock. As it is, they're always complaining I'm not around."

Cathy Bouganian seemed about to speak again, perhaps to state her message a little more forcefully, but her husband cut her off. He was a large, fleshy man with a wide mouth that merged with his jowls to form a perpetual, disdainful scowl. "Why don't you tell us a little more about what you do, Reverend Gauss? For the seniors."

Gauss nodded sagely. Mark Bouganian understood full well that his exalted position in the community required a dollop of charity now and again; he would be a lot easier than his wife.

"We do whatever's necessary to sustain our clients in their homes for as long as possible. For some, that can be as simple as transportation to supermarkets and doctors. For others, it requires cooking meals, balancing checkbooks, paying bills. We've put up new roofs, re-sided homes, hauled fifty-gallon drums of fuel oil on sleds up snow-covered driveways in the dead of winter."

Gauss stopped midgesture, his mouth open, hands spread apart. Then he turned, pointing to a framed scroll on the wall pronouncing the Wayne County Senior Aid Mission an official Point of Light. The scroll bore the signature of George Bush.

"When we got that scroll in 1990, most folks just assumed it was for the good deeds we do. But there was another reason, maybe even more important. SAM is able to put ninety-seven cents out of every dollar it receives back into this community because we use volunteers for almost everything. The mission runs on efficiency. That's important because government money is drying up and our organization is local. Volunteers are at the heart of our operation, individuals sacrificing their own time . . ."

Bill Gauss turned back to the Bouganians, saw Pat Detrick in the hallway beyond. He tried to catch her eye, but she continued on without a glance in his direction. Too bad. With her sturdy build, large sympathetic eyes, and strong, determined chin, Pat Detrick appeared every inch the wholesome volunteer. Gauss liked to confront donors with volunteers, let them know there were people out there willing to do more than write a check.

"Before we take a look around the mission," he continued, "I want you to try to imagine what it's like to be old and alone during a January blizzard. Seriously, try to imagine it. Folks are pretty isolated out here; it's not like Philadelphia. If something happens? If the heat goes off, the water? What do you do if you can't get out and nobody's coming? If you're sick and confused?" He folded his hands, crossed his legs. Time for the clincher. "Every winter, a few of our senior citizens wander out into the cold and die. Or freeze to death in their homes. *Every* winter."

THREE

Pat Detrick strode down the long corridor and went into the empty chapel of the Dreher Community Church without looking into the mission offices on either side. She walked directly to the back of the chapel, her stride habitually firm and smooth, and took a seat in the last row of pews. Raised in a rock-solid, Pennsylvania Dutch household, attending church on Sunday had been as much a part of her child's life as school or play. Pat Detrick had vivid memories of those Sunday mornings, of the preparations, the ribbons in her hair, the spotless dresses, the patent leather shoes and white socks, the hats she wore only on church day.

"Stay clean, Patricia." The first commandment, delivered

by her mother after a scrupulous inspection that included fingernails, ears, and neck.

The Geisheimers (a name she had no intention of reclaiming, divorced or not) never failed to don their best on Sunday. They sat, as a family, in the same pew four rows from the front of the church, and always (even when money was tight) dropped a respectable offering in the collection basket. Pat Geisheimer had carried that tradition into her marriage, but had not understood how much it meant until after her separation. Then she'd come to the austere little church, come to sit on the weekday afternoons when it was empty, to absorb the light streaming through the gold-and-blue panes of the arched windows, to stare up at the plain wooden cross that hung above the altar.

There were times when she'd cried, other times when she was angry enough to tear the cross off the wall, but always, when she finally got up to leave, she'd felt, if not actually renewed, at least strong enough to face the long nights alone. It was during this period that Pat had decided to volunteer for SAM's companion program.

"I feel like I'm in debt," she'd told Bill Gauss. "I've taken so much."

"Music to my ears, Pat," Gauss had replied. "But I want you to take a few days, think it through. The companion program entails a lot of responsibility. Clients become friends. Very sick, very dependent friends. I can always replace a volunteer carpenter, find someone else to drive the shopping van. In a pinch, I've even been known to drive it myself. But when a companion quits, the clients are devastated. And there's no second chance, no way to rebuild the trust."

What Bill Gauss hadn't told her was that devastation cut both ways. That lesson had been learned six months later when Charlotte Keil, who'd buried two children, who'd loved classical music, who'd surrounded her tiny house with lilacs and roses, had died of a stroke in the middle of the night. It'd been a peaceful death, or so Bill

Gauss had insisted, a peaceful death in her own bed after a long life.

"You made it better, Pat," he'd said. "You made it easier. If you can accept the way you feel right now, you'll come out of it stronger. That's what sacrifice is all about. Over time, it builds spiritual strength."

Pat Detrick still wasn't sure about the last part, but, now, a month after Charlotte's death, she was back, ready to start again. She stood up, walked to the front of the church, paused to look up at the cross. After a moment, she nodded, muttered, "Thank you," and left.

"This man, Zeke McTeague," Elaine Gauss told Pat Detrick over a cup of coffee, "he's not nice, not sweet like Charlotte Keil." She took a last pull on the stub of her cigarette, then ground it into an overflowing ashtray. Tall and thin, her narrow features perpetually wreathed in blue smoke, Elaine was the polar opposite of the typical preacher's wife. Born a Catholic in Philadelphia and painfully blunt, she'd raised the hackles of the conservative congregation on more than one occasion. But if her husband had a genius for collecting money, Elaine Gauss had a genius for spending it. She kept track of every penny, fought suppliers over each invoice, demanded discounts they didn't offer their best customers. Though she would never be popular with the Ladies' Auxiliary, never work hand in hand with the flower committee or the choir committee, Elaine was the indisputable brains of the Wayne County Senior Aid Mission, the head to her husband's heart.

"Zeke readily accepts physical aid," she continued after lighting another Parliament. "You wanna shingle McTeague's roof, no problem. Fetch his groceries, fine. But the way I see it, he doesn't want to let anybody into his life."

"Isn't that his right?" Detrick rolled her coffee mug between her palms. She liked Elaine Gauss. She liked the fact that Elaine had maintained her own identity when something very different had been expected of her.

"That's how I look at it, too. But you know Bill. He wants to give it another try." Elaine pushed her chair away from the desk, walked over to the window. She was wearing jeans and a flannel shirt that seemed voluminous over her narrow chest. After a moment, she signaled for Pat to join her. "See the juncos?"

Pat nodded understanding and both women stood silently, watching the small birds forage on the ground below the bird feeder. Slate gray on top, creamy white underneath, the juncos came down out of Canada every year to winter in northern Pennsylvania. According to local folklore, the earlier they arrived, the worse the winter to follow.

"This guy, McTeague," Elaine said, "his heart's just about gone, his kidneys are weak, and his lungs are so congested he can barely breathe. If someone doesn't go out there, make sure he takes his meds, cook him a decent meal now and then, he's not gonna make it through the winter." She took a deep breath, turned to face Pat Detrick. "We sent two male volunteers, retired men not too far from McTeague's age, figured they'd have something in common with him." She shook her head. "Forget about it. Once he found out what they wanted, he sent them packing. Bill thinks if we send a woman, he might respond."

Zeke McTeague, dressed in slippers and a flannel bathrobe, was sitting in front of the television when Pat Detrick knocked on his door. The set was tuned to Channel 28, WBRE, the local NBC affiliate and the only station the rabbit ears perched on top of the TV picked up. Totally absorbed, he ignored the first knock, assuming it had been delivered by one of the volunteers cutting firewood in the clearing behind the house. He was watching Ralph Biondo, WBRE's field reporter, cover the "tragic slaying" of a Monroe County woman. An accidental death, or so the state troopers and the sheriff were saying, one of the four or five sure to occur before hunting season ended.

"The shooter was somewhere in these woods," Biondo whispered dramatically as the camera panned. "Maybe he heard a sound, or saw a flash of movement, maybe he raised his gun too quickly, maybe he fired without taking aim. However it happened, the bullet tore through the trees, passed over that little clearing . . ." he hesitated, letting the cameraman zoom in close, "and crashed through that glass door to kill a mother of three."

At the second knock, this one firm enough to convince him that his visitor wasn't going away, McTeague rose quickly. He was halfway to the door, ready to tell whoever it was to get the fuck out of his life, before he remembered who he was supposed to be. Then he slowed to a shuffle and opened the door.

"Mr. McTeague?" Pat Detrick, a tentative smile fixed to her face, swiftly evaluated the man in front of her, searching for what Elaine Gauss had called "the key to his confidence." He was shorter than she expected, with a full head of gray hair, a stiff, unevenly trimmed mustache, and a pair of unkempt eyebrows that ran halfway up his deeply creased forehead. The dark, rheumy eyes beneath those brows peered at her for a very long moment, then turned downward. "I'm Pat Detrick, from the Senior Aid Mission, and . . ."

McTeague, without a word, shuffled back into the little cabin, found his glasses, settled them on the bridge of his small nose before returning to the doorway. It was beyond magic, as if this miracle had been prepared at the creation, as if it had been waiting to happen all these billions of years later. Everything about the woman was perfect, from the honey blond hair that fell to her shoulders, to her round blue eyes, to her square jaw and wide, athletic shoulders. He raised his nose, as if trying to smell her character, and sensed no physical weakness.

You could take this one back a hundred years, he thought, put her behind a plow while her husband went off to war. She'd get the crop in. Yes, she would.

"Well, I'm Zeke McTeague." He extended a trembling hand, closed his eyes for a moment as her soft palm fell into it. "You wanna come in? I'll put the kettle on, fix a pot of tea."

Pat Detrick started to nod her acceptance, but McTeague was already turning away, shuffling off into the gloom. For a moment, she simply stood there. She'd spent the last few days searching for an opening pitch that would get her through this door and now, just like that, he was inviting her inside. It didn't seem possible.

"Yes, thank you. I'd like some tea." Detrick followed him into the two-room cabin, let herself take a quick look around. Elaine's description of the flaking paint on the walls and ceiling, the uneven floorboards, the soot-stained beams, the small propane cooking stove against the wall opposite the bedroom, had been accurate, as far as it went. But Elaine hadn't mentioned the dozens of photographs that dominated the long wall opposite the doorway. They were in color and black-and-white, some framed and some merely tacked to the wall, the oldest yellow with age, the newest bright and sharply focused.

Detrick moved closer, peered through the dim light. There were no people in any of the pictures, not a single human being, not even a truck or a car. Only roads and highways.

"Them's the places I been." McTeague came up to stand behind her, wishing with all his might that he could see through her eyes, actually be inside looking out. "I was a trucker. Long-distance. Been going over the road since 1947, when I come back from the war." He took another step forward, inhaled the faint, spicy fragrance of her shampoo. His eyes closed briefly, then opened as he exhaled through his mouth. "I just wanted to get it down some way. So's I could remember how it was."

"It looks like you've been just about everywhere." Pat gestured to the clustered images. The roads passed through desert and forest, through mountains and across the plains.

"These must have been taken down South. Isn't that Spanish moss?" She pointed to a group of photos running in a vertical line next to the small window.

McTeague nodded as he stepped back. "Sure is. And that's Louisiana swamp water right there next to the highway. See, I set 'em up in the order of how I took 'em, put the dates in the corner. Figgered that way I wouldn't forget as quick."

"Why aren't there any people?" She turned to look into McTeague's eyes. Swollen by his thick glasses, they seemed even wetter, and slightly opaque, probably due to cataracts. She made a mental note to check with Abby Turner, the Mission's visiting nurse. If Zeke had an ophthalmologist, she'd make an appointment, arrange transportation. That's if she could talk him into going.

"Wasn't nobody there but Zeke McTeague when the picture got took is the reason." He dropped his eyes to the floor, let his shoulders slump. If holding on to her meant playing the fool, he was willing. Eventually he would rise, show himself. Eventually, as he removed the veils, she would see for herself. "Look's like there's been an accident. Damn fool hunters. Buncha drunks, you ask me."

"Pardon?"

"On the TV. Woman got herself shot in her own home. While she was doin' the dishes."

As they turned toward the flickering screen, a chain saw roared into life behind the house. A second and a third followed in quick succession, totally overpowering the set's audio. Zeke wanted to tell her about the do-gooders and the way he felt about them, but he knew it was the wrong time to make Pat Detrick's special position clear. Better to let her view his handiwork, see how long it took her to put it together. Make it a challenge.

On the television, above the legend *Taped Earlier,* two paramedics wheeled a covered gurney down the driveway to the open doors of a waiting ambulance. With a precision obviously born of long practice, they pushed the gurney inside, locked it down, and closed the doors. Then, as if they'd forgotten something, something important, they looked back toward the house before pulling away. A moment later, a man carrying two young boys came through a side door and almost ran to a car parked in the driveway. The man put the children in the backseat, shouted something in the direction of the house, turned impatiently. The face of an older child appeared in the open doorway, another boy. He looked in the direction of the camera, his eyes round with fear, before dashing to the car and diving into the back. The man slammed the car door, then also looked in the direction of the camera. It wasn't much of a glance, but he held it long enough for the crew to clearly record the tears streaming down his face.

FOUR

"He's a strange little man," Pat Detrick told Allen Wayne over a glass of California chardonnay. "Zeke McTeague. He kept insisting that woman who was shot in her home, Melissa Capriella, that she was somehow responsible because she lived so close to the game lands. I tried to pass it off, but he was insistent."

They were sitting in the Mill Room at the Waterview Lodge, one of the oldest resorts in the Pocono region and one of the largest. The Waterview, established in 1887 to serve hunters and fishermen who took the train west from New York City or north from Philadelphia, had expanded upward and outward over the years from this central, rock-solid room with its log walls and low ceiling. Massive, rough-hewn beams hung to within a foot of the tallest customers' heads; the floors, planks of varying widths, were rutted in places, the surface scraped away by a century of traffic. At one end, the farthest from the entrance, piled logs blazed in a massive stone fireplace. At the other, a large, patterned millstone, fully eight feet in diameter, had been set floor to ceiling into the log wall.

Pat Detrick glanced over Allen's shoulder at the millstone, let her eyes trace the sunburst pattern chipped into the rough surface, visualized, just for a moment, the men who'd cut and dragged the stone to the mill in 1794, set it to work for nearly a hundred years before it devolved into an architectural detail. She could, she knew, easily come to think of Zeke McTeague in that way, as a part of history. He'd been everywhere, roaming through America in his truck.

"Back before the Interstates," he'd told her. "Whatever place the load took me. Rain or snow, it didn't matter a tinker's damn. Most nights, I slept by the side of the road."

Pat leaned back in her chair as their waiter approached, set a tossed salad in front of her, another in front of her companion. The waiter's name was Craig, or so he'd said, and he was impossibly young, a student at East Stroudsburg University, one of a number employed by the lodge.

"You know what it sounds like to me?" Allen Wayne asked as Craig hustled off to another table. The room was crowded with hunters discussing the day's glories and frustrations. "It sounds like a variation on the old explanation for rape. That the woman must have somehow asked for it."

Pat sipped at the wine, her second glass; she was feeling good, proud of herself. She'd made contact with McTeague when two others had failed. "I wouldn't take it that far." She picked up her fork, speared a cherry tomato, slipped it into her mouth. The trick here was to pop it without spewing juice all over the tablecloth. Across the way, Allen

smiled at her. He was a good-looking man, tall and powerfully built with a full head of dark unruly hair and a broad
grin that rose to his lips at the least provocation. That they
would never be more than friends had become apparent
after a few fumbling kisses that had failed to stir Pat Detrick's thoroughly dormant fantasies. Then Betty Hoffmann had closed the door altogether.

"Can you imagine," she'd asked, "being naked in bed
with him? Because if you can't . . . Well, it doesn't get better if you force it. Trust me, I know."

The real problem, Detrick thought as she chewed the
successfully crushed tomato, is that I can't imagine myself
naked with anybody. And it's not only that Bradford was
my first and that I stayed faithful for ten years. No, the
worst is that whenever I think about sex, I see him on that
bed, on our bed, see Marianne Todt . . .

At that moment, Carl Rinders walked into the room,
accompanied by a man Detrick didn't know. Carl, one the
lodge's co-owners, managed the restaurant and bar. At
least fifty pounds overweight, he played the part of the fat
jolly host with evident gusto. Carl knew Bradford Detrick,
of course. Everybody knew Fireball Detrick and, by extension, his former wife. Their breakup had made for months
of juicy gossip, endless speculation that fizzled only when
they'd finalized their divorce without going to trial.

"Patricia, how are you?" Rinders slid his bulk between
tables and diners with a freaky, practiced grace, leaned
down to brush her cheek with his lips. Then he nodded to
Wayne, but didn't offer to shake hands.

"I'm fine, Carl," Pat answered. "And you?" She cast the
man with Rinders a quick, curious glance. Of average
height, he was nevertheless imposing. Probably, she decided,
because his own look was frankly appraising, though not
obviously lewd. As if he was undressing her character instead of her body.

"Fine, fine." That said, Rinders put his hand behind his
back, anxious to be away. Then he remembered himself.
"This is Richard Morello, head of security. He was a New

York cop, a homicide detective, before he came to us last month. Rick, this is Patricia Detrick and . . ."

"Allen Wayne," Allen said, extending a hand.

Pat Detrick, as Morello turned, noted that the ex-cop's intense stare extended to her dinner companion. Wearing a navy blazer over gray slacks and a white shirt, Morello seemed completely self-contained, right down to the blue-and-red tie knotted firmly against his throat.

"Ms. Detrick?" He was reaching across the table, his palm outstretched.

Detrick took his hand, watched his thin lips expand into a surprisingly warm smile, noted that his dark, hooded eyes remained perfectly impassive.

"Mr. Morello? Or do I call you Captain? Or Chief?"

"Well, I was trying for Exalted Director of Security Operations, but Carl refused to put it in my job description."

Rinders chuckled appreciatively, slapped his security chief on the back. "Duty calls," he said, turning away.

"Another flatlander," Allen griped at Morello's retreating back. The Pocono plateau, commonly referred to as the Pocono Mountains, rose to an exalted elevation of 2,500 feet, a height from which the natives could look down on anyone, permanent resident or tourist, who came originally from the coastal cities. "You'd think Carl might have found somebody local." The rapid growth of the region between 1970 and the stock market crash of 1987, a period during which the population of Monroe County had nearly doubled, was one of Allen's pet peeves. As was the appearance of malls and outlet centers and fast-food restaurants. Meanwhile, the ebb and flow of outside money determined the year-to-year prosperity of the Pocono Mountains and both of them knew it.

"You sound like Zeke McTeague," Pat said after a moment. "Only his golden age was 1940 instead of 1970."

Allen flashed his easy smile. "I think what I sound like is an old man. And I think what I'll do is console myself with another glass of wine." He uncorked the bottle, pulled it free of the ice-filled bucket. "Tell me a little more about

McTeague. Why did he come back to Pennsylvania if he's been everywhere?"

"Well, Zeke was born here, but I don't see him as attached to the region. No, I think it just happened. He inherited the house, he ran out of money and energy . . . from what I can gather, it all happened about the same time. Then he had his heart attack and that sealed the deal."

"So, your point is that he's simply waiting to die? That he's trapped there?"

Detrick cocked her head to the right and shrugged. Allen Wayne often spoke as if his words carried no emotional baggage. As if Zeke McTeague was some decaying star in a remote galaxy, a curiosity to be observed across million of light years.

"You'll be there, too, one day." She found herself wishing Bill Gauss was around to deliver one of his patented sermons on the nature of sacrifice. Or that she wasn't afraid to appear holier-than-thou. Or that she wasn't constantly surprised by the obvious fact that most people were indifferent to the suffering of strangers. "Anyway, I'm taking him out tomorrow. I asked him what he liked to do, if there was anywhere he wanted to go, and he said he just wanted to get on the road." She laid her fork on the plate beneath her salad bowl. "He said that without his rig he felt like a racehorse with no legs."

Later, after Craig replaced their salads with plates of broiled lake trout and a pair of enormous baked potatoes, the conversation turned to Pat's future. The theory, as she saw it, motivating most of her friends, even Betty Hoffmann, was that now that Pat Detrick's divorce was final, she was supposed to begin a new life. Floundering was simply unacceptable, an affront to their nose-to-the-grindstone values.

"I've been thinking about going back to school. Getting a master's degree."

"In what?"

"In social work." She flinched as she said it, read Allen Wayne's quick smile as condescending. No surprise.

"What you ought to do . . ." Like most men Detrick knew, Allen was quick with advice. ". . . is go into business. You were the real force behind Detrick Motors, Pat. I know you don't believe it, but it's true."

It was true, as far as it went. Back in the earliest days, on that first used-car lot in Scranton, Pat and Brad Detrick had polished and tuned cars, worked the customers, kept the books, fought off voracious creditors. There'd been no division of labor, not when they spent their days lurching from crisis to crisis. Later, Bradford had shown a positive genius for promotion, and their respective roles had hardened. Bradford Detrick became Fireball Detrick of late-night television, before jumping to cable in the mid-eighties. Pat Detrick had remained in the office, crunching the numbers, handling the cash flow, making payroll.

"The problem, Allen, is that I don't want to spend the rest of my life making money. And that's what business is all about. At least, that's what it was for me." She sliced off a piece of fish with the edge of her fork. "Everyone thinks that I was being kind when I agreed to let Brad keep Detrick Motors, but the truth is that I was glad to get out."

The conversation went back and forth for a while, then fell away as they finished dinner, paid the check, shrugged into their coats, left the noisy Mill Room to step into the frigid November night. Despite the intense cold and the stiff breeze, they walked slowly across the frost-covered lawn to the edge of Tamarack Lake. The moon, full and straight overhead in a cloudless sky, edged the dark rolling water with a chill, nearly fluorescent light. Off to their left, in the spruce trees at the far end of the lawn, an owl called repeatedly. Stars, overwhelmed in the center of the sky, shone, bright and hard as diamonds, above the treetops on the horizon.

Pat Detrick drew the night air in through her nose, felt it rush along her throat and burn into her lungs. Her eyes narrowed slightly and a soft smile rose to her lips. This was why she lived in the country, why she resisted Betty's oft-repeated advice, this emotion, so close to what she felt when she sat in the empty chapel, when she looked up at the naked cross. She could not walk away from it.

FIVE

When Pat Detrick finished her shower on the following morning, the first thing she did, even before she picked up a towel, was step onto a balance beam scale next to the hamper. She frowned slightly as the arrow at the end of the beam came to rest in the center of the gauge: 122 pounds, the same as yesterday and the day before, a steady weight, a barrier that she was sure could only be penetrated by the amputation of a limb. Then she cast her steam-blurred profile a sideways glance in the full-length mirror, before turning to face the mirror head-on.

She inspected her body for a long moment, wiped the mirror with a handful of tissues, looked again. Today, her hips weren't too wide, her waist not impossibly thick, the skin beneath her arms didn't hang like pizza dough. Her calves were too thin, of course, but there was nothing to be done about it, no amount of hiking, jogging, aerobics sufficient to swell those muscles.

What I ought to do, she thought as she began to dry herself, is go for liposuction, run a tube from my thighs down into my calves, pump it direct.

Still damp, she hung the towel on the bar, tugged on a white terry-cloth robe, walked into the little kitchen, poured herself a glass of orange juice. There were times when she looked into the mirror, was depressed at what she saw, further depressed by the fact that she was looking at all. Bill Gauss, she was sure, would label the ritual, call it vanity, flash that compassionate, we're-all-sinners smile. Vanity wasn't the point, of course, not on those mornings when she hated every square inch of her flesh, not on mornings when she hated her life. Every woman Pat Detrick knew, including Elaine Gauss, including eighty-year-old Charlotte Keil on days when she couldn't get out of bed, wanted to look good, to be attractive. There was no getting free of the desire, no more than Fireball Detrick could neutrally observe his rapidly balding scalp.

"Unto each a burden is freely given."

The sentence popped, unbidden, into her mind. Surely, it came from Bill Gauss, delivered in the course of a typical Sabbath sermon, a lead-in for the collection plate. No mention, as far as she could remember, had been made of burdens self-imposed, of obligations that could never be discharged. There were times when Pat Detrick watched herself perform the daily rituals, convinced that she had about as much control over her behavior as a lobster dropped into a pot of boiling water.

Well, I guess I'll go put on my face. That's the way her mother inevitably put it. Like the face she woke up with belonged to somebody else.

The phone rang as Detrick set a kettle of water on the stove, turned on the burner. As she picked up the receiver, she took a jar of instant coffee from the cupboard and dropped it on the kitchen table.

"Hello."

"That scumbag did it to me again. I've had enough. I'm coming out there." Betty Hoffmann's tone was sharp, as if she expected resistance and was having none of it.

"Great." Having spent many an hour crying on Betty's shoulder, Pat was in no position to refuse a surprise visit. On the other hand, she wasn't about to change her schedule, either. "When are you coming?"

"As soon as the traffic clears."

"I'll leave the key inside the light over the deck."

"You got a hot date? I'm gonna get in your way? Don't sleep between cold sheets for me."

"Yes, Betty, a hot date with a seventy-three-year-old . . ." She hesitated, searched for the right word. ". . . a seventy-three-year-old stud."

"You going kinky on me, Patricia? We talking role reversal here?"

Detrick spooned coffee into a flowered mug, added sugar, checked the water on the stove. "You want to tell me what happened with Roberto?" Roberto Corrales, Betty's steady boyfriend, an economist with a Ph.D. from Cornell, was married to his job. Turned securities trader, Corrales worked for a small brokerage firm with offices on Broad Street, a bare hundred yards from the New York Stock Exchange. The pressure to generate bottom line profits for the clients was relentless; Bobby's success was inevitably measured against the success of eight other midlevel traders. Everybody in the department dreamed of an eventual partnership, everybody worked twelve-hour days, did research on the weekends.

"I can live with the damned schedule," Betty said. "It gives me a lot of room in the evening when I'm busiest anyway. But I've been looking forward to this vacation for ages and now he tells me to cancel the reservations, turn in the tickets, he's gotta work. It's not right."

Detrick, as Betty went on, took the kettle off the stove and filled her mug. There was role reversal going on here, all right, but it had nothing to do with sex. For the first six months after the incident, she'd been on the phone with Betty almost every night, alternately snarling and crying into the instrument, completely absorbed in her own misery.

"I know he's got ambitions," Betty said. "I know he's got pressure." Roberto was the oldest member of a third-generation American family, originally from Puerto Rico. His father was a fireman, his mother a nurse. Together, they'd put a lifetime of work into his education. He was their breakout child, their professional, and he knew it, as did his brothers and his sisters, his aunts, uncles, and cousins. "But we have to have *some* life together. Truth is, Patricia, I've reached the point where I think of Bobby as my stealth boyfriend."

As Betty continued, Detrick stirred her coffee, took a careful sip, leaned back in her chair, realized that she was feeling good about herself, that she was looking forward to her day, to the night beyond. She glanced out the window, watched a solitary raven drop onto the topmost branches of a green spruce at the edge of the property. Its feathers, glossy and black, fluttered briefly in the wind before gently settling.

"Betty," she interjected finally, "I've got to go back upstairs. You come on out here, relax. I'll try to get back by early evening. If you get hungry, there's what's left of a tuna casserole in the fridge."

After a brief pause, Betty commented, "You're sounding pretty happy today, girl. You get lucky last night?" As if there could be no other explanation.

"Well, I see that fame is goddamn fleeting," McTeague told the flickering television set. At another time, he might have been seriously pissed, might have thrown things, screamed his rage, might have run his rig up against some old lady's bumper and just stayed there until she pulled off the road. But now, buoyed as he was by a renewed sense of purpose, he simply turned off the set, went about his business, telling himself that if WBRE didn't think a hunting accident was worth two days of coverage, that was their business.

He stopped in front of his wall, stared at the photos through bleary eyes, decided not to get his glasses. Now that he was entering a new phase, maybe it was time to put this part of his life, his first career, behind him. It was funny, though, definitely funny; all these fifty years he'd figured his greatest accomplishment was not getting caught, and now his greatest fear was that he'd keel over, die in the dirt without anybody ever knowing. Well, that could still happen, but at least he had a purpose, this slow unfolding. Like the light of sure and certain knowledge slowly unfolding in the eyes of his victims.

Every touch reduces Miriam Swerling, every word the man speaks, the endless questions, each repeated promise: answer and the pain will stop. Now she knows that the promise is about to be kept, that she has been sucked dry, become no more than a dried husk clinging to the strands of an abandoned spider's web.

Still, Miriam tries to remember, to prepare an offering before it's demanded. Above her, a brilliant sun diffuses in the feathery tips of a dozen closely packed cattail reeds. The light surrounds the man's head as he works, shimmers in his dark hair, in the drops of sweat that cling to the stubble on his cheeks the way Miriam, herself, clings to life.

She closes her eyes, retrieves a long-forgotten memory, a Christmas tree, fully decorated and tall enough to brush the ceiling. In the early morning hush, a flood of sunlight through a window bathes the tree, diffusing among the waxy needles exactly as the sun diffuses in the reeds above her head. She is very young, just old enough to creep to the head of the stairs, peer through the banister rails at the feast below.

"You ready, Miriam?"

She wants to say, Yes, I am. Yes. I'm ready to tell you about Christmas. But she can hear in the man's voice neither rage, nor joy, nor lust. Only an abiding affection more terrifying than anything that came before.

The cold mud soothes Miriam's back and her legs. Tears roll ceaselessly from the corners of her eyes. They flow across her temple, beneath the lobes of her ears, into her blood-matted hair. And what she wishes in this last moment of her life is to be once again on those stairs, her eyes filled with the light of that rising sun.

"What's wrong, cat got your tongue?" Before Miriam can answer, the man drops to his knees as if about to pray. "Well, ready or not, here I come."

Nodding to himself, McTeague shuffled over to the stove, studied the fire briefly before adding a log. The do-gooders had filled the 250-gallon tank in the yard with kerosene, but that wouldn't last through the winter, not unless he nursed it along, used it mainly at night or when he was hurting too bad to fetch wood. Prison, when the time came, would be easier. The more he thought about it the more convinced he was. The heat was right there all day, all night, and there were doctors, too, especially for celebrity prisoners. As for the death penalty—well, there was an outside chance he'd live through his trial, but nature would execute his sorry ass long before the State of Pennsylvania dusted off the electric chair.

Or maybe they did it by gas, or injection. Zeke didn't much care. No, what he saw, when he finally settled himself in his rocking chair, pulled a blanket over his shoulders, closed his eyes, were headlines, books, TV specials. He saw his lawyer on the courthouse steps, surrounded by microphones; he saw himself before a video camera, telling his story to Bryant Gumbel or Jane Pauley, heard them call him Mr. McTeague, acknowledge the simple truth, that he was the greatest of them all. The others? No matter what they'd accomplished, the stupid ones like Son of Sam, the clever ones like Ted Bundy, they all had one thing in common: They'd gotten themselves caught. Not one, not a single, solitary one, had deliberately exposed himself, opened his life for inspection, said, "Here I am, boys and girls. Take a good, long look."

McTeague dropped into his chair, closed his eyes, thinking how strange it was that once you made a decision everything else seemed to fall into place. He'd been imagining his confession for several months now, imagining some bored, red-faced cop puffing away on a black cigar. But now that he had his Patricia, now that he had someone truly worthy . . . Well, what he'd do is reel her in a step at a time, sit her down with a tape recorder, give her the whole story, enough detail to write a dozen books. That was the simple part. The hard part, especially for Patricia Detrick, was what he'd do next.

Detrick shifted her Jeep into second as she turned onto Zeke McTeague's driveway. She could hear the dog barking, though she couldn't see it. On her first visit, the animal had stood in the center of the driveway at the very end of its chain until she was right on to top of it, a dirty black dog showing a mouthful of very white teeth. It was she who'd swung her car onto the shoulder of the driveway, pulled far enough into the yard to be out of reach of those teeth. Then it'd sat, still in the center of the driveway, and watched her until Zeke let her into the house.

This time it was McTeague who stood in the driveway, wearing a red plaid hunting jacket, a black watch cap pulled low over his forehead. He was holding the dog off to the side, waving her on.

"She ain't the friendliest," he said as Detrick got out of the Jeep. He was walking toward her, shuffling really, his feet sliding across the gravel.

"What's her name?"

McTeague had to think for a minute. "Becky," he said. "I call her Becky after a used Mack I bought once. Had the name painted over the windshield: Becky. Got the rig cheap and it ran sweet. Best deal I ever made. When I had it repainted, I left the name up there, figured it was good luck."

"Does the dog ever come inside?" Pat walked behind McTeague to the door, then past him as he held it open for her. She took off her coat, hung it on a peg, turned back to face her host. He was staring at her, unembarrassed, as if measuring her in some way, and she instantly recalled the look Richard Morello had given her last night in the Mill Room. "Zeke?" She tried to restrain her impatience, remembering a rule of thumb supplied by Elaine Gauss. You had to take seniors as they were, you couldn't expect change. Adapting was your responsibility; if you couldn't cut it, you were supposed to walk away.

"There's a little house out there, a doghouse," McTeague finally said. "My daddy never did hold with dogs comin' inside and I guess I don't either."

Amazed by her beauty, by the effect it had on him, McTeague barely got the words out. She was wearing a belted sweater that fit her like a tunic, the color somewhere between orange and gold and peach; her cheeks, flushed by embarrassment (at his stare, he knew that, too), echoed the color of her sweater, as did the sheen of her hair.

What was special about it, he decided, was that the drugs they gave him for his heart had cut off his sex drive as surely as if he'd been castrated. And the sex had always been there before, part of the package, centered down in his crotch. This was different, this was pure and there was radiance to it, undeniable radiance, as if he could reach out, find lust in her cheeks, in her hair.

"Looks like you're dressed up to go out," Patricia said, "but I was hoping we could talk a little first. I'd like to get a list of your medications, the names of your doctors."

McTeague decided to let her off the hook. He dropped his eyes to the floor and said, "Take it you don't think I can handle it myself. Take it you think I'm some kinda senile."

"Zeke, I know you're living on Social Security and I know your medications have to run into the hundreds of dollars every month. If you can't afford your prescriptions, there are a number of programs available to help you. . . ."

"Charity." McTeague kept his eyes on the worn carpet. "Man who worked all his life shouldn't have to take no charity. Times, Patricia—" He raised his eyes, looked through his glasses into hers. "Okay if I call you Patricia?" He waited for her nod, then said, "Times, I swear to God, I think I'm too damned expensive to keep alive."

SIX

For the next hour, with the full cooperation of Zeke
McTeague, Pat Detrick rummaged through a shoe box
filled with brown plastic vials, some of which, to her dis-
may, were empty. There were medicines to be taken one,
two, three, and four times per day, to be taken with meals,
at bedtime, upon arising, as the need arose. Some of the
prescriptions had been filled at the Pocono Medical Center's pharmacy, others at local drugstores. Worst of all, the
various medications had been prescribed by four different
physicians, which made the possibility of an adverse inter-
action a serious concern.

After she'd finished, after she'd created a list of

McTeague's prescriptions, how often they were to be taken and who'd prescribed them, she set her pen on the scarred kitchen table and turned to face McTeague who was sitting in his rocker, eyes closed. She was surprised, momentarily, by how small he looked. It occurred to her that he seemed to fade in and out, to sometimes appear sharply focused, sometimes distant, helpless, resigned. Then his eyes opened and she found herself smiling at his frailty. Without his glasses, his eyes were all but invisible behind squinting lids, his mouth, even with his false teeth in place, seemed to fold back on itself, to collapse at the corners like an old sweatshirt.

"Were you sleeping?" she asked.

"Restin'," he answered. "Swear to the truth, Patricia, I keep tellin' myself, Zeke, ain't no sense restin' up for the big rest. Better you should keep your eyes open while they can still see somethin'." He grinned, winked, rubbed his chin. "Guess these old bones don't wanna listen."

Detrick saw it as a request; McTeague wanted to get on the road, had been looking forward to it all morning. She folded her list, tucked it in her purse. "Are you ready?" she asked as she went for her coat.

"Past ready."

They drove out under lowering skies. The temperature was noticeably higher than it had been earlier, the humidity thick enough to shorten McTeague's breath.

"Rain or snow?" Detrick asked. "Which will it be?"

McTeague ran his hands over the Cherokee's leather upholstery, settled himself back in the seat, noted the four-wheel drive and the Jeep's rapid acceleration. He liked vehicles to have a purpose and this one, despite the luxury, was clearly prepared to work, to labor for its master. "Be sleet, then rain," he said. "Weather is somethin' you get good at if you go over the road. Gets to where you can feel it. You know, on your face, like a mask."

They drove past long stretches of mixed forests, forests punctuated by the occasional house, the inevitable strip mall. Detrick, as always, pushed the edge of the fifty-five-mile-an-hour limit on the two-lane, winding road, slowing only for the sharper curves until she came up behind a tractor-trailer, a flatbed hauling five enormous logs. The logs, festooned with red flags, hung a car length beyond the bed of the trailer, forcing the rig to swing wide around every bend in the road.

Detrick sighed. "We're not going to get past him," she said. She glanced at McTeague. He was wearing his glasses now and his eyes, behind them, were huge and wet. His squint had vanished.

"Don't have to worry about gettin' no place," he said, "when you ain't goin' nowhere in particular."

But they did have a destination, a surprise concocted by Detrick on her way over to McTeague's that morning. They were on their way to the Waterview Lodge, to have lunch in the Mill Room, normally a thirty-minute drive that would now run an extra twenty minutes unless the rig turned off. She was hoping McTeague would be intrigued by the age and history of the restaurant, that it would open a pathway into his own history.

Suddenly, as if Detrick had willed it, McTeague launched into a reminiscence. "Got caught in a blizzard once, '56 it was, comin' out of Wyoming into Montana."

"How can you remember the year?" Detrick interrupted. "It was so long ago."

"Took a picture, wrote the year on it so's I wouldn't forget. Anyway, the blizzard come so fast I couldn't make no town before I had'a pull over, wait it out. Snow didn't stop for the most part of two days and the plow didn't come by for two days after that." He stopped abruptly, glanced at Detrick. She was watching the road ahead, leaning back in her seat, completely relaxed.

"Did you have enough fuel to keep the heat going?" she asked without looking at McTeague.

"I run out halfway through the second day. Prob'ly would'a froze to death if I was alone." He folded his hands, set them between his knees. "Had a hitchhiker with me, though, a young lady I picked up in Casper. Lasted right through the snow, she did, kept me nice and warm."

"What does 'lasted' mean?" Detrick asked after a moment.

"Don't mean nothin'," McTeague answered. "Just the fact of it." He turned to face her, his eyes looming behind the thick glasses. "Seems like I never could be with the ladies very long. I ain't been married, ya know. Don't have no family or nothin'. Thing is, Patricia, most I ever been with a woman since I become a man is eight days."

"Eight *days*?"

"Guess I wasn't no lover."

Detrick, despite her curiosity, decided not to pursue the topic. McTeague's intimate revelation struck her as utterly inappropriate. Elaine Gauss had described McTeague, not as fearful or shy, but as a closed book, a man with absolutely no interest in the company of other people. Why then, when they'd spent all of two hours together, was he opening himself up? It didn't make sense and she wanted some time to think about it.

"See them deer?"

She followed McTeague's finger, saw a doe and two young fawns nibbling at the shrubbery beside a white frame house set well off the road. Born that spring, the fawns seemed fragile and tentative. At the sound of gunshots from somewhere deep in the woods behind the house, their heads jerked up, their ears began to swivel frantically.

"Feel sorry for 'em," McTeague continued. "What with everything."

"Do you mean the hunters?"

"The hunters?" He burst out laughing, began to cough, took a clean handkerchief from his shirt pocket and pressed it to his mouth. When he stopped coughing, he carefully refolded the handkerchief, holding it between his hands instead of returning it to his pocket. "What I'm talkin' about is the comin' winter. Be hard on them fawns, but they don't know nothin' about it. Nossir, it's all new for 'em. Only thing they ever seen is summer." He shook his head. "Seems like somebody oughta told 'em what they was gettin' into."

By the time they reached the Waterview Lodge, Detrick's vague unease had disappeared, put to rest by Zeke's recitation of a long anecdote. In the late fifties (this time he didn't pin the year down, a fact not lost on Detrick), he'd been San Diego-bound with a load of beef when he lost his refrigeration in central Arizona.

"Dead of August it was. Temperature up over a hundred by ten o'clock in the morning. The sun turned that tin box into a regular oven, Patricia, and me, I didn't know nothin' about it till I hit the border in Needles. By that time, it wasn't worth gettin' fixed."

He'd rolled down the window then, leaned out into the cold Pennsylvania air as if the memory was still vivid. "The stink of it was enough to send the troopers guardin' the border off to pukin' in the ditch and I tell ya for the truth, them boys didn't keep me there long. No, what they done is pass me through to California, advise me to drop the box in Hollywood. Thought it was real, real funny."

But the California authorities hadn't thought it was funny, especially after the meat packer in San Diego refused the load and the shipping boss in San Antonio decided he didn't want it back, either. The shipping boss didn't want the meat, but he wanted the trailer. And he wanted it clean.

"By then, by God, I'm feelin' like I can hear them flies and maggots back there havin' a feast. Only way I can dodge the smell is by drivin' fast, lettin' it trail off behind me. When I come low on diesel, I had'a pull up to the pumps real quick, get the nozzle in before they give me the heave-ho. Then back on the road, wonderin' just what I'm gonna do. In them days, if you was an independent, you didn't walk away from a load. Nossir, if word got around you couldn't handle problems, the big companies would drop you like a hot dime. And me, my reputation was I'd pull anything anywhere.

"Well, sir, I hauled the load down to the County Health, figured what I was carryin' by then was purely sickenin', but they took themselves a look and said, 'Boy, if the sun sets on your raggedy butt in San Diego, you're gonna wake up in a cell.' Swear for a fact, Patricia, in them times, in southern California, the boys meant what they said. Didn't have to have no good reason, just you was a menace and that was that.

"So what I done—didn't have no choice the way I figured it—was head out into the desert, on Route Seventy-nine, up toward Palm Springs where the rich folks lived. When I got myself far enough out to where there wasn't no traffic, I pulled over, yanked the lock on the fifth wheel—"

Detrick, though she was lost in the story, had to interrupt. "The fifth wheel? What's that?"

"It's what holds the trailer to the tractor." McTeague's tone betrayed no impatience. "See what I done is open the lock and wire the fifth wheel with balin' wire. Just enough to keep it together while I got myself up to speed. Then, I uncoupled the trailer brakes and off I went. 'Bout a half hour later, I spy this overpass just ahead of me and I say to myself, 'Zeke, this is it, make your peace and count your blessings.' I was on a dead flat stretch of ground, goin' full out when I spun my rig and threw the box into a long slide. Then I hit my brakes and the trailer popped loose, slammed into the pilings, split in half like a stalk of celery.

"Me, I ended up out in a field of tomatoes, going backwards until I got hung up in an irrigation ditch. It was dark to what I couldn't see the box, but I could smell it clear enough. That load was all over the highway, twenty tons of rotting cow. Patricia, when I tell you them troopers was pissed off, I ain't tellin' no lie. They slapped me around pretty good, but I just kept mum, took it till they got tired. Insurance company didn't like it much, either, but they paid off just like I figured they would. Made the San Antonio Meat Packin' Company real happy 'cause they figured to lose a bundle on the meat. Always had a load for me after that, whenever I come through."

McTeague, as if he'd planned it, finished his story just as Detrick pulled her Jeep onto the Waterview's asphalt parking lot. She glanced at him, trying to gauge his reaction to the unannounced stop, but the old man was staring out through the windshield, seemingly unperturbed.

"I thought we'd stop to eat lunch. It's on SAM." It was a small lie, a white lie made with the best of intentions. She fully intended to pay the bill herself.

"Seems like they could find a better way to spend their money," McTeague said without turning, "but I could sure do with a good steak. Ain't had a steak since my heart kicked back on me."

"Is that because you're not supposed to eat steak?"

The question was meant as a gentle probe, and it brought immediate results. McTeague shook his head vigorously. "Doc Kellerman give me some kinda food list, but I never paid no attention. It's the pills that're eatin' up my Social Security, makin' it so's I can't afford nothin' else."

He opened the door and stepped out without elaborating. Pat, following, noted his unsteady gait, wanted to take his arm, settled for staying close enough to catch him if he stumbled. McTeague walked with his head and shoulders slightly forward, his knees slightly bent, as if his momentum depended on pure determination. Detrick, following, couldn't repress a smile. The trip had been a good idea; McTeague was out of the house and clearly engaged in something besides his television. Given time, she might even get him to the senior center in Toby-hanna. She might even convince him to renounce his loneliness.

There was a happiness, a joy, that came upon Detrick only when she gave to other people. She could feel it, now, rising into her throat and face like a blush, softening her heart, the physical expression of the essential truth that guided her deepest life. At times, she didn't think she could have a life that excluded these moments, that giving, as Bill Gauss insisted, brought such tangible rewards it ought to be bottled and sold.

SEVEN

McTeague was fading fast and he knew it, sputtering like the last bit of candlewick in a puddle of melted wax. His chest hurt, his eyes hurt, his breath was a dribble of air lost in the muck that filled his lungs. He wanted home, wanted his bed and his pillow, the covers tucked around his body like a shroud. The way things were going, he'd end up in the emergency room before he finished the peach cobbler, his hopes and dreams running out like the flow of his piss through the plastic tube the docs had kept inside him for two long weeks last summer.

He took off his glasses, set them carefully next to his plate. Patricia, on the other side of the table, was giving him a look filled with pity, with understanding, with everything Zeke McTeague despised. In a minute, she'd get up her courage, ask him if he wanted to go home, and he'd agree, no doubt about it. He'd follow her to the Jeep like a puppy dog on the end of a leash.

It wasn't what he wanted, not pity thick as cold molasses. The idea was to keep the do-gooder off balance, bounce her around until she had to put the pieces together. The way it was, the only thing she'd remember was his withered ass going through the door. And what he'd have to do, sooner or later, was shout it in her face: "Hey, I did 'em. I killed them. I killed them *all*."

Still, she was absolutely beautiful. Pity suited her, no denying the fact; it made her happy and Zeke could see that happiness in the glow of her complexion, the fire at the far end of the room reflected in her hair. It was something he'd never understood, though he'd long ago accepted the truth of it. There were people out there, the happiest they got was when they were feeling sorry for somebody else. It was a reality he'd made use of more than once. The do-gooders wanted to find their own good in everybody; they were ashamed of their instincts and their suspicions; they were easy.

But that was back when he'd had the energy of ten men, when he drove fourteen hours at a stretch, hunted the truck stops after midnight, when he wasn't a tired old man with a bad heart, bad lungs, bad kidneys, with only one last chance to get it right.

McTeague stirred his peach cobbler with his spoon, finally brought a bit of it to his mouth. It seemed to have no taste at all, as if his taste buds, one step ahead of the game, had already gone to the grave.

"Zeke, you about ready?"

Before McTeague could reply, a youngish man wearing a suit and tie approached their table. The man smiled at Patricia, said, "Ms. Detrick, nice to see you again. How are you?"

"I'm fine. We're just finishing. Zeke McTeague, this is Richard Morello."

McTeague put his glasses on before taking Morello's extended hand. The look he was getting was all cop and he found himself wishing he'd shaved a little closer, maybe trimmed the forest of hair sprouting from his ears.

"Mr. Morello is head of security at the Waterview," Patricia said. "He was a policeman in New York. Isn't that so?"

She looked up at Morello, gave a him a mock-serious glance that didn't fool Zeke McTeague for a minute. He could feel the chemistry flowing out of her, flowing hard. For an instant he was deeply jealous, but then he realized that the pair of them, if they came together, would open more possibilities for Zeke McTeague then they closed off. The *if* was pretty big, though, because he couldn't read the cop's dead-neutral expression, could see nothing in the sharp nose, the dark measuring eyes, the careful smiling mouth.

"I was a detective," Morello said.

"That's right. A homicide detective. Now I remember." She glanced at McTeague, then back to Morello as the waiter brought their check, left it on the table without being asked. "It sounds very exciting."

"Yeah," McTeague interrupted. "Must have felt real good to put the handcuffs on them murderers." He was feeling a little better now, buoyed, he was certain, by the turn of events. His career had been marked by extreme caution, by a stubborn refusal to improvise; that was why he hadn't ever been caught, hadn't even been a suspect as far as he knew. "Say, you ever gone after one of them serial killers? You know the kind I'm talkin' about? Like Jeffrey Dahmer. You ever go after one like him?"

McTeague slept well that night, which surprised him because he'd taken a long afternoon nap. Usually, naps that ran into the evening kept him awake most of the night, but not this time. He was out of bed an hour and a half before sunrise, turning up the kerosene heater. There was no sense making a wood fire, because he expected to be on the road before it got hot enough to throw any heat. This time the game was going to be a lot riskier; he'd be hunting on private land, would have to leave his truck by the side of the road. Despite all the bravado of the prior afternoon, he wasn't ready for handcuffs and shackles. Not yet. The idea was to be there and gone before sunrise.

Twenty minutes later, after a mug of cold coffee and a jelly doughnut, McTeague got down to work. Though he moved slowly, he kept up a steady pace, the drill, the gathering of materials, getting the truck up and running, seeming a lot easier the second time around. It was raining lightly, the temperature edging fifty degrees, and he took that as a good omen. His breathing wasn't painful, his chest didn't feel as if he'd sucked in a pack of razor blades. On the way out, perhaps by way of celebration, he took the first bump on the drive fast enough to bring his front tires into the air, slam them down into the puddle beyond, thoroughly drench the dog who sat by the side of the road.

He drove very slowly until he reached Route 196, then stopped to wait for a passing car. It was very dark and his own headlights seemed to flare on the slick blacktop. Even with his glasses firmly in place, he couldn't see the edge of the road, not unless he drove slowly enough to attract a lot of attention. But he could see the taillights of the car in front of him clearly enough, could follow at a respectful distance.

His route was torturous, going north to 191, then back south to 390, then north again. Fortunately, there was traffic on the road, hunters most likely, getting into the woods before dawn. Their taillights led him all the way to his destination, enabled him to settle within the boughs of an enormous spruce while it was still completely dark. He snapped off several twigs, cleared a space large enough for the scope and the rifle, then casually swept the windows of the Waterview Lodge.

No luck. The windows of the main building, the few that were lit, had the shades firmly drawn. From this distance, a hundred and fifty yards, he couldn't tell if the occasional silhouette was male or female. He didn't kill men if he could help it.

He let his weight settle back, from his knees to his heels, cradled the 30–30 against his chest. There were lights on around the lodge, more lights around a cluster of two-story frame buildings near the tennis courts, lights along a path winding between a dozen log cabins. As Patricia had explained it, the frame buildings were for the help, mostly kitchen workers and maids; the neatly landscaped cabins, with their covered porches and shingled roofs, were for paying guests only. The cabins were empty now, as were most of the rooms in the main lodge, November being firmly between the fall foliage and skiing seasons, but most of the windows in the staff buildings were lit.

"Seventy dollars a week." That's what Patricia had said. "Seventy dollars plus room and board. That's what they pay their workers." She'd looked around the Mill Room, her gaze seeming defiant to Zeke McTeague. "Tourism is our largest industry and the pay is terrible. It's why our kids, the ones lucky enough to get an education, leave home."

She'd seemed very beautiful to him at that moment, her full mouth pressed into an angry line, her eyes widening, nostrils pinched. The very tips of her ears had flamed red, as had the curving skin along her cheekbones. Now, remembering, McTeague let himself drift, thinking of what he might have done to her in another time, another place, what he might still do to her. If he had the strength.

When he again opened his eyes, a watery sun was rising behind Sheep Mountain on the far side of the lodge. McTeague, who carried no watch, tried to calculate the time he'd been unconscious. He wondered, briefly, if something had popped in his head, some tiny vessel, if from now on he'd shut down from time to time, die in bits and pieces. Then, propelled by a sudden fear that his pickup had been observed, that the local cops were moving in, he brought the rifle stock to his shoulder, centered the scope on a fat, middle-aged woman in a black maid's uniform. Despite her weight and the small red umbrella she held above her head, the woman was hurrying toward the main building through a steady rain. In the instant before he squeezed the trigger, McTeague realized that the hood of his poncho had slipped back, that his head and shoulders were soaked, that he was very, very cold.

EIGHT

"You remember the time you had the fight with Carl Meitzler? We must've been what? Ten, maybe eleven?" Betty Hoffmann sat curled on a pale green couch in Pat Detrick's sparsely furnished living room. She was leaning into a corner of the couch, her right hand resting on the arm, her left flung across the back. As she spoke, she raised her left hand, ran her fingers through her straight, dark hair.

"It was prehormonal, that's all I remember." Pat, in the kitchen, poured boiling water into a teapot. "Except for his look. It was twisted, lopsided . . . like his features were all out of place." She lifted the pot, breathed in the fragrance of the brewing tea.

"I was sure you were going to get beaten up. I was terrified."

Carl Meitzler was a notorious bully with a genius for isolating the weakest of his peers. When he settled on an appropriate target, the net result of his verbal and physical abuse was nothing less than torture. Betty, having caught Carl's attention at church one Sunday when he spied her picking her nose, had been the last of his victims. Meitzler's assault, begun in the church parking lot, had continued at school, finally become shoves, elbows in the ribs, kicks in the rear. Pat Detrick had ended all that. She had attacked Carl Meitzler in the schoolyard at lunch. She hadn't asked Betty Hoffmann for permission to be her champion (Betty Hoffmann hadn't asked for help), but when it was over, Carl Meitzler was running away and he was sobbing. Afterward, Betty and Pat had become best friends, though they'd known each other before only as classmates.

"I was too mad to be afraid." Pat laid the teapot alongside two cups and a plate of toasted English muffins slathered with butter and homemade blackberry preserves. Ordinarily, her breakfast choices were limited to an orange or a grapefruit, maybe a bowl of strawberries if she was feeling exotic and strawberries happened to be in season. "Besides, something had to be done."

"That's not the point."

Pat set the tray on a maple coffee table in front of the couch, went back to the kitchen for cream, sugar, and napkins. "Gee," she called over her shoulder, "why am I not surprised to hear that?" When she returned to the living room, Betty was already sampling one of the muffins.

"Where did you get these preserves?"

"From a native." It was true as far as it went. The jam had been a gift from Charlotte Keil shortly before her death.

"She put them up herself? Like in a mason jar, sealed with wax?" Betty took another greedy bite, chewed, swallowed.

"Drop this on a shelf in Zabar's," she declared, "it sells for fifteen bucks."

"How do you know it was a woman?"

Betty ignored the question. "You were always the confident one. For the whole time we were growing up. You climbed every tree, played ball with the boys, you even shot skeet with your father." Her tone was matter-of-fact, as if ticking off the items on a shopping list. "Me, I kept in the shadows, in *your* shadow. I didn't mind; I was glad to be there. But what I can't figure out is how it got turned around. I think of what you did to Carl Meitzler and I find it hard to believe that prick had the . . . I can't believe he stole your confidence." The epithet referred to Pat's ex-husband. Betty used it whenever she mentioned Fireball Detrick, whom she'd never liked. "What I think, Pat, is that you grew up to marry the bully you defeated when you were a kid."

"We've been through this," Pat said. She added a spoonful of sugar to her tea, stirred, and sipped. "I thought you were here to talk about your own problems."

"I don't have a problem," Betty declared. "At least I won't after I find a lover."

"You're through with Roberto?"

"I didn't say that."

Detrick, the cup and saucer cradled in her palm, leaned back and crossed her legs. "I thought you two had an understanding, that you agreed to be . . . faithful."

"Look, Pat, I'm thirty-three, horny as a cat, and Roberto's never around. Or he comes by at ten o'clock after work and I can see he's so beat all he wants is the pillow." Betty folded her arms across her chest, raised her chin defiantly. "Sex can be very perfunctory. Like, just another obligation, another chore. Hell, girl, I'm not gonna get these years back, am I?"

Though she was tempted to suggest that there were other things to fill your life with, Pat remained silent. In high school, Betty, tall and angular, had always played the part of the ugly duckling. It was only after she'd gone to New York that she'd come into her own, that she'd fallen in love with her own daring.

"I'm going to open an office," Betty continued after a moment. "I've been thinking about it for a long time. I'm going to open an office, hire staff, the whole works."

Betty had begun working in Manhattan's real estate industry almost as soon as she'd gotten to New York. Over the years, she'd risen to the very top end of the residential market. Acting more as a go-between than an agent, she carefully matched buyers and sellers before showing a co-op or a condo. This was a necessity because units valued above three quarters of a million dollars were almost invariably owned by individuals who didn't care to have legions of unmotivated buyers trudging over their antique carpets, who expected buyers (and agents) to show proper appreciation, proper respect, to sometimes wait weeks for an appointment to see the property.

Naturally, the buyers had a different point of view, as did the co-op boards whose approval was necessary before any deal was closed. Bringing all these viewpoints together was the job of the broker and the broker's agents; in practical terms, it meant going to the right parties, meeting the right people, nurturing connections in the corporate and social worlds. To that end, Betty attended virtually every reception given by every mission to the United Nations, regularly dined with executives whose job it was to find housing for the more important executives, religiously attended the opera, which she hated.

"Buyers have never been a problem for me," Betty said. "I could always find buyers on my own. What I needed HH and A for was the listings. But now half the properties coming into the office are referrals from other properties I've sold. People come up to me in restaurants, ask me if I can handle their apartments. Discreetly, of course."

HH&A was Hatch, Hatch & Astor, an upper East Side real estate brokerage, none of whose partners was named

Hatch or Astor. HH&A was in fact owned by two Greek sisters who'd come to New York thirty-five years ago with their father, the ambassador.

"I think you ought to do it." Detrick laid her cup and saucer on the table, picked up a muffin and napkin. "If you can handle the routine."

"Well," Betty admitted, "there's that part of it, too." Her deal with HH&A was simple enough. As long as she produced, she'd keep whatever hours she wished. In practice, this often meant weeks between appearances at the office. "And what I was thinking was that I could use some help, somebody to manage the office, work the banks, get the paperwork out on time." She sat up, tapped Pat's forehead with a long, red nail. "What I'm talking about here is *you*."

"Betty—"

"Don't tell me you can't do it, Pat. Don't insult me with bullshit. You were the brains behind Detrick Motors. Any two-bit actor with a toupee could have handled old Fireball's part." Betty sneered, shook her head. " 'This is Fireball Detrick,' " she mimicked, " 'saying come on down to Detrick Motors. We're on fiiiiiiiiiire.' God, can you imagine?"

Detrick, even after the incident, the separation, the divorce, couldn't bear to hear her ex-husband criticized. She was acutely aware of her reaction, had at one time thought it stupid, had finally come to view it as loyalty—to her past, to her present, to herself. On the other hand, she wasn't dumb enough to debate the issue with Betty Hoffmann, who'd never, in all the years they'd known each other, admitted to being wrong about anything.

"I'm not going to swear you'd fit right in," Betty said when it became clear that Pat wasn't about to respond. "But I will say that in the city there's room for everyone. If you want to do your volunteer work, there's no lack of opportunity. Then again, you might not get the chance, being as I plan to work you to death."

"While you watch?"

"Does that mean you'll do it?" Betty's eyes narrowed. She hadn't come to visit with any real hope of convincing Pat to abandon the Poconos, and now her prey seemed to be within her grasp.

"No, it doesn't mean that I'll do it. But it does mean that I'm enjoying the conversation." Pat popped the last of the muffin into her mouth, licked her fingers, retrieved her tea.

"Try it for a year, Pat. No commitment. If you hate it, you can always come back here. But if things go right, if you decide to stay, you'll retire a rich woman. I promise you." She waved long fingers in a semicircle. "I mean, look around, there's nothing to stop you packing up and walking away tomorrow."

Pat Detrick took her friend's advice, let her eyes drift across the living room. The truth was obvious enough. She was an unemployed, unmarried, childless woman living in a rented two-bedroom house. Except for a dozen family photographs carefully arranged in a short hallway leading to the bedroom, the walls were bare. The new furniture—what there was of it—held no memories. She could put her material life in a suitcase.

"Let me think about it," she said after a moment. "Right now I'm committed to getting Zeke McTeague through the winter. I can't just abandon him."

NINE

Detrick and Hoffmann were on their way to lunch at the Hallburton Inn in the town of Honesdale when Detrick mentioned Richard Morello for the first time. She did it partly to short-circuit Betty's standard speech on the glories of the New York male (the speech Betty gave when she wasn't busy describing New York men as narcissistic predators) and partly because Morello had made a surprise visit to her dream of the night before. In the dream, she'd been sitting behind her lawyer, George Milner, watching and listening as he deposed her husband. Their divorce was not yet final, the terms of the settlement still under negotiation, and Milner, through his questioning, was making the consequences of going to trial very, very clear. In her dream, Brad Detrick had squirmed, wept, then finally disintegrated, leaving her alone in a vast auditorium with George Milner who, when he finally turned to face her, wore Richard Morello's features.

"You sure he's not a drunk?" Betty asked after listening to Pat describe her two conversations with Morello. "Or a slob?" She tapped the steering wheel, stared straight ahead. "Most of the New York cops I've come across drink very hard. And why isn't he married? Where's his family? Why would he give up fifty thousand a year, not counting overtime, to work for an outfit like the Waterview? If those bastards are paying him more than twenty-five per, I'll buy *you* lunch." She turned to her friend, smiled. "No appetizer, of course. And we're drinking the house wine."

It was raining, a persistent drizzle that glistened darkly on the road, on the laced branches of the bare trees, on the hood of Betty's midnight blue Acura Legend. Detrick, cradled by the Acura's wraparound leather seats, stared out the window for a moment before replying. "No, I don't think he's a drunk. He seemed very self-contained. Out of place almost." She took a breath, listened to the tires hiss on the wet pavement. The sedan held the road as if magnetized to the asphalt, rippled over the bumps and potholes. "Like being in this car," she finally said. "Neat and completely self-contained. Completely confident."

Betty nodded thoughtfully. "And you think he's really interested?"

"Yes, I think so. Interested, anyway. That doesn't mean he'll come looking for me."

"Is he cute?"

"Cute? No." Detrick closed her eyes, summoned Morello's image, waited until she could see him clearly before continuing. "More like strong and mysterious. And no spare tire around the middle. And only one chin."

"Not like somebody we know?"

"Not like somebody we don't want to know," Pat said. Through the years, Brad Detrick had seemed to expand, slowly, implacably, adding inches to his waist, flesh to his soft jaw. Toward the end, when he was certain she wasn't coming back, his face had taken on the look of a frightened baby.

"You know," Betty said after a moment, "I never liked the Hallburton Inn. They use arugula in their salad and I loathe arugula. What say we run over to the Waterview, check out the specials?"

"I don't want to chase him." The words came quickly, automatically.

"Why not?" When Detrick failed to reply, Betty shook her head. "C'mon, Pat. Sometimes I find it hard to believe you lived through the sexual revolution. You're an independent woman of independent means. You have as much right to approach the man as he has to approach you. Besides, I want to check him out before I go back to the city, make sure he's not a jerk."

Detrick turned away before the blush rising into her cheeks became apparent. Betty Hoffmann, no matter how well intentioned, wasn't her guardian. Nevertheless, it was clear that they had, as Betty insisted, changed roles, the switch seeming to Detrick at that moment all but complete. When Betty made a quick left into a small parking lot and reversed direction, Pat said nothing. Instead, she mentally reviewed her outfit, the polished flats, the black wool slacks, the pleated rayon blouse, the gray car coat with its sharply fitted waist. As she pulled down the visor to check her makeup in the vanity mirror, she touched the silver necklace she wore, a chain of tiny interlocked swallows that seemed to fly across her chest.

"Relax, you look great," Betty said.

Pat refolded the visor, shook her head. "I think I might have to take that job you offered me. If you become my boss, maybe you'll stop being my mother."

As Betty turned the Acura onto the long driveway leading to the Waterview Lodge, a van bearing the logo and call letters of the local ABC affiliate, WNEP, pulled away from the stop sign at the end of the drive and onto the main road. Both women eyed the van curiously, knowing that WNEP was located in Moosic, one of a dozen valley towns that linked the cities of Wilkes-Barre and Scranton. Moosic was more than forty miles from the Waterview.

"Maybe they were working in the area and just dropped in for lunch." Betty's explanation seemed insufficient before it was fully spoken.

Pat, who'd already imagined every conceivable way in which she might be rejected and was now hoping that Morello would be anywhere but the Mill Room, failed to reply. Betty seemed to sense her rising panic.

"You ready, girl?"

Detrick looked up, realized that she was holding her breath. Meanwhile, Betty, who'd already pulled the keys from the ignition, was grinning from ear to ear.

"Relax, Pat. Try to imagine that you're running your fingers through the hair on his chest, that you're licking—"

"Enough." Detrick opened the door, glanced across the gently sloping lawn, saw a man step out of the woods and begin to walk quickly toward the lodge. Despite the persistent cold drizzle, the man was coatless.

"You know him?" Betty came around the car to raise an umbrella over her friend's head. "And why is he wearing a pink shirt?"

"Believe it or not, Betty, that's Richard Morello."

"You didn't say he wore pink shirts in the rain, Patricia. If you had, I wouldn't have suggested we come. I would have suggested a shrink."

Before Pat could reply, however, Carl Rinders and his brother, Frank, stepped out of the main entrance to the lodge. Also coatless, both men huddled beneath the canopy extending over the walkway, swept the grounds with their eyes, finally spotted Detrick and Betty in the parking lot. Carl Rinders offered a languid wave, then the brothers turned their attention to the rapidly advancing Richard Morello.

• • •

". . . play up the hero bit, safety first, we were prepared. You know how to do it."

Morello was speaking as the two women approached, his voice low, conspiratorial. The Rinders brothers were leaning toward him, looking worried enough to be in need of advice. When Betty and Detrick came within earshot, the conversation stopped and Morello turned to face them. His curly hair was soaked; his dark eyes, as they locked onto Pat's, projected a fierce intensity she hadn't glimpsed before. They held her own gaze so firmly that it took her the better part of a minute to realize that his pink shirt had originally been white, that it was thoroughly stained with diluted blood.

"Ms. Detrick," Morello said. "You'll have to excuse me. I'm having a really terrible hair day."

The statement struck her, initially, as sheer gibberish. By the time she finally understood he was joking, he'd turned and was striding away.

"You heard about what happened?" Frank Rinders asked. He was taller than his brother and twenty pounds lighter, the somber beanpole who kept the books while his round jolly brother charmed the paying guests.

"A woman was shot this morning. One of our workers." Carl Rinders stepped in front of his brother. "By a goddamned hunter." He looked mad enough to spit. "Excuse my language."

"Is she dead?"

"No, she was shot in the arm." He touched his own arm just above the elbow, shuddered noticeably. "God, there was blood everywhere. Everywhere."

"Morello saved her," Frank told them. "He applied a tourniquet, held her quiet until the ambulance arrived. The troopers have been here all morning, the troopers and the reporters." He opened the door to the lodge, waved Detrick and Hoffmann through. "The reporters are coming back at five o'clock. Morello promised to meet them."

"Yeah," Carl said, "he's going to give a press conference, play the big hero."

"He's going to put a positive face on what happened, Carl," Frank responded somewhat brusquely. "Personally, I think it'll be okay. Let the public concentrate on the hero part. Maybe they'll forget the blood."

"What was he doing in the woods on a day like this?" Betty asked as she stepped inside the lodge. "Looking for sick leave?"

"He was investigating," Carl replied. "In the rain, in his shirtsleeves. If you can believe that."

"You know," Betty told Pat when they were seated in the dining room, "you didn't introduce me." She raised her wine glass, sipped thoughtfully.

"I'm sorry." Pat looked down at the table for a minute, then raised her eyes. "There was another hunting accident, just a couple of days ago. A woman was killed."

Betty tilted her head, raised her brows. "Doesn't that happen every year?"

"I suppose so. But that doesn't make it less tragic. The rifles those hunters are using, the thirty-oh-sixes and the thirty-thirties? The bullets can travel for more than a mile and still have enough power to kill."

"You oughta know."

Detrick shook her head vehemently. "I never hunted," she said. "Never. I went target shooting with my father, but that was only because I wanted to spend time with him and there was no other way." She reached out, slid her glass of tomato juice closer, but didn't pick it up. "If I decide to accept your job offer, Betty, hunting season will be one of the reasons why. All those men out there looking for something to kill. It's ugly."

"If you don't like hunting," Betty responded lightly, "I don't think you'll like New York. In New York, the hunters hunt people." Suddenly she raised her eyes, looked over Pat's shoulder, nodded her satisfaction. "Here he comes, Pat. The conquering hero. It sure didn't take him long to change."

Detrick repressed an urge to turn around, another to retrieve her compact, check her makeup in the mirror. A third impulse, to ask if he was coming toward their table, was rendered moot by her friend's widening smile.

"Ms. Detrick, sorry to ruin your lunch."

Detrick reluctantly turned. Richard Morello now wore a black-and-gray herringbone jacket, dark slacks, and a light gray shirt. "You forgot your tie," she declared, the first thing that popped into her mind. She immediately felt like a dithering idiot.

"Carl asked me to lighten up," Morello replied. He seemed determined to ignore the day's shooting accident. "Next, it'll be T-shirts and jeans. Or maybe he'll put me back in uniform." He looked over at Betty, smiled broadly, extended his hand. "I'm Rick Morello."

"Betty Hoffmann," Betty said as she grasped his hand. Her eyes glittered. "And don't think you're getting away before you tell us, in great detail, *exactly* what happened out there today."

TEN

"I don't want to make a big deal out of it, Ms. Hoffmann," Morello said. "The—"

"Betty, please," Betty interrupted. "Betty and Pat."

Morello, who'd seated himself, nodded agreement. "All right. And for me, Rick, okay?" He looked at Pat, settled for a brief smile before continuing. "As a New York cop, I was trained to deal with emergencies and I just happened to be there when Alicia Munoz was shot." He continued to look at Detrick, to hold her gaze. "It's not like I performed microsurgery. I put a tourniquet on her arm, standard procedure for heavy bleeding from an extremity. The woman remained conscious the whole time, but she was very frightened. I tried to reassure her, tell her things were going to be okay. Actually, I think it's fifty-fifty she'll lose the arm."

Detrick continued to look into Morello's eyes. Despite the matter-of-fact tone, his gaze, she finally decided, carried a hint of fear. "Haunted" was the word that came to mind. It was a term she immediately rejected as too dramatic. "If you weren't there," she asked, "would the woman have died?" The question was more baldly stated than she would have liked, but, of course, there was no way to take it back.

Morello looked down at his hands for a moment, then over at Betty. "If I . . . No, if *somebody* didn't stop the bleeding, Alicia most likely would've died before the paramedics arrived. From that point of view, I guess she was very lucky I happened to be there. On the other hand, you can trust me when I tell you that I've dealt with much, much worse."

As the conversation proceeded, Pat, realizing that Morello must have made a special effort to overcome his emotions, to get changed and back to the Mill Room so quickly, finally began to relax. He was looking directly at Betty, his neutral expression devoid of sexual chemistry. That meant he'd come for her, a realization that awakened her own sexual chemistry. "Horny" wasn't the right word for it, thought Detrick, as she sipped at her tomato juice, but she couldn't think of a better one. Ten years of marriage, followed by a year of celibacy, followed by the obvious.

"Frank Rinders told us you were going to play the hero," Betty told Morello. "But it doesn't sound to me like you think you're a hero. What's that about?"

Morello grinned suddenly. "Tell me you're not a lawyer." He continued before Betty could respond. "They worry about everything, these people. Like farmers about the weather. Somehow, Carl got it in his head that a hunting accident in November would ruin the ski season which, I'm told, won't begin until Christmas at the earliest. I made the mistake of advising him to use the incident to generate positive publicity and he nominated me to do the generating." Morello's grin widened. "I'm supposed to tell the media that the Waterview Lodge will henceforth require *all* employees to attend a training course in first aid, including CPR. Guess who's gonna teach the course?"

Betty's laugh was genuine, though the look in her eyes was calculating. "Have you had lunch?" she asked Morello.

Over stuffed filet of sole (Detrick), chicken with capers in a Dijon mustard sauce (Hoffmann), and a New York strip steak smothered with sauteed onions (Morello), they conducted a basic exchange of information. Detrick admitted her divorce, elaborated on SAM and her personal involvement with the mission. Hoffmann proclaimed the glories of Manhattan, the real estate business, the endless race for the brass ring.

"It keeps you alive," she declared over a second glass of wine. "You have no product to sell, nothing beyond your own skill. Being a couch potato is not a possibility."

Curiously, though Betty had clearly intended their lunch as a means to uncover Morello's history, the former detective was the least forthcoming of the three. Instead of answering questions, Morello asked them, mainly of Betty, had her telling anecdotes, one after another, before they'd finished their salad. He did reveal that he'd never worked in Manhattan, that his ten-year stint with the NYPD had sent him bouncing back and forth from Brooklyn to the Bronx until he'd simply gotten fed up with the ugliness.

"I was afraid of becoming institutionalized," he explained, "like a lifer in prison. So I got out. I'm committed to the lodge for a year, but after that . . ." He spoke a little too quickly, as though delivering a response he'd given many times before.

Detrick, as she gradually became aware of Morello's strategy and Hoffmann's acquiescence, began to relax, deciding that Richard Morello's little game was revealing in itself. Of course, there was always the possibility that his probing questions were nothing more than a habit developed in the course of his work—like Betty Hoffmann's skillfully delivered anecdotes—but the further it went, the more convinced Detrick became that Morello had simply decided to keep his past to himself.

The truth, she thought, is that he's interrogating us, putting us to some kind of a test.

The realization annoyed her at first, annoyed her until she admitted that an interrogation was just what Betty had suggested as they drove to the Waterview. And that she, herself, hadn't protested. Now the shoe was on the other foot and if it pinched . . . Well, you didn't judge others more harshly than you judged yourself. Not unless you were a hypocrite and a liar, not unless you were a phony like Fireball Detrick, pillar of the community, who came to church every Sunday, screwed his girlfriend on Monday.

Betty was going on about a former client, Boris Kozorov, who'd come out of the Soviet Union before the end of the Cold War to make a fortune in the produce business. Boris and his wife, Anya, wanted out of Brighton Beach and into a Fifth Avenue co-op; they had the money, but were much too vulgar for WASPy co-op boards that measured individual worth not by the amount of money in a portfolio, but by that money's age.

"They were willing to go two mil for the right spot," Betty said, "and my end, if I could get them in, was two percent. Now there were places I could have put them, triplex penthouses in high-rise condominiums where you can sell your apartment without getting the board's approval. But the Kozorovs didn't want that. They wanted Park Avenue, Fifth, Central Park West; they wanted a prewar building, the older the better; they wanted prestige."

Betty's narrow face became more and more animated as she described her fruitless attempts to make the Kozorovs presentable. "Boris looked just like Nikita Khrushchev—moon face, teeth like tombstones, no hair. I think he used Khrushchev's tailor, too, for his extensive collection of double-breasted suits. The jackets barely came down to his hips. And that's only when they were hanging straight, when they weren't riding up over his fat butt."

Detrick smiled in the right places, nodded from time to time, even laughed once or twice. But it was Morello she studied. His face had again become closed, revealing none of the angry vulnerability she'd glimpsed when they'd been standing outside the lodge.

Maybe, she decided, it was an illusion created by his eyebrows. They were dark and very long, arching sharply downward to frame his eyes. His forehead was flat and smooth, his cheekbones prominent enough to leave his eyes in shadow. Even when he smiled, when his brows lifted, his dark eyes seemed, if not actually cold, at least calculating.

"When it got to the point where I found myself apologizing to my friends, I almost decided to chuck my two percent in the river, go on to something else." Betty put down her fork, dropped her hands onto the linen napkin in her lap. "But then I heard, from a friend of a friend, that the Deutch town house was about to go on the market. Abigail Deutch was old money all the way. Her ancestors went right past the Revolution, past the Mayflower, all the way back to the days when the city was called New Amsterdam. The brick town house she owned outright was not only pre-World War Two, it was pre-Civil War." She paused, looked from Detrick to Morello, leaned slightly forward, drew her companions into the circle. "There's one body of opinion that claimed Abigail Deutch was *older* than her money, that she owned the ship that brought Peter Minuet to the New World. I'm sure she was almost a hundred, stone deaf and nearly blind. And, of course, that town house of hers hadn't had a paint job in forty years. That was probably the last time she threw anything away. The rooms were packed with newspapers, piles of aluminum foil, discarded appliances, broken furniture, four decades of *Time, Newsweek, Life,* and *The Reader's Digest.* Abigail's housekeeper was older than she was; the two old ladies spent their days, from what I could see, chugging Amontillado in the front parlor. That's when they weren't sleeping it off.

" 'The place needs work,' I told Boris when I took him for a tour. 'But you've gotta look at the big picture. The house is eligible for landmark status; if you put it back together, restore it to its original glory, the landmarks committee will have to come to you, tour the premises. You'll get coverage in the architectural magazines, too. Just the fact that the house was built and continually occupied by the Deutch family guarantees its importance.'

"The bunch of them together . . . it was amazing. Abigail kept describing her debut. I don't know the year, but when she told us President Roosevelt attended, she wasn't talking about Franklin Delano. Meanwhile, the Kozorovs were talking, mostly to me for some godawful reason, about Russian politics, comparing pre- and post-Communist governments, the relative benefits of life under Stalin. If that wasn't enough, the housekeeper, who was drinking sherry from a beer mug, complained nonstop about the weather, the butcher, the dry cleaner, the baker, her mother, her father, her five brothers. At one point she gave us ten minutes on the evils of the Truman administration.

"For once, believe it or not, I managed to keep my big mouth shut. Though I have to admit I was tempted to start a fourth conversation, see what would happen. As it turned out, the Kozorovs adored Abigail Deutch, just as Abigail adored them. The deal was signed two weeks later and the Kozorovs are busy restoring their dream town house even as we speak."

Detrick and Morello smiled appreciatively. Betty finished the wine in her glass, then pushed her chair away from the table and stood. "If you'll excuse me," she said before turning on her heel and marching off toward the lady's room.

The awkward silence that followed was thick enough to butter. Morello looked after Betty for a moment, then turned to Pat. "All my dinner stories involve dead people," he said, with an attempt at a smile. "It doesn't make for small talk."

"And now you're back to it." Detrick once again responded with the first thought to jump into her mind. If he's going to do it, she thought, he's going to do it now. And I don't even know him.

"What do you mean?"

"With that woman this morning. You said you came here to get away from all that."

"Oh, right. Funny, I almost forgot. But Alicia isn't dead. That makes a big difference." He let his eyes drop to the tablecloth, finally raised them to meet hers. "Are you always so quiet?"

"Usually."

Morello's eyebrows rose, his full mouth widened into a generous smile. "I don't know, Pat. . . . If the only thing I can talk about is dead people and you don't talk at all, we're gonna have a hell of a long first date."

ELEVEN

The fourth time Betty Hoffmann declared that Rick Morello had "an ass to die for," Pat Detrick finally snapped. "Just suppose," she asked, "that two men were having this conversation, that they were talking about *your* ass."

"If they were talking about *my* ass, I'd have to question their eyesight. Swear to God, Pat, I hit that treadmill six days a week and I'm still losing an inch a year to gravity. Just last week somebody asked me to star in a video: *Buns of Slush*."

"Well, time marches on, right?"

"Can't argue that one."

"Then tell me why the two of us have spent the entire

afternoon talking about a *date*? If we're not still fourteen years old?"

It was seven-thirty and they were sitting in the Cresco Steak House, drinking vodka tonics after an afternoon shopping session at The Crossings, a sprawling outlet mall in Tannersville, and an early movie. Morello's invitation was for Sunday night, four days away, and Pat had no intention of letting a casual dinner become an obsession.

"I wanted to talk about my going back to school," Detrick said after a moment. "To get an MSW." She repressed a mischievous smile, knowing her friend would react badly, looking forward to the response.

"MSW? You're talking about a Master of Social Work?" Betty's voice carried equal measures of disbelief and sarcasm. "Bill Gauss must be doing hypnotism on the side."

"The more I think about it, the more I'm convinced that if I turn away, I'll regret it."

"I'm not talking about the work itself." Betty sipped at her drink as she gathered her thoughts. "The whole country," she said after a moment, "is moving away from social spending. The social work business is in a depression and it's not likely to get better any time soon. Before you spend the next couple of years getting a worthless degree, you better make sure it's what you really want to do."

"I've sent away for some catalogs, to Penn State and Temple University, but I haven't filled out any applications." Detrick stared down at her hands, ran her tongue across her lips, finally declared, "I work with these people at the ends of their lives, listen to their regrets, their fears . . . it makes me want to do something worthwhile with my own life, to look at everything that's happened in the last year as an opportunity. If that sounds old-fashioned, then so be it."

They drove back to the house in silence, the Acura, as it glided through the night, seeming to carry them in a cocoon, to wrap them in its own efficient quiet. Detrick, staring out into the darkness, felt herself to be, if not happy, at least peaceful. Her life was moving forward again, rolling slowly, steadily along.

Maybe, she thought, maybe later I'll understand the how of it; or maybe I'll decide that I haven't done a damn thing, that it was only time healing the proverbial wound.

Thirty minutes later, Detrick, after pulling away her coat, kicking off her shoes, pressed the message button on the answering machine. The tape spun for a moment, then Abby Turner's all-business voice blared from the speaker.

"I was over to see McTeague. He's got a terrible head cold, maybe pneumonia. I tried to talk him into the hospital, but he wouldn't hear about it. Right now, he's on antibiotics. My problem is that I can't get over there until tomorrow afternoon. If you can make it sooner, it'd be a big help."

"That poor old man, right?" Betty said. "Too stubborn to go into the hospital. Too stubborn to have a goddamned telephone. But perfectly willing to rob you of your morning."

Pat said nothing. She recalled a conversation she'd had with Bill Gauss and another volunteer. Martin Veitch had been complaining about one of SAM's clients, Gretchen Cleary, who was in the habit of cursing anybody who entered her home. Though Gretchen's anger was purely impersonal, Veitch (who described himself as a fundamentalist and attended the Church of the Risen Christ, Pentecostal) wasn't sure that Jesus had actually commanded him to tend the terminally ungrateful. Bill Gauss had listened patiently to his complaint, then broken into a merry laugh. "Those darn poor," he said. "No matter how virtuous *we* are, *they* just won't be deserving." That Sunday he'd based his sermon on a single sentence from the Gospel of John: *For the poor you have always with you.*

A breath of cold air from the slightly open window washed across Pat Detrick's face. As she tucked the blankets around her body, drew her knees up slightly, she felt herself being rocked slowly forward, again decided that she was ready to resume her life, to actually create it anew from whatever the future brought to bear. The idea, as she drifted off, seemed to pass across a barrier, to slide from hope to pure conviction, and the last image to impress itself on her consciousness was not that of her naked husband sitting on the edge of their bed, but of the fire at the Waterview reflected in Zeke McTeague's thick glasses. "Gotta admit," he'd told her at one point, "it's lucky you came along. Otherwise I might never have got out past my own driveway."

TWELVE

Though his fever had broken toward morning and he supposed that he'd live to see the sun set, Zeke McTeague felt like he'd been run over by a truck. He lay in his tangled sheets, unmoving, limp as the damp, still atmosphere that hung over the forest outside his door. A few hours earlier, he'd stumbled to the toilet, avoided the shame of soiling his mattress, but then he'd gone right back to bed and he hadn't moved since. He was lying on his right side, his knees curled up into his chest, his mind drifting from the past to the present, mixing them seamlessly together, putting this one's face on that one's body, swapping voices and conversations.

The photographs on the wall across the room seemed to

blend, the roads to connect, as if the highways he'd driven over the decades had been created solely to link the fruits of his labor. There'd been a time, and not that long ago, when he'd thought of the country as one vast cemetery, especially on clear moonlit nights when the world outside his headlights, the forests, deserts, mountains, the whole stunning enormity, had stretched away on either side, a void deep enough to unite the living and the dead.

That was his job, the way he saw it, to unite the two worlds. He could do it, was uniquely qualified because he'd passed his whole life between them, never truly part of the living, breathing mass of human beings despite the fact that he, too, lived and breathed. Even now, as he lay in bed, his memory pulled the bodies of his subjects free of the earth that held them, put flesh on their bones, light behind their eyes. They could smile again, laugh and talk, cry and beg, scream, whimper, and finally know.

If he died without telling, kept his life and his achievements to himself, that would be the end of them. And he felt that he could easily die, right here and now, too weak to resist, too weak even to be afraid.

Suddenly, as if he'd been attacked by an unseen thief, Zeke McTeague began to cry. He cried for his father and his sister who, at the height of his fever, had stood before him again, giants the both of them, enormous, irresistible. He cried for the women of Berlin, saw them as they foraged through the postwar rubble in their tattered clothes, homeless and hopeless, willing themselves into the grave for a candy bar and a pair of nylon stockings. Finally, he cried for all the truck stop whores who'd knocked on the window of his cab, for all the hitchhikers who'd climbed aboard, who'd taken that last ride through the landscape of America.

"Oh, my God, I am . . . Oh, my God . . . Oh, my God, I am heartily sorry . . ."

Though Carol Delman feels her lips move behind the

rough burlap the man has tied across her mouth, she cannot hear the sound of her own voice. Instead, she hears the insistent creak of shifting cargo, an underlying crash that echoes in the half-empty trailer whenever the man hits a pothole or a bump in the road, the unrelenting scream of eighteen tires rolling at high speed over a concrete highway somewhere in western Kentucky.

"Oh, my God . . . Oh, my God . . . Oh, my God, I am . . ."

Carol Delman wants to beg forgiveness for the hundreds of bad checks she's passed in little grocery stores throughout Kentucky, Missouri, and Oklahoma, for the bags of brown dope she's been pushing into her veins for almost twenty years, for leaving her babies, Mary and Duane, in the hands of strangers. She wants to beg forgiveness for each time she's dropped back onto a dirty sheet or leaned across the front seat of a car, each time she's whispered, "Oh, honey, you were sooooooooo good. Why don't you come see Carol again?"

Her prayer is made almost impossible by a pain that radiates from the exact center of her body. The pain has a rhythmical aspect, a pulse that throbs each time the truck passes over an expansion crack in the highway. Carol Delman's effort to anticipate these bumps, to steel herself against the pain that follows, requires almost all of her attention. She has only the tiniest bit left for an Act of Contrition.

". . . for having . . . for having . . . I am heartily sorry for having offended Thee."

Still, Carol knows that she must finish before the man stops the truck, before he again opens the high doors at the back of the trailer, before he climbs aboard. He made that very clear as he wrapped her body, from her shoulders to her ankles, in gray tape, as he knotted the gag behind her head, covered her face with a filthy burlap sack. Not even the explosion of pain when he tossed her into a hollow space between palettes of strapped cargo had prevented her from understanding his final instruction: "Say your prayers, whore."

"And I detest . . . And I . . . And I detest all my sins . . ."

When Zeke McTeague failed to answer Pat Detrick's second knock on the door, she quickly jumped to the most frightening explanation, that he was dead, that he'd died alone in the night. She recalled Charlotte Keil, that she wasn't the one to discover Charlotte's body, that it had been a matter of pure luck. If Abby Turner hadn't stopped by that morning, a day earlier than usual, Charlotte would have been lying on the kitchen floor when Pat Detrick, her phone call unanswered, arrived an hour later.

Detrick pushed the unlocked door wide open, peered into the dusky room beyond. Behind her, the dog barked and then howled. Finally, she saw McTeague on the bed, a shadow beneath rumpled blankets. She held her breath until her eyes adjusted to the gloom and she saw his chest rise. Then she was inside, all business, turning on lights, shucking her coat and purse, crossing quickly toward the bed.

"Zeke?" She dropped her hand to his shoulder, started to shake him, instead shifted her fingers to his cool forehead. "Zeke? It's Pat."

McTeague opened his eyes at the sound of her voice. Though it often took him a long while to get himself together in the morning, this time his mind was unusually clear. Suddenly, he realized that he'd been waiting for her all along, that he'd known she would come, that they were bound together and would be for as long as their hearts beat, as long as either drew breath.

"Well, Patricia," he said after a moment of pure contemplation, "looks like old Zeke really messed it up this time. . . . I feel like a bowl of cold spaghetti. Feel like I been stuck together." He smiled at her, then remembered that his teeth were lying at the bottom of a glass in the bathroom and quickly shut his mouth.

Detrick stepped back, took a closer look at McTeague, decided that his color was good, that a meal and some fluids would hold him until Abby Turner arrived that afternoon. "You wouldn't consider putting a phone in here, would you?" she asked. "Say if SAM agreed to pay the bill?"

"I don't want nothin' that would land me back in the hospital. When my time comes, I wanna go peaceful." He stared at her until he could almost taste the pity she felt. "Say, be good if I got up, hit the john. Seems like I been layin' here for a week."

"Sure, as soon as I take your temperature."

Ten minutes later, with McTeague going about his business, Pat scavenged in the kitchen cupboards for a bag of dog food. She didn't want Zeke to leave the house, not until after he'd been examined by a professional, but the animal had to be fed. McTeague had been adamant.

As she opened doors, Detrick checked the cans and boxes on the shelves, shifted bags of flour, jars of *alfredo* sauce, cans of chili, boxes of pancake mix. She noted, without surprise, that there were no canned vegetables, no fruit of any kind. Later, she would check the refrigerator. If there were no fresh vegetables, she would see to getting them. If necessary, she would cook them herself.

She found the dog food in a cupboard next to the stove, pulled it free to reveal a box of Winchester 30–30 cartridges. The sight of the ammunition stopped her for a moment. Guns, she knew, were as common as milk in the Poconos, but she hadn't noticed a rifle anywhere and the house seemed too small to conceal a large weapon. Not unless it was under the bed or propped behind the coats in the closet.

Curious, Detrick looked through the closet as she retrieved her coat, but found nothing. She put her mind to the problem at hand: how to get the food to the dog without losing a finger. As it turned out, she needn't have worried. Becky dropped to her haunches at Detrick's approach, riveted her eyes to the bowl in Detrick's hands, jammed her muzzle into her food as soon as the bowl touched the ground.

Detrick watched the dog eat, noted her matted, dirty coat, the burrs clinging to her ears. McTeague was too old to care for the animal, that was obvious enough, and she, Detrick, knowing this, could not sit by while the dog suffered. If McTeague couldn't be persuaded to give Becky away, Pat Detrick would have to care for the dog herself.

"You're not going out there to project waves of love in the direction of the nearest senior citizen," Elaine Gauss had declared almost a year ago. "Put it out of your mind." Her smile was almost belligerent. "Bill talks about love, but I say love begins with care. Love for a child, love for a mate, love for anyone. First change the diaper, heat the formula, run the bath. Remember, Jesus *fed* the poor."

The dog gobbled her food, licked the metal bowl, then again dropped to her haunches. She looked at Detrick, tossed her head as if in invitation, ran her snarled tail back and forth across the wet gravel. Detrick retrieved the bowl, took it into the house, refilled it, and came back out. She walked directly up to the dog, her movements as steady and confident as she could make them, squatted and put down the bowl. To her surprise, the animal, before it began to eat this time, paused to run a dry tongue across the back of her hand.

McTeague wasted no time once the door shut behind Patricia. Moving as quickly as his aching body permitted, he snatched her purse off the table where she'd left it and began to rummage inside. He wanted her wallet and he wanted it in a hurry, but the bag was stuffed with enough junk to stock a discount drugstore and he had to proceed very slowly. Even though it didn't seem likely that Patricia would remember exactly where everything was, he needed to be absolutely certain that she'd never know he'd touched her things. At least, not until he was ready to tell her.

He found Patricia's wallet in an outer compartment, her wallet and her keys all by themselves where he should have looked in the first place. After a quick glance between the curtains covering the window revealed Patricia still occupied with the dog, he unfolded the wallet, slid her license and car registration from adjoining slots, and brought them up to his eyes.

The light was dim and the print very small, too small to read. Again, McTeague looked through the window. Patricia was actually petting the dog, running her fingers over Becky's greasy head. "Okay," he muttered to himself, "time to put it into gear."

He shuffled over to a drawer next to the sink, opened it to find a small magnifying glass alongside a pad and pencil. With a grunt of satisfaction at his foresight (he'd always been a planner; that's why he survived, the only reason), he raised the magnifier, then held up Patricia's licence only to find the joke was on him. Instead of a street address, he found a box number at the Sterling Post Office.

Instead of growing angry, as he would have at another time in his life, McTeague calmly checked the registration, found the same useless box number. He considered jotting the address down in case he wanted to send her a post card or a letter, but decided against it. After all, there was no way he could get to a mailbox without her help.

"Zeke," Pat Detrick said as she came back inside, "about the dog, I think . . ."

"That feller we run across day before yesterday," McTeague interrupted. He was sitting in front of the TV, wrapped in a blanket, sitting there unmoving with his back to the door. "The one we seen at the restaurant, the homicide cop, he's gonna be on the television."

On the screen, a slender middle-aged man wearing a black suit was standing alongside a pearl gray sedan, extolling its virtues. The fingertips of his right hand lay gently on the hood of the car.

"He's comin' on right after the commercial," McTeague said without turning. He wondered if the big-city cop would put the facts together, conclude the accident was no accident. But a few minutes later, when Morello's turn finally came, the security chief merely described the efforts he'd made to keep Alicia Munoz alive, then announced that the lodge planned to establish a course in first aid, make the workers pass it before they began to work.

"That tape was made yesterday," Detrick told McTeague. "Look at the rain."

Before McTeague could frame a response, Morello vanished. He was instantly replaced by a dozen state troopers. The troopers, reduced to pale silhouettes by a dense fog, were at the far side of the lake, apparently preparing to work their way into the woods.

"Police say that if the bullet which struck Alicia Munoz came from land owned by the Waterview Lodge, the hunter who caused this tragedy will be charged with the crime of reckless endangerment. It is illegal to hunt on private land without permission in the State of Pennsylvania. That law was written to protect innocent bystanders like Alicia Munoz, a stranger to the region. Alicia Munoz will survive, according to her doctors, but she will never use her left arm again."

As the reporter spoke, her voice grave, the cameraman panned across the hills surrounding the lodge. The fog hung like spun sugar on the treetops.

McTeague wanted to get up, shut off the television. He closed his eyes, felt himself start to drift, wondered if that's what dying was all about, if he wasn't practicing for the big show.

"I'm going to make you some breakfast." Patricia's voice was impossibly cheery. "Any requests?"

"D'ya think," he responded, "that it might not be no accident? What almost happened to that woman?" The day before, when the first reports of the shooting had come through, McTeague had been surprised by the fact that he'd missed, surprised again by the fact that he didn't care. In the endless hours of the night, he'd considered his indifference, finally deciding that it had its root in his dormant pecker. "And what about that other one? You know, Melissa Capriella, the one that got killed in her own kitchen. She was just mindin' her own business, too?"

"I asked you about breakfast, Zeke McTeague. A much healthier topic of discussion."

McTeague ignored Patricia's efforts to organize his immediate future. She was a do-gooder in her heart and if she was going to change, to evolve, to finally open her eyes, it would happen slowly. The most he could do was drop grains of sand between the edges of her ignorance. The rest of it, the pearl, was up to the oyster.

"Now supposin' it was one of them serial killers out there in the woods. Usin' the hunt to cover up what he done. How'd anybody ever know?"

Without replying, Detrick strode across the room, opened the refrigerator door. It was surprisingly clean inside, the work, she supposed, of some other volunteer. She found a carton of eggs on the middle shelf, checked the expiration date. "Maybe," she said over her shoulder, "we could hold off on the murder talk until after we put a little life into our bellies."

THIRTEEN

As the day wore on, though his body lagged behind, a sullen child watching from the sidelines, Zeke McTeague's spirits improved steadily. It was Patricia Detrick, of course, full of surprises, who pulled him up. This woman was all business, as if that other part of her, the cheery do-gooder, was no more than a mask, a disguise she'd used to get in his door. By the time the nurse showed up at two o'clock, Detrick had organized his pills, separated the vials into four boxes—morning, noon, evening, night—labeling them with a heavy-tipped black marker, setting them on the counter next to the sink where he couldn't miss them. Then she'd gotten on the phone to some drugstore, trapped the owner, demanded the price of each prescription, made a list, totaled it up.

"This is only preliminary," she'd told McTeague. "Because I'm not sure you need all of these medications. But if you did take them as prescribed, it would cost you . . . eight hundred and sixty-three dollars and seventy-seven cents per month." She'd grinned at him then, proud of her efficiency, her kind intentions, her noble, do-gooder life. "Your Social Security check, less the Medicare deduction, comes to a little under eleven hundred. That leaves you with three hundred and thirty-five dollars a month for everything else and you can't make it on that. Not without some help."

She was sure because she'd already made an estimate of his expenses—food, electric, kerosene for the stove, a pair of shoes or a shirt now and again. The worst of it, or so she'd said, was the copayment on his Medicare, the twenty percent of the doctors' bills McTeague was supposed to cover out of his own pocket. What he should have done was join an HMO when he retired, finally settled down. Now it was too late: No HMO would accept a man in his condition.

"You're too expensive for the private sector and too rich for Medicaid and there are no public funds anymore, no grant money out there. Food stamps will help—we'll fill out the application before I leave—but what with all the cutbacks . . ." She shrugged. "I'm going to get on the phone tomorrow, call your doctors, try to get a handle on which medications you need, which you don't. After that, I'll hit the private foundations, see what I can pry out of them."

McTeague had nodded from time to time. Patricia was presenting his life to him as if it wasn't his to control, making decisions that weren't hers to make. But he hadn't grown angry. Instead, he'd watched her mouth as she worked, the soft hollow of her throat, the way her full breasts grazed the edge of the table. He'd watched her nibble at the pencil eraser in her hand, shift her buttocks on the hard seat. When she'd crossed her legs, he'd imagined her thighs, imagined the white flesh disappearing into the darker flesh of her groin, imagined the rich visceral stink of her blood.

None of these imaginings had aroused him in the slightest. His own flesh remained indifferent through all his musings. He could remember a time when his pecker jumped in his pants like a frisky colt in a meadow and he couldn't help but wonder if his fascination with this woman, the intensity of his desire to possess her, wasn't a matter of habit, the clankings of an abandoned machine nobody had thought to shut off.

Or, maybe, it was simply a matter of boredom. Zeke McTeague, who used to roam the nation, light and determined as a migrating falcon, was crippled now, a friendless shut-in. The empty hours piled up, smothered him until time itself felt wet and dirty, until the days reeked of the mildew and the white powdery mold growing beneath the claw-foot tub in his bathroom. Who could blame him for welcoming anyone, from rejoicing at any company, from leaping to the obvious, ridiculous conviction: that he could redeem his life, could fly one last time?

He was in the midst of these musings, still wrapped in his bathrobe, still wearing the long johns he'd slept in the night before, when the nurse, Abby Turner, made her appearance. Naturally, Turner directed most of her attention to Patricia Detrick, ignoring him until they'd worked over the problem with the medicines. Until, without ever asking permission, the two women decided to approach his cardiologist, ask him to coordinate Zeke McTeague's treatment. Then Turner jammed her fat gut into his shoulder while she pressed a cold stethoscope against his back, his chest. Ordering him to breathe deeply.

"In through the mouth, Mr. McTeague. And out through the nose."

She took his pulse and his blood pressure, looked into

his ears, wiped his throat with a cotton swab, all the while clucking to herself, shaking her head, prodding, probing. Like she was checking a melon for ripeness.

"You're not out of the woods yet, Mr. McTeague." Finally done with him, she turned back to Detrick while she pushed her instruments into a folding satchel. "I'm not going to be able to get back here until Monday." Her tone was adamant, as if her patient wouldn't be overjoyed at the news. "I still feel he should be hospitalized."

Suddenly, McTeague was filled with an urge to greet the nurse with his 30–30 when she returned, make her grovel, beg for her life, crawl in her own blood for an hour or two before she died. Let the cops find her there, make the arrest, take his confession. It would be over then, the killing phase of his life; it would be time for resurrection, revelation. Time to bring the dead back to life.

"Zeke?" Patricia was talking to him, softly demanding his attention.

"Yes?" He could barely get the word out.

"It's your life. What do you want to do?"

"About what?"

"About going to the hospital for a couple of days. If something happens here, there'll be no way to get help."

"Now, Patricia," he said, "I already told you I wasn't goin' back to no hospital." He could read the acceptance in her eyes, the knowledge that he had a right to control his death, to accept the appointed hour, and he realized that everything he'd thought before, all his conclusions, were simply wrong. This was about Patricia Detrick, about his life taking an impossible, miraculous turn, his dead pecker an open door to something far greater.

"All right," Abby Turner interrupted, "it's your call, Mr. McTeague. Your call and your life. I can't force you to go against your will. Pat, I've got a box of pharmaceutical company samples in the trunk of my car. Why don't we go out and try to match the samples to McTeague's meds? Maybe we can save him a few dollars."

McTeague nodded his encouragement, even managed to

get out of his rocker and shuffle behind them to the door. When Abby Turner, in a voice worthy of a drill sergeant, ordered him out of the cold draft pouring through the open door, he didn't argue. He stepped back, waited for the door to close, then watched the two women through the window. As Turner opened the trunk, he opened her purse. As she read the list of his medications compiled by Patricia Detrick, he carefully copied her address.

An hour later, Detrick set a cup of tea on a table next to McTeague's rocker, sat herself in a worn armchair. She leaned back, let her shoulders settle against the stained upholstery.

"Ugh," she declared with a smile. "I really hate detail work."

"Well, you seem real good at it."

"That's what my ex-husband used to say." She reached for the cup, brought it to her mouth, inhaled the steam before taking a careful sip. Thinking that Brad Detrick had been right, she did have a talent for organizing the minutiae, dealing with the headaches, presenting balance sheets to suspicious bankers. That didn't mean she'd liked it, had done it for any reason beyond a sense of obligation.

"You been divorced? Myself, I never got that far."

Detrick watched McTeague cross his legs, begin to rock. He wasn't wearing his glasses, and his dark irises, cut off top and bottom by narrowed lids, seemed like four crescent moons, waxing and waning in unison. For a moment, she thought she saw something flash in those eyes, something akin to hunger, and she assumed he was reaching out to her through his loneliness.

"Life refuses to be controlled," she said. "No matter how closely you attend to the details." She went on to describe her husband, his manic commercials, the growth of Detrick Motors from a used-car lot in Scranton to the largest dealership in the Poconos. "And what about you? Have you ever been close to marriage?"

"Never had no time for marriage. Always travelin'."
McTeague squeezed his lips together, sniffed as if searching
the air for an intruder. "Did have me a house near St.
Louis and a woman livin' there, but I wasn't home more
than a few days at a time. It was mostly a place to get
mail. You know, in this country you got to have an address. Guv'mint gets real nervous, they don't know where
to find a person."

"Why St. Louis?"

"Smack dab in the middle of the country is the reason.
All them highways reachin' out to everywhere. Like veins
and arteries with blood runnin' through 'em. St. Louis,
now that's the heart." He smiled at her, but his head remained still. "If you're pushin' a rig, leastways."

Outside, as the sun dropped down behind the trees, a
steadily building wind cleared the fog and the dampness.
Detrick, her attention drawn to the rattling window panes,
said, "We'll have to get some plastic over those windows
before winter sets in. Maybe add some putty to the frames."
Then she smiled, got her pad, wrote a hurried note. "See?
Details. My strong point. If you write it down, you don't
forget."

"Brad, he didn't appreciate that?"

She was momentarily startled by McTeague's use of her
husband's first name, by the implied intimacy, as if he was
an old friend already familiar with most of her life. "We
were fifty-fifty partners, Zeke. Brad wasn't my boss."

McTeague pulled the lapels of his robe together, folded
his arms across his chest, spoke without looking up. "Now
this woman, Mariah, she lived in my house in St. Louis.
Mariah was a schizophrenic woman, like Esther, my sister.
Sometimes, when I come by, Mariah'd be there. Other
times she'd be in the hospital. That was when she was
talkin' to herself, actin' crazy. There was other times she'd
be real good, like anybody else. Wasn't no way to predict.
Mostly, I didn't pay her no mind 'cause I was only passin'
through anyway, hangin' around till I could catch another
load."

He stopped abruptly, looked up at Detrick. "You ever know any crazy people?"

Detrick pictured her husband on the back side of a manic episode, sitting on a chair, staring at the crease in his pants. As if the chair was surrounded by empty space, as if any movement would suck him down into the void. "I don't like the word crazy," she responded after a moment. "It has too many meanings. And none of them prepare you for the fact." Nevertheless, she went on to describe her husband's prelithium episodes, days on end when he didn't sleep, other days when he never got out of bed. "Medication saved him, kept him on a fairly even keel. The funny part was that Brad could summon up the manic part whenever he got in front of a camera. Like summoning an evil demon."

"You believe in evil?" McTeague scratched the back of his head. "Most people don't. Not really."

"I guess I'm supposed to," Detrick admitted with a laugh. "Evil and hell . . . they just come with religion and I go to church every Sunday, so . . ."

"That's like most people. They say it with their brains: yeah, evil, definitely. But in their hearts they figure everything can be fixed. That's their mistake. You can't fix evil." He rocked back and forth for a moment. "When you get old, see death knockin' on the door, all the bad things happened to you, all the bad things you done, you wanna reach out an fix 'em, but you can't. They're just gone." Again he paused, stared up into Detrick's eyes. "See, my momma died givin' birth to me and mostly I was raised by my sister. My daddy, he worked down the mill in Anomalink, didn't come home but on the weekends to give Esther money for groceries. Sometimes he'd give punishments, too, specially if he'd been drinkin', but mostly we'd find him there on Sunday morning, asleep on the couch. He'd ask us how things was goin', what we were doin' and the like. Then he'd give Esther some bills, tell her, 'Make it stretch, girl. Money's hard to come by these days.' "

"Didn't you have any friends?"

McTeague read the look in her eyes, watched her begin to pull away, decided it was enough for one afternoon. "Seventy years ago, wasn't nothin' much up here, Patricia. Had a farm over the top of the mountain, the Carpenter farm, but the Carpenters' kids was grown, plus they figured us for trash. No, we was all on our own, Esther and me. Had to make it on our own. We didn't have no radio, didn't get no warning before the big storms hit. Times, I swear, them blizzards come down on us like they was takin' revenge for somethin' we done. Times we didn't get to the Cash and Carry for a week."

Later, when Detrick got up to leave, McTeague pushed himself out of the rocker, led her over to his trophy wall. He pointed to a yellowed photo off to the left, said, "You remember what I told you about gettin' caught out in that blizzard? In Montana? This here is the pitcher I took. That's right where we were." He worked up a good smile, tossed it in Patricia's direction. "And this here . . ." He stepped back, pointed to a much more recent photo on the right side of the wall. The photo was crisp and clear, a two-lane highway running between a tangle of trees and shrubbery. "Now this one I took right close to here. On Route five-oh-seven, 'bout three miles south of Palmyra. Had a woman with me, then, just like when I got caught in the blizzard. Only this one was crazy. She wouldn't stop screamin' so I had to put her out."

Sue-Ellen Mead has no concept of death, she does not fear death or dream of heaven or of hell. Though she vaguely remembers that her mother told her not to talk to strangers, Sue-Ellen does not remember why. Just as she does not remember why her mother failed to pick her up after class at the Blue Ridge School for Special Children, the school she has attended, summer and winter, for the last twelve years. Gripped by terror, she does not even remember the man's offering a ride in his shiny red truck, or taking his hand as she climbed into the cab.

When Sue-Ellen Mead does not scream, she cries. When

she does not cry, she babbles. When she babbles, her voice is wet and husky, her speech thickened by a tongue that has never been under her command.

They drive north along I81, five hundred miles from the western edge of Virginia to the city of Scranton, before turning east. They drive through the late afternoon, through a moonless night under a black sky pierced by sparkling autumn stars. They drive without stopping.

To Sue-Ellen Mead, lying on the floor of the cab with her head jammed beneath the dashboard, the man seems a giant out of a book read to her again and again.

"Fee, fi, fo, fum," she mumbles. "Fee, fi, fo, fum."

His fists and feet bring on her screams; her screams subside into tears; her tears settle finally into scraps of speech. Over and over again.

"You can't understand no more than a damn dog," the man tells her.

It's still dark when the man pulls to the side of the road, shuts down the engine, shuts off the headlights, when he yanks Sue-Ellen Mead out of the cab, drags her screaming through a laurel thicket, down a sharp incline to the banks of a fast-flowing stream. He does not stop when she falls, does not speak until they are far from the road. Then he tosses her to the forest floor, mutters, "Damn re-tard."

Sue-Ellen's lips and chin are covered with shiny snot. Tears glisten on her cheeks. Though she cannot stop crying, she attempts to draw meaning from the man's words.

"Took a big chance with you," he tells her. "Mighta been somebody saw me. Mighta been one of them teachers took down my license number, called the damned police. And now you ain't even worth killin'." He leans down, hefts a rock covered with wet moss. The moss on the rock seems black to Sue-Ellen Mead, like the fur of an animal. "Ain't worth nothin'. Not even your momma's gonna miss you."

Sue-Ellen Mead's tear-reddened eyes glow with sudden understanding. She nods her head eagerly, touches the man's cuff.

"Go ah mommy," she shouts in her excitement. "Go ah mommy."

The man shakes his head in disgust, kicks her hand away. He lifts the stone high above his head, stops long enough to fire off a parting complaint before slamming it down with all the force at his command. "This here is one damn picture," he tells nobody in particular, "that I'm not gonna spend a lotta time rememb'rin'."

Detrick, though she nodded thoughtfully, felt herself grow angry. Yes, she supposed, as an unmarried male of his generation, McTeague's turning for sexual relief to casual acquaintances and prostitutes could be forgiven. But why brag to her about it?

As she walked to the door, pulled it open, McTeague shuffled along behind her. The cold air that rushed in surprised her and she pulled the door shut.

"Well, Zeke—"

"Uh, somethin' I meant to talk about," McTeague interrupted. "Before you left." He peered up at her, his arms wrapped protectively around his sunken chest, then dropped his eyes to the floor. "See, what I been thinkin', the shape I'm in, maybe I oughta try to get it right with the Lord. You know, before it's too late." He lifted a foot, swiped it back and forth across the worn carpet. "What I'm tryin' to say is I'd like to go to church this Sunday and . . . well, damn, I ain't got nobody else to take me, Patricia."

FOURTEEN

"I don't know how I feel about him," Detrick told Elaine Gauss two days later. "One minute he's this frail shuffling old man who wants to be taken to church, the next he's telling me about his schizophrenic common-law wife or his encounters with truck stop prostitutes. If I didn't know better . . . No, if McTeague was a little more sophisticated, I'd think he was playing a game with me."

Detrick hadn't come in to chat with Elaine Gauss. Her original aim was simply to pass an hour alone in the chapel. Unfortunately, she'd arrived to discover the flower committee (a day late) busy arranging flowers for the Sunday service and the choir busy rehearsing for the same event. She'd found herself an empty desk, then composed the periodic report expected of all individual volunteers and group leaders. In it, she'd included her observations of McTeague's physical condition, as well as the continuing problems with his medication. She'd realized, as she worked, that she was merely repeating information already known to Abby Turner, but, with Betty back in Manhattan and nothing special to do, no place to go, she'd continued on without pausing.

When Pat Detrick had walked away from her husband, she'd also walked away from her job of a decade, the one she'd begun two weeks after graduating from college. Leisure had burst upon her like a bomb, the empty hours compounding the emotional emptiness, amplifying her pain until there were times she didn't think she'd get through the night. Even now, she found it difficult to sit quietly in her own home, to curl up with a book, even to watch television for any extended length of time. One of her secret fears was that her work with SAM, her support of Charlotte Keil, was motivated by nothing more than a desire to escape self-examination and loneliness.

"McTeague wants to go to church?" Elaine fingered the report on her desk, Pat's report. Her tone was noncommittal, obviously intended to draw Pat out, to make her define the problem.

"You'll meet him tomorrow, Elaine, assuming he's well enough. He told me that he 'wanted to get right with the Lord.' That's a quote." Pat tilted her head to the left, shrugged. "As if I could refuse."

"And you think he knew that? Before he asked?"

"Well, that's the big question, isn't it? Look, when I went to his cabin that first time, we both thought he'd toss me out. Instead, he welcomed me with open arms and I feel like I've been out of sync ever since."

Neither woman spoke for a moment, neither willing to state the obvious question. Finally, Elaine asked, "Do you want to get out?" She paused, then said, more softly, "It won't get easier over time."

"No," Detrick quickly replied, "I can't do that. He's

too sick, too helpless. But what I can do is set some limits. And make him get a damn telephone. Do you know anything about his family? He claims to have a schizophrenic sister. I'd like to make sure he isn't inventing his past as he goes along."

"A schizophrenic sister and a schizophrenic girlfriend?"

"That's the party line."

"It doesn't seem likely. But the answer to your question is no, I never heard of the McTeague family before Zeke came to the mission."

"Who could I ask? We must have a client or two who's lived in the region long enough to remember?"

Elaine thought about it for a moment. "You could try Claire Pierce. She grew up a few miles north of McTeague's cabin."

"How old is she?"

"Eighty-something." Elaine lit a cigarette, dropped the match into a glass ashtray. "Claire's kind of interesting. Up until three years ago, she was a volunteer. You know, one of those energized old ladies who make everybody else feel like they're goofing off. Then she fell and broke her hip and didn't heal. Now she's facing hip replacement surgery, that or a wheelchair." Elaine spun her Rolodex, flipped through the cards, finally pulled one out and tossed it in front of Detrick. "Claire's a good woman, one of the best. She'll be overjoyed to see you."

Everything about Claire Pierce's life stood in direct contrast to Zeke McTeague's. Everything except her age. She lived with her son and daughter-in-law in a four-bedroom colonial set on an acre of carefully landscaped ground. Two vehicles, a Ford Explorer and a Toyota Camry, both nearly new, sat side by side in front of a pair of garage doors. The chimes, when Detrick pushed the bell, rang deeply from the interior of the house; when the door was opened by Melody Pierce, warm air, flavored with the scent of baking cookies, met Detrick's face. If home, for

Zeke McTeague, was four walls and a kerosene stove, home, for Claire Pierce, was family and friends and loving support.

As if to prove the fact, Claire Pierce sat on a wicker couch flanked by two young boys. She was reading from a book of children's stories, when Melody Pierce ushered Detrick into the small sun room.

Detrick crossed the room, hand extended. "Mrs. Pierce, I'm Pat Detrick. I spoke to you about an hour ago."

"Yes, of course." Her eyes were bird bright, her narrow mouth set in a straight line beneath a beak of a nose. "Boys, you're going to have to find something else to do."

The children grumbled momentarily, but when Claire firmly closed the book, set it on a long table in front of the couch, they scrambled down and dashed out of the room.

"My great-grandchildren," Claire announced as she took Detrick's hand. "Mine for the day."

"How do you take your coffee?" Melody Pierce asked. She remained in the doorway, a heavy woman in her fifties, wearing blue jeans and a blue flannel shirt.

"You don't have to go to any trouble," Detrick quickly replied. "I know I've interrupted your day. Just walking in like this."

"The coffee's already made," Melody assured her. "Around here, there's a pot going all day."

"In that case, I'll take mine with milk and two sugars." Detrick, who rarely drank coffee, understood that she had to accept the offered hospitality. Not to do so would brand her as crass, a flatlander. According to Elaine Gauss, the Pierces could (and did) trace their local ancestors back to the Civil War, thus rendering their beneficence obligatory.

"Sit here next to me," Claire said after her daughter-in-law left them. "I don't hear so well any more." She waited until Detrick was seated, then said, "You're the Geisheimer that married the Detrick boy, yes?"

Detrick, unsettled by the use of her maiden name, by the fact that Claire Pierce knew it, took a moment to reply. "How did you know that?"

"I guess I made it my business to know." Claire barked a laugh. "Folks, when they're being charitable, call me the county historian. The rest of the time, they call me a busybody. Or worse."

Claire Pierce's face was deeply wrinkled; the skin of her jowls sagged against her neck and her white hair was thin enough to reveal a pink scalp. Yet her eyes were sharply focused, her voice strong and precise. The eyes and voice seemed to Detrick as if they belonged in another body, one that wouldn't betray them. "Well, I'm not married to him now. We're divorced."

"Yes, I heard that, too." The old woman hesitated, then said, "Families don't seem to stick together anymore. I've got a son and a daughter, both divorced. They live in California."

They chatted on for a few minutes, exchanging pedigrees, discovering mutual acquaintances. This was also obligatory, this careful distinction between flatlanders and natives. Detrick, though she didn't believe that her great-grandparents' decision to settle in Wayne County conveyed a title in some imaginary aristocracy, had never found a way to gracefully avoid this ritual.

Finally, as if she'd meant to bring the biographical dance to a conclusion, Melody Pierce hustled through the doorway, laid a tray bearing a plate of cookies, coffee, cream, and sugar on the table in front of them. "Mom," she chided, "don't go crazy on the cookies. They're loaded with butter."

Claire stared at her daughter-in-law's retreating back, waited until it disappeared, then immediately bit down on a cookie before adding a spoonful of sugar to her black coffee. "They mean well," she told Pat. "I'm talking about the children. But they don't really understand. I grew up in a time when ladies didn't smoke and didn't drink. When they didn't even go out to work." She dipped her cookie into her coffee, nibbled at the edges. "But we ruled in the kitchen. In fact, you could say food was all we had. Food and laundry."

"I've got news for you, Claire. Even when I went out to work and smoked cigarettes, I still did the laundry."

The old woman fell back against the cushions, curled her mouth into a perfect circle, laughed appreciatively. "Well, there's no winning except for losing, I guess." She laughed again. "You came here to talk about the McTeagues, that's the way of it?"

"Yes. Zeke is living in the family house. That is, if you can call it a house. It's more like a shack. Anyway, he told me he grew up with his sister and that she was schizophrenic and—" Detrick stopped abruptly. What she was doing, she decided, was investigating Zeke, poking into his business. What he chose to reveal to her was one thing, what she pried out of strangers was cut from an entirely different ethical cloth. "He's a client of the mission," she continued. "Elaine told me you were a volunteer, so you know what I'm talking about." She stopped again, ran her fingers through her hair as she collected her thoughts. "I don't know whether I want to stay with him, whether I can be the companion I'm supposed to be. Sometimes, he says things . . ."

Pat shrugged and smiled. Claire Pierce had moved forward until she was now perched on the edge of the couch. She snatched another cookie off the plate, dipped it into her coffee, devoured it whole. "You don't have to explain yourself to me, dear. People have a right to know about other people. I've lived my whole life that way. Besides, everything my uncharitable neighbors say about me is true. I'm nosy; I mind everybody's business but my own."

Claire took a third cookie, this time biting into it dry. "You know, I went to school with Esther McTeague. A two-room schoolhouse in Jericho. She was as normal as anybody else when I knew her. Smart, too. But something happened to her when her mother died giving birth to Ezekiel, died right in the house with Esther watching. Esther was only nine or ten at the time, but she got saddled with raising her brother. In those days, you didn't have to go to school. You didn't show up, that was just one less to educate.

"Now, the father, that'd be Abner McTeague, he was a man of violence and given to drink, but if I remember right, he lived down near the mill in Anomalink most of the time. I suppose he must have given money to those children because they didn't starve and they had clothes on their backs, but I don't recall him being around much. That was probably for the best. Like I said, Abner was a violent man.

"As for Esther . . . Well, I was raised in a time when folks didn't choose between schizophrenia and manic depression. They never used the word psychopath, but they did know crazy when they saw it and that's what Esther became. Her craziness got worse as she got older, much worse. She was in and out of the asylum after Ezekiel went off; sometimes she seemed almost normal, other times . . ." She shook her head. "The farm over top of the mountain was owned by Brian Carpenter and I can remember Brian's wife, Muriel, telling me about hearing Esther in that house screaming. She told me sometimes it went on all night, that she wandered through the meadows talking to the cows. I know Muriel went to the county and the county sent doctors out there, but I don't know what came of it."

Claire paused long enough to clear her throat, sip at her coffee. "You know, dear, after you called me, I began to think about the McTeagues for the first time in years. About the two of them, Esther and Ezekiel, up there all alone in that house. Nowadays, the county'd come along, do something about it. Back then, folks put a premium on staying out of other people's business. Those two children had food on the table, a father who was home often enough to claim a family. I guess folks figured that was sufficient." She raised her eyes to meet Detrick's. "Ezekiel went into the army in 1939, before the war. He was underage, barely sixteen, but he got in somehow. That's how desperate he was to get away."

FIFTEEN

It snowed that night. A two-inch dusting that fell from a calm sky to pile flake by flake on every horizontal surface, to carpet the ground so evenly that it seemed, to Zeke McTeague as he dressed for church, that the snow had always been there. McTeague was standing by the window, watching a red squirrel scatter the fresh snowfall as it foraged in the backyard. The yard was covered by animal tracks, bird tracks, for the most part, that barely penetrated the surface of the snow. Left by the ground feeders, by the sparrows, juncos, and finches. The birds were pursuing the same basic goals the squirrel pursued, the same goals the deer pursued when they arrived before dawn to feed on the shrubs around the house. All were looking for something to eat. And trying their damnedest not to be eaten.

McTeague turned away from the window. He crossed the room to his bed, stared down at the black suit, the white shirt, and the blue tie carefully arranged on his blanket. He'd had a very bad night. His dreams had been filled with his sister, with Esther striding naked through the little cabin, tossing pots and pans, moaning, sobbing, screaming, her dark blond hair flying off in all directions. In the dream, her body had been hairless, his sight blocked by the bars of his crib. But he hadn't been too young to know what was coming, that she'd eventually get to him.

Two questions had perplexed McTeague for all of his adult life. Now, with Esther and his father dead, the questions were beyond answering. Though McTeague accepted the fact that he would never really understand, the questions continued to occupy his attention from time to time. Each was simple enough on the surface, yet their repercussions, over the course of four and a half decades, had ended the lives of more than two hundred people.

McTeague wanted to know, first of all, why Esther hadn't killed him. Back when he was too little to see her fits coming, to get out of her way, to fight back. Was it simply luck? An accident? Or had Esther, even as she carried on long conversations with the empty air, as she pounded her own head into the wall, as she turned to face him with the blood running into her eyes, maintained some tiny bit of control? Had she *deliberately* spared him?

There were times, undeniably, when she'd loved him, others when she'd gone days without noticing him at all. By the time he reached his teens, they'd switched roles altogether. He became the one who bought the groceries, cooked the meals, made sure she took her medication, the one who punished her when she was bad.

The second question was also quite simple: Why hadn't his father just deserted them? McTeague couldn't remember his father ever showing him a moment's affection. He'd never seen his father kiss Esther, or put his arms around her, sit her on his lap. But McTeague could clearly recall the first time he'd observed a schoolmate hugged by her father. The act had seemed mysterious to him, inexplicable, a prelude to something he couldn't even guess at.

If his father had deserted them, had simply stopped bringing the money, the government would have stepped in, taken them away, changed the course of Zeke McTeague's life and the course of so many other lives as well. But Abner McTeague had come back to the cabin, come back month after month, year after year. Pursuing demons of his own.

McTeague shook himself alert, then began to dress. He was going to be a good boy today, on his best behavior. The look in Patricia's eyes when she'd left him the other day had been too close to revulsion. If she walked away now, decided to seek out somebody more worthy of her charity . . . Well, that just couldn't happen. Just couldn't.

When Detrick pulled into McTeague's driveway shortly after eight o'clock, the first thing she noticed was that instead of barking, the dog, Becky, was sitting next to her little house, tail sweeping the snow, tongue lolling off to the side. When Detrick, after parking the Jeep, walked over to retrieve the dog's bowl, Becky did a little dance in the snow, then jumped up to lick Detrick's face.

"Don't mess my coat," Detrick said. She rose quickly and stepped back. "I'm going to need this tonight."

A few days before, she'd told Betty Hoffmann that she didn't want to dwell on her date with Rick Morello, that events would take care of themselves. But now, with that date less than ten hours away, she was becoming more nervous by the minute. Questions like what would she wear spiraled down into what would she say, sank further into whether they had anything at all to say to each other. The more she thought about it, the more convinced she became that a homicide cop who'd worked the slums of Brooklyn and the Bronx lived in a world so different from that of a born-and-raised country girl that he might as well try to describe the atmosphere on Jupiter as try to convey his life experience to her. They would sit there, the two of them, like mannequins, through an endless dinner, politely sipping wine, nibbling at a meal neither wanted to eat.

Still preoccupied when McTeague opened the door to her gentle knock, she was unable to control a double take at the sight of him in his oversized black suit, his faded white shirt with its frayed collar. When she finally realized that the suit had once fit him, she felt a wave of pity. McTeague was literally withering, the bones that held him together pushing up through the flesh of his shoulders, his hips, his chest.

"Guess I look pretty funny," McTeague said. "But what I figure is the Lord won't mind. Bein' as He might not get another chance at me." He stepped back to let her enter. "Once upon a day, this suit was too small for me. If you could believe that." He grinned his broadest grin, stared unblinking from behind his glasses. "I was always a strong man. When I was young, in the army during the war, I was a regular bull."

"I'm sorry, Zeke, you just caught me off guard."

"Bet you was thinkin' about that fella from down to the Waterview. That Italian fella you got a date with."

Detrick, though she managed to avoid a second double take, flinched inside. It was as if McTeague had been reading her mind. She looked at her watch. "We don't get moving, we'll be late. The Lord may not care about your suit, but Reverend Gauss hates to have his service interrupted." Then she glanced down at the bowl in her hand. "Just give me a minute to feed the dog."

That Sunday, Bill Gauss preached a sermon on the parable of the good Samaritan. The Jews and the Samaritans, he carefully explained after reading the short parable, though they'd lived side by side for a thousand years, were social, political, and economic rivals. In light of this, Jesus's decision to employ a teaching that depicted Jews as crass and self-ish, Samaritans as charitable and caring, was revolutionary by any standards.

"If the sermons of Jesus Christ had been created by committee," he told his congregation, "this parable would never have been spoken in public. Remember, Jesus preached to the Jews. Jews were His audience. Bad enough, He commanded them to love their enemies. Now, He was giving their enemies the moral high ground. Beyond that, Jesus was telling them not only that they were to love their neighbors as they loved themselves, but that the word itself—*neighbor*—applied to every human being on the face of the planet."

Detrick, as she listened, decided that it was a typical Bill Gauss sermon, the emphasis on salvation, not sin, on developing social conscience as a necessary precondition to salvation. As a child, she'd been presented, at Sunday school as well as in her own home, with a black-and-white world. Sin was a matter of behavior, the Ten Commandments not subject to interpretation. It was a concept she'd more or less accepted until she went off to college. By her second year, most of her friends—straight or gay—were eagerly committing the sin of fornication on a fairly regular basis. Worse yet, she and Brad were sleeping together whenever possible; if sex out of wedlock was evil, if the act condemned you to burn forever in hell, then she herself was evil, she herself bound for hell.

It was preposterous, she'd concluded. The Bible, no matter how inspired, was meant to be communicated to a particular people at a particular time. If it had been written today, it would be quite different. As it would if written a thousand years from today.

Shortly after the start of her third year at Shawnee College, Detrick had stopped going to church altogether, a decision she'd fully expected to resolve her conflicts. Instead, the next five years, as she'd first graduated, then gone into business with Brad, she'd come to discover that a part of her, at times as insistent as a hungry infant, simply remained unsatisfied by the business of getting and spending. Eventually she'd given a name to this demanding child, called it faith, found her way to a congregation that satisfied her head as well as her heart, a way of life that put conscience ahead of doctrine.

As always, Bill Gauss ended the service with a simple prayer; he prayed for strength and courage in the face of obstacles, for perseverance in the face of all the ugliness tossed up by a world that seemed to revel in ugliness. Then he turned to the faithful and told them, "Go in peace."

Pat, McTeague in tow, glanced at the face of her ex-husband as he made his way out. As always, Bradford had been sitting across the aisle, next to his mother and two sisters. Pat understood his presence as a weekly cross her vanity would just have to bear. His family had been coming to the Dreher Community Church for the better part of two generations. She could not exclude him (though if the divorce had gone to trial, he might have been driven away by pure shame), and no longer wanted to. But she did wish he would stop coming up to her as she stood chatting in the churchyard after services, stop asking how she was doing, stop begging her to come back to Detrick Motors.

When she went outside, Bill and Elaine were standing on the walkway leading to the parking lot, shaking hands with their parishioners. The sun was out and the snow was beginning to melt. In places on the lawn, blades of yellowed grass poked through.

"That was good preachin'," McTeague said after she introduced him to Reverend Gauss. "Pretty near every truck stop in this country has a chapel out in the parking lot and I guess I've listened to a thousand preachers. Mostly they preached about hell and damnation. This here is a whole lot more pleasin' to a man who's got so old he don't remember what sin's about."

"I think I'll take that as a compliment." Bill laughed as he took McTeague's hand.

"A compliment's the way it was meant," McTeague responded.

Pat exchanged a glance with Elaine, then led McTeague to the parking lot where she introduced him to several couples. He smiled at them, shook hands, then seemed to drift off while she made the usual small talk. Detrick, worried about his stamina, watched his dark eyes sweep the the church, the attached wing, the tree line beyond the lawn. Then Brad Detrick approached, and she lost track of her client.

"Pat, how are you?"

It was his typical opening gambit, as if her health was somehow in question. Unexpectedly remembering Morello, she fought a strong desire to throw the ex-cop in her ex-husband's face.

"I'm fine, Brad," she replied. "How about you?"

"Better than ever." Brad Detrick had a reputation for bullheaded determination. Once he set his sights on a goal, he simply dropped his head and charged. Running into the occasional wall had no discernible effect on him other than to provoke a second and a third charge. It was a tactic that had often worked on loan examiners when he and Pat were building Detrick Motors. That it was working less well on his ex-wife these days didn't discourage him in the slightest. "Did I tell you, Barney Turentine is having a nervous breakdown?"

Barney was Detrick Motors' accountant; he and Pat had worked together from the beginning.

"You did tell me that, Brad. You told me last week."

"Yeah, I guess I did." He looked down, swept the snow from the ground with the sole of his shoe, a gesture that reminded Detrick of Becky's tail sweeping the gravel on McTeague's driveway. "The thing of it is," he resumed, "I've hired three people to do what you used to do by yourself. Add up their salaries and benefits, you're looking at nearly seventy thousand dollars a year. It's crazy; I'd rather give it to you; at least you handled problems as they came up. These jerks, they want me to make every decision."

Detrick glanced around the lot, finally discovered McTeague in conversation with an elderly widower named Terence Bannister. "Brad," she said, "my answer is the same as it was last week and the week before. If I decide to take a job, it won't be with Detrick Motors. You were bad enough as a husband. I can't imagine you as a boss."

Brad stepped back, jammed his hands into the pockets of his cashmere overcoat. "For Christ's sake, Pat, I screwed up one time. I admit it."

"Interesting choice of words." The truth, proven beyond doubt by the investigator working for George Milner, Pat Detrick's lawyer, was that old Fireball, not content with the odd affair, was well known at a certain whorehouse in Scranton. Since Milner had used the information to force a settlement, Brad Detrick was fully aware of her knowledge. Nevertheless, he continued to perpetuate the myth that he'd made a single mistake, that she was obliged to forgive him for an impulsive roll in the hay.

Detrick, too angry to continue, turned and walked over to McTeague. She greeted Terry Bannister, a notoriously irascible man, with a quick smile and an even quicker, "Hello, Terry." Then, after nodding at Bannister's muttered, "Howdy," she addressed McTeague. "You about ready, Zeke?"

"Sure am, Patricia," McTeague responded without hesitation. "Terry, I'll be seeing you around."

They walked in silence to the Jeep. As they waited for the car to warm up, Pat, trying to throw off her foul mood, said, "Well, that was certainly fun."

"That your husband?" McTeague asked.

"My *ex*-husband."

"Well, he's sure full of himself. Knowed a lotta truckers with that attitude. Never liked a one of 'em." He cleared his throat, rubbed his hands together. "But say, that fella I was talkin' to, you know him?"

"Terry Bannister?"

"Right. Me and Terry, we went to school together. He knowed my sister, too." McTeague shifted on the seat, finally turned to look into Detrick's eyes. "Feels awful strange to meet somebody who knew me back then. Feels like I come back to something I wasn't expecting."

SIXTEEN

Detrick, partly from stubbornness, partly from pure denial, refused to begin dressing until five o'clock, an hour before Rick Morello was due. On one level, she was still pretending her date was no big deal, on another that even if it was a big deal, she wasn't going to let it control her life. As a direct result, forty-five minutes later, she found herself in a state very close to panic over a broken eyebrow pencil.

"What I'm going to do," she told her reflection, "is turn out the lights, hide in the closet. Wait him out."

Instead, she sharpened the pencil, went back to work, was smoothing her lipstick when the bell rang at six-fifteen.

"Coming." Before turning to the door, she allowed herself a last appraising look in the mirror. She was wearing tan wool slacks, and a cream-colored blouse so pale it bordered on ivory. The finely woven slacks, from a designer outlet in Tannersville, appeared at first glance to be silk. The soft fabric draped her hips and thighs, flaring slightly over her calves, hopefully drawing attention from her waist. The rayon blouse was quite plain; she wore it fully buttoned, concealing the top button with a necklace of irregular amber beads.

"Coming," she called again. She snatched a long, square-cut vest, a sweater almost, off the bed as she passed, shoved her arms through the armholes. The vest was boldly colored, vertical stripes of deep red bleeding into warm brown and smoky orange, each stripe separated by a wavering black line.

"Sorry," she told Morello, pulling the door open. "I got a late start." She saw his eyes flick over her outfit, over her body, read his approval as surely as if he'd put it on paper. Despite herself, she smiled. "Why don't you come inside while I get my coat." Then she noticed that he was carrying an unfolded map in his left hand. "Did you get lost?"

"No, the directions were good, but . . ." Morello flashed a grin. "I don't know if I'm allowed to complain, but I'm used to street lights, intersections. Around here, the forest comes right up to the road; it's like driving through a tunnel. I know they call this area the Pocono Mountains, but I swear I haven't seen a mountain since I got here."

"That's because the Pocono Mountains are really a plateau. The mountain part was made up by the Chamber of Commerce in 1911. To attract tourists."

"Is that true?"

"No," she admitted as she pulled on her coat. "But it was probably made up by the moral equivalent of the Chamber of Commerce. If it wasn't for the tourists, the vacation homes, the region would have the population density of northern Maine." She turned the key in the door. Ragged clouds, propelled by a rising wind, whipped across the full moon overhead. The melted snow, she realized, would be ice within hours. "Rick, uh . . ."

Morello stared back at her, his expression, the way she read it, somewhere between neutral and vaguely curious. He was wearing a gray three-quarter coat, double-breasted. Like everything else about him, the coat was immaculate.

"Your Buick? It's a nice car, but the roads are going to ice up before we get back . . ." She stopped again. Men could be touchy about their cars, about who drove. If Morello took that attitude, it would be a very long night, even if she decided never to see him again.

"You want to take your Jeep, fine by me. I was the kind of cop, I always made my partner drive."

Detrick walked toward the Jeep, her boots crunching the gravel. She could hear Morello behind her. "How did you convince him? To drive, I mean."

"Her, Pat. My first partner was a woman. And what I did was have three accidents in two months. After that, it didn't take convincing. Anna wouldn't let me *hold* the keys. She told me if she got shot, I should call nine-one-one, leave her on the sidewalk until the ambulance arrived."

Detrick had the Jeep running, was about to back out of the driveway when she realized that she didn't know where they were going. She glanced at Morello, read his smile as condescending. Condescending men always pissed her off. She'd met enough of them, factory reps who assumed that Detrick Motors was her husband's show, who looked like they were about to pat her on the head or ass, murmur, "Good girl, good girl."

"I thought we might go to hear Shirley Horn. At Caesar's," Morello said first. "She's a singer and a pianist. A jazz singer. We could have dinner first."

"Which Caesar's?"

"There's more than one?"

"There's three of them."

Morello closed his eyes for a moment, then opened them and smiled. "Caesar's Paradise Stream. On Route Nine-forty."

"Don't tell me—you wrote it down on the backs of your eyelids."

"Pardon?" Morello's smile turned sheepish.

"The way you closed your eyes, then came up with the name."

"Oh, that. A trick I learned at St. Mary's. Catholic schools put a premium on memorization." He turned to look through the windshield as Detrick backed out of her driveway. "It's a useful tool. For cops, I mean. The ability to keep track of the details, remember faces and names. That's how I got to be a detective."

"By remembering details?"

Morello explained that as a patrolman working the South Bronx, he'd made it a habit, before going on tour, to examine the want sheets closely, to match faces on mug shots with faces on the street. Eventually, his arrest record had attracted the attention of detectives assigned to the precinct, then of detectives from downtown, the silks. A gold shield, number 398, had followed.

His explanation broke the ice between them. By the time they reached their destination, one of the splashier honeymoon resorts, a number of biographical details had been established. She and Morello were both divorced, each after a little more than ten years of marriage. Neither had children and both, to a certain extent, felt they were in the process of starting their lives over. Morello's parents, as well as two older brothers and a younger sister, lived in the Woodhaven section of Queens, one of New York's outer boroughs. Detrick's parents had moved to Arizona three years before. She had no siblings, had been born when her parents were nearing forty.

"I think they were surprised when I appeared," she explained. "As if I'd been abandoned on their doorstep. The only thing they really cared about was quiet and, naturally, I kept the house in chaos." She tapped the steering wheel. "I was a loud child."

The economic details came last. Morello told her that he'd inherited enough money when his grandfather died suddenly three years before to render his move from New York to Pennsylvania, when he'd finally decided to make it, relatively painless.

"The money gives me a measure of independence," he told her. "That's for sure. The only problem is I'm not sure what I want to do with my freedom. If anything."

Detrick, engaged by the obvious parallel, then described her deal with her ex-husband, how she'd bought herself ten years of financial independence by insisting on her right to an equal split of their business and property. "I'm not sure the money makes things easier," she concluded. "Most of the time, I feel like I'm spinning my wheels. If I had to go out to work every day, find the rent money . . . Well, you obviously know what I'm talking about."

Morello nodded, then changed the subject. "Sylvia's an artist, a designer; she heads the art department at an ad agency. When my grandfather died, I just walked out, left her with everything we'd accumulated."

"And she took it?"

"Sylvia always had an eye for opportunity." Morello shifted on the seat, unbuttoned his coat. "Me, I like—or *liked*—to hunt down the bad guys. If I'd been ambitious, I would have gone into my father's contracting business. Or finished college, become the lawyer in the family. As it was, I left that particular role to my little sister, the business to my brothers. From what I can tell, they're all happy, if not actually grateful."

Detrick slid the Jeep into a space in the Paradise Stream's nearly empty parking lot. On their way across the snowy lot, walking side by side, Morello suddenly extended his elbow, the gesture a clear invitation. Detrick hesitated briefly, then slid her hand through the gap. She felt his strength, the ropy muscle beneath her fingers, wondered if he was show-ing off, a little boy like her ex-husband. Then she decided that time would tell. They were inside, shrugging out of their coats, before she realized the implications of that last decision.

SEVENTEEN

"John's a retired cop," Morello explained.

"Is that why he talks out of the side of his mouth?"

On their way in, they'd been greeted by a man Morello had introduced as John Hyde, manager of the resort's supper club. Detrick, like most of her native-born friends, favored the locally owned inns over the flashier resorts. It was a small prejudice, one she was aware of and indulged without guilt. Still, watching Morello play the insider at this flashy resort made her feel slightly uncomfortable. Again, she had the feeling she was being manipulated, that Morello weighed and measured every gesture. He was now seated to her left, the chair turned slightly in her direction. His expression was both innocent and interested.

"Cops have a different face for other cops," Morello explained. He was wearing a navy blazer and a fitted blue shirt, open at the collar, that hugged the broad planes of his chest. "You can see it at a party, a wedding, a funeral. Ex-cops talk to each other like coconspirators."

"Are you telling me that all policemen have guilty consciences?"

To her surprise, Morello took the question seriously. "The rules are written to protect the people at the top, the commissioner and the chiefs. They don't apply to the streets. You break the rules often enough, you start to believe that everybody on the outside is looking over your shoulder. You stop trusting." His fingers played with the polished buttons of his blazer. "Another reason I wanted to get out," he added tersely.

The waiter arrived before Detrick could respond. He asked if they wanted a cocktail before dinner, stood patiently while they conferred over the wine list, the dinner menu, finally chose a moderately priced burgundy to go with Morello's steak, Detrick's rack of lamb.

"Very good," he said, turning away.

"Do you think," Morello asked as the waiter retreated, "that he'd say the same thing if we ordered a bottle of screw-top Thunderbird?"

"Most likely, if he values his tip, he'd twirl it in an ice bucket, pour an inch into your glass, then ask you to savor the bouquet. *Very good* is whatever the customer wants."

"Is that the way you ran your company?"

Detrick took a minute before answering. Though Brad was in charge of the showroom and the service department, she'd been acutely aware of customer complaints, this despite understanding that customer satisfaction in the car business, new or used, was only a goal. Like salvation, it was not to be achieved in this lifetime.

"We sold some clunkers," she admitted. "Especially in the beginning." She went on to describe the early years, the frantic scramble to survive, the inevitable trauma at month's end when the bills came due. Morello asked gently probing questions whenever the conversation lagged, his attention so tightly focused on her that Detrick, on one level, felt she was being studied, on another that his interest was deeply flattering. In her experience, most men, when they weren't talking about themselves, were giving her advice. Morello, by contrast, seemed to understand the relationship between patronize and patriarch, that the former implied the latter.

As she continued, she realized for the first time that she was proud of what she'd accomplished at Detrick Motors, that she'd been good enough at her job, had done it long enough to take her competence for granted. No wonder Brad wanted her back; no wonder he was willing to pay seventy thousand dollars a year to get her back.

"I'm sorry if I'm asking too many questions," Morello finally said. "It's a habit I picked up on the job." When Detrick failed to respond, he smiled, scratched an eyebrow, then continued. "You know, when *Miranda* came in, the older cops figured that was the end of the confession. The way they saw it, nobody would be stupid enough to talk to us after they'd been told they had a right to keep their mouths shut and a right to a free lawyer. But in practice, it hasn't changed things at all. The mutts—correction, the *suspects*—all think they can talk their way out of being formally arrested. They make mistakes, contradict themselves, eventually wear down." He looked at her, then picked up his glass of wine and drank. "Interrogation was my specialty."

"Then you're saying I'm a . . . a mutt? Correction: *suspect*." She delivered the question deadpan, continued before he could answer. "Of course, it won't be easy for me to avoid self-incrimination if I don't know what I've been accused of doing."

"I guess what you're accused of," he said without skipping a beat, "is being foolish enough to pass an evening with a man who's spent most of his adult life accumulating bad habits."

A few minutes later, just as their dinners arrived, Shirley

Horn, followed by her bassist and drummer, stepped onto the large stage. She smiled at the applause that greeted her, sat before a gigantic Steinway grand. Then, without looking at the half-filled room, she murmured, "One, two," before launching into an up-tempo version of "Lover Come Back to Me."

Detrick sat back in amazement. Never a jazz fan, she'd been expecting screeching trumpets, honking saxophones, a machine-gun drummer. This woman's voice was pure smoke—insinuating, seductive, quintessentially female in its implied wisdom. Shirley Horn's fingers were so light on the keys they seemed to float, as if she were miming over a player piano.

For the next hour, neither Detrick nor Morello did more than smile at each other. Somehow, even the silence between songs held significance, demanded full attention. When Shirley Horn finally tried to wind it up by introducing her sidemen, Charles Ables and Steve Williams, the audience refused to let her go. She did one encore, then another, finally said, "Now, now, boys and girls, I'll be back. Some things are worth waiting for."

"That was wonderful," Detrick said when the house lights came back up. "Thank you."

Morello spun his coffee cup on its saucer with long slender fingers. "I'm just glad you came with me," he said.

Detrick, with no ready response, sipped her own coffee, let the silence build, decided, in quick succession, that she was powerfully attracted to Morello and that the basis of that attraction was almost completely physical. She took a moment to think back, to remember when she and Brad first met. Had she felt for Brad Detrick what she now felt for Richard Morello? Propelled by youthful ardor, they'd gone at it often enough, but still . . .

"The man you brought into the Waterview," Morello said. "Zeke McTeague. Are you related?"

"Why do you ask?" Detrick smiled as she spoke.

"The way he was dressed, his look. Carl Rinders told me that if McTeague had arrived alone, he— Let me get this right. Rinders said, 'If Pat wasn't there to watch me, I would have eighty-sixed the old bastard on the spot.' "

"That's Carl." Though Detrick tried to fight a rising anger, her mouth tightened. "Next Sunday, he'll go to church, sit in the front pew, play the good citizen for all it's worth." She tossed her head, brought her fingertips to the necklace at her throat. For the next few minutes, she again described, this time in much greater detail, the Senior Aid Mission, its aims, her role, the special problems of destitute senior citizens in a rural setting. Her tone, if not actually defiant, was determined.

Morello's face, though he nodded from time to time, remained expressionless. "I guess crime is the difference," he said when she'd finished. "Between the country and the city for the elderly. Out here, they don't have to worry about getting mugged for their Social Security checks."

Detrick sat back in her chair, folded her arms across her chest. "All right," she said, suddenly impish, "you've tricked me into revealing my inner being. Now, it's your turn. Tell me something I don't already know." She waggled a finger in his direction. "I'm a rubber hose kind of woman. Don't make me use the third degree."

"Something you don't already know? That's what you want?" Morello looked at her for a moment before resuming. "Alicia Munoz, the woman who was wounded at the Waterview? The shooting wasn't a hunting accident. It was deliberate."

"What?" Detrick, who'd been expecting anything else, shook her head as she tried to absorb Morello's words. "What are you saying?"

"While the troopers were searching on the far side of the lake, I questioned an employee, a dishwasher, who was outside the kitchen smoking when Alicia was shot. He was watching her as she came up the walk. I verified his memory of her position when she was hit by comparing it with the blood spatter at the scene. The shot didn't come from across the lake. It came from the woods on the far side of the lawn a hundred yards away. I found the spot

where the shooter knelt, found the imprint of his knees
and toes in the mud just a few feet beyond the tree line.
The view was clear; it couldn't have been an accident."

"What are you going to do?" It was the first thing to
pop into her mind.

"I've already done it, Pat. I called in Donald Barrett,
the trooper assigned to investigate, showed him what I
found. Barrett took it well, didn't try to fight for his original theory. He's gonna hold a press conference tomorrow."
Morello paused. "It gets worse the more you look into it.
Munoz was new in the region. Not only didn't she have
an enemy, she didn't have a friend, either, not outside the
Waterview." He leaned forward slightly, his eyes fierce
now, his smile tight. "All current employees were ac-
counted for, every single one. Of course, somebody might
have followed Alicia up from New York where she used to
live, or even from Guatemala where she lived before she
came to New York. But the shooter, firing from the woods
as if he was a hunter, the use of a rifle instead of a handgun
. . . it adds up to somebody familiar with the country,
somebody local, somebody who killed—who *wanted* to
kill—for the fun of it."

In the silence that followed, Morello signaled the waiter
for more coffee. He continued to look at her as the waiter
filled their cups, his smile gone, his eyes much softer, as if
he wanted to take it all back.

"Why did you tell me this?" Detrick asked. "It wasn't
what I asked."

"I guess I was afraid of that rubber hose you mentioned." When Detrick failed to respond, he added, "I
wanted to give you some idea of what my life was like before I came out here. What I did with my days. Now I'm
trying to put it behind me, but . . . You know, the memory
lingers on. Most of what I do, what I think, it comes from
wading in other people's misery."

Detrick toyed with the watch on her wrist, wondering if
the empathy she felt for him at that moment had been de-

liberately provoked. This despite the fact that a moment before she'd made a conscious decision to lay her own cards on the table. "Maybe we ought to think about getting the check," she said. "You've got a long drive back to the Waterview."

Minutes later, they stood outside, locked in place by the scene before them. The sky above was cloudless now, the moon bright as a headlamp. It bathed the ice collected on the needles of the white pines lining the edge of the lawn, the sheet of ice covering the parking lot, the grass, the curled leaves of the rhododendrons on either side of where they stood. The effect was stunning in its beauty, and intimidating.

"There are so many animals out there," Morello said. "So many animals with no place to hide. It's a miracle anything survives until spring."

Without warning, he leaned down and kissed her. The touch of his mouth was brief and Detrick, though surprised, did not flinch. Instead, she closed her eyes, felt a rising, utterly physical disappointment as he withdrew.

At the edge of the parking lot, a small Ford Bronco spun all four wheels as it fishtailed onto the main road. The high whine of its tires seemed intrusive to Detrick, an assault on the cold light of the moon, the soft crackle of the wind passing over the icy branches.

"Do you think your Jeep can handle this?" Morello asked. "Because the way I see it, I'm gonna have to trade in that Buick tomorrow morning."

"Tell you the truth, Rick, I don't think I'd want to handle this in a helicopter." She knew she wouldn't be able to send him off into the night, even if she got them back to her place in one piece. No, what she'd have to do is invite him to spend the night on her couch, and the couch was much too close to her bedroom for comfort. Though she had no objection, in principle, to love (or sex) at first sight, Morello had opened up just enough to make Detrick want to look a little deeper before she jumped into his bed. "I've got an idea," she said as she took his arm. "They'll salt the roads overnight and the sun will take care of the rest. What do you say we spend a little bit of my settlement, a little bit of your inheritance, and get a couple of rooms here? Tomorrow morning, we'll get an early start, have breakfast at the house before you pick up your car and go to work."

EIGHTEEN

For Zeke McTeague, breathing in the frigid morning air through the scarf covering his mouth, the past twenty hours had been the worst he'd faced since leaving home all those years before. Even worse than the beaches of Normandy, the rubble of Mannheisen and Wiesbaden when he'd been scared all the time, when he wouldn't have given a soiled reichsmark for his chances. It was the memories that did it. Memories he couldn't escape, the memories set in motion by Terence Bannister, the man Zeke intended to kill as soon as Bannister showed himself in the window. McTeague had on three layers of clothing, this in addition to his double-gloved hands, an insulated watch cap jammed down over his ears, a dusty wool scarf pulled up to his eyes. He was prepared to wait forever; the way he saw it, he had no choice.

What McTeague wanted to do was stop the memories, and killing Terry Bannister was the way to do it. That had been obvious from the beginning. Not that Bannister had been the only one to come calling once the word got around all those years ago, the word about Esther, how she was there and willing. How, even if she wasn't, even if she was preaching to the haystacks, she could be persuaded, one way or the other.

McTeague couldn't remember exactly when it began. He'd been four, five, six; young enough to have no words for what he saw, what he heard. But he could definitely remember when it ended; when he'd somehow scrounged the money to buy that old shotgun. After that, at age thirteen, he'd had Esther to himself. She was twenty-two.

The memories, once they got running, had come at him with the power of a freight train. Zeke had been stopped at thousands of railroad crossings over the decades, watched the red lights flashing on either side of some back road, listened to the bells clanging madly. The freights took forever coming across, the loaded boxcars a blur of orange, brown, and gray. Maybe a million pounds on the move, a city in motion.

Well, there was an answer to that all right, a way to stop that train. It was the first answer he conceived after it became obvious that the memories weren't going to stop by themselves, that this particular grade was downhill forever. Just shoot the goddamned engineer, do what he should have done all those years before when he'd cradled that old shotgun against his chest.

"Terry, I find your ass up on the hill again, I ain't gonna be askin' questions. No, what I'm gonna do is blow your head right off your shoulders, see if I can't talk the county into givin' me a damned medal."

Zeke could remember his daddy, when Esther's belly had grown big enough to notice, taking her off in his old

Ford, dust trailing in a long bronze plume as they disappeared down the road. He'd been seven or eight then, old enough to have words for the things his sister did, but not so old that he hadn't been terrified, that the fear ruling his life hadn't jumped him with the ferocity of a bobcat the minute he was alone. As if it was Esther who'd been protecting him all along.

When Esther hobbled back into the house, her belly flat again, something fixed in her so it would stay that way, Zeke had cried openly. It was the last time he'd cried. After that, he'd beaten the fear down with the force of his dreaming, had created himself, a piece at a time, with leftover bits of comic books, stories of Clyde Barrow, Al Capone, Frank Nitti, the Enforcer. When he grew up, he would be the equal of all of these; in his dreams he already was.

Terry Bannister hadn't been the first, hadn't even been one of the pack leaders. Terry was just another pimply teenager out for what he couldn't get from the other girls. But Terry was alive, and they . . . Well, Zeke didn't know where the rest of them were, only that they hadn't stood in that church parking lot, hadn't stood face-to-face with the triumphant Zeke McTeague, the risen Zeke McTeague, and smirked at their own smutty memories.

A light went on inside the Bannister house, behind the drawn shade of an upstairs room. Terry had told Zeke that he lived alone, was proud of his independence, a senior citizen who had the means and the will to take care of himself.

"Sound as a dollar." He'd tapped his chest, sucked in a lungful of air. "Fit as a fiddle."

McTeague shifted his position slightly, stretched his back, worked his fingers, resisted the urge to march up to the house, knock on the front door, show the bastard just who he was and what he could do. Confrontation had been his first impulse once he'd decided that Bannister had to go, confrontation followed by pain. In all the years, he'd never killed in anger or for revenge; his goal had been to make the future, enlarge the present, not clear the past. Not recreate memories that cut like a heated scalpel.

Seen that way, Bannister was not only a violation of everything Zeke had worked to achieve, but a risk. Never kill anybody you know was the first rule of the game. Cops look for connections, somebody with a motive they can understand. That was especially true in the early days, before computers, before the FBI started keeping track of unsolved murders. How many times had he come back through the little towns to find some poor fool tried and convicted for a murder Zeke McTeague had committed, maybe waiting for his turn in the hot seat?

The light in the bathroom went on; a figure moved against the shaded window. It wouldn't be long now because the shades were up in the kitchen and that's where Bannister would go for his morning coffee, his cup of tea, the breakfast he would never eat. McTeague closed his eyes for a moment, brought Patricia Detrick's features into view. He was kneeling out in the cold, had renounced the pleasure of watching Terry Bannister's face when he finally figured it out—all because of Patricia Detrick.

Zeke opened his eyes, took off his gloves, laid the rifle barrel across the rock in front of him, sighted down on the kitchen window. Although his basic goal had taken focus, there were still many questions, a resolution he couldn't yet see. Maybe Patricia, once she knew, would run for her life, get far away, never see his face again. Maybe she'd convince her boyfriend or the cops to snatch his guns, his truck, just leave him in his cabin, leave him to God's tender mercies. Maybe the cops would beat him to the punch, find something he left at the scene, convict him without a confession.

And maybe, if he played his cards just right, played *her* cards just right, Patricia would come to him alone, come to him as a bride, receive his confession as she now received the chalice, as she now received the most basic sacrament.

• • •

When the man removes the rag covering her eyes, the cold glare of a rising moon blinds Corelle Fitzroy. She squints, lifts her bound hands to her face, finally opens her eyes to look out over a field of blossoming white yarrow. The yarrow is so dense, its tiny white blossoms so closely packed, that to Corelle the field seems carpeted, the flowers solid enough to bear her weight. Bounded on three sides by an evergreen forest, the yarrow flows in an unbroken wave to the crest of a steep hill.

"Want you to put this here on."

Despite all that has gone before, Corelle's first thought is of escape. "You got to cut me loose. Can't put on no dress with my hands tied up."

The idea of escape has sustained Corelle, has carried her past those moments when madness declared itself her only refuge. She has been riding in the little cabin in the rear of his tractor for three days and two nights.

The knife he uses to cut through her bonds is long and heavy-bladed. Afterwards, he holds it up for her inspection. "Ain't no place to go, Corelle. Bein' as we're about a million miles from the nearest human." He places the folded white material in her hands, takes a step back.

When Corelle unfolds the material, she realizes that he has handed her a wedding gown, the bodice tightly embroidered with satin lace. She presses the neckline beneath her chin, looks down to discover that the hemline falls to the tips of her toes.

"Bought it for my sister," the man explains. "But she never did get married."

An owl hoots from a tree at the far side of the glade, its call instantly taken up by a rival deep in the forest. The man turns at the sound, turns further at a sudden flash of ghostly white wings. Corelle takes advantage of this momentary distraction. She flings the dress at his eyes, spins on her heel, flees for her life.

She feels, in the first few strides, as if she can run

forever, as if the rocks and roots do not cut into the soles of her bare feet. Then she remembers she has no direction in which to flee, that there are no roads or houses within sight, that she was led blindfolded through the forest.

"Figured a nigger like you'd be proud to be the bride of a white man," the man calls to her back. "Guess I should'a knowed better."

As Corelle runs toward the crest of the hill, the trees alongside the glade seem to her like spectators, like impartial judges at some athletic contest. Over her panting breath, the whoosh and scrape of yarrow stalks against her thighs, she hears his unhurried footsteps.

"You can run, but you can't hide," he shouts. "Believe it was one of your people said that. Joe Louis. Guess old black Joe knew what he was talkin' about."

Corelle falls twice. Twice, she picks herself up and without looking back runs on. When she arrives at the crest of the hill, at the edge of the precipice beyond, the man's joke becomes apparent. Nevertheless, she is not dismayed, not even discouraged. In fact, as she finally surrenders to madness, as she launches herself into the moonlight, she believes with all her heart that she has truly escaped.

The pattern had to be maintained and that was all there was to it. A single shot, an assassin's blow, swift execution from a distance. Death was following Patricia, from the Waterview Lodge to her church; it would continue to follow her until she put all the pieces together. Until knowing made her do, until knowing ruled everything she did, her entire life driven by sure and certain knowledge.

As Zeke watched, the bathroom and then the bedroom lights went out, plunging the house into darkness. Then a fluorescent light blinked twice in the kitchen, finally steadied, and Zeke could see Bannister through the scope, see him clearly. He was wearing a loose robe. A black skullcap protected his bald scalp from the morning chill. He was toothless. As Zeke watched, he rubbed his hands together, held them over the gas stove for a moment, finally turned to face the window before taking a step forward, as if he wanted nothing more than to be a part of Zeke McTeague's destiny.

Zeke held the sights on Bannister's chest for a moment, then slowly raised them until they were centered just above his toothless mouth. Though his eye never left the target, McTeague saw, as in a photograph, his sister lying in the barn, in the hayloft, a filthy rag jammed into her mouth, hands tied to the railing, eyes begging for release.

NINETEEN

"I want to hear *all,* lady. Every lurid, obscene detail. And don't tell me that ass comes courtesy of a pair of push-up underpants."

Detrick's smile expanded into a broad grin. Morello had left only minutes before Betty's call. He'd kissed her again before walking off toward his car. She could still feel the chaste pressure of his lips on hers, the pressure of his hands on her shoulders.

"You're becoming fixated, Betty," she responded. "Too many spankings when you were a child, perhaps? Tell the good doctor."

"Too many as a child, not enough as an adult.

Now it's your turn to play patient. I'm not saying another word until you come clean. Or dirty, as the case may be."

"Well, he walked out the door just before you called." Pat glanced at her reflection in the kitchen window, noted the foolish grin, tried and failed to repress it. She turned her back on her smiling image.

"I'm serious here, Pat. Friends tell each other *everything*."

Once Detrick got started, the words came easily. She told Betty about the music pulling them together, creating a sense of intimacy as if their small table was the only one in the club, about Morello's gently probing questions and his odd response to her demand that he talk about himself. "What Rick told me about Alicia Munoz," she concluded, "I can't argue that it didn't reveal something about himself. But the more I think about what he actually said, the more his story sounds like a warning. You know: Proceed at your own risk." She cradled the phone against her shoulder, opened the refrigerator, removed a carton of orange juice and the plastic box that held her vitamins. "In the meantime, I can't stop thinking about him. As if the warning—the hint of some kind of danger—was part of the attraction."

"It sounds to me like you're smitten, Pat," Betty said. "It also sounds like you won't be moving to Manhattan any time soon."

"Confused is a better word for what I feel. My head's sending one message, but the chemistry is very strong and that's what my body is listening to."

"How about your heart?"

Detrick thought it over as she popped several tabs of vitamin C into her mouth, chased them with a sip of orange juice. "Now that I think about it, my heart doesn't seem to have an opinion. Not yet . . . But we're getting together on Thursday night. For dinner at his cottage on the grounds of the Waterview."

"Don't tell me he's cooking Italian?"

"South American. Rick's mother is Argentinian. And Richard's not his first name. It's actually Ricardo."

"Are you saying we have something in common? We both chose Latino sweethearts."

"Much as I hate to admit it."

The conversation turned to Roberto Corrales, Betty's lover, how he'd shown up the night Betty returned to New York with a bouquet of flowers and reservations at Le Cirque, how his attentions had remained ardent over the intervening days, but it was too soon to know if it would last. "Meanwhile," Betty declared, "it's like a second honeymoon without the first. And I'm enjoying the hell out of it. So what are you doing this afternoon? With your abundance of leisure?"

"Zeke McTeague's laundry."

"Say that again?"

"This afternoon, I'm taking Zeke McTeague to the laundromat so he can do his laundry. While it's washing, we're going next door for pizza. Then, after the laundry is all nicely folded, I'm driving Zeke to Dr. Kellerman's for a checkup. Sound like fun?"

An hour later, she pulled into McTeague's driveway. She was thirty minutes late and tempted to ignore Becky, who pranced in front of her shabby doghouse as if she'd been expecting Detrick to arrive at any minute. But the animal's enthusiasm was contagious, and Detrick, after she parked the car, walked back to the dog, noted the empty food dish before stooping to rub the dog's ears.

"How ya doin', girl?"

Becky reacted by coming up to lick her face. Even as she instinctively pulled away, Pat was struck by the animal's need for affection. Again, she resolved to speak to McTeague, remind him that Becky was a living, breathing creature, that owning her carried obligations. Churchgoing was fine, but he wasn't about to "get right with the Lord" by mistreating one of the Lord's creations.

Inside, she found McTeague dressed and ready, his laundry piled in two plastic laundry baskets. "Zeke," she said, holding out the dog's bowl as if expecting him to take it, "you've got to do a little better by that dog. I don't see why you keep a dog anyway. All those years in the truck you probably never had a pet. Not even a goldfish."

McTeague nodded thoughtfully. He was wearing a Greek fisherman's hat instead of his usual knit cap, the peak jammed down to shade his narrowed eyes. "Becky's my radar," he said. "She tells me when I got company."

Detrick looked at him for a moment. Without his glasses, he seemed oddly blind, as if he was peering into a bright sun. Tufts of gray hair stood out on his face, under his nose and along his jaw, spots he'd missed with the razor. She wondered if you could wear glasses when you shaved, if they'd get in the way, what it was like to be an old man. "Be that as it may," she said, her voice much softer, "Becky's not a radar scope; she's not a machine of any kind. She must be cared for."

McTeague let his eyes drop away from Detrick's as he took the bowl from her hands, shuffled off to the kitchen cabinets. He could feel her sympathy; it poured over him like syrup over a pancake. Hopefully, her emotions would bind her as the doubts piled up, as she put things together, would keep her in place long enough to understand every bit of the deal he was offering.

They fed the dog on their way to the car, Detrick carrying the stacked laundry baskets. When McTeague set the food in front of Becky, she flattened herself on the frozen ground, waited for him to retreat before pouncing on her bowl. Detrick, as she pushed the baskets through the open tailgate, didn't notice; her attention was drawn to the pair of dark wool pants lying on top of the pile. The lower part of each leg, from the knee to the cuffs, was crusted with mud.

"Fell down," Zeke said, coming up behind her. "Fetchin' firewood."

"What?"

"Them muddy pants." He took his glasses from the pocket of his coat, slid them over his nose and ears. "I seen you lookin' at 'em."

"Were you hurt?"

"Just my pride, I guess," he replied as they got into the Jeep. "Went out there with my slippers instead of puttin' on my boots. Just forgot what I was doin'. Lucky I didn't break my neck."

She started the car, pulled out onto the dirt road leading to Route 196, was reaching over to flip off the radio when he stopped her. "I ain't heard the news this morning," he said. "Mostly, come noon, I put on the news."

Detrick nodded, turned her attention to the road, then back to the radio as the newscaster announced the death of Terence Bannister.

Though police have yet to release a statement, sources tell us that Terence Bannister was killed early this morning by a gunshot as he prepared breakfast in the kitchen of his Cresco home. Police believe the shooter's vehicle was parked by the side of the road for a considerable period of time. Anyone who passed over Spruce Cabin Road between five and ten o'clock this morning, and who saw a parked vehicle, is urged to call the police hotline.

McTeague snuggled down in the seat, stuck his toes under the heater. The timing couldn't have been more perfect, not from his point of view. Patricia was staring blank-eyed through the windshield; she looked like she'd been hit with a baseball bat.

"Sounds just like that other one," he said when it became obvious to him that Patricia wasn't about to speak first. "What's her name? The woman who got herself killed last week?" He snapped his fingers. "I remember now. Melissa Capriella. Melissa was in her kitchen, too.

Makin' breakfast when somebody shot her. Just like old Terry."

From the radio's speakers, a chorus of female voices sang the praises of Coca-Cola.

"Terry was your friend," Detrick finally said.

"Wasn't no friend of mine," Zeke said before she could continue. "Hell, I ain't seen him in near sixty years. Least, not before yesterday. Too bad, though. He seemed like an okay fella."

Patricia took a shaky breath, expelled it slowly. "Terry's been in my church for . . ." She shook her head. "He was there before I came. I know his children and his grandchildren."

"Didn't think of it like that. I guess it must hurt pretty bad."

McTeague was about to shut off the radio when the newscaster returned with a segment about Trooper Donald Barrett's press conference that had taken place earlier that morning. The story, delivered without apparent emotion, confined itself to the facts. Alicia Munoz, recovering from her wounds in a local hospital, had been deliberately shot by a sniper concealed in the woods at the edge of the great lawn surrounding the Waterview Lodge. No further information was available, and despite the shouted questions of a dozen reporters, Barrett refused to link the Munoz shooting to the shootings of Melissa Capriella or Terence Bannister. Finally, as in the prior story, anybody with information was urged to come forward.

A few minutes later, Patricia slid the Jeep into a slot fronting a coin-operated laundromat just north of the town of Jericho. McTeague got out of the car first; he walked directly to the back, opened the tailgate, grabbed the two laundry baskets. "Why don't you sit down," he said, "give old Zeke room to operate. If there's anything I know besides truckin', it's laundromats."

Inside, he separated whites and darks, produced a pocketful of quarters, bought bleach and detergent, set the water temperature on a pair of machines. He moved slowly, but efficiently, maintaining a steady pace until he finally closed the washer lids, pushed the coins home.

"Now I'm ready for that pizza," he announced, turning to Detrick. "More than ready. Matter of fact, I'm plannin' to enjoy it twice. Once when I eat it, once when I describe it to the doc. See if he thinks pepperoni and cheese'll clean out my arteries."

TWENTY

Detrick, thoroughly amused, watched Zeke McTeague layer his pepperoni pizza with oregano, garlic salt, hot pepper flakes, and parmesan cheese, watched him push the slice into his mouth, tear it with his yellowed teeth. She'd already spoken to Dr. Kellerman, Zeke's cardiologist, about Zeke's diet. Kellerman had been evasive. He'd suggested, without really saying, that at this stage of the game it didn't matter all that much what Zeke ate.

Behind her, the owner of the restaurant and his wife were having an argument. The husband, a huge man with a belly and butt that swelled his white uniform front and back, kept insisting that it was his pizzeria and if she didn't like the way he ran it, she could stay home with the kids. Finally, the wife broke off, slammed to the back of the kitchen, lit a cigarette.

"The fightin' reminds me."

"Pardon?"

"Reminds me of the war." McTeague laid the crust of one slice on his paper plate, reached for another, began to load it up. "How it changed my life. Made me what I am. Course, the regular army changed my life, too. That's where I went after I left these parts, left Esther. I was sixteen." He paused, held up a shaker of red and white pepper. "Truth to tell, Patricia, I wasn't in such good shape. Just a punk kid who didn't know nothin' but how crazy his life was. The army give me some way to live that folks could call normal, so I guess I gotta be grateful. But it was the war had the big effect." McTeague stopped speaking, began to pepper his slice. He was pretty sure she'd checked him out, became certain when she didn't meet his eyes. That was perfectly fine with him, that she'd recognized the puzzle, was trying to put it together.

Detrick, as she attempted to frame a response, was, indeed, revisiting the guilt she'd felt at Claire Pierce's house, asking questions about McTeague; she found the emotion compounded by McTeague's apparent willingness to talk about his life. There'd been no need to go behind his back, no need to suspect that he was trying to hide something. "Did you see a lot of fighting?" she asked.

"Landed on Omaha Beach, in the second wave. Fought my way damn near to Berlin." McTeague sipped at his Coke, then took a bite of pizza. He chewed judiciously, swallowed, drank again. "See, war is about survival. Leastways if you're on the bottom, a private, like I was. All you know is you wanna live and the only way to do that is kill the enemy. It's like bein' stripped away, like takin' old paint off a fender before you paint it up. After the fightin' stops, you could be anything you want. It's up to you."

Detrick was tempted to ask, *So what did you become?* but held back. The question was too direct; it was ambiguous as well, a question for a psychiatrist, not a nosy social worker. "It must have been very bad," she said.

"Didn't think I had a rat's chance of makin' it through. Friends dyin' all around me." That was a pure lie and McTeague knew it. The truth was that he hadn't made a friend, not in boot camp or in the war, not even in the foxholes he shared with his platoon. "When we come to the German border, at Stuttgart, where there was street-to-street fighting, the captain made me a sniper. After that it got better. Leastways, I didn't have to charge no machine gun nests." Someday he'd tell her about seeing his enemy through the scope for the first time, seeing the man's breath in the air, the stubble on his face, the color of his eyes. It had thrilled him, once he got the hang of it, had brought his pecker to full attention. After a while, it didn't matter whether he was looking at the face of the enemy or the face of an ally. There was only his finger on the trigger, life or death on the line.

Detrick nibbled at her pizza, wondered if she ought to encourage McTeague's reflections or let him go at his own pace. It was obvious that he wanted to talk about himself, that she was his only audience, that she was in fact his last chance. Still, she was afraid he'd get more specific, more graphic, as he rambled on. There was a definite limit to how much she could take, how much of Zeke McTeague's sad, ugly life. She thought of him in that truck, year after year, alone behind the wheel, of his home near St. Louis, his hallucinating lover. How had the man had survived at all? What consolations had enabled him to endure?

"Maybe we should talk about something more pleasant," she suggested. "We can talk about fighting while you fold the laundry. I *hate* folding laundry; I even hate *watching* other people fold laundry."

McTeague nodded thoughtfully. His dark eyes swam behind his glasses. They seemed, to Detrick, wetter and larger than usual, swollen by the lenses, as if he was making an effort to hold them as wide as possible.

"I tell you about this trucker I knew, Dirk Martinson?" McTeague settled back on his seat, resumed eating. " 'Cause if I told ya, stop me right now. I ain't embarrassed to admit that I sometimes forget what I said to who." He paused to swallow, continued when Detrick shook her head. "Well, ole Dirk, he was a drinkin' man, which was bad enough for a trucker, but even sober he didn't have a brain in his damn head. Fact, the only thing Dirk had goin' for him was that he drove fast and hard, one of those good ole boys who run up behind Volkswagens in heavy traffic, lean on the air horn, lookin' like the whale that swallowed Pinocchio's father. Now—"

Without warning, McTeague's face drained of color. He grabbed his chest, felt his breath turn solid in his lungs, tried to speak and found he couldn't form a single word. His glasses dropped into his lap and his eyes squeezed shut as he gathered his strength, willed his fingers to move toward the tablets in his shirt pocket. From somewhere far away, Patricia called his name. He wanted to answer her, tell her what he hadn't said yet, what she meant to him, but he had only enough strength to pop the cap on the vial, shake a tablet into his mouth, settle it under his tongue.

When McTeague opened his eyes, Detrick was on the telephone, calling for an ambulance. He shook his head, managed a languid wave. "I'm okay," he finally said. "Okay . . ."

Detrick looked at him for a full minute before dropping the receiver onto the hook. "Are you sure?" To her surprise, she hadn't panicked, was prepared to administer CPR, keep him alive until the paramedics arrived, do what was necessary.

"You forgot what I told ya." McTeague felt the blood returning to his face, his fingers, his toes; it felt like his heart was reclaiming abandoned territory. "About not callin' no ambulance, not puttin' me back in the hospital."

Detrick nodded as she came back to the table. McTeague

looked much better, but if she wasn't about to take him to the doctor's office, she knew she'd be taking him to the emergency room. Whether he liked it or not. "I didn't even think of it," she admitted as she bent over to retrieve his glasses. "You sure you're all right?"

"Ain't all right and never will be again." McTeague waited for her to sit, then caught her gaze and held it. "That's the fact of it, Patricia." He managed a smile, was pleased when it felt natural. "This bullet's got my name on it."

Detrick let her hands drop to her lap. "I don't think," she said, "that I can just sit here and watch you die." Her blunt tone surprised her; she'd meant to offer an apology. "I think watching you die is simply beyond me."

McTeague looked down at the half-eaten slice of pizza on his plate, found it revolting, resisted an urge to cover it with his napkin. "Then I guess I gotta hope you're not around when the big one hits." He put on his glasses, slid his chair away from the table. "Maybe when I admit that I ain't got the strength to handle that laundry, that if you don't fold it up, it's gonna stay in the dryer, you'll decide I ain't worth the trouble. Bein' as how you already told me how much you hate to fold laundry."

She threw herself into the role of organizer, fetched and folded the laundry, stacked it in the baskets, got the baskets and McTeague into the Jeep. She remained in that role, the one she'd played for years in the back offices of Detrick Motors, when they arrived at Doctor Kellerman's office. With Zeke's permission, she conferred with Kellerman, almost demanded that the doctor forgive the Medicare copayment, that he act as Zeke's family physician, that he coordinate Zeke's treatment.

Kellerman sat quietly while she spoke. Detrick had been in his office before, had asserted the same moral authority, an authority made even more forceful by the fact that she never used the word *obligation*. Instead, she stated the facts calmly, her patient's circumstances, what could and couldn't be done, what she hoped he would do.

"Ms. Detrick," he said when she finished, "I don't give a damn about the copayment. But when it comes to Zeke's overall treatment, he should see an internist, not a cardiologist."

"Zeke didn't have a family physician when he was admitted to the hospital and he hasn't found one since. That means whoever I found would have to start all over again. Look, I promise you that I'll make an effort to scare up an internist, that I'll try to convince Zeke to make an appointment. But in the meantime, Doctor, the harsh reality is that if you don't coordinate his treatment, it won't be coordinated."

It was an argument that brought a smile to Kellerman's mouth. He was a tall, thin man, in his late thirties, with a narrow face and an oddly assertive chin which he lifted whenever he had to make a decision. "I won't be loaded up with indigent patients," he finally said. "I feel I have a responsibility to give something back to the community, but I won't be loaded up." He dropped his chin, tapped the desktop with a blunt finger. "I'm not worried about Mr. McTeague; I'm worried about the next patient, and the one after that."

"I understand, Doctor," Detrick quickly replied. "I won't drain the well." She didn't want to think about Zeke McTeague's face drained of blood, drained to a pale, pale gray. Nor did she want to recall that brief moment when Terry Bannister's features had superimposed themselves, like a rubber mask, over McTeague's. Two old men living by themselves, one taken, the other granted a brief reprieve.

Of course, McTeague's problem was purely physical, a failure of his own system, while Bannister had been killed in an accident, the third—no, the *second* hunting accident of the season. The first had been Melissa Capriella, killed exactly as Terry Bannister had been killed. What would have been the second, the wounding of Alicia Munoz, had been quite deliberate. Alicia Munoz had been shot, according to the newscaster, by a sniper hiding in the woods. The act had been deliberate.

In an instant, Detrick formed a vivid image of Zeke McTeague in a worn, dusty uniform, peering through the telescopic sight of a long, bolt-action rifle. She held that image briefly, as if waiting for him to pull the trigger, then, because the emotion produced by the image was shaded with pure dread, she reminded herself that Zeke McTeague had acted as a soldier, under orders, in a time of war.

TWENTY-ONE

It was just after five o'clock when Detrick and McTeague got back to McTeague's cabin. The sun had already dropped below the trees at the western margins of the yard. Detrick climbed out of the car and retrieved the laundry. As her eyes adjusted to the dark, stars by the hundreds jumped into sharp focus. She dropped her head back for a moment, let her eyes follow the splash of the Milky Way. As always, the mix of emotions provoked by the sight was virtually identical to what she felt while quietly sitting in Bill Gauss's empty chapel.

There were times, she remembered as McTeague came around the car to join her, when the cross in the chapel had seemed as cold and implacable as the stars above her now, when she'd found herself longing for the Catholic crucifix, a body affixed to the polished hardwood. Finally, she'd come to believe that the cross had preceded her little life, as it had preceded the life of Jesus Christ, that the cross would remain in place when she was gone, when all humans were gone. The cross had always been there, waiting for anybody with the courage to climb aboard.

"Gonna be a cold one tonight."

Detrick lowered her eyes, looked over at McTeague. His starlit breath seemed to hover in the night air.

"Zeke, I could use a cup of tea before I head home. You think you could manage that?" She watched his eyes light, his head nod.

"Sure thing, Patricia. Sure thing."

Inside, she set the laundry on the bed, then crossed the room and opened the door of the wood stove. McTeague had banked the fire before they left and there were still live coals in the bottom. She added kindling from a pile stacked beside the stove, adjusted the draft, blew on the coals until the wood caught. When she was sure the fire wouldn't go out, she tossed in a pair of small logs, then closed the door. She turned away to find McTeague rummaging in the cupboards above the sink.

She watched him take down a pair of mugs, fetch the Lipton tea bags from another cupboard. He seemed extremely tired. She was tempted to offer help, but decided instead to let him complete this small task. Still, she hesitated for a moment, observed the rise and fall of his bony shoulders, his obviously stiff fingers separate the tea bags. The stubble on his face was a gray shading against his gray skin.

Finally, she turned away, crossed the room, stood before McTeague's photographs. This time, instead of allowing her eyes to sweep the photos, to be overwhelmed by their sheer number, she began with the photograph in the far left corner, followed McTeague's timeline. The first picture had been taken in 1947; the date written by McTeague was still legible, though the ink was badly faded. The photo revealed a narrow, two-lane road passing over a small brook. The trees alongside the road were dark and bare, the sky above a flat, featureless yellow.

She let her eyes run along the line of photos edging the wall, searching for some indication that human beings had ever been at the sites they froze in time. She looked for a chimney, a roofline, a driveway, a billboard. But she found nothing beyond the roads themselves. Finally, she went back to the photo Zeke had taken after the blizzard in Montana. To her surprise, she noticed features that she hadn't observed in any of the other photos. There were tire tracks on the shoulder of the freshly plowed road, tracks that abruptly gave way to bright, unmarked snow.

Her curiosity piqued, Detrick took a backward step, began to examine the photo closely. Two sets of what were surely footprints—one coming, one going?—ran from the tire tracks to a cluster of trees perhaps a hundred yards from the road. As Detrick studied these footprints, she suddenly realized that McTeague's truck must have backed up before the photo was taken. Or maybe it had been on the wrong side of the road before pulling off. Either way, the vehicle had been deliberately moved before the photo was snapped.

Behind her, the kettle on the stove began to whistle. "Tea's a'comin'," McTeague told her. "Even got some cookies to go with it. Be a regular party."

Detrick nodded absently, let her eyes drift across the photos until she found a second snow-covered landscape. It revealed the same tire tracks, the same two sets of footprints. Something stirred within her, a bitterness she could taste on the very tip of her tongue. She formed an image of McTeague standing in the snow, squinting through his camera's view finder, taking snapshots of nothing.

What's wrong with this story? she asked herself. Why doesn't it make sense, even for a dedicated loner? He told me he snapped these photos so he could remember. Then why not, even if he had some weird phobia about other people, take photos of truck stops, freight yards, his own rig? And why, out of all the millions of miles he'd driven, did these particular roads mean something special to him?

Detrick again stepped back, this time several steps, until she could see the entire wall. How much effort it had taken to assemble the photos, have them framed, arrange them by year, hang them one by one.

"Here's your tea, Patricia."

She turned to find McTeague standing just behind her. He was carrying a dinner plate, holding it out with both hands. A brimming mug of amber tea surrounded by Oreo cookies rested on the center of the plate. "Better take this," he told her. "I think I'm about done for the day."

As he pushed the plate forward with trembling hands, one of the cookies fell onto the gray carpet. Detrick bent to retrieve it. As her fingers gathered the cookie in, she couldn't help but notice that McTeague had put on his leather slippers and that they were spotlessly clean.

TWENTY-TWO

Terry Bannister's wake was more depressing than Pat Detrick, with all of Tuesday to think about it, had imagined. While she'd been expecting a biblical wailing and gnashing of teeth when she walked into the Jericho Funeral Home on Wednesday morning, what she found was a dark stunned silence and a closed coffin. Bannister's children and grandchildren sat clustered together in the little chapel, receiving a steady flow of mourners. Their eyes, as Detrick looked into them, seemed to ask a common question, a question without words, to which no answer could be given. The ordinary consolation of Terry's long, fruitful life had been denied to them. Despite Bannister's age, his death had been unnecessary, an affront. It demanded justification.

The morning edition of *The Pocono Record* had sharpened that demand. A front-page story linked the deliberate attack on Alicia Munoz with the shooting of Terence Bannister. The article pointed out that there was no hunting permitted anywhere near Bannister's house, no high ground a mile or two away from which an accidental shot could have been fired. The shooter had almost certainly been within sight of the home when the trigger was pulled. Further still, both Munoz and Bannister, according to police sources, had been killed by a single shot from a 30–30 rifle.

Statistics prove, Kevin Coughran, the reporter whose byline appeared above the story, wrote, *that hunting accidents almost always involve two hunters and not innocent bystanders. In one study of ninety-six hunting accidents published by the University of Virginia, only two resulted in injury to nonhunters. Yet, since November 26, just ten days ago, when Melissa Capriella was killed in her home, three nonhunters, residing within thirty miles of each other, have been shot, two inside their homes. Though police have pronounced the wounding of one, Alicia Munoz, deliberate, they stopped short of linking all three. The most Donald Barrett, the detective in charge of the Munoz investigation, would concede was that no possibility was being excluded.*

Detrick stayed in the crowded chapel just long enough to shake every Bannister hand, buss the cheeks of the women. Then she went outside to join the mourners. The crowd, perhaps forty or fifty locals, despite the calming presence of Bill and Elaine Gauss, was angry. The tone of their conversations was sharp, their glances penetrating, as if Terry's killer might be among them.

Instinctively, Detrick approached Bill Gauss. The minister stood off to one side, conversing in hushed tones with Stanley and Jane Koehler, two of the more vociferous members of his congregation. Jane, especially, felt that SAM took up far too much of Bill's time, that the poor were adequately served by wasteful government programs.

Though Jane represented a minority opinion within the congregation, her words were given weight by the fact that her family had been attending services at the church since its inception, more than a hundred years before.

"Probably some crazy New York nigger."

The words came from Detrick's left and she turned quickly, expecting whoever made the statement to look away in embarrassment. Instead, Dr. Martin Greenough tossed her a defiant glance, his mouth a tight line the color of healed scar tissue, his flared nostrils two perfectly round black holes.

Greenough turned back to his wife and his mother before Detrick, though she stopped in her tracks, could frame a response. She stared at him for a moment, then walked up to Bill Gauss.

"Looks like you'll have your work cut out for you next Sunday," she said.

Bill looked around, shook his head. Wisps of thinning hair, pushed by a cold breeze, were flying about his scalp. As Detrick watched, he tried and failed to pat them down with the palm of his hand. "I heard what Martin said. I think I was meant to hear."

"And I thought his benediction was just for me," Detrick replied. She nodded a greeting to Jane Koehler, shook hands with Stanley.

"People are afraid," Jane declared. She was a tall, broad-shouldered woman with a preference for vivid down-filled overcoats that added to her bulk. "You can't blame them." She looked directly at Bill Gauss as she spoke, almost daring him to dispute her claim.

"Let me get this right, Jane." Gauss didn't raise his voice. "You agree with Martin. You think Terry Bannister was executed by a . . . a 'crazy New York nigger'?" He slid his hands into the pockets of his coat. When Jane Koehler failed to reply, he took a deep breath, said, "In point of fact, all the Western religions hold individuals responsible for their actions. What's unique about Christianity is that it holds them responsible for their feelings, too."

"What I think, Bill," Jane replied sharply, "is that over the last couple of decades we've been overwhelmed by migrating, big-city trash."

"Let us bow our heads and pray," Pat said lightly. Without a little bit of help, she didn't think either one of them would back down.

"Pomposity," Bill Gauss said, echoing her tone, "is the prerogative of the ordained. I learned that in my first year at divinity school."

Jane smiled at Detrick. "The man has style," she admitted. "And knowledge." Her smile widened. "I really hate that."

They began to discuss Terry Bannister, concentrating on his fierce independence. At eighty-one, Terry had still driven, handled all the cooking and cleaning in his small home, shoveled his own snow. He was an inspiration, they agreed, a role model, not only for other senior citizens, but for everyone who knew him.

It was typical small talk, a massing of clichés that ignored Bannister's legendary fiery temper, ignored the sentiment commonly expressed by his six children: Thank God he's healthy enough to care for himself.

"Terry was the epitome," Stanley Koehler finally said, "of the rugged individualist." He looked at his wife, waited for a nod of approval. "A dying breed, I suspect."

Minutes later, the Koehlers drifted away and Elaine Gauss, who'd been standing off to Detrick's left, talking to Kurt and Evelyn Schneider, came over to join her husband. "All clear?" she asked.

"Now, now," Bill Gauss responded. " 'And charity for all,' remember."

"That's what you should have told Jane Koehler." Elaine took her husband's gloved hand, hunched her shoulders. "So, how's our boy, Pat? You make up your mind yet about Mr. McTeague?"

Detrick shook her head. "I'd have to say I'm still confused. Have you ever been to his home, Elaine?"

"No, I only saw him in the office."

Detrick quickly described McTeague's wall, the carefully arranged photos, the empty roads. Her description
was succinct, as if she was still at Detrick Motors, discussing cash flow with a loan officer.

"That's sad," Bill Gauss responded. "That he had nothing else worth preserving, nothing more important in his
life."

"That's what I thought at first." Detrick paused, let her
eyes sweep the crowd in the parking lot. They were standing under a glaring winter sun, in their Sunday best, and
the buzz of the conversations around them pressed on her
ears with the persistence of swarming honeybees.

"At first?"

Detrick turned to Elaine, met her dark eyes. "At first I
thought it was sad . . . No, it *is* sad. But I'm starting to
think it's also crazy. There were other pictures he could
have taken; there were places he'd been to—truck stops,
repair shops, freight yards—that had to mean more to him
than an empty road." Detrick felt her voice begin to go
shrill. She frowned, let her eyes drop away from Elaine's,
shifted her attention to Bill. "It's too much work for too
little result. I'm talking about the photos, taking them,
framing them, mounting them on the wall. There has to be
some other motivation besides nostalgia, something he's
not telling me."

"It sounds like an obsession." Bill Gauss shifted his
weight, pursed his small mouth. "How many pictures are
there?"

"I can't be sure," she admitted. "But there's got to be a
couple of hundred. He's got them hanging floor to ceiling."

Before Bill could respond, they were joined by the Clark
family. The youngest, two-year-old Joseph, tugged at
Elaine's coat, then stretched his arms overhead. Elaine
picked the boy up, cradled him against her shoulder. "Fu-
nerals scare the little ones, don't you think?"

Detrick barely heard the conversation that followed. Instead, she remained preoccupied with McTeague. Bill
Gauss had used the word *obsession,* but failed to suggest

what McTeague might be obsessed about. Or what part photos of empty roads might play in that obsession.

What you have to do, she told herself, is make up your mind. In or out. Detective is not a role that suits you.

But even so, she had the feeling she'd already gone too far to back away. She tried to imagine the look on McTeague's face if she told him that she wouldn't be back, tried to imagine how she'd explain her decision to him. *Well, Zeke, the problem is that you're just too creepy for a do-gooder like me. I prefer my sick and dying to have a bit more dignity.*

Elaine had told her that McTeague wouldn't make it through the winter without help, a bleak view reinforced by the incident in the pizzeria. Detrick could still see McTeague's bloodless features, his trembling hands scrabbling for his medication. No, she couldn't just walk away; in a very real sense, an almost frightening sense, she was trapped.

"Pat."

Detrick turned at the sound of her name, found a smiling Rick Morello, flanked by the Rinders brothers, walking toward her from the entrance to the funeral home. She watched Morello for a few seconds before taking a step toward him. At that moment, he seemed very strong in his black overcoat and maroon scarf, and very confident in his movements, a rock to be leaned on.

"One of the Bannister grandkids, Bobbie Bannister," Carl Rinders explained. "He works as a security guard at the lodge. Part time, when he's not going to college. We came to pay our respects."

After politely inquiring about her health and the health of her parents in Arizona, Carl and Frank Rinders moved away, leaving Detrick and Morello standing together in the parking lot.

"I missed you," Morello said without preamble.

Detrick searched for a witty rejoinder, something casual and sophisticated, searched an apparently empty brain. Finally, she simply told the truth. "I missed you, too."

Again, as he had in the Caesar's parking lot, Morello offered his arm, waited for Detrick to lay her fingers in the crook of his elbow. As they strolled toward Morello's Buick, Detrick noticed her ex-husband standing with his mother on the lawn in front of the funeral home. He stood with his hands on his hips, his fleshy jaw thrust forward, his mouth curled into a tiny circle. To Detrick, he looked exactly like a petulant child about to throw a very major, very public tantrum.

TWENTY-THREE

"I've got to get back," Morello explained. "I'm on the clock."

Detrick nodded her understanding though she didn't release his arm. "Did your press conference make the Rinders stop worrying?"

"You mean about the shooting?"

"Yes."

"It did until Donald Barrett called the shooting deliberate. Carl Rinders is afraid the paying customers will decide that someone has it in for the lodge, that it had nothing to do with Alicia."

"Then he must be happy about that story in the *Record*. The one that linked the three shootings."

"Serial killer in the Poconos?" Morello shook his head. "I don't think the implications have reached them yet. They're too busy worrying about the weather over the Christmas holidays, if they'll be able to make enough snow to get all the ski runs open."

"And what about you?" Detrick asked. Behind her, the crowd stirred as Terry Bannister's eldest daughter, Maureen, stepped out of the funeral home. Detrick watched Maureen light a cigarette, toss the match away.

"I have no opinion about the weather three weeks from now," Morello replied.

Detrick laughed. "I'm talking about the serial killer theory."

"I was hoping I wouldn't have to have an opinion about that, either," he responded. "But Donald Barrett's developed a crush on Mary Shatner, our social director. Mary won't give him the time of day, so Barrett shows up every night to buy me a drink, engage in a little cop-to-cop conversation. Hoping to run into her accidentally." Morello thrust a key into the lock. "See what comes of being a cop? You lock your car no matter what, even if there's a hundred people standing around to watch it."

"Wait a minute." Detrick laid her hand on the door of the Buick, as if to hold it closed. "You haven't answered my question."

He sighed. "The troopers recovered slugs at each scene, all thirty-thirty caliber, but they were too deformed for an exact match. In fact, the only piece of useable evidence right now is a pair of leg casts."

"Explain that, please. What are leg casts?"

Morello's mouth tightened slightly as he gave her what she took to be a penetrating cop stare. "It was raining the day Alicia Munoz was attacked. The shooter knelt in the mud, apparently for quite a while. I found two parallel imprints, including knees, shins, and the toes of a pair of hiking boots. The troopers made a plaster cast of the imprints, hoping to eventually match them to the shooter." He managed a half-hearted smile. "Look, I have to get back," he said, "before some native defiles the indoor pool."

Pat shook her head. "Not until you answer my question. I want to know if *you* think these shootings are related."

Morello's eyes hardened momentarily and Detrick knew he was about ask her why it was so important. Instead, he took a deep breath and shrugged. "Yesterday," he told her, "I walked about fifty yards into the woods, then turned back toward the lodge. Pat, there's trees and shrubs everywhere. I couldn't even *see* the lodge. There's no way you can fire a shot from that kind of dense forest and have the round travel more than a few dozen yards without hitting something. That means—not just in the Munoz case, but in the Bannister and Capriella cases as well—that the shooter was within clear sight of his target. Which makes it murder."

"But why, Rick? What's the motive?"

He replied without hesitation. "Pleasure, most likely. Sexual pleasure, if the shrinks have it right."

She finally stepped away, let him open the door, get inside. She'd obviously said something wrong, trespassed on some prickly personal territory, even though her questions had nothing to do with his personal affairs.

"I'll see you tomorrow?" He reached through the open window to take her hand, his smile suddenly genuine.

"Tomorrow night. I'll bring the wine." It wasn't until Morello's Buick reached the end of the lot, had turned onto the main road, that she associated his talk of leg casts with Zeke McTeague's muddy trousers. She turned back to the funeral home and was momentarily blinded by the glare of the sun on the mortuary's slate roof, a glare that reduced the individuals in the crowded parking lot to narrow silhouettes. Instinctively, she brought up her hand to shield her eyes and saw, in the shadow of her palm, Zeke McTeague as he'd stood three days before, stood in deep conversation with Terry Bannister who now rested inside. Who rested inside his coffin.

• • •

On the night following Terry Bannister's wake, after a long phone call to Betty and a fruitless effort to concentrate on the evening news, Pat fell asleep shortly before midnight. Curiously, though she held Zeke McTeague's image in her mind throughout the conversation with Betty, his name was never mentioned. She had wanted to talk about McTeague, about his photos and his crazy sister, about his muddy trousers and spotless slippers, about a growing suspicion she couldn't seem to dismiss. But the image of McTeague that persisted, that refused to be banished, was of the ashen-faced old man in the pizzeria, of McTeague after he'd taken his medication, his closed eyes, the rattle in his chest as he tried to draw breath.

So she and Betty had talked, instead, about Rick Morello and Roberto Corrales, about New York real estate, about Terry Bannister's wake, the anger engendered by his death, serial killers in the Poconos, anything but Zeke McTeague. Even when Betty suddenly declared, "Something's bothering you, Pat. I can taste it," Detrick had merely replied, "I think I'm a little nervous about my date tomorrow night. You know, going to his place, having dinner . . ."

By the time she actually fell asleep, she had almost come to believe that Morello was at the core of her restlessness, that her real problem was somehow missing out on the sexual revolution, that if she made that simple decision to drag Rick Morello into bed, she wouldn't be worrying about Zeke McTeague, serial killers, muddy laundry. Then she'd begun to dream.

Detrick dreamed of a snow-covered road, of falling snow driven nearly horizontal by a howling wind. Beside the road, a slight figure wearing an army uniform held a weapon, a rifle, at the ready. The barrel and stock of the rifle were camouflaged by narrow gray bandages. The bandages hung vertically, despite the wind, like frayed handkerchiefs on a clothesline. Detrick stood behind this figure, directing his attention to parallel rows of footprints on the far side of the road. Suddenly, she realized that she couldn't feel the snow against her face. At first she was puzzled. But gradually a sense of safety, of protection, overcame her curiosity. It was as if she'd been granted some kind of immunity, a reprieve, perhaps, in light of the job she was required to do. With a slight nod, she finally tapped the soldier's helmet, leaned forward, whispered in his ear. "We'll wait it out for as long as she lasts."

At that point, Detrick woke up. She was calm at first, as if the emotions of the dream had simply carried over into her waking life. Then, as she put McTeague's words and stories together with Terry Bannister and the news video of Melissa Capriella's husband pushing his children into the car, she grew more agitated. She'd watched that video on McTeague's television; he'd even called her attention to it, insisting that Melissa Capriella had participated in her own death by choosing to live in a home that bordered the game lands.

Enough, Detrick told herself. She got out of bed, went to the bathroom, washed her face. It was a little after three and she was tempted to take down her Bible, read the Psalms, as she had in those first months after the breakup of her marriage. Instead, she dropped down into her bed, shut off the light, decided to close her eyes and hope for the best. Thirty minutes later, she fell into a deep sleep and again began to dream. In her dream, Detrick saw John Kennedy, Jackie at his side, driving through Dallas in an open Cadillac. Kennedy was waving, smiling that narrow sardonic smile that passed for sincerity. The crowds lining both sides of the street waved back at him, cheered ferociously, like parents at a Little League baseball game.

As the motorcade drove into the center of town, the crowds grew deeper and Kennedy became more and more animated. He rose to his feet, spread his arms, raised both hands above his head as if about to break into song. At this point, Detrick realized that it wasn't John Kennedy in the car; it was her former husband. She was about to raise her voice in protest, to warn the crowd, denounce the fraud, when the front of Brad Detrick's head exploded forward, a cloud of blood and brain matter that grew in size until it engulfed her field of vision.

Detrick sat up in bed, gasping, ran her hands over her face, through her hair, momentarily surprised to find her palms free of blood. Then, when she finally realized that she'd been dreaming, that she was now awake, she groaned softly. She walked into the kitchen, turning on the overhead light as she passed through the living room, and filled the teakettle, took a mug off the shelf, added a bag of mint tea and a spoonful of sugar. Her work had long ago taught her that not every problem can be solved. Sometimes you have to cut your losses, accept the consequences. Her own ego had temporarily obscured the basic message; now life itself, in the form of Zeke McTeague, had broken through her denial. She could no longer imagine herself nursing the old man through the winter, not when he inspired dreams of bloody death. Tomorrow morning, she would tell Elaine Gauss. She would put McTeague behind her.

The kettle began to whistle on the stove, the lid to rattle as the water came to a boil. Detrick waited until the whistle became a shriek, then filled her mug. For a moment, kettle in hand, she stared into the mug, watched the tea bag release pale green tendrils. Finally, she began to consider exactly how she'd explain her decision to Elaine.

Well, you see, Elaine, I suspect that Zeke's one of those serial killers. I think he may have walked into the woods, knelt in wet mud with a freezing rain pouring down, and tried to murder Alicia Munoz. Never mind his heart condition, the fact that he doesn't drive and the Waterview is twenty miles away. Forget that he can barely shuffle along, that he can't see worth a damn.

The problem, of course, was that as soon as she put words to her suspicions, they sounded idiotic. If not downright paranoid.

Detrick sipped at her tea. She breathed deeply, decided to tell Elaine part of the truth, the part she was sure about.

Zeke McTeague frightened her. Maybe she couldn't put words to her emotions. Maybe she couldn't devise an explanation that seemed rational, even to herself; that didn't mean her fear wasn't real. There were times, in McTeague's presence, when she felt like an animal approaching a baited trap, the bait being poor, pitiful Zeke McTeague and his effect on her conscience.

I can't get past it, Elaine. I've tried telling myself not to be judgmental, and I know that Zeke needs assistance, but I've got to get out.

Elaine wouldn't be happy to have McTeague dumped back into her lap, but she'd accept it. After all, Detrick was a volunteer, not an employee. No, the problem, for Detrick, was that she would have to go to McTeague's cabin one last time, watch his bloated eyes swim behind those glasses, his mouth work silently, hope he didn't collapse before she got out of there.

TWENTY-FOUR

Now that it was really the last time, the last, *last* time, Zeke McTeague felt that everything he did was touched by a . . . Well, he wasn't exactly sure what he was feeling as he brushed the few teeth he had left. He was sad, yeah, sad for sure, but there was something else, too—a kind of magic that made every little task important, as if he'd never done any of it before, never spent a minute in this body. As if his hopes had already been realized, his new life already begun.

It was spiritual, he finally decided, definitely spiritual. He'd have to make sure he explained that to Patricia when the time came, that there were all kinds of spirits out there and you could pick any one of them, capture its strength by making it happy. It was just a matter of knowing what they wanted.

He thought of his sister before she went crazy, his sister kneeling by his side at the foot of the bed, teaching him to pray. Esther had been real big on the Bible, reading it out loud every night after dinner. They never did get to church, of course, because their father wasn't a man for church, even when he was around. Abner McTeague was a man for the bottle and for sleeping it off on Sunday morning.

McTeague chuckled at his little joke. It was very early, just five o'clock, yet with all the work ahead of him, he figured he barely had enough time for a cup of coffee and a slice of buttered toast. Fully dressed, he set water to boiling on the stove. Then he turned up the kerosene heater and let the rush of warm air play over his hands. For a moment, he felt nothing, thought nothing, but then an image formed. He saw Esther naked, the small thrusting caps of her breasts, the lacy pubic hair. She was beating him, though for what he couldn't remember, beating him while she prayed for his salvation.

With a jerk, McTeague roused himself, went back to the stove, checked the water. He took down a mug, added a spoonful of instant coffee, another of sugar, told himself to forget the past, that he was moving into a future, a real future with real possibilities.

After a final glance at the rapidly boiling water, McTeague shuffled over to the refrigerator. He took a loaf of white bread from the bread box, dropped a single slice into a battered toaster, and pushed the lever down. The acrid smell of burning metal rose to his nostrils, a familiar odor. The toaster reminded McTeague of himself. Despite some deep internal flaw it continued to function.

McTeague thought of his own cousins, of all his mother's relatives, coal-mining folk out of the Lackawanna mines in Scranton. They'd gone off to West Virginia, to Matewan County where they'd come from, shortly after McTeague was born. Just packed up and left. For McTeague, this was another of the mysteries that had guided his early life, to be wondered at, but never explained. Like his father's stubborn support, his refusal to either desert the family or be an actual father. Like Esther's not having killed him or, better yet, his not having killed Esther.

He'd been maybe eleven years old the night he'd gone after her with the knife. This after years of praying for someone to rescue him, making every kind of bargain with the Lord in return for a savior. Finally, he'd given up, waited for her to fall asleep, grabbed a carving knife, tiptoed over to her bed. She'd awakened then, seen the knife, known exactly what he intended. Her eyes had rolled in her head; her hands had jumped across her chest, arms covering her breasts. As if her throat wasn't a sufficient target.

They'd stayed that way for a long time. McTeague could still recall making the decision to spare her, to let his sister, his only real family, live. After that, Esther had stopped beating him. He'd wondered, as time went by, whether her new attitude came as a result of her being moved by his mercy, or if she was guided solely by the glint of moonlight on honed metal. Maybe she carried that image inside, the knife in his hand, maybe it had been printed on her brain, maybe she resurrected it whenever she was tempted to pound him. By that time, however, there was no way she could tell him.

Despite the bitter cold and a relentless wind that peppers her back with sharp grains of newly fallen snow, Amelia Baldi finds herself not only content, but actually focused. Up to now, she's been obsessed with the pure injustice of her calamity, reminding herself between visits from the beast named Zeke McTeague, that she'd been after Dave for three weeks, had told him, "Get the car fixed, Dave, before it stops running altogether." If he'd listened to her, she'd be home now; it was that simple. At home with her husband, with her infant son, with her dog, with her cat, with her life.

McTeague carries Amelia over his shoulder, in a fireman's carry, because she can no longer walk. His hands grip the backs of her legs while her head hangs, jaw slack, to the top of his belt. Though he avoids the deeper drifts, the snow rises to McTeague's knees and every step is a struggle, a determined push against resistance, a lurch as their combined weight drops forward.

With each each jolt, each step, blood shakes free of Amelia's face and hair to fall onto the piled snow. As if the snow had been waiting all along, as if the snow were a living organism, each flake a cell, the tiny drops of blood instantly expand. They pass through every shade of red as they grow, from crimson to scarlet to a pure glowing pink the color of a baby's cheeks.

Amelia Baldi evaluates the small circle of snow beneath her eyes as she would if she were still able to capture it with her ancient camera. It is clear to her, as McTeague trudges forward, that she'll have to wait until noon, until the midwinter sun is as high as it's going to get, the light as flat as possible, before she begins. Then she can lean forward, give her head a shake, catch a myriad of drops in various stages of expansion. As long as she continues to move into the light, she can explore a half dozen exposures and several different films before the scene is compromised by shadow.

You've got to probe every millimeter of the frame with a light meter, Amelia tells herself. Don't get lazy. If you can't find a way to compensate for the high contrast, the sun will bleach your whites, blacken your reds, play you for an utter fool.

Process as Composition, she decides as McTeague reaches a stand of aspens beside a frozen, snow-covered stream. That's what I'll call it if I get the colors right. Process as Composition. Or Snow Drinking Blood.

As Zeke McTeague, some three hours later, guided his aging pickup from Route 196 onto the Interstate, he realized quite suddenly that his earlier sadness had simply faded away. He'd done everything a man could do in pursuit of his chosen path, everything; now he had to put that phase of his life behind him. The future was beckoning, rushing him along with the flow of traffic toward . . . He closed his eyes, imagined Patricia entering his cabin, the astonished look on her face, knowing she had no options, that she'd never had options, that he'd always been the master.

The sun was strong through the windshield and McTeague pulled his cap a little lower on his forehead. What he felt at that moment, to his surprise, was hope, pure childish hope. It was more than he'd expected, certainly more than he deserved, yet he embraced the emotion without reservation. He'd done it all and there was still more to do; he was truly blessed.

McTeague took I84 east to the next exit, Route 390, then headed south. Ten minutes later, he pulled over at the entrance to one of the hiking trails running through Promised Land State Park. Hunting wasn't allowed in the state parks, and it was too cold and too early for hikers; he didn't expect to run into a soul, as he tossed the bag lying on the seat alongside him over his shoulder and made his way along the path, and he didn't.

A few hundred yards into the park, McTeague found an old hemlock that had fallen several years before, opening a small grove to sunlight, the sunlight itself sparking the growth of young trees and shrubs around the rotting trunk. He found cat briar and blackberry as he made his way toward a stand of hemlock saplings. Thorns plucked at his jacket, his pants, the sack he carried over his shoulder, but he stubbornly kept on. When he reached the saplings, he set the bag down, dropped to his knees, waited for his heart to quiet before he got to work.

The branches of the young evergreens swept to the ground, hiding a small hollow at the center of the grove. McTeague put his rifle and the box of cartridges into the space. Then he covered the pile with the sack, added broken branches, handfuls of loam, whatever he could scoop up.

Back on the path, he stared into the saplings, searched for any trace of his efforts, found nothing. Soon the snow would end all chance of discovery before spring, plenty long enough. He began to retrace his steps, reminding himself that he wasn't finished yet, that he still had plenty to do. The walk seemed much longer going out, as did the drive back to his cabin. On the way, he tried not to think about what came next, what was going to happen to his little truck. To his way of thinking, even though it sounded stupid, this was a true crime. The little truck had worked hard for him, been loyal in a way human beings had never been loyal; he'd loved it, loved every one of his trucks, mourned their passing, found thoughts of them gutted for spare parts, finally crushed and sold for salvage unbearably sad.

He pulled the pickup into the barn, closed the doors behind him, then opened a five-pound bag of sugar and removed the gas cap. The plan was to pour the sugar into the tank with the engine running. The sugar would coat everything from the fuel pump to the carburetor to the valves to the cylinders with gasoline-flavored syrup. Once down, the engine would never run again.

But he couldn't make himself raise the bag, let the sugar run down into the tank. Even though he knew he should disable the vehicle in a way that would convince a good mechanic that it hadn't run in years, he put the bag of sugar on a shelf and shut down the engine.

"Guess everything wants to live," he told himself before he opened the hood, popped the distributor cap, and closed the gap on the points with a small screwdriver. Then he scrambled the spark plug wires and adjusted the fuel mixture on the carburetor until it was feeding pure gasoline into the engine. The truck didn't come close to starting when he cranked the ignition—that was to be expected—but a careful inspection would probably reveal what he'd done.

Be that as it may, McTeague didn't hesitate once he made up his mind. He ran the battery down, left the lights on for good measure. Then he flattened the tires and removed the single license plate. He was tired now, but his heart felt okay, which was just as well because he still had more to do. Moving slowly, he pulled the knit cap down over his ears, jammed his fingers into his gloves, swept the barn free of tire tracks before sliding his battery charger, air pump, jumper cables, and license plate into a plastic trash bag. He tossed the bag over his shoulder and walked a few yards into the woods, finally tucking the bag into a hollow space between two enormous boulders where he could find it again.

As he made his way back to the cabin, he thought about all the good things to come, about Patricia, the hard-ass cops with their hard-ass looks, the public reaction to his confession. The first book about Jeffrey Dahmer had been out within weeks of his arrest. They'd probably get his out within days. After all, Dahmer had been a looney-bird amateur, a schizo just begging to be caught and punished, nothing compared to Zeke McTeague. Dahmer ate hunks of his victims, kept a hand in the refrigerator where the cops would be sure to find it. The man hadn't begun to understand that the taking had to be completed, that finishing paved the way to new beginnings.

McTeague paused in the doorway of his cabin, let the warm air rush over him before stepping inside, closing the door, pulling off his cap and coat, his gloves and scarf, his sweater. He hung each garment on pegs nailed into the wall, taking his time about it, before turning on the television, settling back in his old rocker. In fifteen minutes, the news would come on. With a little bit of luck they'd have footage of his latest effort. If not, if it was too soon, they'd be sure to have it by six o'clock. Zeke McTeague could afford to wait; he had all the time in the world.

TWENTY-FIVE

Detrick saw the lights of the police cruisers in her rearview mirror before she heard the sirens. There were three of them, coming up fast and so close together they might have been cars on a speeding train. She pulled onto the shoulder of the narrow two-lane road and watched them go by. When the cars turned west some three hundred yards away, she asked herself if she knew anybody who lived on Oak Kiln Road and was distinctly relieved when she realized that she didn't. She carried this relief (along with a sense of having, in a very un-Christian manner, foisted her troubles on someone else) all the way to the Dreher Community Church where she found herself totally unprepared for the scene that greeted her as she came over a shallow rise and glided toward the small white building at the bottom of the hill.

Ahead, in the parking lot, five state trooper sedans formed a protective semicircle around a volunteer ambulance. The ambulance and all five police cars had their emergency lights on; the revolving lights cut intersecting swatches of color across the white brick of the Dreher Community Church.

The effect on Detrick was hypnotic; the piercing lights seemed to chop at her concentration, to separate her thoughts, leave them unconnected. She was at the very edge of the parking lot, having come to explain her decision to abandon McTeague. Oddly, though her eyes remained unfocused, refusing to pick the scene apart, her sense of hearing was intensified. She heard the hiss of the Jeep's heater, the hum of the fan, the engine turning over beneath the hood, the slight chug of the exhaust; she heard voices as well, laughter from the troopers standing behind their cruisers, an intense, though muted, conversation between several detectives. The detectives wore overcoats and had their hands jammed into their pockets; the troopers wore leather coats and flat-brimmed western hats.

Later, she'd come to ask herself how long she would have remained there in her parked car if left to her own devices. As it was, she estimated that she sat in the entrance to the lot for several minutes before one of the troopers detached herself and strolled over to the Jeep.

"May I help you, ma'am?" The officer—her nameplate identified her as Trooper Koposky—stared at Detrick through mirrored sunglasses.

"I'm here to see Mrs. Gauss. I work at the mission. Can you tell me what happened?"

"We're sorting that out now, ma'am." Koposky pulled a small notebook from her back pocket. "What did you say your name was?"

"Patricia Detrick." She drew a breath. "Trooper Koposky, are you going to tell me what happened?"

"Are you related to anyone in the building?"

"No, I'm not."

"There's been a shooting, ma'am. I can't say any more than that. How do you spell your last name?"

"D-E-T-R-I-C-K. You can't tell me if anyone's been—" She started to use the word *killed,* changed it at the last second. "—if anyone's been hurt?"

"Sorry." Trooper Koposky stepped back, let her hand drop to rest casually on the butt of her holstered gun. "I'm afraid you're going to have to move along."

Detrick started to put the Jeep into gear, stopped herself. There was no way she was going to leave, carry the burden of uncertainty until the news filtered down to her. "Elaine and Bill Gauss are good friends of mine. If something has happened to them . . ." There was no expression at all on Koposky's face, and no possibility that she was going to disobey orders, reveal anything to a stranger. "Can you tell me," Detrick asked on impulse, "if there's an investigator here named Donald Barrett?"

Koposky, as if expecting Detrick to abruptly disappear, continued to stare. Then she pointed to the detectives, said, "Yeah, Barrett's here."

"Unless you can help me, I'd like to talk to him. He's in charge, right?"

The trooper took a second to think this over, finally said, "You wait here," before turning away. She walked over to the detectives, tapped a man wearing a gray tweed overcoat on the shoulder. They spoke for a moment, then the detective began to walk toward the Jeep. He smiled as he came, a tall handsome man with a thick head of very blond hair. His eyes were the featureless blue of the December sky.

"Miss Detrick," Barrett said as he came alongside the Jeep. "You're Rick Morello's friend?"

"Yes, I'm trying to . . ." Faced with someone likely to provide a definite answer, Detrick found herself unable to ask the question. She saw Terry Bannister's closed coffin, considered his mutilated head, the need to keep the sight of that shattered head from his family and friends.

"Nobody was hurt, thank God," Barrett told her. "Somebody fired a bullet through Ms. Gauss's window, but it missed her by several feet." He glanced behind him. "I've gotta leave, Ms. Detrick," he said, still smiling. "Duty calls."

"Is it about . . . Is it something about Oak Kiln Road?"

Barrett's expression turned quizzical. "Why do you ask?"

"I saw three police cars turn up there a few minutes ago."

"Yes, well . . ." He shifted his weight from one foot to the other, again glanced at the detectives standing behind him. Finally he turned back to Detrick. "Do you know a woman named Florence Clark?"

Detrick shook her head. She felt close to tears and yet instinctively knew tears would be totally inappropriate; if she cried, she would be forever disgraced in Barrett's eyes. "No, I didn't know her. Is she . . . ?"

Barrett nodded. "Look, if I'm gonna beat the reporters to the scene, I better get going."

"Wait." Detrick put a restraining hand on the detective's arm. "Did it happen like all the others? Like what happened here this morning?"

"That's the way it seems," he said, not bothering to hide his distaste. "But we still have to investigate." Like Koposky, he dismissed her by stepping back. "You say hello to Rick for me. He surely thinks a lot of you."

At any other time, the praise would have thrilled her. Now, she barely heard it. Despite a sense of relief so powerful it would have shaken her knees if she'd been standing, threads of thought continued to weave through her mind, each going its independent way, refusing to tie together. "Sergeant Barrett—"

"Donny, please." A web of fine wrinkles sprouted at the corners of his eyes.

"Would it be all right if I went into the church, sat for a little while?"

Barrett frowned slightly. Then he nodded. "Park off in that corner. I'll tell the troopers to let you through."

• • •

If Detrick hoped to discover some kind of refuge inside the church, to isolate herself from the harsh realities unfolding outside, she was sharply disappointed. The revolving lights on the police cruisers in the parking lot whipped across the chapel's blue-and-amber windows, stained the unadorned walls of the church with splotches of light. Detrick had made her request on impulse; now she wished she'd driven away. Her thoughts had finally jumped into focus, setting on a single object, Zeke McTeague.

She paced the rear of the chapel, back and forth from the north to the south walls. In all her life, she'd never known a single individual who'd been deliberately wounded or killed; murder was something you read about in the papers, a fact of somebody else's life. Now it seemed that violence trailed in her wake. She'd driven Zeke McTeague to the Waterview and Alicia Munoz had been shot on the following day; she'd taken McTeague to church and Terry Bannister had been murdered on the following day. And now Elaine Gauss had been shot at three days later. It could *not* be coincidence.

She stopped pacing and briefly stared down at the floor before taking a seat in the last pew. *It cannot be coincidence.* On the one hand, she wanted to run out the door, confront Donald Barrett, demand that he arrest McTeague. On the other, she didn't know Barrett, couldn't be sure, once he heard a description of McTeague's physical condition, that he wouldn't dismiss McTeague as a suspect. After all, McTeague *was* a sick old man. At times he seemed actually feeble. It was hard to imagine him crouching in the early morning cold, waiting for his victims to show themselves.

Until now, Detrick realized as she leaned forward to rest her elbows on the pew in front of her, she'd been making intuitive judgments. Judgments, she realized, driven by McTeague himself. It was McTeague who'd drawn her attention to the news video taken at the Capriella house, the scene of the first murder, suggesting that Melissa Capriella was partially responsible for her fate because she lived alongside the state game lands. The next day, he'd deliberately brought up the subject of serial killers with Rick Morello.

Closing her eyes, Pat remembered that she'd gone to see McTeague at the request of the nurse, Abby Turner, on the day after Alicia Munoz was wounded. That was when she'd seen the box of 30–30 cartridges. The box had been lying in the cupboard, right behind the dog food where McTeague had put it. And it was McTeague who'd insisted that feeding Becky could not be put off. That same afternoon, he'd asked her, point blank, if she thought the Capriella and Munoz shootings were deliberate. She'd dismissed his question at the time, as she'd dismissed much of what he said, as the product of his odd, lonely life.

Again she saw McTeague in conversation with Terry Bannister outside the Dreher Community Church. Their conversation, she remembered, had been lively, but after Bannister's murder, Zeke had insisted that he and Bannister weren't friends. And it was Zeke who requested that she turn on the radio in the Jeep so he could listen to the news. Could he have known the station would report Terry's murder? And yet, hearing the announcement, he hadn't seemed upset, not even ruffled. Instead, he had impassively compared the death of Terry Bannister to the death of Melissa Capriella. And that same afternoon, he'd described his wartime training as a sniper. That was three days ago, the day after she'd taken him to church and the last time she'd seen him.

Detrick drew a deep breath. Though she was still certain that McTeague was the sniper who'd been terrorizing the county, the facts she'd gathered seemed extremely thin. The rest of it—McTeague's subtle manipulations; his gaze, now piercing, now unfocused; the wall of photos and their effect; tales of passengers in his truck who screamed and had to be put out—were infinitely harder to communicate.

Pat looked down at her hands, found them lying flat in her lap, two dead fish waiting to be wrapped. The metaphor evoked the shadow of a smile. Immediately after her separation from Brad, she'd felt herself whipped back and forth between anger and self-pity, had once actually wished that she could flop down, lie in her bed as cold and unmoving as a flounder on a pile of ice. The image had formed as she waited for service in a fish market near Mount Pocono and she'd later come to understand it as a turning point, the moment when she'd finally seen the relationship between self-pity and self-indulgence, how expensive that package really was.

Well, she wasn't going to fall into that particular trap again, wasn't going to revert to the petulant child nursing her grievances, no matter what the consequences. And there would be consequences, because there was only one place to go for help, one individual to approach, and that was Rick Morello.

Detrick closed her eyes, tried and failed to imagine the new track her life would take, finally decided to ease off the drama. There was work to be done and no one else to do it. She rose, eased out of the pew before again looking up at the cross, offering a silent thank-you.

TWENTY-SIX

After a quick drive home, she hesitated only long enough to fill her coffee maker before going to work. She took a stenographer's notebook, a number two pencil, and an eraser from the center drawer of her desk, carried them to the kitchen table, sat, and began to write. Her intention was to get everything, no matter how silly, no matter how amorphous or paranoid-seeming, out in front of her where she could see it. One thing for sure. Although McTeague had no alibi for any of the killings, there was no smoking gun here, no concrete admission of guilt on the part of Zeke McTeague. If Morello—and Barrett after him—was to be convinced, he would have to be overwhelmed by an accumulation of small details. It was up to her to present those details fully and coherently.

Ninety minutes later, when the well of her memory finally went dry, Detrick set down her pencil. She had written three pages of notes. Her handwriting was very precise, in direct contrast to the phrases on the page which seemed to her the rantings of a paranoid. She reminded herself that Morello hadn't been there, hadn't seen the wall of empty photographs, McTeague's wet eyes swimming behind those glasses. Notations like, *McTeague flashes between sinister and fragile, threatening and helpless (without transition)* were probably not going to help.

She stood abruptly, turned away from the table. There were times during her reign over the back offices at Detrick Motors when she'd faced problems that seemed insurmountable, especially in the later years. Brad, at the very pinnacle of a manic personality swing, would order hundreds of vehicles, even during a recession, leaving his wife to meet payroll when those vehicles sat on the lot unsold. Over time, she had learned that she couldn't always beat a problem into submission. Sometimes she had to create a little space, give her mind room to work.

After finishing her coffee, washing the pot and the filter basket, she decided to take a shower. Passing by the couch in the living room, she glanced out the window, caught a flash of lawn, the woods on the far side, and imagined McTeague kneeling out there, licking his lips while he waited for opportunity to knock. Instinctively, she ducked, as if she could see the bullet on its way, still had time to avoid its impact. Then, despite an urge to curl up into a ball, she tiptoed across the room, closed the blinds, one by one, pressed against the wall. By the time she finished, her heart was pounding and she had to force herself to go through the rest of the house, yank down the shades, pull the curtains together.

She was in the bedroom, closing the shutters, before she realized that Zeke McTeague had no way to find her, not unless he was psychic. Her driver's license showed only the post office box she'd rented after leaving Brad, and her phone number and address wouldn't be listed in the phone directory until next year because she'd moved into the house too late to be included in this year's edition. McTeague had never been to SAM's offices, so he could not have gotten her address from that source, either.

Detrick sat on the bed and began to consider a question that had not occurred to her before, but that now seemed painfully obvious. If McTeague was not targeting her, if he didn't plan to kill her, why had he revealed himself? Melissa Capriella, a stranger to Detrick, had been killed before she and McTeague had met, so he'd already been set on his present course. If he'd continued to attack individuals entirely unknown to her, if he'd confined his conversation to trucking anecdotes, she would never have suspected him. Yet McTeague, the man who'd fiercely rejected three other volunteers, had begun feeding her bits and pieces almost from the moment she'd walked through his door.

Maybe, Pat speculated as she rose and began to undress, he wants me to know he's going to kill me. Maybe he wants to torture me psychologically, the way it usually happens in the movies, to chase me, knife in hand, through the woods behind his house.

Given McTeague's physical condition, the image, when Detrick tried to construct it, seemed ludicrous. Yet the question that provoked the scenario remained valid. McTeague was not crazy; he didn't see things or hear voices like his sister. He must have a reason for playing this game with her.

It wasn't until Detrick emerged from her shower, with no answer to her original question, that a second, more practical question rose into her consciousness. How, she asked herself, does McTeague get from his house to the homes of his victims—twenty-five miles in the case of Melissa Capriella—unless he owns a vehicle? All along, she, like everybody else at the mission, had been assuming McTeague was trapped in his little cabin. Another tribute to his weak heart and shuffling gait. But there was no reason he couldn't have a small truck or a car stored in the dilapidated barn on his property. No reason at all.

And there was no reason, she decided as she slipped into a robe, wiped the bathroom mirror free of steam and began to blow-dry her hair, why somebody—meaning herself—couldn't disable that vehicle, couldn't, for instance, take an ax and drive it through the radiator. Without a vehicle, he would never again leave his home unaccompanied.

The more she thought about it, the more practical the solution became. It could be done immediately, without help from anyone; she could waltz up to his house, turn things around, play the hunter instead of the deer. She could even make a virtue of the act by hoping against hope that she'd find no vehicle. McTeague's immobility would proclaim his innocence.

She put the hair dryer on the edge of the sink, walked to the closet in her bedroom, took down a small box tied firmly with a piece of twine. She slid the twine over the edge of the box, then removed the cover and stared down at the gun inside. Her father had taken her into his den, given her the little Seecamp .32, along with a box of hollow point cartridges, on the night before he and her mother left for the Arizona suburbs. The clear, typically male implication, which Pat had found entirely insulting, was that she needed a weapon now that he wouldn't be around to protect her. This despite the fact that she still had a husband at the time.

She'd wanted to protest, refuse the gift, but it was a farewell dinner and her mother, apparently innocent, was in the kitchen, undoubtedly hoping to maintain the politely placid atmosphere that shrouded her entire life. Her father wouldn't have understood, either, would have found his daughter's resentment unfathomable.

So she'd taken her father's offering, tossed it on a closet shelf, forgotten it completely. Now, she picked up the automatic, released the clip, and let it drop into her hand. Detrick was too familiar with guns to be afraid of them.

Her father collected antique revolvers, had taken her out to the firing range, taught her to use everything from a single-action revolver to a twelve-gauge Remington. But she didn't particularly like guns, the proof being that she hadn't fired one since high school.

No, she told herself, this is not a Hollywood movie and you are not Sigourney Weaver incinerating the aliens. You're a bleeding heart and you'll act like one. You'll go back to work, get your scribbled notes together, take your case to the proper authorities, let the state handle it. As if to prove her determination, she turned on the radio and searched the dial until she found a news broadcast that confirmed what she'd known all along. Florence Clark had been shot and killed from ambush as she sat down to breakfast in the safety of her own home.

Tamarack Lake was frozen over, the ice a glistening sheet running to a horizon so black it might not have been there at all. Detrick could see individual stars reflected in the surface of the ice, hear the ice groan and crack in response to the water moving beneath it. Within a few weeks, the surface of the lake would be dulled by snow, tracked by snowmobiles and cross-country skis, but for now it carried every available light, the stars and the moon, the amber lamps surrounding the lodge, the headlights of passing automobiles flickering through the trees.

It was beautiful, of course, relentlessly beautiful, but at the same time entirely unwelcoming, as if the lake's beauty was meant for some other class of being.

Detrick shut down the engine, slipped the keys into her pocket, firmly repressed a wave of self-pity. It was a perfect night for romance, for an arm-in-arm stroll by the shore of the frozen lake. A perfect night to watch the moon rise above the trees, to watch its elongated twin move across the ice. That wasn't going to happen now. Rick Morello had met Zeke McTeague, seen the old man fumble through a meal, shuffle across the room; Rick's reaction to her carefully reasoned argument would certainly be indulgence of the sort a parent might show to a fibbing child.

Well, that's very interesting, Patricia, but do you really think McTeague had the strength for it? If he did, he oughta move out to Hollywood because that old guy's the greatest actor I've ever seen.

If Rick Morello does that, she told herself as she opened her car door, if he laughs in my face, I'll take my case to Donald Barrett. And if I can't make Barrett listen, I'll go out to McTeague's on my own. I'll do anything but live with this knowledge.

As she strode across the parking lot, down the narrow path leading to Morello's cabin, Detrick felt good about herself. Sacrifice, self-reliance, nose to the grindstone: Strength implied purpose, a willingness to accept the burden, whatever it was, whatever the consequences. Nevertheless, when Rick Morello opened the door, she took one look at his small enigmatic smile, the light in his eyes, and muttered, "Shit."

TWENTY-SEVEN

Morello's smile vanished; his eyes narrowed and he raised his chin as though he were farsighted and wanted to get a better look at his guest. "What's wrong?"

Detrick forced a smile. "The sniper," she said as she walked past him into the cottage, "the one who wounded Alicia Munoz and killed Terry Bannister. What would you say if I told you I know who he is?"

Morello came up behind Detrick. He took her arm, gently turned her until she was facing him. "You've got my attention."

"Then what would you say if I told you the sniper was Zeke McTeague?"

Her second question had the anticipated effect. Morello's face seemed to fall apart, his mouth, cheeks, eyes and eyebrows to fly in different directions, like a small flock of birds looking for a place to perch. "The old man you brought to lunch at the lodge? That's who you're talking about?"

Detrick stared up at him for a moment, then slipped her hand into her purse, removed her notes. "Do you think we can sit down, maybe have a glass of wine?"

"Actually, I thought you were bringing the wine." His face had recovered, found a neutral, determined set.

"Oh, Lord, I forgot all about it."

"In that case, you'll have to settle for a Heineken."

Detrick nodded, let herself drop into a brown club chair next to a high-backed love seat. Although the chair's upholstery appeared to be in good condition, the springs had obviously seen their best day, and she sank down until she was certain her buttocks were brushing the chocolate brown carpet. Morello stepped into the kitchenette, pulled two green bottles from the refrigerator, and set them on the counter separating the kitchen and the living room. Detrick, watching him as if this routine chore were a command performance, started to speak, then decided to wait until they were both sitting down. A moment later, Morello put a glass stein on the table next to her, then, cradling his own glass, sat on the couch.

"That chair," he observed, "it's not in the greatest shape. Maybe you'd like to move."

"Why don't I just say what I have to say, Rick, and get it over with."

"Shoot." He grinned self-consciously. "Poor choice of words."

"The worst," she readily agreed.

For the next fifteen minutes, she made her case, made it without interruption, consulting her notes as she went along. She began with McTeague's trips to the lodge and the Dreher Community Church, the shootings that followed each, emphasized McTeague's encounter with Terry Bannister. When Morello failed to react, she proceeded to the box of cartridges she'd found in his cupboard.

As she went along, Detrick became more and more convinced that she was right, that the bits and pieces of Zeke McTeague's life formed a cohesive whole. Her voice reflected her confidence; she ticked off the various items as if reciting a mathematical formula. McTeague, she explained, had been a sniper during World War II, had described his training and experience in detail to her. He'd been the first to suggest that the shooting at the lodge might be the work of a serial killer, had even brought up the topic of serial killers with Morello the time they'd met. Finally, she described the mud-caked trousers placed on top of the laundry basket where she was certain to notice them, McTeague's explanation about falling in the rain, the spotless slippers on his feet.

"I don't know anything about serial killers, where they come from, how they develop," she said, dropping her notes to her lap, "but I can tell you that McTeague's mother died at his birth and he was raised in complete isolation by a schizophrenic older sister. His childhood experience, which I verified with a woman who knew his sister, must have been pure hell. But when he described it, he was oddly calm. It was as if his life had happened to somebody else."

Detrick stopped abruptly, having suddenly decided not to go beyond the facts she'd assembled, not to argue their sickening implications. Morello was looking down at his folded hands when she finished; he held that posture for a long moment.

"What about Melissa Capriella, the woman who was killed in her home a couple of weeks ago? And Florence Clark? How do they connect to you?"

"They don't." Pat sipped at her beer. "Melissa was murdered before I met McTeague. As for Florence Clark, I think McTeague was showing off, demonstrating his power. I also believe it was his way of increasing the pressure. The pressure on me, of course."

Morello nodded. "What you say about the Capriella woman makes sense," he declared, "because I guarantee that McTeague, assuming you're right about him, didn't take up the profession of murderer at age seventy-plus."

"Of course." Detrick ran the back of her hand across her forehead as another piece of the puzzle slid into place. "He's been at it for a long time. I should have known."

"Be that as it may, why did he alter his plans after he met you? Why would he decide to target individuals known to you? It's as if he wants you to put it together."

Detrick put down the glass. "I've been trying to answer those questions for the last six hours. And, yes, he does want me to know; I'm sure of it." She shifted her weight on the chair, but only sank deeper. The cushion seemed to fold around her legs. "Look, let the psychiatrists deal with his motivation. As for myself, the idea is to stop him. People are dying, Rick."

Morello raised his glass, drank, then, still holding the glass, said matter-of-factly, "What you say, Pat, it's very compelling. But there's something you need to know. I had a call from Donny Barrett about an hour ago. Barrett told me he has a suspect down at the barracks, that he expects the guy to cave any minute."

Detrick's first reaction was anger. Why had he allowed her to ramble on, make a fool of herself? The explanation that sprang to mind—that he was merely indulging her, a proud daddy listening to his daughter recite lunatic poetry—did nothing to improve her state of mind. She was halfway to demanding her coat, when Morello went on.

"Barrett's suspect, he's Florence Clark's nephew, Coleman Poole. Poole's an ex-con. He had a rifle in his van, a thirty-thirty registered in his own name, when Barrett picked him up. The rifle was slick with gun oil because it had been recently cleaned."

Pat shook her head as she tried to absorb the information. "What was his motive?" she asked.

"Money, according to Donny. Poole was Florence Clark's only relative. He stands to inherit her mortgage-free house and whatever she has in the bank." Morello sipped at his beer. He seemed surprised to find it empty. "Poole admitted this to Donny. That he was her only relative and he expected to inherit. That's why Barrett's so certain he's gonna get a confession."

"That doesn't explain Terry Bannister and Elaine Gauss," Detrick responded stubbornly. "Or any of the others."

Rick shrugged. "Cover-ups or tragic accidents. That's what Barrett wants to go with. Poole attacked Munoz because . . . Look, Pat, Donny Barrett's under a lot of pressure to make an arrest. This guy, Poole, he's the perfect patsy. A greasy-haired, tattoo-covered biker who spent five years in prison for attacking another man with a baseball bat. I'm not saying Barrett knows that Poole's innocent. I'm not even saying that Poole *is* innocent. I'm just saying that it's real easy to use a violent ex-con to buy yourself a little time."

Morello was interrupted by the shriek of a smoke alarm. He glanced into the kitchen, then back at Detrick, grinned and said, "So much for the paella," before jumping up. Pat, trapped in the sagging chair, took a bit longer. By the time she joined him in the kitchen, Morello was scraping away at the bottom of a heavy skillet with a long metal spoon. "Charcoal, anybody?" he asked cheerfully. He stepped over to the sink, ran the outside of the pot under cold water before setting it on the porcelain. Then he popped the cover on the smoke alarm and removed the battery.

"Fortunately," Pat said, waving at a cloud of malodorous steam, "we're within a hundred yards of a decent restaurant."

Without warning, Morello took her in his arms and kissed her. Detrick, much too stunned to frame an immediate response, felt her body do so. Her arms instinctively circled his ribs, locked onto the broad muscles of his back. When he finally stepped away, she found her knees so weak she nearly stumbled.

"I'm crazy about you," he said. "I can't stop thinking about you." Then he stopped, as if that explained everything.

Detrick searched, briefly, very briefly, for some retort, some flippant, dismissive remark. When nothing came to mind, she took his hand, brought it to her cheek, held it fast. "I can't help but sympathize," she told him. "Because I've been having the identical problem."

The Mill Room was nearly empty. Their waiter, a young woman Morello introduced as Miriam, had a pair of vodka tonics on their table within minutes. Morello held one up, paused.

"Here's to crime and punishment," he said. "Especially punishment."

"Does that mean we're going to get back to Zeke McTeague?" Detrick, despite a persistent tingling in her breasts and belly, had no intention of letting go.

Morello set his drink down, scratched his right eyebrow. "Tell me something, do you think McTeague has targeted you?"

"No," she replied without hesitation. "He doesn't know where I live and has no way to find out. Plus, if he was really after me, why would he let me know he was coming? Physically, he's no match for anyone. The only way he succeeds at what he's doing is by sneaking up on his victims."

"Then you don't have to move. Which is just as well, because I hate the idea of you going away, even if it's only temporary." He sat back in his chair, crossed his legs. "Let me tell you something about Donny Barrett. In personal injury investigations, unless you have an eyewitness to identify the perp, you have to find a connection between the killer and the victim. A connection and a motive. That would even be true in serial killer investigations. What Barrett did in the Munoz case was check the whereabouts of every employee at the Waterview who knows her. He even sent one of his detectives to New York to interview her relatives. When those efforts came to nothing, he worked forward to Terence Bannister and backward to Melissa Capriella, again looking for some connection."

"And a cover-up was the best he could do?" Detrick snorted her contempt.

"That's not the point." Morello leaned forward. "The point is that you've found a connection in Zeke McTeague. The rest of it, all the little hints, don't amount to much. But that McTeague was at the Waterview the day before the wounding of Alicia Munoz, that the killing of Bannister and the attack on Elaine Gauss occurred within days of his meeting them, is compelling. I'm not in charge of the investigation, but if I was, McTeague would have to prove himself innocent before I'd let him off the hook."

Detrick started to speak, then stopped herself. Now that her secret was out in the open, that it hadn't been rejected out of hand, she felt nearly overcome with relief. To bear the burden of stopping McTeague alone, she realized, might well have crushed her.

"There's one item you can supply that'd be a big help," Morello continued. "Tell me how McTeague gets around. What kind of car is he using? Donny's already gotten a couple of hundred calls on the hot line. Maybe some good citizen noticed McTeague's vehicle parked by the side of the road and has phoned in a description. If Donny has something in his files, he'll be a lot more receptive to your idea of a geriatric serial killer."

TWENTY-EIGHT

Detrick felt the blood rush into her face. "I don't know that McTeague has a car," she admitted. "I've never seen one there." She went on to describe the barn, her tentative plan to get inside, disable any vehicle she discovered.

"So what you're saying . . ." Morello fell silent as Miriam approached the table, order pad in hand. He opened his menu, glanced inside.

"As if he didn't have it memorized," Miriam said to Detrick. "He eats here every night."

Detrick caught a hint of resentment in the waitress's voice, found herself wondering if Miriam wasn't attracted to Morello, if she hadn't been rejected or, worse, ignored.

"When you're right, you're right, Miriam. I'll have the

penne in vodka sauce. And ask John to please toast one of those doughballs he passes off as loaves of Italian bread."

"And for your salad, sir?"

"House dressing."

Morello was back to his buttoned-up persona, a fact not lost on Detrick. Somehow, she found it comforting.

"I'll have the lamb chops, well done," she said. "The house dressing will be fine."

They watched Miriam walk away. Detrick sipped at her vodka tonic; Morello toyed with the buttons on his shirt. Finally, she said, "You were about to ask me a question."

"Right. About how McTeague gets around. You're saying that if McTeague doesn't own a vehicle, he couldn't be the . . . the Pocono Sniper."

Detrick grimaced at the epithet currently being used by the media. "That's the way it looks." Her tone was firm, as if she'd made up her mind about something. "He's too irascible to have a partner. And he's too weak to steal a car. So I have to see if there's one inside that barn."

Morello raised a hand, palm out. "I don't want to say the wrong thing here, but if you want me to go out there with you, it wouldn't be any problem. If you want me to go alone—"

"I don't think we should do anything until we hear from Donny Barrett. If he gets a confession . . ." Detrick finished her drink, set the glass on the white tablecloth.

"A confession would let McTeague off the hook? If Poole admits to it, you'd be satisfied?"

"I wouldn't have much choice." She looked into Morello's eyes. "But it wouldn't get me over the feeling that Zeke's manipulating me, that he has something specific in mind for me. That was why I went to the mission this morning. I'm supposed to take Zeke to church on Sunday, but I'd decided to tell Elaine that I'd had enough and I wanted out. As for you going to McTeague's by yourself . . . Zeke has a dog he keeps chained outside. The dog—Becky's her name—likes to bark. He'd know you were coming."

• • •

After dinner, at Morello's suggestion, they strolled to the Waterview's Lenape Room, a cocktail lounge/supper club named after the Indian tribe that'd been driven from the region more than two centuries before. A Thursday night and between seasons, the entertainment was confined to the efforts of Paul Morgan's Mountain Swing Band, a local group that played catering halls when it couldn't find bookings on the nursing home circuit. Their music, though it claimed kinship with that of Benny Goodman and Count Basie, was really based on pirated Lawrence Welk arrangements.

Detrick, faintly amused, followed Morello to the bar, ordered a glass of white wine, settled down to listen. "If you hadn't taken me to hear Shirley Horn," she said after a few minutes, "I'd accuse you of being tone-deaf."

"Not fair," he responded. "It's a wonderful band to dance to. Whatever beat you pick, they're right on it. At one time or another."

As if to prove his point, he took her hand, led her onto the dance floor just as Morgan, a middle-aged maestro with a Skitch Henderson goatee, lurched into a turgid version of "Twilight Time." Still amused, Detrick didn't get the point until she settled into Morello's arms, his right hand cupping the small of her back. When she was younger, she might have pronounced it all, including her physical reaction, a seduction. Now she saw Morello's obviously calculated scenario as an invitation he was giving her plenty of time to refuse.

"When I was first promoted to detective," Morello said, "I had to learn to read people, know when they were lying. It's not hard to do, but it takes concentration. There's a little gap, an empty space between the time someone decides to lie and the time they begin to speak. If you train yourself to watch, you can see the gap clearly." His fingers tightened on hers, led her hand down onto his shoulder. "There's a kind of unexpected benefit to knowing when people lie. By process of elimination, you also know when someone's telling the truth. The thing I'm getting to, Pat, is that when I look at you, I don't find that gap. You're not manipulating me; you have no ulterior motive. You're just yourself."

It was nearly two hours later when Pat Detrick, lying with her head on Morello's bare shoulder, a leg casually thrown over his thighs, noticed the blinking green light on the answering machine. The bedroom was lit with candles and the machine was set on a tall chest against the wall, but even so, she felt, one of them should have seen it long before this.

As she watched, the tiny bulb flashed over and over again, as if determined to persist until acknowledged. Though Detrick wanted to ignore it, to return her attention to the trail her fingers continued to blaze through the matted hair on Morello's chest, every burst spoke to her of bullets smashing panes of glass, closed coffins. Of Zeke McTeague. A moment before, she'd been thinking of Betty Hoffmann, of the question Betty had posed: *Can you imagine yourself naked with this man?* When the time finally came, there'd been no moment of truth, no reflection, no decision to make.

"Your answering machine's blinking," she finally said.

Morello took so long to respond that she thought he might have fallen asleep, but when he did speak, his voice was steady and focused. "Yes, I know. I've been trying to ignore it." He smiled, pulled himself to a sitting position. "I want to hold onto this minute." He reached over, cupped her breast. "And anything else I can get my hands on. I feel like a kid trying to make Christmas last until New Year's." He sighed. "And now for the bad news," he said, getting up from the bed.

"Partner, we are booking Coleman Poole for the murder of Florence Clark even as I speak. Got ourselves a neat

little statement that's gonna put the mutt in jail for a long time to come. Speak to you."

When Detrick left an hour later, the temperature outside was twenty-two degrees and falling. It was snowing softly, the surging cold wringing the last drops of moisture from the atmosphere. The WBRE meteorologist would call it a dusting and that's the way it would appear in the morning. The snow would drape every branch, line the interlaced stems of the enormous forsythia in her backyard, beckon to her until she thrust her feet into a pair of boots, took a walk out into the stillness of the woods, let herself be overwhelmed.

Maybe something would come to her, some inspiration, and she'd know what to tell Elaine Gauss. Right now, she couldn't justify spreading rumors about Zeke McTeague, that he was a killer. Not with somebody else under arrest. But if she didn't, if she wrote off her unwillingness to return to McTeague as a conflict of personalities, Elaine would certainly send another volunteer; the mission's nurse, Abby Turner, would continue to visit; McTeague would have ready targets no matter what happened to his vehicle. If he had a vehicle.

Detrick switched on the defroster, felt a rush of heated air slide across her face, decided that her dilemma wouldn't crunch like the numbers in a Detrick Motors ledger. And she very much wanted to work through the problem, put it behind her so she could luxuriate in the insistent warmth sweeping up from her belly to her breasts, the ache in her thighs. She was halfway to being in love with him, hopelessly in love, head-over-heels in love. It was not a time for thoughts of murder and murderers.

TWENTY-NINE

When she awakened from a dreamless sleep at six o'clock the following morning, she discovered Zeke McTeague still dominated her thoughts. After fifteen minutes of tossing beneath the blanket, she decided to take the bath she'd considered the night before. She brushed her teeth, brewed a cup of tea, set her cup on the lid of the commode before running the water, adding a capful of bath oil while the tub filled.

The groan of satisfaction that rose from her chest as she slid beneath the steaming water, felt it rise, liquid and oily, to cover her body, had nothing whatever to do with McTeague, however. It spoke only of Rick Morello, of the night before, the nights to come. When she and Rick had parted, neither had set a time to meet again, even bothered to say, "I'll call you tomorrow." There'd been no need for it, no need for reassurance.

The mood was seductive enough to last through four reheatings of the water in the tub, until her toes were wrinkled at the tips. It would have lasted still longer, perhaps until the moment she left for the mission, if she hadn't turned on the television as she went to the refrigerator for a glass of orange juice. The local news was just finishing and the anchor, a middle-aged woman with teased black hair and a relentlessly perky smile, was recapping the top stories. Or, rather, she was recapping a single story as footage of Coleman Poole, flanked by two burly troopers and surrounded by reporters, played across the screen.

Poole, short and at least forty pounds overweight, glared at the reporters and their cameras as he shuffled forward. To Detrick, he seemed slightly bewildered by the handcuffs and shackles that bound him. She watched him shake out his shoulder-length hair, then spit on the pavement. According to Morello, Poole had served time in prison for attacking another man with a bat. Detrick thought she could see that in him, that uncontrollable rage. Poole was not a man accustomed to being helpless.

"Once again, an arrest has been made in the murder of Florence Clark. The alleged sniper's name is Coleman Poole, Ms. Clark's nephew. While details are still sketchy, Sergeant Donald Barrett, speaking for the State Police, confirmed the rumor that Poole has given a statement to investigators. Sergeant Barrett refused, however, to link Poole to the murders of Melissa Capriella and Terence Bannister. He described both investigations as 'ongoing' and 'intense.' "

• • •

The morning sun had done its work and the parking lot of the Dreher Community Church was free of snow. Anxious to get through the conversation with Elaine and Bill Gauss, Detrick parked the Jeep close to the wing housing the mission, then, as she stepped out, noticed a pickup truck backed into a slot at the corner of the lot farthest from the church. Two young men squatted next to the truck. They were trying to start a balky chain saw, one of three laid in a row on the asphalt. She recognized one of the men, Samuel Abbington, another volunteer. She waved at him, got almost to the door before remembering that she'd seen him at McTeague's the first time she'd gone out to the cabin. He'd been part of a team cutting the deadfall behind the little house into firewood. On impulse, she turned and walked across the parking lot. To her surprise, as she grew closer, her heart began to beat more rapidly.

"Morning, Miss Detrick." Abbington rose to his feet. He was a handsome boy, his blond hair cut short, his smooth, open face unmarked. Elaine Gauss sometimes referred to Samuel, not without fondness, as the mission's poster boy.

"Good morning, Samuel." Detrick thrust her hands into her pockets. "How are the folks?" Abbington's parents were strong supporters of the mission.

"They're fine."

The second boy rose. He stood several inches shorter than Abbington, with narrow features and bushy eyebrows that reminded Detrick of McTeague's. Abbington introduced him as Gino Cappadone, adding, "From St. Mary's."

Detrick nodded hello, accepted a quick smile before turning back to Samuel. "You've been out to Zeke McTeague's place, right? I remember seeing you there."

"That's right. Gino was there, too. We cut up an old maple, bucked it and split it. Took us two days. Nasty old guy, that McTeague. Didn't even say thank you."

"Yeah," Cappadone added. "Didn't wanna let us use

the barn to store the tools overnight. Gave us a hard time about it."

"But he did let you? Finally?" Detrick rocked back on her heels, tried to brace herself.

"Only after I explained that the mission was closed and we were on our way to a party and we had nowhere else to keep them." Abbington flashed an embarrassed grin. "A white lie. We could've taken the tools back to my folks' house, stored them in the garage, but we were in a hurry."

Detrick nodded, smiled. When she spoke again, she detected a slight tremble in her voice. "Why did McTeague want to keep you out of the barn? Did he have something in there he didn't want you to see?"

Abbington shook his head, looked at his buddy. "You notice anything, Gino?"

"He had an old pickup in there, a Chevy, but I wouldn't say it was worth protecting. Hadda be at least ten years old."

"Yeah, right," Abbington said. "Now I remember. It was filthy. And one of the tires was flat. McTeague told us he liked to sit in it, remember the good old days when he drove all around the country taking pictures."

The interior of the chapel was empty when Detrick took a seat at the very end of the front pew. She needed to prepare herself. Convincing Elaine Gauss (and Bill, too, there was no way around convincing Bill Gauss) would not end the problem of Zeke McTeague. Bill would never abandon a helpless old man. Not on the basis of her suspicions, not on the basis of his own suspicions. Somebody would be going out there to take McTeague shopping, do his laundry, make sure he was still breathing.

Pat closed her eyes, saw Abby Turner, medical bag in hand, step out of her Dodge, heard the crunch of Abby's boots on the gravel driveway as she strode toward the cabin. A walking target, that's what she'd be. As would anybody else approaching that house. Pat's father had been a hunter. Over the years, he'd brought back dozens of skinned deer. Pat, fascinated, had studied the carcasses stored in the basement freezer. She knew exactly what a bullet from a hunting rifle could do to flesh and bone. The exit wounds had the look of explosions.

THIRTY

Despite a firm decision to march into Elaine's office, just get it over with, Pat lost her nerve at the last minute, neatly sidestepping into Abby Turner's empty cubicle as if that had been her destination all along. She sat down, picked up the phone, glanced at the posters on the wall, a pair of identically framed Ansel Adams prints. The expansive landscapes, each an intricate play of light and shadow on a barren range of sharply peaked mountains, spoke to Detrick of nature at its most inhuman. Even the gnarled Sequoia in the foreground of the photo closest to her represented no more than a grudging concession, a reluctant acknowledgement of the living planet.

But then wasn't that what McTeague had done, in his

wall of empty roads? Without any pretense to art, the old man had done exactly what Ansel Adams had done, created the same emotional effect. The difference was that Adams had started where McTeague left off, added beauty to the loneliness.

A revelation slammed into her with the force of an oncoming train. For a long moment, she could not breathe. McTeague's photos filled her mind, the great jumble of them, peopled at last, peopled with the bodies of his victims.

He told me that he took the pictures so that he could remember, she thought. Then she added the part he'd left out: *So he could remember what he'd done, who he'd killed, how he'd killed them. Each photo was a memento, each recorded his life's work, his triumphs.*

McTeague had spoken to her of evil, had raised the subject, insisting that true evil existed and could not be altered in any way. He'd been very certain of what he'd said, she suddenly knew, because his knowledge came of personal experience.

"The bastard," she muttered when she found the breath to speak. "How could he do it?" A second questions immediately rose into her mind: *Dear God, how can I stop him?*

As Detrick punched a number into the phone, as she waited for Morello to answer, her mouth tightened and her eyes narrowed. She felt a pure rage beginning to build.

"Hello."

"Rick, it's Pat."

"Pat, I tried to call you a few minutes ago."

"I'm at the mission." She hesitated, reminded herself her outrage would not stop McTeague, that she had to work purposefully, could not be diverted by her emotions.

"Is this about McTeague?" Morello's voice was noticeably softer.

"Yes," she admitted. "I found out a few minutes ago that he has a pickup truck in his barn."

"That's opportunity."

"What?"

"The vehicle gives McTeague opportunity."

"Well, there's something else. Two somethings, really. I was thinking about the second shooting, Alicia Munoz. You said the killer knelt in a cold rain for a long time. I didn't think that McTeague could endure that exposure, the man's so weak. Now, I remember that on the evening after the shooting at the Waterview, I got a call from Abby Turner, the mission's nurse. Abby told me that McTeague was ill. She asked me to drive out to his cabin and make sure he was okay. Rick, McTeague was sick *because* he knelt in the rain, because he got soaked. That's when his pants got muddy, the pants he made sure I noticed."

"All right, it fits, though it isn't exactly evidence. What else?"

"I have to tell Elaine and Bill Gauss about McTeague; I have to warn them even though I know it won't do any good. It's like you said, Rick, my suspicions aren't evidence. I might have a chance with Elaine, she's the practical one, but I'll never persuade Bill to abandon McTeague. That means someone has to—"

"I know what it means."

"And what I'm beginning to think is that someone has to be me." Detrick felt suddenly weary. "What I was hoping was that you've spoken to Donny Barrett, that he has a rock-solid case against Coleman Poole."

Morello didn't respond immediately; Pat, listening to his noticeably more rapid breathing, felt her heart take a pronounced nosedive.

"I can't help you there, Pat."

"You didn't speak to Barrett?"

Another hesitation, then, "Yeah, I spoke to him. The jerk." Morello's tone soured. "According to Barrett, Poole admitted that he's been doing crank on and off for the last couple of weeks and—"

"Wait a minute. What's 'crank'?"

"Speed. Methamphetamine. The drug of choice for bikers." Morello took a deep breath, let it hiss between his teeth. "Anyway, the problem is that Poole can barely remember where he was yesterday, so he's having a hard time putting together an alibi for any of the shootings except the last ones."

"You mean Poole has an alibi for the time of his aunt's killing?"

"What I'm saying is that Poole has a girlfriend named Rose D'Angelo who told Donny Barrett that Poole was sleeping in her bed yesterday morning. That's the good news. The bad news is that D'Angelo has a string of prostitution and drug possession arrests in Scranton. She's a biker's lady, so lying to the pigs for her man is a matter of honor. Maybe she's telling the truth and maybe she isn't. There's no way to be sure."

"So the police have nothing," Detrick said, almost to herself. "Nothing at all."

"What Donny has is a fairly damning statement. Poole admitted he was glad Florence Clark was dead and he was looking forward to spending her money. He told Donny that he always hated his aunt. He called her the Ice Bitch."

Detrick could feel the indignation rising and fought to control it. "Is that Donny Barrett's idea of a confession?"

"Pat, I was just there to listen." He hesitated briefly, as if trying to pluck something positive from the heap of bad news, then said, "The forensic unit is going over Poole's van with a fine-tooth comb. Inside, outside; top and bottom. They're trying to match soil on the vehicle with the soil collected near the killings. Plus, Donny has the leg casts. That's what he's counting on."

"Pardon?"

"Remember I told you the troopers made casts of the impressions where the shooter knelt in the woods? Outside the Waterview?"

"Oh, right."

"Donny claims the casts fit Poole's legs and the prosecutor's gonna go with it."

It was Detrick's turn to hesitate; she glanced at one of the Adams prints on the wall, closed her eyes, and saw McTeague pointing at the blizzard photo, nodding his head as a teacher would at a slow, but willing, student.

When she spoke her voice was barely audible. "Rick, what if those pictures on McTeague's wall, all those photos, what if they were tombstones in a cemetery? What if they were trophies, records of his past deeds?" At that moment Pat felt a sorrow powerful enough to overcome her outrage. Her chest began to heave, tears to spill from her eyes. Finally, she said, her voice tight with emotion, "What am I going to do?"

Morello's reply was incisive. "Warn your people at the mission, then take your case to Donny Barrett. For now, there's nothing else to be done. One thing certain, you can't go out there alone. You *can't.*"

The naked anxiety in his voice sobered her. "When I was a kid," she said, "maybe ten or eleven, I watched a kid named Billy Hennison trap a squirrel in a cage. The animal went crazy, running from side to side, bouncing off the bars. Now, I know how it felt. I'm stuck with this; I can't get out of it. The funny part is I'm beginning to think trapping me was what McTeague planned all along."

"Maybe so, but it's a trap you can avoid. You don't have to play his game. If going out there is what you decide you have to do, Pat, take me along. Tell him I'm a trainee, a volunteer who needs a little hands-on experience. McTeague might not believe it, but he'll have to live with me. He has no alternative except to throw us out." When Pat didn't respond immediately, Morello went on. "Look, there's a couple of things we can do right away. First, we can take our case to Barrett, lay it on his doorstep. I wouldn't expect him to take it seriously, not when he's committed to another suspect, but if I put it just right, I can probably force him to cover his ass by poking around into this. Maybe if McTeague feels a little heat, he'll break cover."

"Yes, all right. That sounds all right." Detrick plucked a tissue from a box on the desk and wiped the tears from her face. "What was the other thing?"

"You described a McTeague photo taken somewhere close to here?"

"On Route Five-oh-seven, near Palmyra."

"You also told me the photos were dated, right?"

"Oh, of course. I should have thought of that myself. We can check with the police, see if any . . . see if anything happened in Palmyra around that time."

"If we come up empty," Morello warned, "it wouldn't prove much. If he did bury somebody in the woods, the body might not have been discovered. But at least you'd be doing something. You wouldn't be waiting around for the worst to happen."

"That's if I can remember the year, which I don't at the moment. Just that it was somewhere in the seventies."

"Give it time, Pat. I've worked with hundreds of witnesses. Details come back to you over time. In fact, being as I have this pertinent experience, I thought I might come over to your place this afternoon, see if I can't help the process along."

THIRTY-ONE

Zeke McTeague was a guy who liked to work his fantasies; for him, it was a matter of principle. He had little regard for the man who simply drifted, let his pitiful daydreams run their own course, settled for whatever fragments happened to meander up out of the sink of his unconscious. In fact, McTeague no longer used words like "fantasy" or "daydream" to describe the endlessly reworked thread of memory and aspiration, past and future, that had driven his thoughts as he barreled along America's roads. No, Zeke McTeague now thought of his daydreams as *My Autobiography*.

And something else had been added, too. Something

added and something subtracted. All those years of hiding, of never telling a soul, never sharing, they were done now. Now he would offer his life to any man with the courage to aspire. In some ways, he already had.

That was the addition. The subtraction . . . well, the subtraction was easy enough to explain. No more victims, no more secret lovers; the past could no longer be applied to the future. In a very important way, Zeke McTeague had renounced perfection even though he fully understood that he'd never gotten it quite right, not once.

It should have made him sad, the way he figured it. He should be spending his days locked in bittersweet thoughts of all that might have been, all that would never be. That hadn't happened, although a very short time ago (before he'd gone out to the game lands, before Patricia came into his life) sorrowful had been a distinct possibility.

The trick was to have something you had to do before your heart exploded. And not something phony—not bathtub aerobics for seniors or plopping your bony ass into a rocking chair, what's gonna happen next on the soaps the only reason you bother to get your ass out of bed in the morning. No, your something had to be important enough to push you up out of that chair, away from the tube, had to make you roll up your sleeves, be sure you got it right.

That was why he was standing in front of his trophy wall when the dog began to bark, why he was reviewing the earliest photos, getting the names in order, the places, what they told him, what he did to them. If he messed it up in his autobiography, confused the names, the places, somebody out there, some asshole reporter, would write a book, tell the world that Zeke McTeague was a phony, that his life never happened.

"Coming," Zeke called a moment later when he heard a knock on the door.

As he shuffled forward, McTeague yanked off his glasses, stowed them in a shirt pocket. He figured it was most likely one of the do-gooders, maybe with a basket of cookies. Pat Detrick, his Patricia, wasn't due to take him to church for another forty-eight hours.

"Hello, Zeke."

Though he tried to keep the triumph out of it, McTeague couldn't repress a smile. Even the sight of the ultimate do-gooder, Reverend Bill Gauss, standing behind Patricia, his pastor's face arranged in that pious half-grin, half-grimace, couldn't dampen his spirits. Something inside McTeague, something very young and only partially human, even by his own reckoning, screamed: *She knows. She knows everything.*

"Hi, Zeke." Gauss's voice seemed to come from a great distance, as if observing the fact that he had no place here, no real part to play. "I figured since you visited my house last Sunday, I'd return the compliment. I would've called ahead, but you don't have a phone."

McTeague stepped back. "You wanna come inside, I'll make us some tea."

By the time he got them settled in the cabin's only chairs, McTeague knew that he was not to be confronted, that, for today, everything important would remain unsaid. Which was fine with him. The unspoken accusation charged every gesture, the slightest sound, with meaning. Their suspicions filled their eyes with malice, righteous anger, bitter fear so powerful he, Zeke McTeague, a man who knew something about fear, could taste it in his own mouth.

So he left them to stew in their conspiracy while he made the tea, carried it back into the room, all the while wishing that he hadn't missed Reverend Bill's dearly beloved, that he'd splattered her brains all over the cheap paneling.

"Heard somebody took a shot at your wife the other day," he said as he sat on the edge of the bed. "Seen it on the television."

"Why don't we switch seats. Seeing as we're uninvited guests." Gauss stood abruptly. "Say, did you know Florence Clark?"

"Never laid eyes on her." McTeague stayed where he was. "But this Pocono Sniper business got me interested. Seems like that's all they talk about on the news. Like we finally done something smart enough to notice." He looked in the preacher's eyes, stifled a laugh at the idea of this soft-bellied asshole playing the role of Patricia's defender.

"Smart enough?" Gauss arched an eyebrow, looked up at the ceiling, then back at McTeague. "I'm not sure what you mean by that."

Patricia broke in before McTeague could reply. "I'm going out to see Becky. Should I take some food with me?"

She was looking directly at him, making no bones about how she felt, and that was all to the good. He had Patricia hooked now; if she wanted to fight, well . . . the fight was why you went fishing in the first place.

"Have to admit," McTeague said, "the dog could most likely use a little dinner. Being as I've been feelin' too peaked to get out much and feed her lately."

It was raining softly as Detrick strode across the driveway. The sky above was the color of tarnished pewter. All trace of the prior night's snowfall had vanished, replaced by the steady drip of rain, the cheerless sigh of the wind.

"Becky? It's me, girl." Remembering the animal's ferocious challenge to her first visit, Detrick carefully announced her approach. The dog was inside its little house, out of the rain. It wouldn't do to surprise her.

Finally, Becky's head emerged, muzzle to the dirt, in an attitude of pure submission. Pat studied the empty plastic bowls half buried in the mud. "All right, girl, it's all right. I won't leave you here. Come on out." Becky continued to advance, emitting a low, pleading whine, the cry of a hungry pup, as she came. Her fur was matted tight enough to show her ribs. Swiftly, angrily, Pat unhooked the chain attached to the dog's collar. "Come, girl. Let's get you safe."

When she swung the Jeep's tailgate open, Becky jumped

inside without being told, without any encouragement, as if she recognized the obvious, that this was her only chance. She curled up immediately, didn't react when the tailgate closed.

McTeague and Bill Gauss were examining McTeague's photos when Pat walked through the doorway. She stopped short, tried to control her outrage as she listened to McTeague prattle on.

"Been just about ever'place in the lower forty-eight, Reverend. Been to Canada, too. Always rollin'. Hell, if I wasn't pullin' twenty-five ton, I felt like I might just up and float away." McTeague's bony shoulders were rolling with laughter. "Lemme tell ya some more 'bout them truck stop ministers. In case you're lookin' for tips." He slapped Gauss on the back. "Every big truck stop got itself a ministry, mostly just a trailer home set up on cinder blocks in the parkin' lot. Inside, ain't much more than a few chairs, a cross, pamphlets in a rack, and nat'rally some preacher man always ready to bring your sinnin' soul to Jesus. Like they knowed tomorrow you'd be movin' on, they wouldn't get no second chance." He scratched the back of his head, glanced over his shoulder at Patricia on the other side of the room, tossed her a broad wink. "Many's the time I prayed for the strength to stop my sinnin' ways, but I couldn't get it right, nohow. Them truck stop Annies come knockin' on the door and you been travelin' all alone for a couple weeks . . . Well, took a stronger man than me to resist the devil."

This crow has an eye for death, an eye for death and a nose for death and four hungry chicks to be fed. Though she fears the man pushing through the half-grown corn, as she fears all humans, the motionless heap of flesh he drags behind him inspires her. She hops from her nest, rocks back and forth, cocks her head, then finally issues a sharp summons to her clan.

McTeague halts, looks up for a moment, finally tries to

bury his growing depression in anger. He hauls Sonia Alcibedar to her feet, shakes her until her eyes open. "See what's gonna getch'ya?" He points to a dusky shadow perched in the topmost branches of a huge oak at the edge of the field. "Old crow's gonna getch'ya."

Sonia Alcibedar does not respond and McTeague, disgusted, lets her fall to the soft earth. On the horizon, five crows beat heavy, patient wings against a stiff crossbreeze. They pass directly above Zeke McTeague and Sonia, but only Zeke McTeague sees them. He pauses to watch the birds settle into a sugar maple at the edge of the field, to listen as they call back and forth.

After a moment, he grasps Sonia's ankles and trudges forward. As always, now that it's finally over, he feels deeply regretful: He's again failed to get it right; he'll never get it right; he's risked his life for nothing.

He wants to tell himself that he won't do it again, won't take that terrible risk with so little to be gained, but he's been at it too long and he knows better. Just as he knows that what he feels at this moment will pass away, that for the next month or two, he'll be just another trucker hauling freight over the roads of America.

When McTeague reaches the edge of the forest, leans Sonia Alcibedar against a heap of piked rocks, the crows move in. They come through the trees, hopping from branch to branch as if unwilling to expose themselves. McTeague watches them come. He stands with his legs apart, his hands on his hips, just a bit out of breath. "Guess you want you dinner," he tells them. "Guess you think you're entitled."

The crows settle in the trees around Zeke McTeague and Sonia Alcibedar as if trying to prevent their escape. McTeague imagines them to be witnesses, judges in black robes. The idea not only pleases him, it inspires him to one last effort. He kneels in front of Sonia Alcibedar, pulls her head forward with his left hand as he opens her eyes, takes a good look inside.

At first McTeague sees nothing. Sonia's pupils remain

fixed; she does not blink. But then, little by little, as his fingers close around her neck, as his thumbs press into the hollow at the base of her throat, something rises in her. It is not life, exactly, or even the yearning for life, but McTeague nods in recognition before raising triumphant, mischievous eyes.

"What will ya do," he asks the screaming crows, "if I decide to bury the bitch?"

Detrick willed herself not to react to McTeague's little speech, though she was sure it had been delivered for her benefit. She reminded herself that she was not here to convince Bill Gauss of anything, but to let him make his own decisions, draw his own conclusions. The effort to convince that had taken place back at the mission had been, in Bill's case, entirely unsuccessful. Not surprisingly, Elaine had been easier. Sitting in her office, the shattered window covered with a plywood panel and a sheet of plastic, the plastic billowing softly in the draft, Elaine had listened carefully, then raised the only pertinent question: "What are we going to do?"

"Well, we're not going to desert him." Bill had hovered over his wife. "Not on the strength of what I've heard here." He'd given Detrick a reproachful look, as if to say, *Don't we have enough problems?*

"You know, Bill . . ." Elaine had waited until her husband turned, then continued. "When I heard the shot, I thought, *If you can hear it, it's already missed you.* I must have remembered that from some movie. You know, that it's the one you don't hear that gets you." She'd lit a cigarette then, shaken out the match, dropped it into an overflowing ashtray. "Funny I should remember that."

"Elaine . . ."

"No, forget it, Bill. One of us has to go out to McTeague's and right now I'm too scared." Then she'd burst into tears.

They'd finally worked out the present compromise: Pat and Bill Gauss show up unexpectedly, no further visits scheduled before Sunday morning services. In the mean-time, Pat would probe, see if she could interest the police in her suspicions, rummage through back issues of the *Pocono Record*, try to insert a human being, alive or dead, into one of McTeague's photos.

It was the last aim that finally got Detrick moving. She closed the door, crossed the room to stand next to McTeague, to let her shoulder brush his while she ran her eyes over the wall of photos, finally pointed to a blacktop road curving through dense forest. "This one, Zeke. This is the one taken south of Palmyra?"

McTeague peered at Detrick through narrowed lids. He'd forgotten his false teeth, left them soaking in a glass of cloudy water. Now, he knew, his mouth was a crater, lips turned inside like they wanted to crawl down his throat, find their way to the other end, suck him inside out. "Yessir," he replied after a long moment, "that's it, all right."

"Didn't you tell me you had somebody with you on that trip?"

"Don't recall sayin' that." McTeague let his eyes drop, not because he feared her question, though he was content to let her come to that conclusion, but in an effort to conceal a growing, almost paternal, pride. The way she went after him, let him know what she thought, how quick she'd put things together . . . the way he saw it, he'd be a damn fool not to be proud. The next time out, she'd come alone. Next time she'd be his. "Course, lately I'm havin' trouble recallin' my own name." He turned to Bill Gauss, said, "Maybe I better take that chair. Feelin' a bit on the peaked side."

He shuffled across the room, hit the seat with an audible thump. No need to fake it. His breath was rattling in his lungs, as it had been doing all day, as it would tomorrow. He touched his chest, looking for the pain, expecting it, but his heart remained steady.

"You okay?"

McTeague nodded. Reverend Bill was sitting in the

other chair while Patricia checked the pantry, his medications, made little notes to herself. She hadn't questioned his lie, another plus. Anybody else, any fool, would have jumped down his throat, stormed out the door, ended the game before it was over.

"Fine, fine," McTeague said. "Lookin' forward to Sunday. Hear what you got to say about someone takin' a shot at your wife. Seemed like a real nice lady that one time I met her."

A few minutes later, as Patricia was putting on her coat, she turned, fixed him with a stare. "By the way," she said, "I'm taking Becky with me. She hasn't been fed."

"Well, now—"

"No argument, Zeke. If you find that you miss the dog, I'll bring her along when I visit."

McTeague watched Patricia fit the ends of the zipper on her coat together. Though her mind was obviously somewhere else, her long, slender fingers worked precisely, proclaimed their own confidence, their independence. Meanwhile, her eyes had him pinned in the chair, the look she was giving him pure cop.

"Long as you're comin' back," Zeke finally told her, "guess I can live with the rest of it."

THIRTY-TWO

"When I was a boy, living over toward Moscow," Bill Gauss said as he stepped out into the mission's parking lot, raised his collar against the persistent drizzle, "my neighbors, an elderly couple, the Muellers, kept a dog named Sparky. Sparky was even older than the Muellers, in dog years anyway. That old dog couldn't see, couldn't hear, couldn't outrun anything faster than a rather clumsy eight-year-old, my age at the time. Sparky—" Gauss stopped abruptly. His smile turned suddenly apologetic. "I'm going on," he said softly. "As I've been going on since I got into the car. Well, Pat, the only thing I know for sure is that Ezekiel McTeague is an ugly little man. The way he kept returning to Elaine's close call? I had to remind myself that he spent his whole life in a truck, that he grew up in isolation. Small wonder he hasn't mastered the social graces." Gauss tried a smile, gave it up when she returned his gaze without comment. "I admit that the photos are very strange. Like something out of a gothic film. The emptiness . . . it has an effect, but I don't know exactly . . ."

"Bottom line," Pat said grimly, "you're going to continue support."

"Abandoning the man is simply unthinkable."

"But you're not going to send anybody out there alone, right?" Her tone was unequivocal, its businesslike quality necessitated by the fact that she was still fighting an anger so intense she didn't dare give it expression.

"I don't want to, but, heaven help me, I can't devise an explanation for sending out two volunteers when we're spread so thin."

"If you send a volunteer out there without informed consent, you're going to be responsible, Bill. Morally and legally."

Gauss sighed. He took off his glasses, rubbed his eyes. Later, he would go into the chapel, give himself up to prayer, hope the answer would come to him.

"Look," Detrick said, "I'm willing to go with you, but I'm not going alone."

"Then you're absolutely sure about McTeague?" he asked, the skepticism apparent in his voice.

"I know. McTeague knows I know." Despite her best efforts, Detrick's voice began to rise. "I know he knows that I know. He knows that I know . . ." She slapped the steering wheel. "There's just no end to it."

Gauss lifted his chin, pursed his lips. "I can't go with you on Sunday morning. If McTeague's to come to church . . ." He stepped back, lifted a hand. "Give me a day to think about it, Pat. I'm sure I'll come up with something."

• • • •

She was halfway home, still trying to get hold of her thoughts, when Becky raised her shaggy head over the backseat and licked her lips. Startled, Pat gasped, felt her heart jump into high gear. "You scared the hell out of me," she told the dog's reflection in the rearview mirror. As if in repentance, Becky dropped out of sight, leaving Detrick to the slick road, the soft splatter of rain on the windshield. A forest of hemlocks and mixed pines lined both sides of the road. It was dark beneath their boughs and Detrick flipped on the Jeep's headlights, tapped the gas pedal, remembered that Rick Morello was already at the house. She was almost home when she managed to trap a pair of intersecting thoughts, to hold onto them long enough to make an association.

The anger she felt at that moment, she decided, was identical to the rage she'd felt decades before when she'd come riding to Betty Hoffman's rescue, when she'd stood up to Carl Meitzler, the schoolyard bully. Then, as now, she'd been driven in part by righteous indignation of the sort she'd later come to distrust. But there was something else as well, a far more primitive element that smacked of pure survival. She would not sit back, passive, play the victim's part. Nor would she wallow in self-pity, as she'd been doing for more than a year. Somehow, McTeague would have to be confronted.

As she rounded a long curve, Pat saw Morello's green Buick parked in her driveway. She pulled the Jeep in behind the Buick, was about to open the door when she noticed that the car was empty. Then she saw Morello come out of the woods to the left of the house. He was wearing a damp trench coat and a pair of very muddy loafers. When he saw her, he paused momentarily, flashed a guilty grin before walking over.

"Is that your pathfinder outfit?" Pat, as she rolled down the window, couldn't resist the jibe. Morello's soaked hair was standing on end. He looked like Frankenstein's bride.

He ducked through the window, kissed her once, then

again. "Maybe," he said, "because someone—whose name shall not be spoken here—was late, her neglected visitor was forced to play the part of the bear in the woods."

"Is that true?"

"No, it's not." Morello straightened. "I was looking for any sign of McTeague, just in case he pulled off the impossible and got hold of your address." He frowned, laid his palm on the Jeep's roof. "It looks clean to me. I— Hey, what's with the dog?"

Detrick finally opened the door and got out. She walked to the back of the Jeep, unlatched the tailgate, swung it open. "Her name's Becky. She used to belong to McTeague."

"You went out there?"

"With Bill Gauss. I'll tell you about it later, after I get Becky fed. Here, would you carry this?" She handed him the half-empty bag of dog food she'd taken from McTeague's.

Morello sniffed, reached out to scratch Becky's ear. The animal was completely passive. "Fed and *bathed*. She smells like she's been swimming in the septic tank."

Detrick watched the dog jump down. "I think McTeague was going to let her die. She had no food, no water."

"Why would he do that? Why did he get the dog in the first place?"

Morello's question went unanswered. Detrick unlocked her door and strode inside the kitchen. She took a pair of metal bowls from the cabinet above the stove, filled one with water, the second with dog food, put both on the floor. Becky sniffed at her food, then looked up at Detrick and wagged her tail.

"It's okay, girl. Go ahead."

The dog cocked her head to one side, waited for a second, then buried her muzzle in her food. Morello put his arm around Detrick and both watched the dog eat. Then Morello took a deep breath. "I wouldn't expect a country person like yourself to know this, especially a God-fearing, righteous country girl like yourself, but in the sex clubs on the West Side of Manhattan, and there are many, many sex clubs on the West Side of Manhattan, the latest rage is naked dog bathing."

"Naked *dog* bathing?"

"That's right, Pat. I got it firsthand from a nymphomaniac vice cop. Naked dog bathing is definitely *au courant* among New York sophisticates." He cleared his throat, let his hand slide up to cover her breast. "Of course, that's only in the straight clubs. The S and M clubs are very, very different. In the S and M clubs they do naked *cat* bathing."

Two hours later, over a pot of strong coffee and a plate of chocolate-chip cookies, they finally got to work. Morello wanted to prepare a statement from Detrick, the way he'd prepared affidavits from witnesses when he was a working cop, to put her suspicions in writing, hand the resulting document over to Donny Barrett.

Barrett, Morello told her before they began, would be quick to recognize the implicit threat of such paperwork. Once Detrick's statement was placed in the case file, any failure to act on Barrett's part would blow up in his face if McTeague came under suspicion later on. It was a risk an ambitious cop like Barrett couldn't afford to take. At the very least, even if he placed no credence in her story, Barret would have to send one of his investigators to check the lead, thereby generating enough paperwork to cover his ass.

So they went at it for most of the evening, Pat in her gray sweats, Morello in a T-shirt and pair of red briefs while his pants, socks, and shoes dried by the radiator. They worked on her Apple computer, worked their way through several drafts before she was, if not satisfied, at least appeased.

"Every time I see it like this . . ." She held up the two single-spaced sheets of paper, stared at them for a moment before laying them next to the printer. "A few offhand remarks, a box of cartridges, a pickup truck in a barn . . . I feel like a fool."

Morello stood and stretched. "That's only because of McTeague's age and his heart condition. Back him up ten years and the man would be a prime suspect. Look, I never investigated a serial killer, but I know someone who did, a lieutenant named Brock. If I remember right, he got so desperate at one point that he consulted the feds, listened to their serial killer lecture."

"Did he find the killer?"

"Not because of anything the FBI told him. What finally happened was one of the intended victims escaped and the perp was apprehended at the scene." Morello walked over to the sink, filled a glass with tap water. "Anyway, Brock told me something I never knew. He told me that most serial killings are never solved, that they start and stop for no apparent reason. You said McTeague's got photos dating from 1948 on his wall. When I first heard that, I thought he couldn't possibly have gotten away with murder for all that time. But since he dumped the bodies so far apart, it's like a serial killing that never got started. I mean how would anybody link the victims? Even if the victims could be identified. If—"

Morello stopped abruptly as Becky, who'd been sleeping a few feet away, rose, then began to whine softly. She trotted over to the door, looked back expectantly.

"I think she's trying to tell us something," Morello said.

"She's telling us that she had a life before McTeague tied her in that yard. A life with someone who cared enough to train her." Pat flipped on the outside lights, opened the door to a fog thick enough to hide Morello's car fifteen feet away.

She watched Becky disappear into the fog, then turned back to Morello. "You have fog lights on the Buick, Rick?

Because if you don't, you're going to have to stay the night. Which is just as well, because for the first time since I left my husband, I really don't want to sleep alone."

"Actually," he admitted with a sheepish grin, "I wasn't planning to go anywhere."

THIRTY-THREE

At ten o'clock on the following morning, after an early phone call to set up an appointment, Pat found Elmer Crown perched on a stool at the Newfoundland Diner. Close to eighty and semiretired, a tiny man made tinier by age, Elmer was hunched over a cup of coffee at the end of the counter farthest from the door, an unlit cigarette dangling from the corner of his mouth. Elmer's scalp was baby-smooth and spotted, his small, narrow features obscured by a mass of deep wrinkles. As she watched, he wiped the lids of his dark eyes with a crumpled napkin and turned to face her.

"C'mon over, Pat. And buy an old man who's too old for a goddamn drink a goddamn cup of coffee."

She took off her coat, hung it on a hook. Elmer Crown was as close as the Poconos came to an actual historian. He'd grown up in Wayne County, a student-athlete, covered World War II for the *New York Times,* moved on in the post-War years to the *Philadelphia Enquirer* where he'd served as city editor until his resignation twenty-five years ago, following the death of his wife. Then he'd come home, remarried, bought a house near Pocono Springs, and gone to work for the *Pocono Speaker* at half his former salary.

Elmer's final career choice had branded him, if not a fool, at least an eccentric. FIve years after moving back to the Poconos, he'd self-published two books on the region, one a genuine history, the other a chronicle of famous Pocono ghosts. Rumors about the expense involved had kicked his reputation into a downward spiral and jokes about his use of a vanity press were passed about like doughnuts before a deadline. Elmer had responded by peddling his literary efforts to every tourist shop in the region, his profit per book ten times the royalty offered by mainstream publishers. Within two years, he had his investment back. That was two decades ago and both volumes were still displayed on racks (provided, naturally, by the author, publisher, and distributor) in a hundred little stores. Right next to the cash register.

"How have you been?" Pat approached Elmer cautiously. Crown had been one of her husband's drinking buddies, had even created Fireball Detrick's tag line—*We're on fiiiiiiiire*—at the tail end of a night of serious boozing.

"My doctor says I can't drink and I can't smoke and I can't eat anything that tastes like it belongs in a human mouth. As opposed, say, to the mouth of a rabbit." Crown scratched at his unshaven jaw. "Christ, I can't even fart without fattening some doctor's bank account. I tell ya, Pat, old age is a disease. It's not fair you should get sick, too."

"You're in your eighth decade. You've got a wife who

loves you, children who tolerate you, and you're physically, emotionally, and financially independent. Some would say that you're lucky."

Crown shook his head in disgust. He waved the counterman over, ordered coffee for Pat and a chocolate doughnut for himself. Then he turned back to her, stared defiantly for a moment, said, "That's like expecting the survivors of the *Titanic* to be grateful."

"I imagine that many of them *were* grateful."

"And I imagine them spending the rest of their lives tossing rocks through church windows." He folded his arms, flashed a triumphant smile. "That's the difference between us."

"I'll drink to that." She repressed a fond smile. She'd always liked Elmer Crown, had found his professed cynicism devoid of small-town hypocrisy. Elmer expected the worst, was seldom disappointed. Once, drunk, he'd called her Saint Patty, wanted to know if she'd chased the snakes out of Ireland before she'd come to rescue the Poconos from itself.

"Brad's still in love with you." Crown again wiped his eyes. He was wearing a plain brown suit, a yellowing white shirt, and a green-and-gold striped tie. His typical uniform. "I don't think he can help it."

Pat thought of Morello, felt a warm glow spread through her, hoped it wouldn't rise into her face. "You're wasting your time, Elmer. Having survived the shipwreck, I'm not looking to buy a return ticket."

"That's what I told Fireball, but . . ." He picked his doughnut off the plate, looked at it, then set it back down. "I got sugar, too," he muttered.

Detrick pulled his plate toward her. "As long I'm paying," she said before taking a bite.

Elmer shook his head. "Once you realize women have no hearts, it's impossible to believe in anything." He pulled several folded sheets of paper from his jacket pocket, laid them where his doughnut had been a moment before. "When you called me yesterday, asked me if a body had been discovered near Palmyra in '79, I didn't ask any questions, right?" He waited for her nod before continuing. "Well, now I'm asking."

"It's not something I can talk about right now." Detrick, who'd been expecting a cross-examination, took another bite of his doughnut.

"For Christ's sake, Pat. I been in the news business fifty-five years. At this late date, you want me to forget I'm a reporter? We're talkin' about a murder here."

"True enough, Elmer, but now that you've taken out those copies, I know I can take a trip to the *Speaker*'s morgue, look up the information myself."

To Detrick's surprise, he burst out laughing. "Don't try to play hard-nosed with me. I know you too well." He snatched the remains of the doughnut, stuffed it into his mouth. "I did you a favor; now I'm claiming a favor. *Quid pro* goddamned *quo*."

"I don't have anything you can use." Although she was tempted to knock Elmer Crown off his seat, take the papers and run, she spoke in the dead-neutral voice she'd previously reserved for loan officers in time of crisis. "Not yet." She tapped the counter. "And if I should learn something . . . something significant, the first place I'm going with the information is to the police."

"And the second place?"

Detrick slid her hand over the counter, picked up the folded papers. "You, Elmer. You're the second place."

Elmer Crown grinned triumphantly, then got down to business. "Ya know, you got the location right, but the year wrong. That's what threw me at first. The body was found in April 1980, not in 1979. But it was right where you said it would be."

"Which was?"

"A hundred yards into the woods off Route Five-oh-seven. Three point six miles south of Palmyra."

Detrick unfolded the pages, skimmed a dozen stories about the accidental discovery of a decomposed body by two unlicensed fishermen working their way toward a secluded stream. Within a few days, a pathologist had determined the body to be female, death to have been caused either by strangulation or stab wound, the body to have lain in the woods for at least six months. But no identification had ever been made, despite a police check of missing person reports from as far away as New York and Philadelphia, despite the extensive publicity given the discovery of the corpse.

"I didn't get the year wrong," she said. "The body was found in the spring. It lay there over the winter."

Crown watched her refold the articles, stuff them into her purse. "I don't know if you heard, but I'm updating *Great Pocono Ghost Stories.*"

"I'm sure your publisher is waiting with bated breath."

"I'm my own publisher." Crown sniffed. "Anyway, what I'm thinking is I'll include your victim. I mean it's perfect, right? A woman murdered, left to rot in the forest? On foggy nights she rises up to demand . . ." He dropped his head, stared at his lap for moment, then raised his eyes to meet Detrick's. "I think I'll make it that instead of justice, she demands a name on her gravestone." He nodded eagerly. "Yeah, that's it. She's stuck on the earthly plane until she has a real identity. I'll call her the Route Five-oh-seven Ghost."

THIRTY-FOUR

When they strode into Donald Barrett's small office at the Swiftwater State Troopers barracks, the sergeant's expression flipped from welcoming to wary to something approaching afraid. Detrick, as she watched the transformation, as she took his hand when he rose to greet her, felt a rising wave of sympathy. Morello hadn't told Barrett that she was coming. Now, faced with her presence, Barrett knew something was wrong, that Morello's omission had been deliberate.

"Ms. Detrick, why don't you sit down."

"Pat," Detrick replied before complying. Barrett's Formica-topped desk, though piled high with paperwork, was nevertheless well organized. The telephone was clean, a white mug bearing the green logo of the Philadelphia Eagles sat within easy reach of his left hand, a plastic organizer holding pens and pencils, a gray stapler, a small box of assorted paper clips, were all dust-free.

"Anybody want coffee? A stale doughnut?" Despite his initial reaction, Barrett was smiling.

"Just came from lunch," Morello said. He took the matching chrome-framed chair next to Pat, tugged at his trousers before crossing his legs. His face, she noted, showed nothing, was as closed as she'd ever seen it.

"So, what can I do for you guys?"

"We've got a suspect for you," Morello said. By agreement, he was to play the advocate, Detrick the innocent bystander.

"A suspect in what crime?"

"The ones you're currently investigating."

Barrett's face flushed red. His blond eyebrows lifted. "C'mon, Rick—"

"Maybe you better take a look at this."

Morello, like an evil magician producing a scorpion from a hat, slid Detrick's statement out of his briefcase, let it drop from his hand to fall directly in front of Barrett. With no choice in the matter, the trooper lifted the stapled sheets and began to read.

Pat shifted in her seat, crossed and recrossed her legs before she got hold of herself. The passive role she played here felt entirely unnatural, though it was she who'd suggested it. Barrett, she'd reasoned, would be unlikely to accept the conclusions of a lowly citizen, whereas Rick's credentials were already established.

"Let me read it again," Barrett said after he'd gone through the material once. "Maybe it'll make sense this time around."

"Better check these, too." Morello again reached into his briefcase, retrieving the photocopied articles supplied by Elmer Crown. Instead of dropping them in front of Barrett, however, he laid them gently on the desk, as if afraid they might shatter.

Pat watched Barrett's face tighten as he reread her statement, skimmed the news stories. He was going to resist, she decided, try to sweep the implications away. Her job, and Morello's as well, would be to outflank him, to strip away his options, manipulate him until he ran out of choices.

"I look at this." Barrett held up the pages, shook them at Morello. "And I don't see anything. I don't see what you're driving at."

"You don't see McTeague as the Pocono Sniper?" Morello sounded genuinely surprised.

"What are we talking about here?" Barrett looked at the papers in his hand. "Emotional flip-flops, a pair of muddy pants, a box of cartridges behind the dog food. For Christ's sake, Rick, the old man catches a cold and it's supposed to prove he's a murderer?"

Morello nodded. "McTeague was there," he said. "He was at the lodge on the afternoon before Munoz was shot. He was at the Dreher Community Church, having a conversation with Bannister the day before Bannister was shot, three days before Elaine Gauss was attacked."

"Coincidence," Barrett said stubbornly. "It happens."

Pat expected Morello to finally react—hadn't he told her that detectives instinctively mistrust coincidence?—but he remained calm. "And the photo? The body? McTeague's admission that he had a passenger in the truck?"

"You want me to investigate a fifteen-year-old killing, I'll be more than happy to check the file, do a little research. But what happened fifteen years ago doesn't make this old guy the Pocono Sniper. For one thing, the MO's are completely different. The body found in 1980 was strangled, stabbed, and probably mutilated." Barrett met Rick Morello's steady gaze. "The killer liked to work close up. He transported the body, made an effort to cover the murder. Doesn't sound like sniping to me."

"Killers get old, too," Morello replied. "They have to settle for what they can physcially accomplish. Just like everybody else."

Barrett laid both palms on the table, rose to his feet. He hesitated for a moment before turning his back, addressing the filing cabinets behind him. "Look, there's something going on here you don't know about. Tomorrow morning, Coleman Poole gets formally charged with the two additional counts of murder and two counts of attempted murder. For the Bannister killing. He confessed to his cellmate, made a statement against penal interest. Put that together with the proven facts, that he's been roaming the area freely, sleeping in his truck, that he hated his aunt and knew he'd inherit if anything happened to her, that he carried a thirty-thirty under the seat, that a van similar to his was spotted in the area of the Bannister killing, and you have enough to secure an indictment." Barrett turned back to face Morello. At no time did he so much as glance at Patricia Detrick.

"And his motive?" Morello asked. "Not for Clark, for the others."

"Does cover-up sound too cold-blooded?" Barrett's thin mouth jerked into an angry smile. "Coleman Poole is a suspect in two unsolved homicides that took place after his release from prison, one a contract killing. The story going around is that he pulled off the contract hit for three hundred dollars. Now, figure Florence Clark's estate at roughly sixty thousand dollars. What do you think a guy who commits murder for three hundred dollars would do for sixty thousand? Fillet his grandmother? Decapitate his baby sister? How about fire off a few rounds at a bunch of strangers?"

"And that's what you're going with? A jailhouse snitch and a rumor?" Morello nostrils tightened as he drew a breath.

Barrett folded his arms. "You know my job, Rick. I investigate, present the results to the County Prosecutor. Carringford decides where to take that evidence, what charges to bring."

Morello impatiently waved him off. "Get to the bottom line, Donny. The goddamned punch line."

"Carringford's gonna ask for the death penalty."

The sentence burned in Pat's nostrils like the stink of a cheap cigar. Get it together, she told herself. Show some courage. The game isn't over. McTeague can't win.

"You got a book deal yet?" Morello leaned forward. "You going on Larry King tonight?"

"This guy murdered three people, Rick. And he shot at two more. What to do you think we should ask for, probation?"

"What I think is that you should investigate the lead I just gave you. What I think is that you should cover your ass in case the defense gets hold of this material and you're asked about it when you testify."

Morello drew his lips back over his teeth in imitation of a smile. Barrett dropped into his chair. Now that the cards were all on the table, he seemed to relax. For the first time, Barrett looked directly at Patricia Detrick, weighed her for a moment before asking, "Is that the way it's gonna be, Ms. Detrick? If I don't investigate McTeague, you'll take your suspicions to the defense?"

Detrick, now that it was finally her turn, found her mouth almost too dry to speak. She took a deep breath. "I'll take my suspicions," she told Barrett, mildly surprised by the strength of her voice, "wherever my conscience tells me to take them."

Detrick and Morello began their ride back to the Waterview in silence. The deal they'd gotten was, in Detrick's opinion anyway, the best they could have gotten under the circumstances. When Barrett had declared that no judge would sign a search warrant based on coincidence and innuendo, Morello hadn't argued. In fact, he hadn't made any comment at all. He'd just sat there, waiting, like a big cat contemplating a very trapped mouse.

Barrett, inspired, perhaps, had rushed on: "What I'm willing to do is drive out to McTeague's place tomorrow afternoon, talk to him, get a feel for where he's coming from. If it goes anywhere, I promise I'll run with it." He hadn't bothered to add the obvious: *And if it doesn't, I'll write a report, stick in the file, have it ready to cover my butt. In case some lawyer yanks my pants down.*

"Tomorrow," Morello finally said as they approached the lodge, "you're supposed to take McTeague to church, that right?"

Detrick stared through the windshield. The sun was dropping fast and the glare on the pavement was making it difficult to hold the Jeep in a straight line. Her hands tightened on the steering wheel. "I have to call Bill Gauss when I get home. To see if he's found someone to go with me."

"What if I went with you?"

"To church?"

"To pick up McTeague, then to church." He smiled, laid his hand on her shoulder. "I'd like to be there when Barrett shows up."

"Rick, are you Catholic?"

"No, I'm not." His fingers slid up to caress the back of her neck, wind through her hair. "I don't have any trouble believing in a single creator for the universe. Although I don't see why it couldn't have been created by committee. My problem is believing in a creator who gives a damn about human behavior."

"I see." Pat flicked her turning signal, slowed for the turn into the Waterview's long driveway. "Do you think, between now and tomorrow, you can work out a different answer to that question?"

"Why?"

"Because everybody who goes to the Dreher Community Church knows me by my first name. If I show up with you, I'm going to have to introduce you around." She smiled now, suddenly happier than she had any good reason to be. "When folks hear that Italian last name, that's the first question they're going to ask you: 'Morello? Are you Catholic?'"

THIRTY-FIVE

It was one of those days, McTeague decided. One of those days when he didn't want to move a muscle, when the bed and the pillow, the wool blankets and the soiled sheets, were more than he could handle. One of those days—which were rapidly becoming all of his days—when he didn't give a tinker's damn for the past or the future, for what he'd done or what he hoped to do.

McTeague didn't hurt anywhere, not in his chest or his back, not in his elbows, knees, or knuckles. His lungs were taking air, more or less, and his heart was beating evenly, neither pounding against his ribs nor skittering off like a mouse at the silhouette of an owl.

You got no excuse, he told himself for the fifth time. And you got work to do.

Nevertheless, he lay there, eyes open, watched the gray light swell, become dawn, become the fully risen sun falling smack on his face. His mind drifted as he waited for strength . . . no, not strength, as he waited for *desire* to return.

He thought of Esther and how, one Halloween, she'd taken it in her head to decorate the cabin. It hadn't made sense to the seven-year-old McTeague because they'd never had so much as a Christmas tree before that time. But he knew that once Esther got something in her head it took a long time working its way out; plus, even in the best of times, she didn't take to interference. So what he did was stay out of her way, hide himself in a chair by the stove while she snipped away at sheets of black and orange paper, decorated the little house with spiders and black cats and leering pumpkins, strung webs of gauzy cotton over dirty windows.

When she'd finished, when she'd put away the scissors, hung her apron on a nail by the stove, they'd danced. Esther had cranked up their mother's old phonograph, had taken him into her arms, waltzed him around the room. Over and over and over again. McTeague could still remember the feel of her thin dress against his cheek, the warmth of her belly, the solid crush of her breasts. It had been one of the happiest moments of his very unhappy childhood and the memory of it now was enough to get him out of bed.

He went to the bathroom first, took care of business, then shuffled over to the bureau next to his bed, opened the bottom right drawer, removed an ancient photograph, the oldest in his collection. The photo showed a young woman, a teenager who looked older than her years, standing in the shade of a large tree. The trunk of the tree rose behind her, its lowest branches just visible at the top of the frame. Next to her, staring into the camera with the wide, frightened eyes of a trapped animal, a small boy stood at attention. His head came only to the girl's hip and he had to reach up to hold her hand.

Very carefully, McTeague laid the photo on a rickety end table next to the sofa. He made a cup of coffee, a plate of toast, covered the toast with butter and jelly, ate quickly. The dishes went into the sink, to be handled later. A quick shower, as close a shave as his failing eyesight allowed. Finally, he got down to the only real task he'd set himself, the one thing he had to do before Patricia came to him.

He knelt beside his bed, grabbed the handle of a suitcase hidden underneath, found that he could barely move it. On another day, a day without Patricia, he might have spent an hour dwelling on his demise. Now, inspired, he dragged the suitcase to the kitchen table, hoisted it up, dumped the collection of knives and the single whetstone inside onto the table.

There were knives of every description, boning and slicing knives, skinning and scaling knives, single- and double-edged knives, a dagger, a stiletto, even a cheap jacknife. A few of them had been employed in the course of his life's work, but most had served as mere visual aids, elements of the vision he'd been trying to perfect for more than fifty years.

As McTeague sat down, pulled the whetstone toward him, lifted the first knife, ran its already polished edge over the surface of the stone, he admitted to himself that perfection had never been a possibility. No, it was trying that mattered, seeing perfection out there, dangling before him like a ripe peach in the very topmost branches of a tree. You could see it was too far up, that the branches were too slender to support your weight, but you went climbing anyway, put everything you had into obtaining the prize.

That was what he'd tell Patricia when she came to him. She wouldn't see it, of course. Not at first. But she'd listen, remember, maybe think about it over the course of her life, come finally to understand.

• • •

It was a gorgeous day, so lovely and unexpected on this second week of December that Detrick, as she stood outside Zeke McTeague's little cabin, instinctively raised her face to the sun.

"I feel like a target on a shooting range." Morello had come around the Jeep to stand alongside her. "The one with the squinting bad guy."

Smiling, she looked up at him. "I'd bet my bones," she said, "that McTeague has some kind of a surprise for me. But it won't be a rifle. It won't be a threat to me personally. Not yet."

"I'd feel a lot better," Morello said as they walked toward the front door, "if you had said *us,* instead of *me.*"

McTeague opened the door as they approached. He'd been expecting Patricia to bring along some protection, but the appearance of the former detective came as a surprise. A very pleasant surprise, now that he thought about it.

"Zeke, you remember Rick Morello, don't you? From the Waterview Lodge?"

Patricia's voice carried—what? McTeague searched for the right words. Certainty? No, confidence. Well, he'd make her pay for that confidence. Just as he'd make her pay for dragging her ex-cop boyfriend into Zeke McTeague's business. She was supposed to come to him alone, as a bride to her bridegroom. Instead, she'd betrayed him. "Sure do. You're that homicide fella." He offered his hand, peered through scratched glasses. The cop's dark eyes carried a simple message and so did the power in his grip: *You hurt this woman and you die.*

At least that was the way he read it as he stepped back, let them pass into the house, get a good look at what should have been for Patricia's eyes alone. "Been sharpenin' my knives," he told them. "The doc said I should try to keep busy, find somethin' to do. Told me havin' a goal in life helps you live longer."

THIRTY-SIX

McTeague, calmer now, but no less determined as he stood slightly off to the side and watched Patricia introduce Morello to the departing congregation, had to admit that what he felt at the moment was jealousy. The emotion surprised him. It had been a very long time since he'd wished for a normal life, to be a part of the human tribe. Patricia was standing to the right of Bill Gauss, trying to appear relaxed though she betrayed her nervousness, published it by touching the buttons at the end of the cop's sleeve from time to time, by plucking at them as if trying to remove a loose thread. The cop was much cooler. He flashed the same smile over and over again, extended his hand, raised an eyebrow when some fool asked him if he was a Catholic, said, "Well,

I *have* been a Catholic. But not since high school." As if he'd rehearsed the line.

What got to McTeague was the permanence. Patricia was telling her friends that this man, this cop, was now part of her life. She was telling them to get used to it. Meanwhile, Zeke McTeague, who wanted to absorb her the way a plant absorbed sunlight, was off by himself, his false choppers clacking away like a ticker tape machine on benzedrine.

McTeague took a step back, leaned into the shadow of an open doorway. The sun was pouring onto Patricia's honey brown hair as if it existed for no other purpose, accenting every toss of her head, every gesture.

His jaw now stilled by a tiny smile, McTeague folded his arms across his chest and closed his eyes before retrieving one of his most precious memories. In an instant, he was again striding onto a sandy beach outside Painters Hill on the Atlantic coast of Florida, plunging a shovel into the hollow between two high dunes. The sand, wet beneath the surface, had offered more resistance than expected; it packed on the blade of his shovel, stuck fast when he tried to dump it. Despite an effort that had sweat running from the back of his neck to the depths of his crotch, the sun had already cracked the horizon before he dropped Marlene Harrod's body into the shadows at the bottom of her grave. For just an instant, it had bathed her dead-white flesh in pale orange light. As if trying to restore her to life.

"Zeke, you all right?"

McTeague opened his eyes to meet hers. "Sure am, Patricia." He straightened up, took a raspy breath. "Wouldn't be the worst thing if we got in the car, though."

She looked back at Morello just as her ex-husband, Bradford, walked out of the church. Brad stopped abruptly when he saw her, chewed at his upper lip before speaking. "Pat, how're you doin'?"

"I'm doing fine." She slid her hand into the pockets of her coat, raised her shoulders as if to ward off a blow.

Brad was wearing that petulant look again, eyes narrowed, nostrils flared. Morello came over to stand beside her. "This is Rick Morello," she said, as if that explained everything Brad needed to know.

Brad sucked in a deep breath; with an effort, his face dropped into its normal set. "Brad Detrick here." He grabbed Morello's hand, pumped it hard. "You're that security guard I heard about."

"That's right." Morello's grip tightened. "And you're the guy I saw on television. You were very, very . . . effective."

Morello's mouth curled into a smile that Pat labeled cruel. His eyes were darker than ever. She glanced at McTeague. He was leaning back against the door frame again, his mouth slightly ajar, watching the exchange with naked curiosity.

"That's a hard man you got," the old man said without looking directly at her.

Pat Detrick searched for a penetrating rejoinder, found nothing sharper than *takes one to know one,* didn't say it. Finally, she muttered, "I'm really getting sick of this game."

"That's 'cause you ain't done nothin' to end it." McTeague poked a finger into his chest. "Leastways, nothin' right."

"So, Pat, when're you coming back to work for me?"

She turned back to find Bradford standing with his thumbs hooked into the lapels of his cashmere overcoat, as if daring Morello to guess its cost. The contrast between the two men couldn't have been more obvious. Bradford's thin blond eyebrows and short lashes were so light as to be nearly invisible. His eyes had the sightless petulance of an unblinking doll's, while Morello's sharply angled brows and high cheekbones kept his dark eyes in permanent shadow. She found herself wondering if two men so physically different could share a common flaw, if maybe she'd come home one evening to find Morello soiling their bed.

"I think we ought to get going." She gestured to McTeague. "Zeke's getting tired. It's been a long morning for him. And we have a lot to do."

• • •

Donny Barrett's unmarked car was already parked in front of the barn when Detrick turned the Jeep into McTeague's driveway. Barrett stood outside, leaning against the car door, wearing a gray tweed topcoat over a charcoal suit. This in direct contrast to the pair of uniformed troopers in the backseat of the Ford sedan.

"Seems like we got ourselves company," McTeague said. "If you'd of told me, Patricia, I would'a made sure I had some cake in the house. So's we could have a little party."

"They want to talk to you," Detrick said as she helped him out of the car.

"Talk about what?"

"Just look at it this way, Zeke," Morello called from the other side of the Jeep. "If you're innocent, you have nothing to worry about."

McTeague was tempted to respond with a taunt of his own, something about washing his pecker in Patricia's blood. But his play here, as he understood it, was infirmity, if not actual humility. He shuffled over to Barrett's Ford. "What could I do for you?"

"Thought we might have a little talk inside," Barrett replied evenly. "About a photograph you took in 1979."

McTeague unzipped his jacket, fished out his glasses, made a production of cleaning the lenses, fitting them to his face. He looked at the cop for a long moment, finally said, "Don't wanna make trouble, but it don't appear to me that you come here to look at old pictures. Maybe you better tell me what you got in mind 'fore we go inside. Unless you got a warrant."

"No warrant," Barrett admitted. "I'm just here to straighten out a few things." He tightened his mouth; his blue eyes grew cold as marble. "Before they get out of hand."

"What kinda things?" McTeague, who found Barrett's anger amusing, looked over at Patricia. She stood next to Morello, leaning into his shoulder, staring right back at him.

Barrett coughed into his hand. "The kind of things," he said, "that don't go away by themselves." He coughed again, waited for McTeague's full attention. "The kind of things it's better to talk about in private."

"That why you brought a gang with you?" McTeague flipped a hand at the uniformed troopers. "Case you gotta fight your way inside?"

"Look, McTeague, it's Sunday and I want to get back to my kids. So, either let me inside or tell me to get off your property."

McTeague nodded. The last thing he wanted was to send this cop on his way. He turned without another word, led Barrett across the yard, opened the door, stepped aside.

"What the hell?"

"Them's my knives I collected when I was goin' over the road." McTeague shut the door, felt his world narrow down, felt the ghosts flowing through the still air of the little cabin, Esther in the lead. The ghosts were demanding release, as they had many times before, and McTeague wanted to tell them to be patient, that their time was rapidly approaching. "I take 'em out once in a while, sharpen 'em up. Helps me remember."

"Remember what?" Barrett's hand dipped toward the table, then jerked back. He turned to face McTeague.

"Helps me remember when I was young and strong. 'Fore my heart went south."

"How's your heart right now?"

"Still pumpin'." He shuffled across the room, tapped the Palmyra photograph. "This here's the picture."

Barrett stared at the photo, the date in the corner. "Ms. Detrick tells me you had a passenger in the truck when you snapped that shot."

"Ain't never said nothin' like that. Patricia must'a heard me wrong."

"I see." Barrett folded his arms across his chest, tipped his head back to stare at McTeague along the length of his nose. "And you weren't at the Waterview Lodge the day before Alicia Munoz was shot? Weren't at the Dreher

Church? Didn't have a conversation with Terry Bannister the day before he was killed? And you don't have a truck parked in the barn where nobody can see it? Pat Detrick got everything wrong, did she?"

McTeague forced a sigh, shuffled across the room, turned on the television. "Didn't kill nobody." He settled himself in his rocking chair. "That's my bottom line. What's yours?"

"I'd like to have a look around. With your permission."

"You do that, Sergeant. Look anywhere you want." McTeague began to rock back and forth, easing into it. He was tired now, ready for a nap. "And when you get done with your fool's errand, you tell Patricia to stay away from here. Tell her Zeke McTeague don't wanna see her no more. Tell her he's got better things to do with the little time he's got left."

THIRTY-SEVEN

Across the road, beneath the branches of the taller trees, pockets of highbush blueberry, swept by the angled winter sun, clung to the last of their leaves. The narrow, curled leaves were a pale yellow streaked with red and so dry they rattled in the wind. Detrick found her eyes riveted to the shrubs, the narrow pools of color, as if she might find answers there, solutions unavailable to the police, solutions to convince the police.

"I'm gonna make it simple," Barrett said. "We looked everywhere; we found nothing. No gun, no ammo, not even a map. The pickup in the barn has two flat tires and it won't start, period. I put Ray Trager on it. He built his first hot rod when he was twelve. John swears that truck hasn't been started in years. No means, no motive, no opportunity. Beyond that, McTeague's a first-class suspect." The bitterness was evident in his voice.

A red squirrel began to chatter from the branches of a nearby oak, its call a mix of rapid-fire chucks, barks, and moans. From time to time, the little animal stopped abruptly, flicked its tail, listened for the cries of its competitors before launching into another chorus of the same combative song.

"What about the knives?" Morello asked. "The knives on his table?"

"So the guy's a jerk," Barrett shot back. "So what?"

"And the photograph?"

"I checked the photograph closely, Rick. There's nothing there. No road marker, no landmark, nothing to prove it was taken within a hundred miles of where that body was found." Barrett opened the car door. "Look, it's been nice, but I gotta get home before my ex-wife goes ballistic. I was supposed to take the kids Christmas shopping." He climbed out, stepped up to Detrick's open window. "McTeague asked me to give this to you. Said it would explain things. He also asked me to tell you not to come back."

She took the photo from Barrett's hand, watched him stride over to the Ford, get inside, hold a quick conference with his two companions before pulling away. She stared after the sedan until it disappeared, then glanced at the photo before passing it to Rick Morello. Thirty feet away, the squirrel, as if aware of her gaze, flipped its tail once, then again, then ran straight up the trunk of the tree, a blur of orange against the deeply grooved bark. The animal ran as if it had no intention of ever stopping, was determined to rush skyward, rocket off into the sunset.

"You recognize the people in this picture?" Morello asked her. "It must have been taken sixty years ago."

Pat took her gaze from the squirrel, turned, kissed Morello. "It's McTeague, standing next to Esther, his sister."

"She looks very much like you."

"That's the point, isn't it? McTeague rejected two volunteers before I showed up. I couldn't understand why he accepted me. Now I know." She put the Jeep in gear, pulled onto the road. "Let's go home, walk the dog, have some dinner. Let's do something *normal*. Maybe I can shake the feeling that I've been kidnapped to an alien planet."

An hour later, over plates of fettucini smothered in an impromptu cream sauce, Morello turned the conversation back to McTeague. "If it wasn't for those knives, I'd have to say we misjudged him."

"That's one of the reasons they were out on the table. So I'd be sure."

"And what's the other reason?"

"He wanted to warn me."

"You mean the knives were there as a threat?"

"Yes, but not to me, of course." Detrick set her fork on the plate, wiped her mouth. "Of course."

"Of course?" His features darkened. "Don't play with me, Pat. Because the way I feel, right now, I'm liable to make a side trip, put a pillow over that bastard's face, push down real hard. Somehow, I don't think there'd be an autopsy."

She shook her head. "You won't do that. You can't. You've had enough murder. Murder is why you left New York." Her tone was flat. "McTeague knows the mission won't abandon him, that somebody will show up, even though I've been excluded. That's what the knives were all about. If I don't play my part, he'll use them on Bill Gauss, Abby Turner, whoever comes to help him." She felt tears well up in her eyes. "He's been ahead of me all the way. Setting his trap. I remember thinking last week that if I could just disable the truck, he'd be finished, that he couldn't get out on his own. The joke is that he'd already disabled the truck, gotten rid of the gun, the ammo I saw in the cupboard." She bit her lower lip, shuddered. "And then there's Coleman Poole. Sitting in a jail cell, accused of murder. A lucky accident, from McTeague's point of view, but the jury's going to believe that the shootings have stopped because the real killer was arrested."

Morello reached for her hand, but she pulled away. "Tell me more about serial killers, Rick," she demanded. "Tell me how they choose their victims."

"They live in their fantasies." Morello reached out again, this time found her fingers, claimed them. "The fantasies come first, before the killing begins. They're like visions to an artist—the perfect killing, the perfect victim."

"The ideal woman?"

"Unless you're gay. If you're gay, you kill the ideal man."

Detrick freed her hand, picked up her fork. "The last part of it was really the best. Banning me from the cabin. It was ingenious."

"You think he's finished with you?"

She spun her fork in the pasta, watched flecks of butter-streaked sauce flip over the edge of the plate, drop onto the tablecloth. "Finished? I don't think he's really begun."

"Then what does he want?"

"He wants to bare his soul." The bitter irony forced a smile onto her face. "Then, if he happens to be in the mood, he'll kill me."

She'd said it as a joke, but hours later, sitting up in bed while Morello slept beside her, Detrick felt herself settle into something approaching certainty. She remembered Morello's cool reaction to her comment about McTeague wanting to confess, to reveal himself, his true colors.

"Tell me, Pat," he'd asked, "why, since you've been totally unable to predict McTeague's actions up to this point, you think you know what he's going to do next? Tell me how you know he didn't bury that rifle in the woods behind his house, that he can't get to it whenever he wants, that he isn't loading it right this minute?"

"McTeague's been feeding me bits and pieces all along," she'd replied. "He *wants* me to put it together. That's part of the game." Morello's expression remained skeptical. "You remember what you told me about homicide investigation, about trying to make connections? Well, there was no way to connect Melissa Capriella, the woman he killed before I met him, to Zeke McTeague. They were complete strangers. If he'd continued to kill strangers, nobody would ever have suspected him."

Morello had finally nodded agreement. "It's hard enough to suspect him even now."

"Exactly. But then I came waltzing into his life, the do-gooder from the Senior Aid Mission, and for the first time in his life he changes the pattern. Now he can be connected to the attacks."

"But only by you."

"That's the whole point. If he merely wanted to kill me, I'd never see it coming. No more than any of the others. But if he doesn't merely want to kill me, then he must want something else." Detrick had looked down at her plate for a moment, then up at Morello. "Baring his soul. That's what he's been doing all along. Showing me little snippets of his life, because he eventually plans to show me every single ugly detail."

"Then why didn't he just come out and do it?"

"Toying with me is part of his game. Like killing Florence Clark. The way I see it, Zeke targeted Clark before I walked into his life, so it wasn't a big problem for him to stop there last week on his way to the mission. Not for a great and powerful man like Zeke McTeague." She added, "It's hard to be the unsuspecting victim of a man who's virtually told you that he's a killer."

"And what about the category of *suspecting* victim?"

It was a good question and Detrick, looking down now on her sleeping lover, still had no answer beyond, "McTeague's a feeble old man. Without the element of surprise, he's almost helpless."

The room was warm, the winter quilt much too heavy. Morello, in his sleep, had thrown it off and now lay naked on the blue cotton sheet. Detrick slid down beside him, laid the fingertips of her hand against the back of his neck, ran them along the ridges of his spine, over his buttocks, the wiry black hairs covering his thighs. Finally, she closed her eyes and allowed herself to absorb the heat of this body.

She lay there until she was certain that sleep would not come. Then she got up, went to the window. The moon was still above the trees; it swept the withered lawn, washed the brown grass in pale, cold silver, an unearthly, uninhabited scene. But she knew better, of course, knew that the forest was fully alive, fully inhabited, that shrews and voles and mice and rats moved through the darkness, that owls, raccoons, skunks, and bobcats sought their flesh, that death nourished life and there were no vacations.

THIRTY-EIGHT

Though Zeke McTeague, too, noted the clear night and the full moon overhead, he wasted no time in philosophical speculation as he worked to get his little truck up and running. McTeague had been on an emotional roller coaster since Patricia Detrick drove away, thinking he'd maybe made a big mistake giving Esther's photograph to that cop, asking the cop to tell Patricia, *Don't come back*. What if Patricia took old Zeke McTeague at his word? What if she hadn't gotten the point at all? What if she was telling herself that she'd done her Christian duty, taken her suspicions to the proper authorities, that now she was out of it? What if Patricia wasn't Esther's child, the way he'd been thinking, but just another helpless cow, no better than any of the cows he'd butchered over the years?

All afternoon and into the evening he'd bounced from fear to rage like a mouse between the paws of a cat. But in the end, as it always had in the past, rage won out. Rage was his protector, his oldest companion; rage had carried him through long nights huddled in the forest, listening to Esther call his name, her voice sounding in his ears like the howling of wolves.

The way out, his escape, was to do and not to think. He understood that instinctively. Patricia Detrick had to be shown the price of desertion, that what the army called *dereliction of duty* carried a severe penalty, an end-of-life sentence. If he didn't feel up to it? Well, that was just too bad. Because anything, even death, was better than sitting in his rocker, listening to the howl of crazy Esther's ghost.

A calm had settled over McTeague once the basic decision was made. As he'd known it would. For the next two hours, he concerned himself with the practical. While his dinner cooked, he made coffee and filled a thermos, gathered tools and stuffed them into a burlap bag. At the last minute, instead of going to his collection for a weapon, he lifted a heavy-bladed kitchen knife from the drawer next to the sink. He wiped it carefully before dropping it into the bag.

As he ate his canned stew and his canned carrots, Zeke thought about all the ways a knife can cause pain. He'd known women to fall apart at the first appearance of a blade, to piss themselves, to vomit with terror. Given time, it was possible to bleed a woman until she withered like a fallen leaf. It was also possible to take her life with a single thrust, take it silently and so fast there seemed no barrier between life and death.

After dinner, Zeke had dropped, fully clothed, onto his bed. He didn't turn off the light, get under the blankets, or even take off his shoes. His mind was filled with thoughts of blood, of how he might subdue the woman he intended to hunt despite his being a feeble old man, about what he would do, minute by minute, if he managed to bring it off.

Comforted, somehow, he had fallen into a deep, dreamless sleep from which he awoke nearly six hours later. For a long moment, he didn't know where he was or why he was sleeping with his clothes on. Then he propped himself up on one elbow and saw the burlap bag where it sat on the floor.

He'd gotten up immediately, up and out, pausing only to put on his coat and hat, jam his hands into a pair of gloves, and shoulder the bag containing his tools. The cold ate into him as he put his truck back together. Despite a mechanical expertise developed in the course of breakdowns a hundred miles from the nearest garage, it took McTeague almost an hour to get the pickup started. By that time, his feet were so numb he could barely depress the gas pedal.

As he sat there in the dark, waited for the heater to blow warm air, McTeague unfolded a map of northeastern Pennsylvania. This would be the first time he'd traveled to the little house on Cedar Creek Road in the dark. If he made a wrong turn, he might drive ten miles before he figured it out, found a crossroad. If the road wasn't marked or he couldn't make out the street sign in the dark, he'd be driving in circles until daybreak.

McTeague, as he carefully flattened the creases on the map, recalled his first year at the Dreher School, Miss Alger pulling down a roll-up map of the United States. "You are *here*," she'd told her three first-graders while the older kids worked math problems. "This is *Pennsylvania*." Her pointer had traced an irregular rectangle. "These are the *New England States*. These are the *Middle Atlantic States*. *Pennsylvania* is a *Middle Atlantic State*."

Miss Alger had been strong on remembering. Remembering and penmanship. She didn't care for interruptions and she'd frowned when he raised his hand, even though he's never raised his hand before. "Yes, Ezekiel. What is it?"

The eyes of the other children had seemed to pierce the back of his head. He was sitting in front, as usual, a near-sighted boy who'd never had his eyes examined. "Please, ma'am, them black lines. Are they roads, ma'am?"

"No, Ezekiel, they are not. Those are rivers. As you would have learned, had you been patient."

Later, during recess, Miss Alger, all smiles away from her lessons, had taken him to the side. "Are you interested in roads, Ezekiel?"

"Yes, ma'am."

"If I give you a road map of Pennsylvania will you promise to learn the names of all the cities? You can ask your sister to help you."

By that time Esther was too far gone to even help herself and Miss Alger must have known it. Still, over the next couple of years, he'd learned the names of the cities and the little towns, and the roads that ran through them, puzzling over the map whenever crazy Esther was out of the way. Then, one afternoon Esther had found him kneeling in the barn, found the map lying unfolded in a pool of sunlight. McTeague, who knew what was going to happen next, had tried to jump to his feet, snatch up the map, and run. All at the same time.

He'd failed, of course. And, of course, that night Esther burned the map, his treasure, in the center of the yard. She made a big production out of it, lighting the unfolded map in a half-dozen places, adding twigs and small branches until she had a pretty decent bonfire going. Then she took him by the hands and they danced around the fire, danced beneath the moon, danced until his own voice had joined his sister's in that primal howl. He could hear it still, in-human, speaking of no emotion he could name; he would always hear it.

The roads were deserted when he finally got going, which was just as well because the effort to get ready had taken its toll and he was driving erratically, drifting from one side of the road to the other. Just south Cresco, three deer bolted across the road in front of his little pickup, there and gone before his foot moved off the gas pedal.

Show some heart, boy, he told himself. That was what his father had said whenever he complained about Esther. That, or *Show 'em you're a McTeague.*

The small, one-story house on Cedar Creek Road was dark when McTeague, his headlights off, glided to a stop. Moving quickly now, he shut down the engine and opened the door. The cold hit him hard, hard enough to make him wish momentarily for his rocker, but he got out anyway, pausing only to heft the bag of tools before he trudged through the shadows toward the door at the rear of the house.

McTeague wasn't surprised to find the door secured by a spring lock instead of a deadbolt. He knew the locals were too proud of the low crime rate to realize how isolated their little houses were, how the surrounding forest gave aid and comfort to the enemy. No, the surprise was that the door was locked at all. Chuckling softly, McTeague withdrew a heavy screwdriver from his tool bag. He slid the blade between the lock and the frame of the door, then levered the screwdriver with both hands until the door popped open.

It was warm inside the house. McTeague, as he waited for his eyes to adjust to the darker conditions, took off his coat and dropped it near the door before removing the knife from the bag. Very early in his career, McTeague had broken into homes from time to time. Despite the obvious danger, the thought of his unsuspecting victims asleep in their beds, maybe dreaming some happy dream, had thrilled him no end. Then one night he'd been attacked by a dog as he made his way toward an old Nebraska farmhouse, attacked and severely bitten. After that, after twenty-eight stitches in an Omaha emergency room, he'd kept his eyes focused on the road ahead.

Slowly, despite his madly beating heart, McTeague,

knife in hand, edged from the kitchen into the living room, then stopped again to look and listen. The room smelled of furniture polish and potpourri, of stale cigarette smoke and garlic from last night's dinner. Clothing, a jacket, a sweater, a pair of sneakers, lay scattered about the room. A plastic ashtray on a table next to a long couch overflowed with cigarette butts.

McTeague absorbed the reality of the life he was about to take as if he could truly possess that life, as if by adding pieces of somebody's else's life he could at last make himself whole. That was impossible, of course, a lesson he'd learned decades before, a lesson he remembered as he crossed the room, as he entered the short hallway leading to the bedrooms, as his hand tightened on the hilt of the knife.

The first door he came upon was slightly ajar. McTeague, peering in, saw posters on the wall, rock and movie stars he didn't recognize, an adolescent's room. He heard soft snoring, then a creak of bedsprings and a few seconds of quiet before the snoring resumed. For a long moment, he struggled with the desire to slip inside, wet the blade of his knife, but he didn't know if the sleeping child was a boy or a girl. He didn't trust his own strength, either, didn't know if he had the energy to handle two in one night.

Purpose, he told himself. *You got to remember Patricia and why you come here.*

He took a reluctant step, then another, wishing with all his heart that he was again young and strong. By the time he reached a second door, this one closed, he was too excited to do more than press his ear against the wood, make sure all was quiet, before turning the knob, pushing the door open far enough to slip inside. Cool air from an open window played across his hands and face as he shut the door behind him, took a good look around. The room was sparse, a bed, a bureau, a vanity table with a plain mirror on top. The walls were bare except for a large wooden cross above the bed. Even the blanket that covered the sleeping woman was a dark, uniform blue.

McTeague, driven by a rush of adrenaline, clutched the knife to his chest as he crossed the room, then dropped to his knees by the side of the bed. He wanted to wake the sleeping woman, look into her eyes when she recognized him, absorb her terror; he wanted to add her fear to the dark pool of fear he carried within himself. Closing his eyes, he lowered his face to the back of her neck and drew the smell of her flesh into his nostrils.

He held that position for as long as he dared. Wanting more, always more. As he raised the knife high above his head, opened his eyes, found his target, he thought of Patricia asleep in her own bed, of how desperately he wanted her, of her cruel betrayal. Then he slammed the knife down through the blanket, between the woman's ribs, deep into her heart.

THIRTY-NINE

When the phone rang at ten o'clock the next morning, Detrick and Morello were at the kitchen table waiting for a pot of coffee to finish brewing. Detrick's first reaction was to let it ring, to shut out whatever nightmare was trying to crawl into her life. She looked at Morello, said, "You see how he tightens the noose?"

"You don't know . . ."

Detrick picked up the phone on the fourth ring. Her half-whispered, "Hello," was followed by Elaine Gauss's voice, choked with sobs.

"Oh, Pat," Elaine cried. Then she repeated, "Oh, Pat."

Detrick felt her heart sink. How could she have been so stupid? Like everybody else, she'd been tricked into believing that McTeague was trapped, tricked by Donny Barrett's hot rod mechanic. "Elaine, try to tell me what's happened. Did somebody . . ." She paused, tasting bile in the back of her throat.

"It's Abby Turner. She's been killed in her bed." Elaine again burst into tears. "Her daughter, Kay, found the body and called me. Look, I've got to get out there. I've got to help Kay through this. I know you and Abby were friends—I was hoping you'd come over."

Detrick hesitated. Lying didn't come easily to her: she needed a moment to gain control of her voice. "Yes, of course," she said. "Just give me a couple of hours." Again, she hesitated. "Elaine, was Abby shot? Was it like the others?"

"No, she was stabbed. Oh, Pat, Kay told me the knife was still in her back."

For a long time after hanging up, Detrick was unable to speak. She sat with her eyes on the table between herself and Morello, her arms wrapped around her chest. If she'd been just a little sharper, she told herself, she'd have gone to McTeague days ago. Instead of wasting her time with Sergeant Barrett. Now McTeague had punished her for her tardiness. As he would punish her further if she didn't give him what he wanted.

"Pat?"

Morello's voice seemed to come from far away and she thought of how strong he'd been, how willing to listen, to help where he could. "It's Abby Turner, the mission's visiting nurse," she finally said. "Abby's been killed. Stabbed in her bed. In her sleep, I hope."

"You can't know that it was McTeague."

Detrick kept her eyes on the table. "Just a coincidence? That it?"

She heard Morello draw a deep breath, then say, "I want to know if you're going out there." His voice carried an edge unfamiliar to Detrick, a cynical, bitter quality that reminded her of Barrett's parting comments.

"Tell me what you would do." She raised her eyes at last. "In my position."

Morello lifted his mug. His hand was shaking. "I can't get past the typical male response," he admitted. "I want to beat the fuck out of him, get his signature on a confession, details he couldn't know unless he'd been there."

Detrick split the muffin in her hand with a fork, dropped the halves into her toaster. "What happens if he dies in the process?" She turned. "I keep seeing those photographs on his wall. And I wonder what they were thinking. You know, in the moments before they got into his truck, before he . . . killed them. They deserve to have names. At least that. At least they deserve to have names." She fought to control her tears. It was too early for grief. "I'm repeating myself," she whispered.

"Giving them names," Morello responded, his voice tight, "will not give them life." He drew a breath. "Punishing the murderer is all you can do, but it isn't enough. It was never enough." He pushed the chair back, raised his chin, ran his tongue across his upper lip. "I want you to promise me you won't go out there alone."

"And you? Will you make the same promise? That you won't go out there alone?"

"I promise," he replied. "For now. Not forever."

"Then, yes. For now, I promise, too," she said, knowing full well that they were both lying.

It's funny, Zeke McTeague thought when Rick Morello, gun in hand, pushed the door open, stepped inside, how the things that happen to you in your life, the things you aren't expecting, can turn your bullshit upside down, black into white, fear into hope.

McTeague had returned from Abby Turner's home at three A.M., had staggered into the bathroom, stared at the pasty-white face in the mirror, decided that he hadn't given up the ghost, that the ghost was all he had left. The pain had eased off a bit after he took the pill, the nitro, but it hadn't gone away. No, instead of vanishing, the pain had smoldered in his chest, burst into flame every hour or so. Even now, six pills later, it felt like someone had rammed a fist up his ass.

"You plannin' to shoot me?" The words came out in little puffs, so softly that McTeague could barely hear them in his own ears.

"Stay in the chair," Morello said. He tucked the automatic into the waistband of his trousers, closed the door behind him. "Keep your hands where I can see them."

It should have cheered him, the cop voice, cop command, but the pain was too sharp, too insistent. "Think you better get to the point," McTeague said. "Bein' as I'm not feelin' up to no long conversations."

"Where are the knives?"

Morello took a step forward, then stopped. McTeague could see the wheels turning, the big cop trying to work out the problem, how to threaten somebody who's halfway to dead. "My collection's in a suitcase under the bed. You want, you can borrow it." He lowered his eyes, waited for his breath to catch up to his brain. "Don't come with instructions, though. You gotta work 'em out for yourself."

"You think you're beyond pain? That what it is?"

McTeague rocked back in the chair. "No sense in makin' threats, mister. Threats are for the future. Whatever you gotta do, you gotta do it now." He raised his eyes to meet Morello's, saw defeat, the face of an actor who's wandered onto the stage without a script. "Me, I need to rest. I gotta get strong before my company shows up, catches me unprepared."

She ran a bath once Morello had left, ran it as hot as she could stand, lowered herself into it, laid her head against the edge of the porcelain tub. The course of her relationship with Rick had been changed; she was sure of that even if she didn't know where that change would lead. Once again McTeague had reached into her life, given it a cruel tweak, a preview of the show to come.

As she pulled herself up, began to soap her body, Detrick noticed Becky lying with her head in the doorway. The dog's coat was clean, her eyes clear and expectant, as if she'd never belonged to Zeke McTeague, was living proof that escape was possible.

The phone rang while Detrick was shaving her legs. She started to answer, to step out of the tub, then checked herself. It's probably Elaine, she thought, wondering what's happened to me. Or Rick making sure I haven't gone out to McTeague's.

Instead of either, after the answering machine rolled through her programmed message, Detrick heard Betty Hoffmann speak. Betty was again squabbling with her boyfriend, Roberto, and the outrage in her voice rang so hollow that Detrick, listening, wanted to cover both ears with a towel. She thought of Abby Turner, cut down while her daughter slept in another room. Abby, who loved her daughter ferociously, would never see Kay's life unfold, and Kay, whose father had walked out on his family years ago, would lose her only anchor. Kay's life had been forever altered by Zeke McTeague; she would take this pain to the grave. By contrast, Ricardo's devotion to his work, his neglect of Betty, was pure melodrama.

She switched on the small TV in her room as she shrugged out of her robe. Half expecting news of Abby's murder, she was taken off guard by the face of WBRE's weather forecaster and the words *Emergency Snow Advisory* as they scrolled below a graphic of the eastern half of the United States. The graphic was pure white to the northwest, green from Ohio to the coast, then blue over the ocean, the colors separated by curving red lines. The lines (isobars, she recalled) were edged with blue triangles; the apex of each triangle, the point, faced outward like a weapon. A large red *L* in northern Missouri was echoed by another in southern Louisiana. To the east, a clearly outgunned *H* sat on the Pennsylvania-New Jersey border. As she watched, the graphic went into motion. The Missouri low pushed at a steep angle through Indiana and Ohio, the Louisiana low rushed to the coast then turned north, the Pennsylvania high fled into the Atlantic.

"Batten down the hatches, folks, because this system's not going anywhere soon."

Detrick put her robe back on, walked to the front door, and let Becky out. The sky, now the color of wet slate, was rapidly lowering, billowing downward like a deflating balloon. Detrick knew that she didn't have a lot of time, that the storm might break at any moment. As soon as the dog finished and trotted back inside, Detrick went directly to her bedroom, stripped off her robe, laid out a set of quilted underwear, a pair of flannel-lined corduroy pants, a silk turtleneck, and a heavy wool sweater. There was always the chance that she'd have to leave McTeague's, to walk out if the snow became too deep for the car. When she finished dressing, she found her down parka and shook it out. She put on a pair of insulated boots, laced them to the top, left the parka on a chair near the door and walked back into the bedroom.

The little Seecamp was right where she'd left it on the closet shelf. With no hammer and no sights, no external safety, the gun seemed only half formed, an artist's rendering of a deadly weapon. Detrick released the clip, laid the automatic on the bed, picked up the box of cartridges, and removed the cover. The bullets inside shone out as if the light had been there all along, a genie waiting for release.

"Damn," Detrick whispered. "Damn, damn, damn."

She was still holding the box, holding it cupped in her hand as if it might explode at the slightest movement, when the phone rang. The sound jerked her to attention, stiffened her shoulders. She was afraid now, and she knew it, knew also that she was supposed to be afraid, that it was part of the game. Though she told herself to let it ring, she picked up the receiver and brought it to her ear.

"Hello?"

"Pat, it's Rick."

"Hi."

"I've been busy helping Carl. What with the snow coming, the lodge is booked solid for the weekend. You'd think it would make him happy, all those skiers so early in the season, but the good news has thrown Carl into overdrive. Even though he's got four days to get ready, he's trying to stock up on everything from booze to bacon."

She saw the opening and seized it. "Talk about stocking up," she said. "I've got to make a quick run to the supermarket before the storm gets really bad. I was just about to leave. Why don't I call you tonight?"

For a moment, she thought Morello would lash out, maybe threaten or forbid her. It was clear to her that he knew exactly where she was going, what she intended to do. She heard him exhale into the phone. The hiss of his breath seemed to her as startling as a sob.

"All right, Pat," he said. "I'll speak to you tonight. Take care."

FORTY

Patricia Detrick pulled the Jeep to a stop at the mouth of Zeke McTeague's driveway and turned off the headlights. The steady rattle of sleet on the hood, the roof, seemed almost friendly, a toddler shaking a favored toy. But when she zipped up her parka, stepped outside, took a hesitant, sliding step toward the cabin, the weather closed around her. The chatter of ice falling on the gravel driveway rose to a near scream, and as she lowered her head, forged a path into the wind, she remembered a video she'd seen years before in Sunday school. The tape had been taken by a local resident, a missionary just returning from a posting in Ethiopia. Toward the end of the tape, after the usual shots of grateful children coming to the school, converts offering their souls to the Lord, the missionary had recorded the descent of a horde of locusts. The insects had come by the millions, dropping from the sky in an appropriately biblical cloud. As they devoured fields of wheat, stripped the orchards, the click of their mandibles had overpowered the missionary's breathless narration, the whir of wings, the wailing of the farmers as they slapped at the insects with burlap bags. The terrible sound had poured from the speakers to fill the small room until, one by one, the children had covered their ears, squeezed their eyes shut.

The sight of McTeague's house, the pale seductive light in the single window, brought her to a momentary halt. She took off the glove on her right hand, put her hand in the flap pocket on the front of the parka, gripped the little gun. There was no silhouette in the window, nobody standing guard, but still she approached the house from the side, worked her way across the front, squatted down before looking through the window.

McTeague was in his rocking chair. His eyes were closed, his jaw slack, his mouth open. A glistening line of saliva ran, unbroken, through the dirty gray stubble on his chin, down along the folds in his neck. It had puddled on the collar of his blue flannel shirt, a dark spreading stain that nevertheless demonstrated life.

Last chance, Patricia, she told herself. Last chance to turn around. With a start, she realized that there were no witnesses here, that she had made her intentions clear to no one. If she failed, if she turned away, started the Jeep, turned the heater full up before backing away, her shame would remain private, personal, a secret she would carry into the grave, but a secret nonetheless.

She again looked into the cabin, found McTeague in the same position, one hand on his lap, the other hanging down alongside the chair, fingertips nearly brushing the floor. He'd taken out his upper plate before he'd fallen asleep, had laid it on the table next to his rocker; it rested there, a curving line of yellowed porcelain tombstones.

She crawled beneath the window, then rose, pulled the

automatic from her pocket, and walked quickly to the entrance. She wasn't surprised to find the door unlocked. She wasn't surprised, either, to find Zeke McTeague's eyes now fully open, his fingers pressing his false teeth into place.

"You're lettin' the heat out." McTeague snapped his upper and lower teeth together several times, then, satisfied with the fit, he nodded once, stiffly. "And bein' as I'm feelin' poorly, I don't need me no chill."

Detrick closed the door, stepped forward. The sleet hammered against the roof, echoing in the room. The sound enveloped, as if they stood beneath a waterfall.

"You gonna kill me?" McTeague raised his left hand, pointed at the gun Detrick held. "Now, your boyfriend, he wanted to shoot me in the worst way, but he didn't have it in him. You know, that door between wantin' what you want and gettin' it? Your boyfriend couldn't push it open."

"And you, Zeke, you stepped through it? Stepped through the door?"

McTeague nodded. He was surprised to find himself short-tempered, peevish. He'd been anticipating something entirely different. Triumph at the very least, maybe even joy, joy followed eventually by transformation. Meanwhile, his mouth was dry and sour, the pain in his chest insistent; his breath tasted like a mildewed sock. "Long time ago," he replied. "Never looked back, neither."

"And what was on the other side?" She shifted the gun from hand to hand as she unzipped her jacket, slipped it off. She dropped the automatic into her pants pocket, rubbed her hands together. "It's cold in here," she said without waiting for an answer.

McTeague set the rocker in motion again. "Heater don't throw much heat. And I ain't had the energy to get the wood stove goin'."

It was the simple truth and Detrick could see it clearly. McTeague's complexion was ghostly and his bloodless lips had the look of long-healed scar tissue. He'd lost weight in the last twenty-four hours; his skin hung across the bones of his face, sank deep into the hollows of his cheeks. His eyes had dropped back in their sockets, as if looking for a way out before the ship sank out of sight.

"You want to go to the hospital," she said, "I can probably get us out of here." Her tone was so matter-of-fact it was almost taunting. "If you wait, you're going to be trapped."

"That bad, eh? Look like I'm about ready for the old boneyard?" He laid his palms on the arms of the rocker, began to push himself erect.

"Stay in the chair, Zeke."

McTeague froze halfway up. He held himself still for a moment before dropping back onto the seat of the chair, cursing inwardly. Even that little effort had him chugging like a winded horse. "You gonna shoot me if I get up?"

"I don't have to shoot you, Zeke." Now that she was inside, committed, she felt an insane urge to hurry, as if she could fast-forward the video, rush through the previews, the opening credits. "And you know it."

When McTeague failed to respond, she deliberately turned her back. She opened the wood bin. Inside, she found split logs, kindling, and newspaper, all neatly stacked.

"Do-gooders done it for me," McTeague called from across the room. "Remind me to thank 'em."

She shook down the ashes in the stove, stacked a handful of kindling over a row of rolled newspapers, adjusted the flue before putting a match to the paper. The dried branches and twigs caught almost immediately and she added several small logs before slamming the door. Then she walked over to the sink, filled the kettle, and set it on a burner.

"You makin' tea?" he asked. "This here a social visit?"

"Turn your pockets inside out, Zeke." She leaned back against the refrigerator door, folded her arms across her chest. Her voice carried an edge of weariness; she could hear it herself, was almost certain that McTeague would pick up on it, use any weakness to gain a perceived advantage.

"That ain't friendly, Patricia. You know I wouldn't hurt you."

She shook her head. "It's kind of late for a relationship based on trust, don't you think?"

"You only believe that because you ain't looked hard enough at what I already told you. But you'll know before too long. Know why I wouldn't hurt you." McTeague, the lie spoken, managed after an effort that had him panting, to reverse the lining of his empty back pockets. He twisted in the seat, wiggled the flaps at Detrick. "You satisfied?"

"Now your front pockets. Then roll up your sleeves, pull up your trouser cuffs, pull your shirt out of your pants."

McTeague did his shirt last, saved it deliberately, figuring it was as good a way to get started as any. He tugged it free of his trousers, trapped the tails beneath his chin, then unbuttoned his long johns, working downward from his throat to his navel. "See what I mean?" he asked.

His narrow, fish white chest was lined with horizontal scars. Some, a few, were raised, but most, and there were many, were no more than flat pale strips against his bloodless skin. "You know who done this?" he asked.

"Esther." It wasn't a question, the way it came out, just a statement of fact, an observation that might easily have been neutral.

"Old Esther," McTeague chuckled, "she had a way with sharp edges. What she'd do, when she was of a mood, was make the cuts real shallow, wait for the blood to bead up, lick it off." He ran a finger, from his left to his right nipple, across the surface of a raised scar. "I was just a little kid, didn't know nothin' about keepin' clean. Got my share of infections."

Detrick felt her stomach lurch, as if it had glided into an air pocket, been sucked downward. "And, of course, everybody knew. Your teachers and neighbors, everybody knew."

"Course they knew." McTeague snorted, was about to continue when the steady pounding of sleet on the roof and the windows abruptly eased. A moment later, it was gone, vanished, replaced by the moan of the wind in the chimney, the creak of swaying trees, the rattle of bare branches.

Detrick glanced through the window, thinking the storm was over, that she would be able to leave, to make a run for it if she found she couldn't bear the horror to follow. Then she saw that it wasn't over. The sleet had merely changed over to snow, the sharp crystals become small gray shadows running in swarms behind the glass. Again, she felt the urge to hurry the process, get it done. "Tell me what it is you want, Zeke. Tell me what you want and I'll tell you what I want. Let's make a deal."

FORTY-ONE

McTeague leaned back into the rocker. "You think to bring a tape recorder? Along with that little gun?"

"Is that what you want to do? Confess?"

"Now don't be rushin', Patricia." He lifted his chin, managed to put some of the fire, the power, back into his voice. "Do-gooder like yourself got to make allowances for an old man. In the bureau, the bottom drawer—a tape recorder and bag of cassettes. I don't wanna lose nothin'."

McTeague watched her straighten, glance over at the bureau. "And maybe you should serve up some tea, maybe toss a couple big logs on the fire. That way, once we get to goin', we won't have to stop."

"That's a good idea." She folded her arms across her

chest, smiled. "Setting things up, I mean. But there's something I need to know, before I get started. Terry Bannister, Melissa Capriella, and Abby Turner. Are they on your list of revelations? Because, if they're not—"

For the first time, McTeague laughed. "Piece of luck there. Old bad-ass Coleman Poole gettin' busted for them shootings. Kept the devil at bay, is what it done. You see that trooper, that blondie? See them blue, blue eyes? Figured he was Dirty Harry. Already solved the crime and didn't want no part of Zeke McTeague." He stopped abruptly, eyed her again, remembered a time when his stare would freeze a woman in her tracks, make her beg for mercy. "I ain't plannin' to hold nothin' back." he said. "This here's my story I'm gonna be tellin'. My only story."

"And you're going to tell all of it?" Detrick insisted. "Including what you've done over the past few weeks?"

"Course I am." McTeague grinned, laid his hands in his lap, wished with all his might that his pecker still worked, that he was still young and strong, that he could do this the right way. "Don't you trust me, Patricia?"

Detrick fell to work. She dropped a log onto the fire, poured their tea, added milk and sugar before carrying the mugs to the small table next to McTeague's rocker. Then she found the little tape recorder and the cassettes in McTeague's bureau. Without taking her eyes off McTeague, she plugged the recorder into the wall, tore the plastic wrappers off the tapes, inserted a tape into the recorder. Finally, she turned the unit on, then off. As she worked, she considered, for the first time, just how easy it would be to kill Zeke McTeague. The pillow Rick suggested would do the trick nicely. Or she could drag the old man into the woods, let him sit out there in his long johns until she was sure he'd never get back. Nobody would ever know.

She tried to put these thoughts out of her mind, told herself that she had a task to perform and she ought to get it done as quickly as possible. McTeague wanted her to react, wanted her rage, her despair, to watch her twist in the wind of her own emotions.

"Better put a label on that tape," McTeague instructed. "A number or somethin'. 'Cause if my heart holds out, there's liable to be a bunch of 'em."

She found a pen in her purse, carried a chair across the room and set it on the far side of the table. As she sat down, a quick, clear image formed in her mind. She saw Zeke McTeague lying under the snow in the driveway, a shadowy, indefinite form soon to become invisible, a snow-drift. His right arm stretches upward, palm out, a suppli-cant's gesture, the gesture of a drowning man begging for help. It's too late, of course. The snowflakes no longer melt in his hand; instead, they puff up to form a tissue-paper blossom, a rose in winter.

"You ready now?" Detrick pressed the record button, watched the tape spin. A tiny red bulb next to the recessed microphone began to blink steadily. Nodding, she held it up for McTeague's inspection. "This okay?"

McTeague grunted his approval, shifted in his seat, slid his fingers beneath his belt. "Hands won't get warm no more," he announced. "Don't seem to matter how hot it is."

"That's what you have to say? You got me here to talk about your chilly fingers?"

"You're pissed off, I can see that. Good reason for it, too." McTeague, though he'd been rehearsing this mo-ment for weeks, felt a powerful reluctance to begin. He wanted to own the moment, hold it in his hands, cradle it lovingly, tenderly. He peered at Patricia through narrowed lids. He wasn't wearing his glasses, and her face was little more than a blur. "All right." He took a deep breath, ran his tongue over his lips. "Let's start with you."

Detrick crossed her legs, laid her hands, one atop the other, on her right knee. She started to speak, thought bet-ter of it.

"You know, the kinda life I lived," McTeague contin-ued, "I never thought much about gettin' old. There was always a load goin' someplace, another load to pick up, truck stops along the way. I didn't take it no further, didn't see the need; I was too busy makin' my life to want to pass it along, let somebody else carry the memories after I was gone. Then I had my heart attack and I started to think different." He paused, plucked his glasses off the table, settled them on the bridge of his nose, over his ears, looked straight across at her. As always, he found her utterly beautiful. "Get right down to it, Patricia, what I done, bein' as I didn't have no children, was pick you to bear the glad tidings. Folks talk about John Wayne Gacy and Ted Bundy like they was some kinda gods, but I say that Gacy and Bundy were assholes. Just like all the rest of 'em that went and got themselves caught. You see what I'm gettin' at? Me, I lived a whole life, done everythin' they done, more, and I'm still walkin' around."

"But not for long." Detrick slid the mug of tea off the table, sipped at it, then drank deeply. She looked over at the wall of photographs behind McTeague. It would be daybreak before they got finished. "Once these tapes get to the police, you'll be just another animal in a cage. Where you belong."

"That's real spunky," McTeague said. "I like that." He gripped the arms of the rocker, pushed back. "But see, gettin' arrested, that's part of the deal. Way I figure it, the cops'll have to keep me alive for the trial, so I'll most likely be in a hospital, instead of a cell." He cocked his head to one side, closed his eyes, let his thoughts flow. "What I'm gonna do is plead insane, claim my childhood turned me into a killer. Be right dramatic when I take off my shirt in that courtroom, show the jury Esther's handiwork. By that time my book'll be out so the whole country's gonna be watchin'."

Detrick rose. She went to the door, opened it, let the cold air, the wet prickle of blown snow, cool her down. She told herself that she was helpless here, that McTeague had already set the conditions, predetermined the outcome. Even if he died before morning, even if she killed him, she could not leave Coleman Poole sitting in jail. No, the tapes would have to go to the police. Eventually, they'd make their way to the press, eventually some reporter would write the book.

She closed the door, was halfway across the room when she realized that it might be possible to relegate all the material affecting the Pocono region to a single tape. If McTeague didn't make it through the storm, the other tapes could be destroyed. The confession would still be sensational, but the furor would be mostly local. Eventually it would die down. With McTeague gone, there would be no fuel to add to the fire.

"You gotta stay close, Patricia, else the recorder won't pick up your voice." McTeague was holding the tape recorder on his lap. He pressed a button, then set it on the table. "And, see, it's important that your voice be there if you're gonna bear my glad tidings. Once the tapes get to be public, folks know that other voice belongs to Patricia Detrick? Bet you could figure it out for yourself, Patricia. My name and your name, they're gonna go down in history."

"In that case, maybe I'll write a book of my own. *Dawn With The Devil*. How does that sound?" Detrick regretted the words before they were out. In spite of her instincts, she was sparring with McTeague; she was giving him what he wanted.

"Ain't no skin off my nose. Get yourself a million dollars. Go on the television, become famous." The old man's eyes were wide with pleasure. "Hide out in your house, or move somewhere people don't know you. It's all the same to me, because no matter what you do, you're gonna carry me into your grave. You'll never be shut of me. Never." He leaned all the way forward, gripped the edge of the chair as if about to push himself erect. "When I first saw you standin' at that door, I thought to myself that I was seein' Esther's child. Not Esther, not crazy Esther dancin' naked in the snow, but Esther's child somehow grown into a woman and sent to me. I felt like that moment had been waitin' a million years to happen, like it'd been waitin' for-ever; I felt like my life had always been comin' toward this, but I was too ignorant to know it. That's when I decided to let you know, to make the tapes, to pass my life on."

Detrick leaned forward, pushed McTeague back into the chair. More sparring, more helplessness. The points were piling up. "You murdered Melissa Capriella before you ever met me, Zeke. What was that about?" She held her breath. If he admitted to the one shooting, it would be enough. She'd turn the tape recorder off, try somehow to get out through the storm.

"First things first." McTeague rubbed his shoulder. "I wanna get the why of it out of the way, the general part. In case I don't live long enough to write the whole book."

FORTY-TWO

McTeague jammed his fingers into his shoulder, cupped the sharp bone, grabbed at the pain running in waves through the flesh of his right arm as if he could hold it off, apply a tourniquet for the nerves. But the pain kept right on coming, pushing through his chest, making the turn into his arm, hot, liquid, a fire in the blood. His hand dangled at the end of his arm like an anchor at the end of a chain.

"You all right, Zeke?"

For a moment, McTeague thought he could actually see the words, read them instead of hearing them. Patricia's voice seemed to float across the space between them. Then, without answering, he released his shoulder, groaned despite his best intentions as he fumbled a nitro tablet into his mouth, held it beneath his tongue, waited for the pain to subside.

It took longer than it should have, endless minutes with his eyes squeezed shut, thinking that Patricia hadn't repeated her question, that she was just sitting there, waiting to see what happened, wiling him to die. He knew he couldn't blame her, but it made him sad to think about it anyway. She was so wrong. What he offered wasn't a curse, it was a legacy. If he could make her see his life for what it was, maybe she'd come to his funeral, watch his coffin slide into the pit, drop a flower on his grave. That would be something, he figured. That would be a pure triumph.

He imagined her, years later, standing on the grass at the foot of his grave, head bowed in contemplation. A breeze flicks at the hem of her dress, a stray wisp of hair caught beneath the brim of her hat. She holds a white rose in a gloved hand, holds it high; the blossom rests against her lips. There is nobody else present, no minister, not even Gauss, the chief do-gooder. Only the bones in the boneyard, the rows of anonymous tombstones.

When McTeague finally opened his eyes, Patricia was sitting quietly, hands resting in her lap. Staring at him like he was a lab rat at the tail end of a failed experiment. "S'pose you was hopin'," McTeague said. "Hopin' to get off the hook."

Pat started to respond, then abruptly changed her mind. The bone and cartilage of McTeague's face had come forward, as if there was nothing left beneath his skin, neither muscle nor fat nor even blood, as if he'd consumed himself. She'd first seen that look in the nursing home where both her grandfather and grandmother had died. It had seemed to her then, as it seemed to her now, irreversible.

Still without speaking, she again stood, walked to the door. The ground outside, the little she could see of it, was already covered with several inches of snow. Worse, when she raised her eyes, the snowflakes hung before her like a curtain, reflecting the light coming over her shoulder, revealing nothing beyond. Even with the auxiliary fog lights on the Jeep, there was every chance that she'd drive off the side of the road, end up trapped in a ditch until the plow came through.

"I might be able to get us out of here." She was amazed at the even tone of her voice. At that moment, it seemed to her that she'd spent her entire adult life being practical. "And then again, I might not." She closed the door, turned to find McTeague with the tape recorder in his hands, thrusting it forward in a gesture that she, despite herself, found brave.

"Time's wastin', Patricia, and we got ourselves a long way to go." McTeague put the recorder on the table, waited with growing impatience while she banked the glowing logs in the stove, added wood, adjusted the flue. When she was finally sitting on the other side of the table, he tried to clear his throat, managed only a rattle that even he found ghastly. Still, he persisted.

"When I try to think about why it all happened, where it began," he said, not looking at her now, "it gets blurry. I know for a fact I killed Esther in my mind a thousand times. My old man, too. And I killed them boys that come up for Esther, killed 'em every way there is to kill somebody. In my mind." He paused to catch his breath. "But I never done nothin' real except warn Terry Bannister off one time."

"Was that why you chose Terry? Because you'd already dreamed it?" She picked up her mug, sipped at the cold tea. She would have to cook something later, feed herself, feed McTeague, play Earth Mother to McTeague's Doctor Death.

"Thing is, about them old days," McTeague ignored her question, "they could'a gone a lotta ways. I mean, things happen a little different, maybe I never do no more than run over a cat, slap my kids around. But when the army put that rifle in my hands, told me to pick my target, it was like I got introduced to myself, like a voice in my

brain said, 'Zeke McTeague, this here is Zeke Mc-
Teague.' " He leaned forward, tucked his hands, fingers
extended, between his knees. "Now the thing about it, Patricia, ain't nobody forced me to listen to that voice. The
army put it out there, give me a chance, but it was me who
went down the road. Way I see it, everybody got a time in
their life when they get to choose a road, and most of 'em,
what they do is take the easy way, do everything right and
proper, go off to the church every Sunday, have babies,
complain about the goddamned weather. Me, I done the
opposite. . . ."

McTeague's whispered voice droned on. She wondered,
as she waited for him to get down to specifics, if somewhere along the line, perhaps on one of those rare days
when he got to school, he'd been forced to read "The
Road Not Taken." But, no, it didn't seem possible, not
that long ago. Robert Frost would have been a young man
in the 1920's, his poetry unknown, even though he undoubtedly had white hair, wore plaid work shirts, red wool
jackets . . .

"Patricia? You there?"

"Sorry, I was drifting." The apology, the explanation,
came unbidden, and Detrick, as she watched McTeague
shake his head, watched his sunken lips frame a black
semicircle that she took for a frown, supposed that she was
a perfect example of McTeague's cowardly citizen. If it
wasn't from a sense of duty, a sense of obligation, how did
she get here? At any moment, she might have refused, with-
drawn, claimed the status of noncombatant. McTeague
had laid out his snares, but he hadn't forced her to step into
them; in fact, he would undoubtedly have applauded her
for avoiding the trap.

"I think you wanna pay attention, Patricia."

"The tape recorder's paying attention. That's what it's
there for." The temperature in the room was rising steadily
and she could feel a prickle of sweat bead on her scalp.

"Patricia?" McTeague could sense her resistance, see it
in her eyes; she was trying to run away. That was all right

with him. There wasn't any place to go. She'd proven that a minute ago when she opened the door.

"Just continue, Zeke."

A gust of wind shook the cabin as McTeague resumed his narrative. The wind rattled the windows, pushed a chill draft across the floor. A tendril wrapped his ankles, slid beneath the collar of his shirt. "Before the war come to an end, I had me enough kills to know that sittin' off at a distance, maybe a hundred, two hundred yards away, wasn't gonna cut it. So what I done, after the Germans surrendered, was get myself transferred to the MP's and volunteer to stay on. Patricia, there wasn't nothin' left to Berlin once the Russkies got done with it. Rubble and pieces of buildin's about to become rubble, no water, no electricity, no fuel. The *fräuleins* they'd do just about anything for food or something they could turn into food, cigarettes, chocolates, like that. Mostly all the young men were dead, so the *fräuleins* were on their own, them and their brats." He cleared his throat, this time managed to bring up some phlegm, swallowed it, then drank a little tea. "You know, live or die, nobody really gave a damn that first winter. Nobody was countin', keepin' score. In the American sector, the MP's were the police. There wasn't no one else to turn to."

"Just you, right? Uncle Zeke to the rescue?"

Again, McTeague ignored her. "That first time," he said, "I remember it like a woman remembers her first lover." He stopped, cocked his head, grinned at her. "I heard that once, read it someplace, that women never forget their first man. Is that true, Patricia?"

"You feeling better, Zeke? That what you're telling me here?"

"Guess I am, now you mention it." McTeague set the rocker in motion, turned his head away, gazed off at the door. "Won't say I wasn't scared that first time, Patricia. You can dream about somethin' all you want, but it ain't the same as doin' it. I was brave enough in my dreams, but when the time come, when I found some *fräulein* off by herself, I was scared enough to pee my pants. I'd wake up in the morning, tell myself, 'Today's the day, McTeague.' But come midnight, I'd be lyin' in my cot, still a virgin. Then, one night I got called to a barracks brawl on the other side of the city, a real bust-up, must'a been twenty-five GI's involved, tore the barracks all to pieces. After we put it together, got the scene under control, me and the boys snuck us a few drinks before I headed home."

McTeague closed his eyes, listened to the drone of his own voice; he called the night back to him.

It's cold in Berlin. Snowflakes dance in the arc of the Jeep's headlights; the Jeep's canvas top flaps in the wind like a crippled bird in a chimney. The roads have been cleared, but the lots are still heaped with rubble. Slabs of concrete lay across one another, held together by reinforcing rods and steel beams that protrude, in places, like the bones of some decaying animal. Here and there, a building remains standing, or a piece of a building, and McTeague knows there are people living behind the boarded widows, huddled around scrap metal stoves. In the daylight, they come out, the women and the kids, to pick apart the carcass of their city, scavenge for firewood, a torn blanket, a dented cooking pot. Occasionally—whether pulled by gravity or unbalanced by the work of the scavengers themselves McTeague doesn't know—the rubble shifts as the women work and traps them. McTeague has been called upon to supervise the rescue effort on several occasions. He enjoys the work.

McTeague is within a mile of the barracks when he sees a child standing by the side of the road a hundred yards ahead. He slows, wondering if he should pick the girl up, take her to a government shelter, knowing she might not survive the night if he doesn't. As he draws closer, however, the figure edges to the curb and McTeague realizes that his initial judgment was wrong. She is not a child at all, but a tiny, middle-aged woman, the years apparent in her lined face and the gaps in her smile. Her lips are painted a deep crimson, the blob of color a shocking contrast to her torn gray coat and shapeless black hat, her pale German skin. Still, her intentions are clear.

When the Jeep comes to a stop, the woman opens the door, hops in without permission. " 'Ello, soldier." She points to herself, says, "Inga."

McTeague takes a pint of bourbon from his coat pocket, offers it, watches her drink. He views her aggression as a sign, even though he realizes she's just a whore trying to get out of the cold, and he tells himself she's so small that she couldn't possibly escape him, couldn't possibly hurt him. Already, his erection strains against his trousers.

As he unzips his jacket, reaches for his wallet, withdraws a five-dollar bill, the woman stretches forth a tiny hand, frail as a sparrow, and grasps his penis. "Ja," she says, her head bobbing rapidly. "Ja, ja." Her hands, even through his uniform trousers and his underwear, McTeague thinks, are very cold. As cold as death.

She guides him as he drives, pointing left and right at intersections, repeating, "Ja, ja," as he makes the turns, finally directs him to the curb in front of a long, single-story brick warehouse. The western half of the building has collapsed and the lone window in the eastern half is covered with a sheet of battered plywood.

"Bring whiskey, okay, soldier?"

Again she smiles and McTeague can see her tongue behind the gaps in her teeth. He follows her inside, waits for her to light a candle, start a fire in the tin stove. The room is bare except for a mattress and a pile of blankets, a few pots on the floor by the stove. It smells of dust and mice, of flaking plaster and mold and cheap perfume. Finally, her task completed, the woman turns to face him. She takes off her coat to reveal a blue, summer-weight dress that falls to the tops of her knees.

"Lie down," McTeague says. His voice, as he hears it, is choked with fear. He feels as if he has something caught in *his throat, a sharp, unyielding object that he's afraid to cough up. Still, when she doesn't respond, he gives her a little push, repeats, "Lie down."*

"Ja." The woman nods to herself, finally drops to the mattress, rolls onto her back. She pulls the hem of her skirt to her waist; her crimson smile, as cold as the air in the room, leers up at him. "Fic-fic," she calmly announces before drawing her legs apart, raising her hips. "Ja."

A rush of sound, a roar, fills McTeague's ears as he falls to his knees. When he takes her throat in both hands, her watery blue eyes widen and her hands grip his wrists. But she doesn't really fight him until the very end, until, finally, her body thrashes beneath him, passionate at last.

That night he sleeps as he's never slept before.

FORTY-THREE

"I run outta there so fast, Patricia, that I left that damn bottle with my fingerprints on the glass. Didn't remember about it till the next day after reveille." McTeague opened his eyes to find Detrick up and pacing. He, himself, felt calm, oddly peaceful. For a moment, he wondered what he'd said to upset her. Then he chuckled. "Them first few weeks, I felt like any minute I'd be arrested, that one of my MP buddies would put a hand on my shoulder, lead me off to the stockade. But you know what, Patricia? Nobody ever come. In fact, far as I can tell, nobody even cared. That's when I learned there's women in the world that the world don't want. What do you think of that?"

She turned on him in a fury. "Life wants life," she spat. "Everybody counts."

"That include me?"

"That includes . . ." Pat started to answer, then changed her mind. Instead, she plucked a photo from the top corner of McTeague's trophy wall. "I want you to give them names," she demanded.

McTeague's eyebrows shot up. "You mean a decent Christian burial wasn't enough?"

She stared at the blinking red light on the tape recorder, found herself craving the machine's indifference. She thought of Morello, remembered how casually, how proudly, he'd added the word *homicide* to the word *detective*. As if there were no price to pay.

"Just get to it, Zeke. Remember, it's your legacy."

McTeague held the photo at arm's length, nodded. "I recall this one. Honey-Bee Sue-Ellen Prescott from Fracsville, West Virginia. She went too quick to suit me." His eyes met Patricia's. "By then I had me some experience. Enough to be sure that slow is better."

"I want the names and the places," she said. "I want to know if all the dates are accurate. I don't want to hear what you did to them."

"Devil in the details, is it?"

She took a step toward McTeague, glared down at him. "You got me here, Zeke. It was your doing. Now, let's get it finished."

"And what you gonna do, Patricia? If I wanna take my time? You gonna take out that little toy gun and shoot me?" McTeague scratched the stubble on his chin, examined his fingernails. "Be a hell of a turnaround, wouldn't it? A *woman* killing Zeke McTeague?"

"You're sure that I won't?" Detrick, as she turned away, again saw the figure in the snow, saw the upraised hand. She found herself wondering how hard he'd resist. If she grabbed his arm, yanked him upright, began to drag him toward the door. "You want to live," she said, her voice so soft she might have been speaking to herself. "If you really thought I was going to kill you, you'd beg for your life." When McTeague didn't respond, Detrick, her voice still a near whisper as she chased the idea rolling through her mind, continued. "All this business about not going to the hospital, no telephone in the house. There wasn't a drop of truth to it, was there? You don't want to die."

She was looking directly into his eyes now, past the dusty reflections on the surface of his glasses, beyond the half-formed tears on his lower lids, the streaking red veins. "What do you have in mind for the future, Zeke, courtesy of the State of Pennsylvania? Angioplasty? A bypass? Maybe a heart transplant?"

McTeague's lips tightened. He closed his eyes, started to turn away, but when Detrick gripped his jaw, he offered no resistance.

"Would you beg, Zeke? If I dragged you out into the snow would you *beg* for your life?" For the first time, she saw the rage simmering just below the flat brown surface of McTeague's eyes. His anger seemed to her, at that moment, all encompassing, his effort to conceal it monumental. "Would you take a chance, run the risk? I mean, a do-gooder like me would never leave you to die in the snow, right?" She grabbed McTeague's arm, pulled him to his feet. He seemed almost weightless.

"Enough, Patricia." McTeague let himself go limp, waited patiently for her fury to subside. He won. When she dropped him back into the chair, he looked up at her, said, "Guess you got it right. If you put me to the test, I'm gonna beg for my life. Score one for you."

She stepped away, drew a shuddering breath. Though she knew the answer, she couldn't stop herself from asking the question. "If you love your own life, how could you have taken life from someone who never harmed you in any way?"

"You missed the whole damn point," McTeague said. His voice betrayed no emotion. "First I done it because the army told me to. Then I done it because I had to." He snorted contemptuously, made no effort, now that he was safe, to conceal the anger rolling through every cell in his body. "Then I done it because I liked to."

It was as if she'd reached a plateau and, bone weary, needed to rest, to gather her strength. Later, she would remember little of McTeague's narrative. She fetched for him, carried the old photographs to his chair, laid them in his hands, returned them after he was finished. Whenever the tape recorder shut down, she flipped or replaced the cassette; new tapes were precisely labeled, full cassettes returned to their plastic cases, the cases dropped into her bag.

Detrick handled these objects delicately, pulled the photos from the wall with her fingertips, held the pen so lightly that at one point it dropped from her fingers to rattle on the table. She carried that same delicacy into her other tasks: as she tended the fire, as she prepared and served a meal of fried eggs and chili, buttered white bread and canned string beans, as she washed the dishes, placed them in the drain beside the sink. Through it all, McTeague's voice droned on, his tone calm and measured, as if he, too, was conserving his strength. She was aware of McTeague's voice, as she was equally aware of the steady moan of the wind over the eaves, the sharper hiss of the wind through the white pines behind the house, the roll of snow-muffled thunder in the distance.

It was just after ten o'clock and she was standing in front of the sink, wiping her hands on a towel, when, for no reason apparent to her, she recalled a long-forgotten quotation from the Book of Genesis. *This is the book of the generations of Adam.* She tried to visualize the rest of the verse, a favorite trick to jar her memory, but the words refused to come. Instead, she remembered a second phrase: *Now these are the generations of the sons of Noah, Shem, Ham, and . . .* The name of the last son eluded her, but she knew that a chronicle of the Hebrew people followed each verse, that the author spoke of life flowing into life, stubborn, unrelenting. Just as McTeague spoke of death flowing into death, of blood demanding blood, of a line that rippled through shadow, that persisted equally, that would in no way be affected by the arrest of Zeke McTeague.

"Zeke?"

McTeague looked up at her as if trying to place her voice. He took off his glasses, wiped his eyes with the back of his sleeve. "I was just gettin' goin.'" His voice sounded vaguely apologetic.

She glanced at the wall of photographs, was surprised to find that McTeague was nearly a third of the way through them. "I want to know if anyone ever escaped."

"Depends on how you look at it." McTeague laid the photo he was holding carefully on the table. He stared at it before turning to face her. "The first rule was not to get caught." He shook his head. "Meant, for a fact, that I had to control myself, had to pass on by if things wasn't quite right. From time to time, I had a woman in the cab looked like trouble, like she maybe had a gun or a knife in her bag. When that happened what I did was put her off at the nearest truck stop. Made sure there was plenty of folks around when I did it, too." He settled himself against the back of the rocker, stretched his legs. "As for the rest of 'em . . . see, what I done was keep a hammer in the pocket on the door next to me, a tack hammer like an upholsterer would use. Course, I wouldn't show it right away. No, what I'd do, if I had me a whore for company, I'd do a little grabbin', talk about what kinda games we was gonna play when we settled down for the night. If I had me a hitchhiker, I'd keep my hands to myself, flash 'em a sweetheart smile, play the radio. Sooner or later, unless folks been goin' over the road pretty regular, they get tired in a truck, start to drift." He grinned up at Pat, touched the center of his forehead with a grooved, yellow fingernail. "Thing about it, Patricia, is when you make your move, you got to make it hard and fast, right smack in the middle, no hesitation. You bring it off just right, you own 'em."

"And if you don't?" She looked down at her hands, found her fingers wrapped in the dish towel. "If you didn't?"

McTeague laughed. "Had a woman, one time, she jumped right out through the door. We was goin' about sixty at the time. Never did find out what happened to her." His face turned suddenly grave. "Funny thing about it is no cop ever come askin' questions. Not once, in all them years. It's like I was protected, like somethin' was watchin' out for me." He tapped his knee for emphasis. "Tell you for a fact, I ain't never believed in no god, no Jesus, nothin' like that. But there's times when the desire comes on me so hard and so quick I feel like I'm standin' out in a Texas hailstorm. Like somethin' inside me is callin' the tune. Somethin' inside me that isn't me."

He wanted to tell her about the trickiest part, getting his girls into the sleeping compartment behind the cab, tying them down, taping their mouths shut, doing all of it without being seen by anybody else and while they were still strong. By comparison, the disposals were much, much easier—a short hike in the woods, a few minutes with a spade if the earth was soft, or a thicket by a river if the ground was too rocky or frozen. One time, he'd left a hitchhiker named Lena Lennison sitting in a rocker on some farmer's porch. A thousand miles from where he'd picked her up.

"I'm tired," McTeague finally admitted. "Think I need me some sleep." Though he tried to control it, to resign himself, his voice, a whisper really, carried a measure of regret. This wasn't the way it was supposed to go, not the way he'd dreamed it, but now that he was here it all made sense. He'd imagined that he could do with words what he'd done with knives and hammers. He had underestimated the strength of Patricia Detrick. It was too bad really, because he could almost smell her blood.

"I want you to talk about Terry Bannister and Melissa Capriella first," she said.

"You figurin' I might not wake up?" McTeague read the answer in her eyes, the way her hand fluttered up to cover her mouth.

"I don't want to take the chance," she told him. "I don't think it matters very much any more. To you, I mean."

McTeague shrugged. "Sounds about right." He settled himself in the rocker, crossed his legs. "Sure, I done 'em. Figured I was makin' like Custer's last stand. Keep on fightin' till the cops caught up with me. Then you come along and that changed things considerable." He let his eyes close for a moment, felt sleep beckon, finally repeated, "I'm tired, Patricia."

"Just a few minutes more, Zeke, and you can rest." It was a lie, she thought, of the sort that Morello might tell in the course of an interrogation.

She began by having McTeague describe the disabling of his pickup, where he'd hidden the rifle and the other incriminating evidence. Then she shifted to the attack on Melissa Capriella, the first attack, and slowly worked forward, through the wounding of Alicia Munoz and the murder of Terry Bannister, before an exhausted McTeague begged off. "Ain't no point in this, Patricia. Even a damn fool like that blondie trooper could figure this one out." When she didn't immediately respond, he added wearily, "We could always get back to it later."

"Okay, Zeke. Give me another five minutes and I'll put you to bed." Detrick shut down the recorder, then got up and began to search the house for hidden weapons, the living room and kitchen first, then the bedroom. Though her search was thorough and systematic, her mind continued to drift. Instead of concentrating on what she'd achieved, maybe raising a self-congratulatory mental toast, she picked at what was missing, the puzzle piece called justice which had apparently been left out of the box.

All along, she'd been expecting some . . . She searched for a word, finally settled on *catharsis*. The intimate de-

tails, the revelations, the horrors, were supposed to have
torn her apart; they should have been transforming. Meanwhile, the only thing she was sure she felt was vaguely un-
easy. As if there was something she hadn't done, some
challenge she'd failed to meet. As if, just maybe, she'd
missed the whole point.

McTeague was asleep in the rocker when Detrick concluded her search by taking all the cutlery from a drawer
near the sink. She looked around the cabin for a moment,
then walked to the front door. With both hands full, she
had a difficult time working the knob, but she finally managed to give it a half-turn, only to find the door's outward
swing blocked by snow. With a sigh, a shake of her head,
she jammed her shoulder against the wood and forced the
door open.

Although snow continued to fall thickly, the air surrounding McTeague's cabin was eerily still. The wind had
vanished, but the silence, as she tossed the silverware up
and out, struck her as overwhelmingly violent, in no way
an indication that the storm was drawing down, but only
a pause while it gathered strength. As if to confirm her
judgment, a bolt of lightning ran straight across the sky,
from cloud to cloud. It brought Zeke McTeague's little
yard into sharp relief. The spidery black trees, the low
barn with its pale sagging roof, a glistening peaked ocean
of snow that barely covered the windswept driveway yet
rose in a long undulating drift against the house.

McTeague was still asleep. His head was lying on his
left shoulder and a drop of saliva bubbled in the corner of
his mouth.

"Zeke? Do you want to get into bed?"

McTeague opened his eyes to find Patricia walking
toward him, shoulders square, her stride firm and bal-
anced. He recalled one of his first impressions of her, that
she would have been at home on a farm, that a hundred
years ago she would have pulled a plow if that's what it
took to get a crop into the ground. "Guess so, Patricia."

He tried to push himself up, failed, made a second, more determined attempt that barely got his buttocks off the seat of the rocker. "Looks like I need me some help," he finally admitted.

She offered her right hand, felt McTeague's cold fingers close around her palm, found his touch utterly repulsive. As soon as she got him to his feet, she let go, leaving him to stand or fall on his own. "You can handle this?"

McTeague responded by shuffling forward. He was free of pain now, his body not up to even that small effort. When he reached the bed, saw the piled sheets and blankets on the mattress, he pulled up short, drew his hands into his chest. He felt Patricia's eyes on the back of his head, smelled, faintly, the odor of coffee on her breath as her fingers settled on his shoulder, urged him ahead.

"Just a few steps, Zeke." Again she was repulsed by the touch of his flesh. Still, she continued to guide the old man forward and when he couldn't do more than sit on the edge of the mattress, she lifted his feet onto the mattress, lowered his head onto the pillow.

I'm done now, she thought as she stood erect. *I've done my duty.*

She was about to turn away, perhaps make herself a cup of tea, when McTeague, after a sharp dry cough like the snap of a branch, abruptly stopped breathing.

Detrick, as she'd been trained to do, put her fingertips to his throat, took the carotid pulse, finally told herself, *His heart is still beating.* Then, before she could form another thought, McTeague's eyes opened wide. They made a single terrified circuit of the room before settling on hers. His voice, when he spoke, was so soft it might have been no more than a final exhalation, yet Detrick heard the words clearly. "Esther," he whispered. "Esther, help me."

Pat's head jerked back as if to avoid a blow, as if she could avoid the words themselves, as if she could avoid her next thought: *Let him die.*

McTeague's face was as dingy as the sheet beneath his

head, his lips a darkening purple. As she watched, unable to move, his fingers curled into his palms, his back arched, forcing his chest away from the mattress. Finally, his brown eyes turned briefly inward before snapping shut.

Again, Detrick heard the command: Let him die.

It won't take very long, she told herself, won't amount to more than a lazy nap on a snowy afternoon. Far, far less than he deserves. And you don't have to do anything; you don't even have to watch. If you walk away, make yourself that cup of tea? By the time you inhale the rising steam, squeeze a few drops of lemon into the cup, it'll be all over. Later, maybe tomorrow night, maybe next week, you can make a postcoital confession to Rick Morello. You can make your lover proud.

As she dropped to her knees, tilted McTeague's head sharply backward, cleared the mucus from his throat, as she pinched his nostrils closed, fitted her lips over his mouth, blew her own breath down into his lungs, Patricia Detrick recalled the image she'd held so clearly a few long hours before. She saw McTeague lying in the snow, led to his death, another object to check the wind, saw his arm extended up and out, the supplicant rejected. How dramatic it had been, how utterly trivial. Her life, she knew, would begin from this point, the course of it determined by what she did here. And she would not live a trivial life.

When she awakened, hours later, the sun had long ago risen. Although a gusting wind howled in the white pines alongside the house, the ragged cloud cover was torn by shafts of dazzling sunlight. The storm was over and yet the air was heavy with drifting snow. It chattered on the windowpanes, sounding, to her, like the gnawing of mice in the cabin's walls.

McTeague was sitting in his rocker. His lips, when he realized she was awake, spread to form an infant's toothless smile. "Still kickin'," he said. "Thanks to you."

"You should have stayed in bed, Zeke. The plow'll come by any time now."

"Won't be quick enough to help you none." McTeague raised his right hand, pointed the little Seecamp .32 at her chest. "Nice of you to bring this along. Don't think I could manage nothin' more strenuous."

"Does it make you happy? To have me like this?" Her voice carried no emotion beyond plain curiosity.

"Not as much as I want it to," McTeague admitted. "Seems like the last thing you do in your life oughta feel a damn sight better." He tried to nod, but even that effort was beyond his abilities. His body felt dead, all of it except for his tongue and his lips and his fingers wrapped around the small pistol. It was a miracle that he'd gotten from his bed into the chair, that he'd found the strength to take the gun from the table.

Suddenly angry at Patricia's stubborn composure, McTeague said, "You think you know it all, right? College-educated woman like yourself, you think you got old Zeke figured out entirely. But old Zeke's still got a trick up his sleeve. You remember old Florence Clark?" His voice broke on the last word. It crackled like dry leaves in a stiff wind.

"Yes, I remember."

"Well, I never done her. Nope. I was in a big hurry that day, what with the preacher's wife and dumpin' the evidence. Didn't have the energy to be shootin' no strangers." McTeague paused long enough to absorb the expression on Patricia's face. He'd expected, if not anger, at least repulsion or fear, but her features remained impossibly composed. As if he was simply playing into her hands. "You don't believe me?" he finally demanded.

"Why you didn't tell me this before? When the tape was running?"

McTeague dropped the gun to his lap and shook his head. "Never could abide a rat. Besides which I know I'm goin' out. One way or the other." He picked up the gun and looked at it. "These here tapes, I mean 'em to inspire the next generation. Way I see it, there's a fair chance that

Poole could make the jump. You know, from profit to pleasure."

"And you're certain that Coleman Poole shot Florence Clark?" Detrick sat up straight in the chair. It was time to get this finished.

"Don't know nothin' of the kind. Just seems like he's a mean sunnabitch and he had a good reason." McTeague tried and failed to clear the phlegm from his throat. "What I do know is that I didn't go nowheres near that Clark woman." He waved the gun in her direction, said, "If I was gonna lie about it, I wouldn't have waited. I would'a put it down on the tape."

"But you did lie on the tape. If you're telling the truth now, then you lied on the tape."

McTeague snorted. If she didn't believe him? Well, not only didn't he have the energy to convince her, it didn't matter all that much anyway. "Only reason I'm tellin' you now is because you won't be tellin' nobody else."

Pat thought of what Morello had said about Rose D'Angelo, Coleman Poole's lover, that she might be telling the truth about Poole's alibi and that she might not. There was just no way to know for sure. She felt suddenly tired. "I guess you tricked me," she said. "All this time I've been worrying about Coleman Poole. I've been thinking he's a scapegoat, just somebody to take the pressure off the police and the politicians. Now I have to deal with the possibility that he's a murderer. And I'm helping to set him free." It was cold in the room, the fire in the wood stove undoubtedly reduced to a few glowing coals. If she hurried, she knew, she could lay newspaper and kindling over the coals, tease the fire back to life. Otherwise, she would have to start from the beginning.

"Yeah, that's right, I tricked you." McTeague's jaw was slack, his open mouth a black hole in his face. His laughter was soundless. "Guess I gotta take the shame."

"That's right. Trick me once, shame on you. Trick me twice, shame on me." Detrick slowly extended her right hand, palm up, toward McTeague; the movement struck her as sensual, even languid, a gesture appropriate to a southern belle on a hot summer's day. Nevertheless, her voice when she finally spoke was as cold as the howling wind outside the little cabin. "But the joke's on you, Zeke. The joke and the shame and the trick. Because the gun's not loaded. It was never loaded."

FORTY-FOUR

When Coleman Poole's attorney, Susan Brandt, having just secured a dismissal of all pending charges against her client, emerged from the Wayne County Courthouse, the mass of reporters clustered at the bottom of the steps raised their cameras and microphones as if offering a toast. Brandt, a smile playing at the corners of her mouth, came to a full stop at the sight, trapping Poole in the doorway. Poole, his face barely visible above his lawyer's shoulder, started to push by, then, seeing the mob below, he, too, broke into a smile. Finally, as if reacting to an offstage cue, the pair began their descent.

"Like royalty," Donny Barrett muttered to Morello and

Patricia Detrick, who stood beside him on the sidewalk. "Like this is what it was all about from the beginning."

Neither responded, although Morello's hand tightened on Detrick's arm. It was bitterly cold; the sun for all its brilliance seemed, to Pat, without energy. On the horizon, a few small clouds drifted beneath a painfully blue sky; directly before her, a halo of frost surrounded the heads of the reporters, as if all were exhaling from a single pair of lungs.

"You'll be next," Barrett declared to Pat Detrick. "Better try to pick up a few pointers." Then he turned, added, "Excuse me, I have to go puke," before walking away.

She looked up at Morello, found his features composed, his thoughts hidden. He'd had that same look on his face as he pushed through the snowdrifts covering McTeague's driveway three days before, a clownish hero in a long black overcoat and shiny rubbers. By then, McTeague had been dead for hours; by then Detrick had arranged McTeague's corpse on the floor beside his rocker, had closed his eyes, covered his body with a brown woolen blanket.

"At long last this monstrous farce has been brought to an end," Susan Brandt said to a small forest of microphones when she'd reached the bottom of the steps. "And while the prosecution must be credited for promptly bringing Ezekiel McTeague's confession to the attention of the court, this rush to justice would not have occurred in the first place had the police not been so anxious to find a scapegoat."

Detrick started to turn, only to find herself held fast by the grip of Morello's hand. "You want to leave?" he asked, obviously surprised. It'd been she who'd insisted they come.

"No, no. It's just hard to hear."

"I know what you mean." Morello let go of her arm and slid his hands into his coat pockets. The movement was very precise, as if he had practiced before coming out. "One goes down, another comes up. Back in my cop days, when I was a cynic, I used to tell the boys it was good for business. Especially after I had a few beers."

Donny Barrett had spent the better part of six hours poring over the tapes supplied by Detrick on the afternoon following McTeague's death, growing more and more angry as the truth became more and more apparent. Finally, when Detrick described McTeague's little joke, his final trick, Barrett had come off the chair. If Morello hadn't been been there, Pat was certain that the trooper would have struck her.

Later, with the County Prosecutor, James Carringford, present, a still-smoldering Barrett had argued that with McTeague now dead, the tapes should not be turned over to the defense until the details of his confession had been verified. "I mean, what is he saying here? 'I snuck up through the woods; I took aim; I shot somebody.' It doesn't amount to a hill of—" He'd taken a quick glance at Detrick before finishing the sentence. "—a hill of shit."

Initially, Carringford had gone along, but the next morning, two different trooper search teams, bearing evidence gathered in Promised Land State Park and the woods behind McTeague's cabin, had returned to the barracks within fifteen minutes of each other. They had McTeague's rifle, his license plate, the air pump he'd used to get the little truck up and running.

"The state accused Coleman Poole of mass murder," Brandt told the reporters. She was a small, notoriously feisty woman who usually practiced in the nearby city of Scranton. "On no physical evidence whatever." Her gloved hand slashed the air. "They ignored Coleman Poole's alibi, dismissed it out of hand, while they clung to the vicious lies of a jailhouse informant. They vilified him in their public statements, leaked bits and pieces of a so-called confession, demanded, actually *demanded,* the death penalty. All without a single piece of incriminating evidence."

Morello shifted his weight, muttered, "I've got to buy a pair of insulated boots. My toes feel like frozen fish sticks." Detrick, too, felt restless. She knew she was looking for completion here, knew also that she would find just the opposite. Twenty feet away, Coleman Poole, his hair freshly cut, his egg-shaped body stuffed into an overcoat a size too small, blew into his cupped palms. Though his ears and his tiny nose were bright red, he remained expressionless.

"Do you intend to file a lawsuit against the county?" a reporter holding a WBRE microphone demanded of Poole when Susan Brandt paused long enough to draw a breath.

"Mr. Poole is considering the possibility of litigation," Brandt announced before her client could reply. "But whether or not he goes forward, make no mistake, we consider the police and the Wayne County prosecutor's office responsible for this travesty of justice."

Carringford had reacted to the physical evidence in the only way possible. The prosecutor had those portions of McTeague's confession dealing with the local attacks transcribed and forwarded to Susan Brandt along with a note declaring that the state would not oppose a motion to dismiss. Though Detrick's name had been left out of it, her reprieve, according to Barrett, would be decidedly temporary.

"We have to pass the tapes along to the jurisdictions involved in the various killings. Probably clear a couple of dozen homicides in the process. The bad news, for you, is that the passing part is going to come from the Attorney General's office in Harrisburg. They have no reason to protect you down there." Barrett flashed an angry smile from behind his desk before adding, "Of course, if you're in a hurry for your fifteen minutes of fame, I could leak the tapes this afternoon."

Detrick, who had already had an appointment with Elmer Crown, an appointment she felt obliged to keep, had taken the news calmly. "And what about Coleman Poole?" she'd asked. "Does he just walk away?"

She'd asked Morello the same question over dinner on the prior evening. His answer had been so similar to what Barrett now told her that she was forced to accept it. Even if McTeague had been telling the truth about the murder of Florence Clark, and there was no way to know that, it didn't mean Coleman Poole was guilty. The only real evidence against him was an alleged confession to a jailhouse snitch in which Poole claimed responsibility for all the attacks, a confession now clearly discredited.

"Rose D'Angelo has the answer," Morello had insisted. "If she's lying, then Poole set up his alibi before his arrest. I don't think he would have done that if he hadn't killed his aunt."

Barrett had added, "I went out to see D'Angelo yesterday. She basically told me to go—to drop dead."

"Mr. Poole, are you bitter about your arrest?"

The inevitable question came from a woman Detrick failed to recognize, one of a dozen reporters from New York and Philadelphia who'd been assigned to cover the finale of the Pocono Sniper killings.

Though his head remained still, Poole swept the crowd with his eyes. The rumor, as reported in the *Pocono Record*, was that he'd already hired an agent, that his agent had already cut deals with *The Star* and *Hard Copy*.

"I'm happy to be outta jail," Poole declared. Then, after a nudge from Susan Brandt, he added, "I just wanna get my life back together, have a decent meal, a decent night's sleep without a death sentence hangin' over my head. This has been a terrible experience for me."

Detrick shoved her hand into Morello's pocket and curled her fingers around his. "I'm beginning to enjoy this." She waited for him to turn, to meet her eyes. "The questions, the little speeches—it has the feel of ritual."

"Yeah, well, life goes on." Morello, his shoulders hunched, leaned toward her. "And it doesn't get any prettier."

Despite her apprehensions, Patricia Detrick had gone to see Rose D'Angelo. That, too, had seemed an obligation. Although without credentials of any kind, neither cop nor reporter, Pat couldn't imagine why D'Angelo, holed up in a dilapidated trailer park near the town of Moscow, would speak to her. In the days after Coleman Poole's arrest, a dozen reporters had come out to the Summer Breeze Trailer Park in search of an interview. None had been successful.

D'Angelo had been outside shoveling snow when Detrick made her way along the narrow lane running through the park. She was a tall, raw-boned woman with a yellow-green bruise covering the right side of her face from cheek to jaw. Gloveless despite the intense cold, her knuckles where they gripped the shovel had been red enough to draw Detrick's attention as she pulled to the curb.

For the next several minutes, Pat, as if preparing for a quick escape, had remained behind the wheel. Then D'Angelo, still gripping the shovel with both hands, had walked to the edge of her property and fixed her with a hard stare.

"Bitch," she'd declared, "you come outta that car, I'm gonna bury this shovel in your goddamned skull."

She had searched D'Angelo's eyes for some glimmer of the truth. She'd found, instead, a rage that defied further investigation. After a moment, she'd put the Jeep in gear and driven away.

The crowd of reporters fronting the courthouse began to drift off. That, too, seemed, to Pat, part of the ritual.

She watched their collective breath separate into a dozen individual streams as they slid into the vans lining the far side of the street, and felt an incongruous satisfaction settle over her.

"I think," she told Morello, "that's it's actually going to be finished."

"In spite of Florence Clark?" Morello asked. "In spite of what's going to happen when your name's made public?"

"No, not in that sense." She removed her hand from Morello's pocket. She drew the hood of her parka down over her forehead. Despite the parka and the heavy wool sweater beneath it, the cold was beginning to penetrate her chest. "But I don't feel smaller now. Even though I can't control what's happening."

"In prison they say, What doesn't kill me makes me stronger. Is that what it's about?"

"Something like that."

Poole and Brandt, as if waiting for the reporters to change their minds, to return, stood alone for a moment. Then a red van, a commercial model with no windows in the rear, pulled to a stop in front of the courthouse. Rose D'Angelo was behind the wheel. And though she looked directly at Patricia Detrick, her steady gaze betrayed no sign of recognition.

Poole and Brandt turned to face each other. They shook hands and smiled broadly. Then Brandt turned back to the courthouse and Poole made his way to the waiting van and Rose D'Angelo.

On a sun-drenched ledge above the courthouse entrance, a line of pigeons stirred briefly before diving into the icy wind. The birds glided down along the steps, straight toward Morello and Detrick, then wheeled up and away. As they rose, the sun briefly illuminated their furiously beating wings.

"How do they know to turn that way?" Morello asked. "All at once. It's as if they're all connected to the same pigeon brain."

"The pigeons stay in formation because of the hawks."

Detrick waited for Morello to nod, then added, "The larger hawks, the broad-wings and red-tails and the harriers, take pigeons in the air."

"In that case, Patricia," Morello said as he took her arm and led her away, "it's a wonder the pigeons find the courage to fly at all."

ABOUT THE AUTHOR

Stephen Solomita is the author of ten published novels, including the acclaimed Stanley Moodrow series. A native New Yorker, he currently divides his time between New York and the Pocono plateau in northeastern Pennsylvania.

From master of suspense

Stephen Solomita

comes another edge-of-your-seat thriller—
when a killer targets the most prominent citizens
of a small Poconos town, one by one—
and none of them are talking,
even to save their lives

Coming in August 1999 from Bantam Books

Read on for a sneak preview of the text . . .

As Clarry Neumark was escorted to her table by an unsmiling maître d', she could feel the appraising glances of the diners in the Rockdale Country Club's Oak Room skitter across her face and body like Japanese beetles over the leaves and petals of a blossoming rose. The Oak Room was not only the most expensive restaurant on the Pocono plateau in northeastern Pennsylvania, its clientele was strictly limited to Rockdale members and their favored guests. Apparent in the eyes of the Oak Room's patrons was the sad fact that Clarry Neumark, obviously not a member, didn't really qualify as a guest either. Nevertheless, Clarry swept across the room with her shoulders held wide, her step firm, her expression serene. She'd already been run through the mill when she'd changed from her uniform into the black wool dress she now wore, then tottered through the Swiftwater State Trooper barracks on unfamiliar three-inch heels. One trooper, a female who couldn't readily be accused of sexual harassment, had brought down the house with a single comment.

"Hey, Clarry, don't tell me you caught the hooker patrol tonight."

On the other side of the room, James Leacock rose to his full height, well over six feet, and favored Clarry with a broad smile. Nearly ten years Clarry's senior, Leacock was an excessively handsome man with a wide brow and sharp black eyebrows that angled down to graze the corners of his blue eyes. His nose was straight and firm, his mouth generous, his jaw prominent without being assertive. His full head of light brown hair, just beginning to gray at the temples, looked as if it had been molded instead of cut.

"Clarry . . ." Leacock reached out to momentarily squeeze her hand.

"Sorry I'm late." Clarry waited for the maître d' to pull her chair out, then smoothed the back of her dress as she sat. "I got hung up in Clark Summit." A Pennsylvania State Trooper for nearly ten years, Clarry had been appointed to the Bureau of Criminal Investigation's forensic unit a year before and assigned to gather evidence at crime and accident scenes. "It was unavoidable."

His smile narrowing but still prominent, Leacock nodded judiciously as a busboy arrived to fill Clarry's water goblet. The goblet was crystal, as were the wineglasses and the polished facets of the enormous chandelier hanging from the ceiling overhead.

Having decided not to be the first to speak, Clarry fixed her eyes on the polished surface of a silver bud vase set in the exact center of the table. She'd come to put an end to their relationship, a goal in her estimation best postponed until the end of the meal, her first at the Oak Room.

After the busboy withdrew, Leacock slid a bottle of white wine from a silver ice bucket, then displayed the label for Clarry's inspection. Clarry dutifully read, *Domaine Michelot Buisson*.

The words meant nothing to her and she wondered, as she'd been wondering almost from the day she'd met Jimmy Leacock, what it was about him that had attracted her in the first place. Clarry hadn't heard from Leacock in more than a month, had been surprised when he'd called to invite her to dinner. On one level she'd been hoping he'd just vanish; on another she'd been thoroughly pissed. Although she'd come to think of the womanizing Jimmy Leacock as Peter Pan with an erection, she was stung at being unceremoniously dumped.

They made small talk throughout the meal, occasionally lapsing into silence as they ate. Clarry had a second glass of wine with her chicken Kiev and rosemary potatoes, then accepted Leacock's offer of a brandy with her coffee. When the waiter served the

Hennessy a few minutes later, she followed Leacock's lead, raising the snifter to let the fragrance rise into her brain as she rotated the snifter between her fingers. As usual, it smelled like paint thinner to her.

"Well, I guess it's time to get down to business," Clarry squared her shoulders, raised her chin until she was looking directly into Leacock's eyes. She was nearly five ten and a hundred and forty pounds, with a square face and light brown eyes spread far enough apart to be noticeable. As a cop, she'd learned to use those eyes, to drill them into the eyes of belligerent civilians as if she meant to tunnel through to the other side.

It didn't always work, of course, as it wasn't working now with Jimmy Leacock, who was smiling and shaking his head. "I hate that look," he observed. "I always expect it to be followed by a right cross."

"If telling you that I don't want to see you again is the psychological equivalent of a punch in the mouth, consider yourself knocked out."

Her message delivered, Clarry leaned back in her chair and finally relaxed. Thirty-two years old and single, she'd only had six lovers in her life, including Leacock, and this was her first formal good-bye.

The right corner of Leacock's mouth jerked slightly and his expression hardened for a moment. He said, "I think we both know that whatever we had for each other is gone." Then he raised his brandy snifter in a toast. "To us. Individually, if not collectively."

Clarry sipped at her brandy, swallowed, waited for the predictable heat to rise into her throat. It wasn't possible to catch Jimmy Leacock off guard. She'd known that going in, but was still glad that she'd made her point as firmly as possible. "If it's over and been over," she observed, "then why did you insist on this dinner?"

Leacock took a moment to consider the question. His best quality, in Clarry's opinion, was that whenever they were together he always gave her his full attention. As if she was the most important thing in his world. And most likely, until he moved on to his next conquest, she was.

"I didn't think," he finally said, "that you'd come to hate me."

"One thing about you, Jimmy, you never waste your time. So why don't you move the show forward by answering my question?"

Finally, he showed a flash of annoyance. "You're a very literal woman, Clarry," he said.

"It's a cop thing, Jimmy. And if I remember right, it used to turn you on."

Leacock shrugged his shoulders, then flashed a sheepish grin. "Would you consider the possibility . . ." He raised a hand defensively. "The *remote* possibility that I asked you here because I think a lot of you and wanted to do something nice for you?"

It was Clarry's turn to appear sheepish and she bit the bullet with characteristic fortitude. "As a matter of fact," she admitted, "I didn't."

"Clarry, have you heard about the DRP?"

"Pardon?"

"The Delaware Regional Police Department."

"Oh, right. Some townships in Monroe County

are trying to organize a police force. There's been talk about it at the barracks."

"Four townships. Delaware, Jefferson, Butler, and Pocono Falls. It's a done deal."

Clarry straightened to allow the waiter to set a parfait dish of hot cherry cobbler topped with vanilla ice cream on the table. As Leacock's dessert was served, Clarry noted that his side of the tablecloth was immaculate while, as usual, hers was thoroughly stained. There were times in her relationship when she'd longed to see a bit of spinach caught between her lover's teeth, a drop of gravy on his shirt. It hadn't happened, she decided, because Jimmy Leacock would never suffer the loss of control.

"So what's it got to do with me?" she asked. "The Delaware Regional Police."

"The department is in the hiring stage and they're looking for a detective." Leacock picked up his tea-spoon and dipped it into the ice cream. "They've already signed a man up, a retired New York cop named Grogan. He had an edge because he grew up in the region."

"That what it's gonna be? Two detectives?"

Leacock shrugged, said, "It's a small department," then began to work his way through the ice cream to the cherry cobbler below.

"I heard the pay is less than I'm making with the state."

"True enough. But you won't have to worry about shifting Peter to a new school every couple of years."

Clarry nodded agreement, then turned to her

dessert. Her thirteen-year-old son, who'd attended four different schools in the last seven years, was rapidly entering adolescence, perilous time under the best of conditions. Meanwhile, pursuing a policy designed to prevent corruption, the state insisted on transferring its personnel from time to time.

"You and Peter," Leacock said, "have a great relationship. In spite of everything." He touched his chest with the fingers of his right hand. "I just thought, since I'm on the Crime Commission charged with forming the DRP, that you'd want me to make the offer."

As Leacock's voice trailed off, Clarry felt her initial surprise begin to dissipate. Though she currently held the rank of detective, her assignment to the forensics unit had long ago ceased to be challenging. Small police departments were limited in many ways, but as a detective with the DRP she'd get to field every kind of complaint.

"Jimmy," she finally said, "the rumor going around is that the DRP's giving locals a hiring preference."

Leacock straightened in his seat, one side of his mouth curling into a sardonic smile with which Carry was quite familiar. "I told you, Clarry, that I'm sitting on the Crime Commission. Besides, you're a Pennsylvania native. You grew up in Bucks County, an hour away. Plus, we need another woman on the force. We've got one and we need another. That's the truth of it."

"You forgot the part about how you know I can handle the job."

"Convincing Carroll Woods—he chairs the commission—that you'd make a great detective was the least of my problems." He leaned forward, covered her hand with his own, then favored her with a fond, tender gaze that over time she'd come to associate with mild sexual arousal.

"I'm grateful, Jimmy," she insisted as she picked up his hand, then pushed it to his side of the table. "Really I am. Just not *that* grateful."

To Clarry's surprise, Leacock began to laugh. After a moment, now completely relaxed, she surrendered to the alcohol running through her bloodstream and joined him. What she didn't anticipate, however, as she made the decision to lay an application before the DRP's hiring committee, was that she would neither see nor hear from James Leacock for more than a year. And even then she would have to seek him out.

As he yanked his left foot from the yielding earth alongside the narrow walkway, he told himself that he'd made a mistake and that there was nothing he could do about it. The shoes would have to go, of course, but that wouldn't necessarily help him. In a few hours the cops would be all over this garden, his footprint found, photographed, and filled with plaster of paris. What he should have done, considering that it was four-thirty in the morning and dark enough to walk into a tree, was slap on a pair of cheap shoes and not gone out in his Ferragamo tasseled loafers.

Briefly, he considered running his hand over the soft earth until he found, then obliterated, the print his shoe had made. But, no, that wouldn't work. He'd worn these clothes, the suit, the tie, the polished dress shoes, because he needed to make a good impression on his host. Otherwise, he'd have come in a plastic raincoat, rubbers, and a shower cap.

He consoled himself by remembering that if his enterprise went well, he could always buy another pair of two-hundred-dollar shoes. And another, and another, and another.

Still, he took great care to steady himself, stretching out his right arm to graze the shrubs that lined the walkway, his left to graze the brick wall of the Blue Heron Lodge. Then he took a careful step forward.

He continued on until he turned the corner of the building, then hesitated long enough to square his shoulders and draw a deep breath. Some twenty feet ahead curtain-filtered light poured through a pair of french doors to illuminate a concrete patio hedged with sharp-leaved holly. The effect, after the darkness of the pathway, seemed almost magical, a scene that might have been taken from a fairy tale he'd once upon a time read to his daughter. A fairy tale that had failed to raise the slightest glimmer of recognition in her eyes.

Maybe, he told himself, it's because you won't be

taking this path again, because next time you'll be coming through the front door.

Without further hesitation, he walked into the light, then stepped through the partially open door. As he closed and latched the door behind him, the mingled odors of furniture oil and pipe tobacco filling his nostrils, Winston Rollok, seated behind a wooden desk large enough to serve as a coffin, slowly turned. Rollok was a powerful man. Despite the heavy jowls and a layer of fat that ballooned his gray suede jacket, his strength was evident in his broad back and thick hands. It wasn't difficult to imagine him, even with his mouth hanging open, his eyes widened in surprise, as he'd once been, the high school hero, center on a basketball team headed to the state championships for the first time in its fifty-year history.

"Good morning, Winston," he said as he crossed the room to stand before an open safe. "How are we on this glorious September morn?" He watched Rollok's shoulders stiffen, his narrow lips clamp down as he struggled to put the pieces together. "Oh? Are we in a bad mood? Did we miss our cup of tea? Was our morning poop unproductive?"

Having apparently come to some sort of a decision, Rollok responded by pushing a thick white envelope to the edge of the desk. "Take it and go."

"What's the rush, Winston? You don't like my company? You think I'm an asshole?"

Instead of snatching the envelope, he began to circle the room. His eyes took in the woodcuts, a collection of biblical scenes dirty and dark enough to be originals, as Rollok claimed, and the eighteenth-century copper weathervanes, a centaur extending a bow and arrow, a soaring eagle, a puffy-cheeked Gabriel blowing on his horn. Finally, he stopped before an oil painting of an early steamship, its sunlit sails furled over twin smokestacks, plowing through a dark, roiling sea. A brass plaque beneath the painting named the ship, the S.S. *Commander*, but not the artist.

"You've done great for yourself, Winston," he said. "Just great." And that, of course, was the understatement of the century. Rollok had seventy-five, maybe a hundred grand on the walls. And this was only his office. The man's house, he knew, was a virtual museum. "Considering how low you started and the low road you've taken in life."

Rollok leaned back in his brown leather chair but did not look up. Instead, he busied himself with a meerschaum pipe, its yellow bowl carved into the shape of a turkey. "How fortunate for you," he said. "My doing well. How very, very fortunate."

"Shit." The man shook his head in disgust. The way he saw it, making the money was all right, even making it the way Rollok had. But the transformation from poor boy to country squire was too repulsive to contemplate.

Rollok jammed the pipe stem between his teeth and fumbled in his pocket for his lighter. "Why don't you take the money and go?" he said. "What is it that you want?"

Instead of responding directly, he slid the knife from its sheath, pressed it against his right thigh, and took a step forward to grab Rollok's chin with his left hand, to yank it back so hard the stem of Rollok's pipe snapped like a twig beneath a hard-soled boot. "What is it I want?" he asked as he slammed the knife through the back of the chair, through bone and muscle, through Rollok's lungs and into the center of his heart. "What I want, Rollok, is more and more and more. I want to catch up."

SUE GRAFTON

"Once again, the finest practitioner of the 'female sleuth' genre is in great form...."
—Cosmopolitan

"Ms. Grafton writes a smart story and wraps it up with a wry twist."
—The New York Times Book Review

"The best first-person-singular storytelling in detective novels."
—Entertainment Weekly